HEAVEN and HELL

HEAVEN and HELL

Arthur Altman

St. Martin's Press, New York

For my wife, Sandra, and for my
grandmother, Maria (nee) LoConti.

HEAVEN AND HELL. Copyright © 1990 by Arthur Altman. All rights reserved. Printed in the United States of America. No part of this book may be used or reproduced in any manner whatsoever without written permission except in the case of brief quotations embodied in critical articles or reviews. For information, address St. Martin's Press, 175 Fifth Avenue, New York, N.Y. 10010.

Design by Glen M. Edelstein

Library of Congress Cataloging-in-Publication Data
Altman, Arthur.
   Heaven and hell / Arthur Altman.
     p.   cm.
   ISBN 0-312-04326-0
   I. Title.
   PS3551.L7937H4   1990
   813'.54—dc20   89-77996
                                                                                 CIP

First Edition

10 9 8 7 6 5 4 3 2 1

Cast of Characters

Major Characters

Alcibiades LoConti—Al, an Assistant District Attorney, Bronx County, New York City
Renee LoConti—his wife
Vince LoConti—Al's brother
Pericles, Peppy Gennaro—Al and Vince's uncle
Ray and Elizabeth LoConti—their children

The Serial Killer

Ronald DePew

The Police

Carleton—a cop suspected of murder
Pete DiCerrechia—Al's best friend
Detective Marty Doolan—an undercover officer
Sergeant Denny Driscoll—13th Narcotics
Detective Timmy Flanagan—an old time Homicide Detective
Detective Carl Gutierrez—an expert

Detective Elrod Harrison—DA's squad
Rory O'Donnell—an Irish emigré whom Al knew since their teens
Aloysious X. McDaniel ("The Hat")—Inspector-Assistant Borough Commander
Cornelious "Connie" O'Toole—a senior chief with a secret link to the Hat
Detective Morrie Shapiro—Flanagan's partner
Balthazar "Bill" Solwin—CO 13th Narcotics
Lt. Allie Boy Spano—Al's cousin
Ruella Watkins—a friend of Al and Renee; widow of Denny Watkins
Officer Richie Zemberelli—a legend
William Wotter—an ex-marine whom Al also knew since youth

The District Attorney's Office

Fazio ("Frank") Caporosso—District Attorney of Bronx County
Jimmy Farrell—narcotics DA who started with Al
Terry Hanratty—best trial man in the office
Dave Hornbein—good book man
Johnny O'Boyle—Bureau Chief Homicide Bureau
Carmine Riccaldo—one of the Grand Inquisitors
Maurice Slefner—the other Inquisitor

Organized Crime Figures

Santa Giacamo—bicycle riding bookie
Jimmy Clams Grimaldi
Mrs. Grimaldi—his wife
Guido Insalata ("The Admiral")—boss of the Bronx
Carlo Ogdalente (aka Charlie "the Plant" Oakdale)—in the Admiral's employ
Mildred Oakdale—Charlie's wife
Dominic "Micky" Varino—the Admiral's son-in-law
Susan Varino—the Admiral's daughter

The Judiciary

Judge DiGrande—judge
Judge Finch—trial judge
Judge Samuel Flay—Mr. Judicial Notice
Judge Marty Honig—judge of the Criminal Court
Judge O'Neill—one of Al's favorites
Judge Ned Rothman—judge of the Criminal Court
    Minor Judges
Conmy
Fleck
Gruck
Termi
Tiernan

The Members of the Bar

Joey Cassossa—an ethical and excellent lawyer
Howard Caven
Jim Fisher
Reynard Foxworth
Sy Gold
Marty Guildern
Fast Frankie Hammon
Quiet Marvin Pollard
Rhinequist

Drug Dealers

Biaggio Blaze Squerente
Chaparall (aka Mervin Greene)
Chingo (aka Fidel Vicun)
Mr. and Mrs. Ferro
The Jamaican
Tommy Jassy
Jimmy Nofrio
Paulie "the Brain" Carver

Medical Examiner's Office

Dr. Linda Cristen

Others

Raul Alquerido—an Argentinian drug dealer
Anselm—an accountant from the North Bronx
Adian Bard—a rapist-killer
Elias Baruba—a Queens politician
BB balls Berghaus—a police supervisor
Bix—charged with murder
Mrs. Blanchard—a victim
Blatt—a cop in the 13th narcotics
Boremisano—a police supervisor
Captain Bourke—a police superior
Leon Brastock—charged with murder
Sy Brazberg—former chief of Homicide DA's office
Sgt. Brutti—US Army intelligence
Ronnie Bucchiossi—Morris Park stickup team member
Carmine—a mailman
Ronald Coleman (aka Muhammad Aktwi)—a psycho defendant
Cozzella—a detective NYPD
Trevor Cunard—a married man from suburbia seeking sex
Cuzzi family—an organized crime family
Sgt. Danforth—an intelligence NCO US Army
Daniels—a detective NYPD
Rick Dano and Marguerite Dano—suspected of dealing drugs
Lenny DeStefano—a victim
Connie DiCerrechia—Pete's wife
Augie DiFillippo—detective NYPD
Dinefresio—a witness
Lt. Richard Drelko—police supervisor
Elva Dunis—murderer
Alicia Endicott—murderer
Mr. Endicott—victim
Enzo—waiter in the Last Supper
Herb Faeroe—Bureau Chief Criminal Court Bureau

Dorothy Farquier—senior citizen
Paddy Fay—bartender in the Old Bailey
Sgt. Feldman—Ronald DePew's platoon sergeant in the Army
Tommy Finley—Bureau Chief of the Narcotic Bureau
Mervin Flohic—a dicky waver
Jackie Fratello ("Graves")—a Bronx undertaker
Uncle Peppy Gennaro
Jimmy Gerello ("Giraffe")—a burglar
Gladys—a waitress
Marty Gorshbein—her ex-husband
Sarah Gorshbein—encounters DePew
Sadie Gracowski—a girlfiend of Allie Boy Spano
Milberg Greenway—Bronx politico boss
Roosevelt Greg—murderer
Heriberto Guzman—charged with murder
Helen—a friend of Vince LoConti
Imelda—a barmaid
Inez—a gogo dancer
JoJo—owner of a bar and restaurant in the Bronx
Woodrow Johnson—an oldtime burglar
LeRoy Joseph—Morris Park stickup team member
Margaret Keefe—widow resident of Manhattan
Kevin and Maynard—friends of Leon Brastock; charged with murder
Kiernan—priest at Good Shepherd
Davey Kirshenbaum—a witness
Vincent La Magna—father-in-law of Rick Dano
Randy La Tourde—detective NYPD
Pat Lawless—member of the lathers union
Lenahan—a police superior and Zemberelli's commander in the national guard
Bob Livgrum—DA stenographer
Lucky Luciano—mentioned as a prosecution model
Luis—a Cuban gang leader
Capt. Mac MacNamara—an underling of O'Toole
Miles Macomber—a telephone listing
Mr. Maheny—president of Mother Nature's Farms, the milk company employing Vince LoConti and Richie Zemberelli
Mancuso—a cop from Manhattan
Ipsy Mankevich—an informer from the 1940's

Fred Margolis—a witness
Matarda—a friend of Allie Boy Spano
Kelly McKnight—public relations NYPD
Jimmy McLaren—officer NYPD
Ricky McNaughton—robber and murderer
Mrs. McNeill—encounters DePew
Dolores, Margaret, and Ruth McPort—encounter DePew
McSherry—detective NYPD
McTigue—a bartender
Denny McVeigh—detective NYPD
Myron Mercus—an attorney
Mike—a bartender
Millie—a waitress in the Last Supper
Mincione—a detective
Moltry—an army Captain
Victor Moore—a defendant
Morales—sharp cop from Manhattan
Joseph Mroz—charged with murder
Dewey Mulligan—friend of DePew
Sean Mulligan—Dewey's father
Mulvey—detective NYPD
Lucy Munoz—a witness
Georgie Nastolden—a criminal who ran into the Inquisitors
Paul Neumann—attorney for the PBA
Nevins—a kid driving a car in the 40's
Nora—a transit worker's wife
O'Brien—a murderer
Angela O'Brien—his wife
Heather Goldstein O'Grady—wife of Hughie and friend of Peppy Gennaro
Hugh O'Grady—friend of Peppy's
Jimmy O'Shea—member of the lathers union
Didi O'Sullivan—stickup team member
Raoul Ortiz—member of the Young Sinners
Mrs. Owen—Al's neighbor
Mrs. P—a voice on the phone
Attilio Otto Paulumbo—relative of Richie Zemberelli
Perrottas—neighbors of the Grimaldi's
Jimmy Phelan—a reporter
Otis Poquay—murderer

William Portman—murderer
Henry Quade—member of the stickup team
Marvis Qualkeeve—criminal partner of McNaughton
Quirel—an ADA
Jonah Quoe—an ADA
Hamshooz Rajehvi—a link to an old crime
Cheech Rodriguez—wanted by the DA's squad
Feliciti Rodriguez—Cheech's mother
Octavio Rolezon—charged with murder
Ira Schmorkler—sharp detective
Serquez brothers—charged with murder
John Servetter—US Attorney Southern District of NY
Jimmy Shaugnessy—detective NYPD
Sybil Shields—rape victim
Louie Shifaggi—golfer who finds a pair of legs
Mike Shupinsky—owner of a grocery store
Dr. Silver—friend of Mildred Oakdale
Ira Silver—member of stickup team
Sol—boss of Sarah Gorshbein
Dr. Stein—ME
Sue Stein (no relation)—driver for ME's office
General Stroessner—head of state—Paraguay
Sgt. Talbot—44 IU
Teach—name picked up on a wire
Claude Temoles—recidivist victim
Captain Arthur Thornwood—NYPD Intelligence
Migdalia Torres—Bronx housewife
Officer Trowbridge—NYPD
Umberto—works for the Admiral
Rose Underwood—Bronx senior citizen
Valdez—undercover cop
Martha Valles—murder victim
Jesus Vasquez—Bronx defendant
Emmanuel Vildar—Bronx victim
Denny Watkins—deceased husband of Ruella
Lou Ann Wilson—Bronx prostitute
Cosimo "the Joker" Zemberelli—older brother of Richie

HEAVEN and HELL

MAY 1988

WHEN THE THIRTY-THREE-FOOT RV exited the Major Deegan Expressway, it proceeded down a service road, stopped opposite the Four Four precinct, and waited. It was as if a dinosaur had come back from the millennia to visit the city. Onlookers stared.

It was 5 P.M. and the northbound Deegan Expressway seemed to be one vast parking lot, jammed and clogged to a standstill by the gorge of traffic exiting the city on this Friday afternoon.

Driver Ray LoConti, a nineteen-year-old, long-haired blond, looked out at the milling crowd of black and Hispanic onlookers. Some seemed to be laughing at the youth and his situation.

Suddenly the hostile, staring crowd was abruptly parted by the awesome menace of police lieutenant Allie Boy Spano. At six-four and two hundred and forty pounds he commanded respect. Lieutenant Allie Boy had just finished his tour. He got up into the vehicle and with the five other occupants they all drove south.

The three men seated in the rear of the RV played cards on a table fastened to the floor. Ray LoConti's father, forty-four-year-old Alcibiades LoConti, attorney-at-law, sat next to him. Years ago he had grown tired of telling everyone that his first name was pronounced AL-see-bye-a-dees.

"Just call me Al," he had said then, and always repeated it now when he was newly introduced.

The police lieutenant, Allie Boy Spano, aged forty-nine, stood directly behind the two LoContis. There was a shocking resemblance between Allie Boy and Al. Even though they were first cousins, the resemblance in their dark eyes and tanned facial features was that of twins. Alcibiades LoConti, six feet tall and two hundred pounds, smiled with pride at his son's mastery of the colossus that he was driving.

The six men were en route to Montauk Point on Long Island's eastern end. They had chartered a boat and were to spend the next three days fishing for shark.

"Rough day, Loo?" one of the card players shouted from the back, greeting Allie Boy with the police slang for the lieutenant's rank.

"Usual fuckin' horror show," the lieutenant said.

Al LoConti only smiled.

His son drove through the crowded streets as he headed toward the southbound Deegan Expressway.

These masses of humanity, their ebb and flow, these street people and their third world faces all made young Ray LoConti ill at ease. He was raised in fresher waters, a product of suburbia. He sweated as he steered the RV through these strange, threatening, Bronx passageways.

The lieutenant seemed to sense the boy's uneasiness.

"Don't feel bad, kid," the lieutenant said. "I got twenty years on this job and feel safer swimmin' with those sharks we're goin' after than bein' out there."

"You're always huntin' predators, Loo, even when you're off duty," another of the card players teased.

Alcibiades LoConti smiled then looked over at his son. He was sinewy, with strong muscled arms. Alcibiades watched with pleasure as he observed some of his own mannerisms in the boy, his son whom he had lost but had now regained. Al smiled again. The boy truly had his mother's face, yet where the mother was beautiful, Ray was strong and handsome.

Ray braked for a red light and sighed. "Beats me why anyone would want to work here."

"We all did plenty of huntin' in these waters, even your old man," Allie Boy answered. "Some we got and some we didn't. But most we got," LoConti said softly.

Ray drove past Yankee Stadium then proceeded onto the Deegan south.

"I never want to be involved with that kind of work," Ray said.

"It wasn't so bad. Every day was different and I was . . . I was much younger then," the father answered. "When you live it it's one thing when you look back—well . . . time clouds your memories. You don't remember the bad, only the good."

"You must of seen it all, huh, Pop?" Ray asked.

"I had many many cases. . . ." Al's voice trailed off.

"Which were the best, I mean, which were the most interesting?" Ray asked.

"They were all interesting. Some were—" he paused and stared out at the passing traffic for a second. "There were three that stood out above all the thousands of others. Three that involved a lot of investigation and three that took many years to resolve."

The traffic stopped completely and then picked up again at a five-mile-per-hour crawl. The backup from the George Washington Bridge to the Cross Bronx Expressway to the Deegan Interchange caused by the hordes escaping the city on this Friday was finally having its effect.

With his foot alternating from the brake to the accelerator, Ray glanced at the service road and watched a group of kids jumping from the spurting stream from an opened fire hydrant. The water burst out into the street.

"What were those three cases about?" Ray asked.

"One involved a mass murderer . . . . a kid named DePew, of all names," Spano said. "The second involved a pair of legs that were found at a Bronx golf course. The body belonging to those legs was not found for a long, long time. Not until after your father and many cops really sweated. And the third case, Ray, involved a beautiful girl who was murdered by just one bullet. She had a boyfriend. A young married cop."

"Were all of them finally solved?" Ray asked.

"All except one." Allie Boy Spano placed his hand on Ray LoConti's shoulder. "Your old man has been through ten Goddamn meat grinders, kid, you should be real proud of him. Real proud."

Ray looked over at his father and winked.

Alcibiades smiled and winked back as the traffic continued to crawl south in Bronx County.

INSIDE THE COURTHOUSE AT 161st Street and the Grand Concourse, twenty-seven-year-old Alcibiades LoConti raised his right hand and took the oath as an assistant district attorney. It was Monday, August 10, 1970, and he stood as one of thirteen new assistants in the Office of the District Attorney of Bronx County, the office ruled by the iron hand of the legendary the Honorable Fazio "Frank" Caporosso.

Unlike most of the other newcomers, Alcibiades was not a 1970 law school graduate. He had finished law school in 1968, and then one week after his bar exam he had entered the army as a lieutenant. He had been promoted to captain and decorated for his bravery in Vietnam. While still on active duty he had applied for a position with the Bronx DA. Al had heard of the office's reputation for excellence. After he was honored with the appointment, he had celebrated with his wife and best friend, Renee, for two days. They had dined at the Last Supper, a bar and restaurant owned by Al's uncle Peppy, and then went to the theater in Manhattan. They had taken a trip on the Circle Line, drank red wine together in small cafés and returned home to make love.

As the Honorable Frank Caporosso came down the line, he shook each man's hand warmly.

"Welcome to the office, Al," he said.

Al thanked him. The DA, Alcibiades observed to himself, was like one of the best officers he had served with in the army. He had flamboyance and real charisma, and his words made you feel as if you were the most important man in the world.

Today Al LoConti, father of a son, Raymond, thirteen months, and a daughter, Elizabeth, just three weeks old, felt that he was the luckiest and happiest man alive. After the ceremony, he walked out of the office with Jonah Quoe and Detective Elrod Harrison. Detective Harrison drove them across town to the Criminal Court of the City of New York, Bronx County, which was housed in two century-old buildings on 161st Street and Third Avenue. They entered the main building. The subway cars of the Third Avenue El squeaked as the train made a turn past the court buildings and the Four Two precinct. Neither the shrill grinding of the steel wheels on the iron train tracks nor the grimy courthouse interior dampened Alcibiades's optimism. He felt he was now enlisted in a new and different war.

Al walked into the DA's offices on the fourth floor of the courthouse. On the short ride over Detective Harrison, an experienced black man with fifteen years on the job, had hit it off with Al and Jonah Quoe. Elrod introduced the two new assistant DAs to Herb Faeroe, the Bureau Chief. Faeroe's small cubbyhole of an office was packed with lawyers and police officers. He beckoned to one of the officers.

"Get Terry Hanratty over here to give these guys an orientation," he ordered. The officer grabbed a phone and made a call.

"After Hanratty shows you around, LoConti will go to arraignments today and Quoe goes to the complaint room. Welcome and good luck. Remember, always prosecute firmly and forcefully and if you have a question, remember that the common denominator is the human equation." Faeroe finished and returned to his office.

Harrison grinned and shrugged his shoulders in response to Al and Quoe's puzzled looks.

"Hanratty is a real good DA," he told both of them. "He'll give you a good rundown."

Terry Hanratty arrived. He was Al's height, six feet tall, blue-eyed and fair-skinned. They shook hands warmly after Elrod Harrison made the introductions.

Then motioning them to follow, Hanratty left the offices and entered the cage elevator in the hallway.

On the way down he explained that the clerks' offices were all on the ground floor and that the other three floors held the courtroom or Parts of the court. This courthouse handled all adult offenders. A second courthouse, diagonally behind this one, held the arraignment part, the complaint room, and handled all youths between sixteen and nineteen charged with crime.

Hanratty explained and lectured while they walked across to the arraignment building.

"Just think of the criminal justice system as a sewer responsible for processing all the shit and scum in this city. The criminal court is like the first intake valve. Ninety-nine percent of all the shit flows in this court first by way of arrest. The sewer is full of holes and overflows regularly. It can't handle the volume and the politicians won't spend money to provide the courtrooms or the jails to house the criminals. So the DAs are really just shit sifters. In the complaint room and at arraignment you try to separate the serious stuff from the rest of the crap that the cops drag in. The way you do that is to plea bargain. Car thefts and your warehouse burglaries wind up misdemeanors. Pocketbook snatches too. Gambling and prostitution are bullshit and get violations and fines. Robbery, serious assault, rape, and sodomy all go over to the grand jury for indictment and prosecution by the Supreme Court Bureau. Small drug cases up to double sales of heroin get pleas here. Serious drug cases and investigations are handled by the Narcotics Bureau. The Rackets Bureau handles corruption and organized crime. So they do a lot of investigation. But even though I hear you were an MP officer, LoConti, you'll never see the Rackets Bureau. Your name ends in a vowel, and that makes you ineligible."

Alcibiades flinched. Hanratty saw it and continued.

"We got a Complaint Bureau across town that provides access to the citizenry. Mostly nuts come in, but because the DA is elected it is a good service. If you get sent there permanently look for another job. The DA staffs it with clinkers, you know, pigeons that can't fly. But the woman who's the Bureau Chief is a sharp prosecutor and a good boss. The Homicide Bureau is the class of the office. The best trial guys go there. There's no hacks in Homicide. Murder cases that come in here get remanded. But even if you guys make it to Homicide—and there are guys in this office for ten years who haven't—you'll find that even murder cases are plea-bargained. Supreme Court plea bargains your property, your genitalia, and your ass. Narcotics Bureau plea-bargains with the guys who put shit worse than cyanide in our society, so why shouldn't the Homicide Bureau bargain away the value of your life. The shit just oozes out of the sewer at every level. And the prison system, which is at the far end of the intake, is just a temporary holding pen, solidifying the shit until it's more lethal and offensive and then spewing it back here on the streets. It don't mean a fuck."

Alcibiades was a little shocked at Hanratty's cynicism and description but what the man said seemed to make sense.

They entered the Arraignment Building and walked upstairs to the first floor. Hanratty watched as Al surveyed the building's interior.

"Those windows ain't been washed since World War I," Hanratty said, noticing Al's glance at the large iron and brass-rimmed windows on the first floor, which bordered Third Avenue and the elevated subway train.

Al nodded as the three entered the complaint room. A line of police officers were waiting for their interviews with a DA concerning their arrests and the writing up of the DAs' green sheet summarizing their cases. From here, Hanratty explained, an officer would then go to the arraignment Part and wait for his case to be called. The complaint or court papers would be brought to the court by the court personnel, as would the DAs' case files.

Al listened attentively because he wanted to learn the ropes quickly.

Jonah Quoe was dropped off to assist in the complaint room and Alcibiades was brought into the arraignment part, just as Faeroe had ordered. The ADA there introduced him to the judge then handed him a batch of case folders.

Hanratty had Al watch how the DA handled his arraignments for about ten minutes. Then he patted Al on the back. "It's all yours now. Have fun." He and the DA on duty then left, chuckling.

Things were happening real fast for Al.

The bridgeman called the next case. Al flipped open the DA file. He was alone in front of a crowded courtroom. Battle-tested police, cynical defense lawyers, and pompous, arrogant court personnel were all watching him. Relatives of the defendants crowded the spectators' benches. The room was an indoor arena buzzing with heated conversations in both Spanish and English.

The bridgeman pulled a yellow backed file, the color representing a felony case. He then began.

"People of the State of New York against Jesus Vasquez. Charge 140.20 Penal Law, Burglary Third Degree, premises, Yangzee Warehouse, complaint of Officer Trowbridge. Defendant represented by the Legal Aid society."

The bridgeman then turned to Alcibiades. "People's position on bail or parole?"

It was sink or swim for Al LoConti. He knew everyone was watching him.

'Don't step on your dick, young Captain,' he muttered to himself.

He swallowed and kept his voice firm. Acting almost by rote, he flipped open the case folder and read the green sheet. The bail recommendation was $500. He looked at the defendant's yellow sheet stapled underneath the complaint and found fourteen other arrests listed.

"People request $2,500 bail. Defendant has fourteen previous arrests," he stated loudly and firmly.

The Legal Aid lawyer almost went through the roof.

When he was finished, the judge set the bail at $1,000 and smiled at Al. This kid will keep his head above water, the judge thought. "Next case."

When his first day was over, Alcibiades left and walked out front of the courthouse. Two uniformed police officers and two plainclothes officers were standing outside the main entrance. A black female officer stood beside them.

The two uniformed officers grabbed Al, mussed his hair, and pulled his tie while the others smiled.

After roughhousing him they all dragged him across the street to the Piggly Wiggly, a cop's bar across from the Four Two. The uniformed officers were Al's cousin Allie Boy Spano and Pete DiCerrechia, Al's best friend since boyhood. The two plainclothes officers who also went along were William Wotter, another close friend, and Rory O'Donnell. Al had known O'Donnell since he had emigrated to New York from Ireland as a teenager in the late fifties. O'Donnell had been with the 199th Light Infantry in the slaughter in the Ashau Valley in Vietnam in 1965 and was on his third marriage.

When they got to the bar, they all ordered drinks. The bartender was a retired sergeant from the Four Four. He knew them all, and he congratulated Al too.

Alcibiades had one drink, shook hands all around, then left. Before he reached his car two blocks away, O'Donnell had finished his fourth Jamieson's and beer chaser.

On the same day that Alcibiades LoConti was being sworn in as an assistant district attorney in the Bronx County Courthouse, Ronald DePew, age thirteen, stood in the boiler room of an apartment house on Southern Boulevard in the South Bronx.

Ronald had murdered five people in the last six months, and none of those murders had been solved. He had left no clues and the police had not even connected the murders to one perpetrator.

Around two in the afternoon, Ronald walked next to the wall behind the boiler and peered through a peephole into the clubhouse of the Young Sinners. Four members of the Young Sinners' gang were inside. Against the wall a young girl dressed only in black panties and a black brassiere sat on a couch.

She was sixteen years old and the gang leader's woman. The other gang members were teenagers too. Luis, the leader, wore a green army fatigue jacket and a black beret. A metal miniature of the flag of Cuba was clipped to the front of his beret.

Luis stood up and rolled a marijuana cigarette. He took a long drag off it, keeping the smoke deep within his lungs, and then released it, then inhaled again until the glow at the cigarette's end brightened into a vivid hunter's orange. He passed the joint to the girl and after she inhaled she passed it to Chingo, a gang member seated on the couch at her side. Chingo inhaled, closed his eyes, and touched her breast. His hand moved slowly. It caressed and fondled.

Luis stood in front of them as they played, and rolled another joint. Ronald watched as he smoked and then heard him call softly to Chingo. When Chingo looked up, the leader nodded toward the door. Chingo obediently stood up and left. Ronald heard the clubhouse door open and then close after Chingo passed from his sight.

Ronald then focused his attention on the other two gang members, who were nodding out on a battered couch against the far wall. Seated side by side, their heads drooped and almost touched. The two were far away in a state of total narcosis, in heroin-induced dreamworld. Ronald became excited when the now-topless girl leaned forward and unzipped Luis's fly and crammed his member in her mouth. Ronald saw Luis, standing there, almost indifferent, inhaling the marijuana as the girl squealed and performed her ministrations.

After Luis climaxed, Ronald watched as the two drank from a bottle of wine. The girl then dozed on the couch. Luis drank the rest of the wine and smoked more pot. After a while he fell asleep too.

Ronald's moment had finally arrived. He slipped into the clubhouse room and walked swiftly and silently behind the sleeping leader. Then he thrust an ice pick into the soft tissue of Luis's skull, behind his ear and an inch below the elastic fabric at the bottom of his beret. He quickly walked away from the body and killed the two sleeping junkies in the same manner. Luis's corpse was still jerking spasmodically when he returned to the couch and placed the bloody ice pick on top of the beret.

The girl slept on. Quietly Ronald walked behind the couch. He was professional. He extracted a piece of piano wire from his pocket. The ends of the wire formed two handles wrapped in black electrician's tape. He clenched the handles and crossed the wire to form a loop over the sleeping girl's head. As it landed on her shoulders, he placed his hands together.

When his thumbs touched, he snapped his hands apart and the wire snaked tight. The girl's head was almost severed before she felt the wire biting into her flesh. Her body convulsed twice and then she died.

DePew removed her panties. She was now completely naked. After fondling her for a minute or so, he heard a noise. He tiptoed to the door and listened. Hearing nothing, he surveyed the scene, then left the clubhouse.

Outside on Southern Boulevard, he walked in front of a police car that was stopped for a red light. The driver of the car was a young, black officer named Ruella Watkins, six weeks out of the academy.

"What's that white kid doin' in this neighborhood?" she asked her partner, Allie Boy Spano, a two-year veteran.

The partner, a stocky, muscular white officer, glanced at DePew. "Who gives a fuck?" he answered, and stepped on the accelerator as the light changed.

DePew went home without further incident.

Chingo came back to the clubhouse later because he liked the girl. When he opened the door he flinched and almost threw up at the slaughter. He recovered quickly. Realizing that no one was left alive, he stripped the junkies of their drugs and money. Then he removed the leader's wallet and emptied it of seventy dollars and twenty-two heroin-filled glassine envelopes.

Both Chingo and Luis had been in America for two years. Before that, both had spent time in a Cuban hospital for the insane. Chingo knew that Luis had been responsible for three unsolved murders in the Bronx. The police had termed them gang-related.

Chingo stuffed the cash and drugs in his pockets, then left, closing the door quietly. He gave no thought to the identity of the slayer of his fellow Young Sinners.

Chingo went to St. Mary's Park off Brook Avenue and sold the heroin he had gotten. Ronald DePew went to his home in the East Tremont section of the Bronx and turned on his family's television. There were no news flashes yet concerning the massacre at the Young Sinners' clubhouse.

Two days later Johnny O'Boyle, deputy bureau chief of the Homicide Bureau, stood inside the Young Sinners' clubroom. Johnny was only five-seven yet, he had an aura of power. His jet-black hair was combed, parted, and styled in the fashion of his idol, the late President John F. Kennedy. His manner was different. He was curt, abrupt, and respected by all the Homicide detectives yet truly liked by only a few.

O'Boyle gave directions to the forensic photographers and detective investigators like a director at a motion picture studio. His authority was unquestioned. He had tried forty-five complete murder trials and lost but three.

O'Boyle had a file of three other unsolved random murders in the Bronx over the last seven months. While the weapon had never been an ice pick or a sharp wirelike object, something of the utter senselessness, the utter horror connected the crimes in his mind. The police, of course, had made no linkage.

O'Boyle hoped he was wrong.

When the medical examiner and forensic team were finished, O'Boyle left. He paused and chatted with the first officers on the scene, who had responded to the building superintendant's call. The stench of the bodies decaying for two days in the August heat had led him to the clubhouse.

Neither Allie Boy Spano nor Ruella Watkins could add anything to Johnny's knowledge. The investigation, like the investigation in the other murders, would produce no leads.

On August 19 Police Officer William Wotter of the 13th Narcotics Division was looking out of a second-floor window of a burned-out building. The 13th was an elite unit created to assault the narcotics scourge on all levels. One of three such units in Bronx County, its prescribed area was not limited by either precinct or even county boundaries.

Wotter watched as the junkies approached a drug seller who stood in the alcove of a nailed-up doorway in front of a closed bodega. He radioed reports of the sales to his backup team of Rory O'Donnell and Lieutenant Balthazar "Bill" Solwin.

One of the buyers finally went around the corner in the direction of the backup team. Wotter radioed his description.

"The junk's in his right front pants pocket," Wotter reported. O'Donnell and Solwin grabbed the buyer, searched him, and placed him under arrest. They retrieved the heroin from the man's right pants pocket.

The impetuous O'Donnell left Solwin with the buyer and ran around the corner after the seller. The seller spotted him, although O'Donnell wore an old army fatigue shirt and dirty pants.

Still grieving over the dissolution of his third marriage, O'Donnell had consumed the greater part of a quart of Irish whiskey and two six-packs the evening before. He couldn't even get near the young Hispanic.

William Wotter watched as the gap between the drug seller and his partner widened and then saw O'Donnell stop, exhausted. Wotter took a long good look at the seller's young face. If he ever saw Chingo again he would not forget him.

A pair of legs wrapped in a green plastic trash bag were blood-drained white. A pair of shoeless feet stuck out from the green plastic bag.

The first foursome out this morning of August 13th, 1970, from the Split Rock Golf Course were four Bronx contractors. One of them, portly Louie Shifaggi, drove his six iron 150 yards into a sand trap. When Shifaggi, known as Louie Shitface to his friends, went to get his ball, he found the plastic bag. When he opened it he found the legs.

The entire front nine had been closed and Officers Pete DiCerrechia and Richie Zemberelli waited around standing guard over the legs.

DiCerrechia, twenty-seven years old, cursed silently as he observed Inspector Aloysious X. McDaniel approach.

"Watch it, Richie, the fuckin' Hat is comin'," he said.

Zemberelli snapped to attention and saluted as the Hat walked up. The Hat was the assistant borough commander. Even now, though it was only seven-thirty in the morning, you could smell the stink of liquor on his breath. The Hat returned Richie's salute. He was followed by a group of eight detectives and two uniformed police captains from the borough command.

The Hat was furious. There had been a string of murders in the Bronx in the last week and the police had no leads on any of them. He jumped up and down and yelled at DiCerrechia and Zemberelli.

Everyone feared the Hat. Young cops like Pete DiCerrechia had heard the hundreds of stories that made up the Hat legend. They ran from the numerous beatings he administered to Italian bookies to the time he hauled in a rabbi for double parking. Despite his psychotic behavior, he was immune from discipline. It was rumored that the Hat must have the book on some of the highest brass in the department.

The Hat continued to scream at DiCerrechia and Zemberelli.

"Hey, Inspector," DiCerrechia shot back irreverently, "we didn't kill this one. Why take it out on us?"

DiCerrechia's colossal balls caused the Hat to stop. Everyone was terrified of the Hat. His insane rages and behavior were legendary. No one had dared to defy him. The other detectives and police brass just gaped. Even the Hat was too stunned to reply. He turned and started giving directions.

Richie Zemberelli was thirty-two years old and had been a cop for seven years. It had taken Richie six years to get through Columbus High School. In his fifth and sixth years he was known as a super senior. Richie had passed the test to become a cop the only way he knew how—he let his older brother, Cosimo "the Joker" Zemberelli take it for him. Cosimo had squeaked by and Richie had been sworn in.

Richie's fellow officers soon found out that he was far, far from being bright. So he became the focus of innumerable practical jokes. Hardly a week went by that Richie wasn't being dispatched to West Farms to an area near the statue of a Civil War soldier armed with a musket. Richie was always sent there on the same complaint. "Man with a gun."

Richie always searched with commendable intensity. Sometimes he would surreptitiously patrol West Farms seeking the "man with the gun," but the collar eluded him. His constant vows to "Get that motherfucker with the gun" became a legend in the department.

He was deluged with magazines of every description, the result of false subscriptions. He unknowingly joined the Book of the Month Club on two hundred occasions within thirty days. He received a summons for not licensing his dog, and he received six false notices from the IRS concerning tax audits.

And yet Richie enjoyed his life. He had two steady girlfriends in his old Morris Park neighborhood. Richie was smart enough to tell each of them that he was married though he was not.

Richie perked up when he saw that one of the captains with the Hat was Lieutenant Colonel Lenahan, his National Guard battalion commander. Richie had been a sergeant first class in the National Guard, and he had proudly worn seven stripes. Richie was the chief battalion cook and Lenahan loved him.

Lenahan motioned him over. Richie joined the brass as DiCerrechia stood in silent guard.

Richie's chest puffed with pride as Lenahan introduced him to the Hat, who was barely courteous.

"Just what we need today, another fuckin' murder," the Hat grumbled toward the legs.

"Uh, excuse me, Inspector," Zemberelli piped up. Everyone turned toward him. "This can't be a murder."

"*What!*" the Hat shouted.

"To be a murder you have to have a body, you know, *corpus*

delictus, like they said in the academy. You only got a set of legs here and no corpse. No corpse, no murder."

The assemblage guffawed. It was another Zemberelli classic.

They stopped when the Hat patted him on the back and shook his hand enthusiastically. Richie had solved the Hat's problem. This would not be classified as a murder unless a body was found. With any luck, the Hat thought to himself, the body would be found in Manhattan or Queens and they would have the case.

Richie smiled, delighted at the Hat's praise. Then his smiles turned to utter disbelief at the Hat's next statement.

"My boy, you just made Detective Third Grade."

SANTA GIACOMO, A BOOKIE from Morris Park Avenue, parked his battered Chevrolet in front of the brick home of his boss, Guido Insalata, the Admiral. He had come to pay his condolences and to offer his services to his patron at the time of his grief—the murder of the Admiral's son-in-law.

Dominic "Mickey" Varino had been found in an Orchard Beach parking lot with two holes behind his ear. There was a rumor that the Admiral was behind it, but Santa Giacomo gave it no mind.

When Santa Giacomo rang the bell, the Admiral himself answered the door. He welcomed his underling graciously and offered him a glass of wine. Santa Giacomo accepted. As they drank, Santa Giacomo made the customary offerings of condolences and aid. The Admiral, the ruler of organized crime in the Bronx, thanked him profusely and then ushered him out the door.

Santa Giacomo was an eccentric, a lover of opera and fine art, a man with knowledge of the classics, a man of wisdom, of intelligence. Yet the Admiral still had not forgiven him for refusing to exploit his friendship with legitimate businessmen, such as the uncle of the new assistant DA from Giacomo's neighborhood, Alcibiades LoConti. The uncle, Pericles "Peppy" Gennaro, owned the Last Supper Restaurant on Morris Park Avenue. The Last Supper was a landmark. Winning Yankee baseball teams had celebrated there. Peppy Gennaro hosted the Giants, Knicks, and celebrating politicos on all levels. Despite repeated hints from the Admiral, Santa Giacomo refused to involve his legitimate friends in his other world.

Santa Giacomo drove away in his battered Chevy, a tribute to his lack of ostentation. In deference to the Admiral's loss, he did not bring up his displeasure at the continued insults from the Hat when he picked up his weekly envelope. He sighed as he turned onto Morris Park Avenue from Eastchester Road; it was good to be back home.

It was strange that the Admiral had been at home alone, unprotected by his platoons of bodyguards. Santa Giacomo was convinced in his heart of hearts that the murder of Dominic "Mickey" Varino would remain a mystery to everyone for all time.

Later that afternoon assistant DA Johnny O'Boyle was briefing the DA on the murder of the Admiral's son-in-law. He had been ushered into the enormous office of the District Attorney of the County of Bronx, the Honorable Fazio "Frank" Caporosso. Everyone was nervously respectful in the presence of the District Attorney.

Four homicide detectives assigned to the case sat around the conference table. They were all subdued. Johnny O'Boyle and Sy Brazberg sat opposite them. Brazberg was chief of the Homicide Bureau. Caporosso himself stood behind his desk looking at the assemblage like a bank president addressing his subordinate directors.

As he began he addressed his remarks to the next in the chain of command, Brazberg. "I'm concerned about an organized crime bloodbath with the Cuzzi family, Sy. Do you think I have anything to worry about?"

Brazberg was sixty-five years old. His pension was secure. He could have retired tomorrow, and the DA's flamboyance never intimidated him. He had jumped out of just as many airplanes as the DA in World War II and had done so with the weight of sixteen additional years.

"I left my fuckin' crystal ball upstairs, Fazio," he said. "How the hell do I know? Ask these other guys. Maybe they can fucking tell you."

The detectives stared down at the conference table. O'Boyle squirmed uneasily. Only Brazberg could show such insubordination without retribution.

Brazberg was pissed off. Today was his granddaughter's birthday, and he didn't want to sit here with a bullshit briefing where no one had any answers. His twenty years of experience as the head of the Homicide Bureau had taught him that the odds of solving an organized crime hit were less than hitting the Irish sweepstakes.

"Listen, Fazio, Johnny O'Boyle has got a briefing for you so I'll let him tell you what he knows. Johnny, do your schtick."

"Thanks. First as we all know, Dominic Varino is the Admiral's son-in-law. Dom, or Mickey as they call him, was found in the trunk of a Buick in the Orchard Beach parking lot last Sunday morning. He had two twenty-two slugs behind his right ear." O'Boyle paused.

"The ME ruled out suicide." O'Boyle smiled. Brazberg guffawed. The DA just stared.

O'Boyle continued. "Needless to say, there are no prints. The car was stolen from a dentist on Pelham Parkway. Varino's car, a 1970 Toronado, was found two blocks from his girlfriend's house on Country Club Road. She of course tells us she's never heard of Dominic Varino. So the detectives show her some snaps of her and Varino together. The snaps come from the "Commissioner's Organized Crime Task Force."

O'Boyle paused, poured some water from a beaker on the conference table, and sipped. Then he continued. "She then tells us that he stopped by on Saturday night. They visited for a while, if you know what I mean, and then he left about ten-thirty P.M. We figure he was picked up right after that, killed, and dumped."

Then, turning to the DA, he said, "I realize a lot of this information is known to you, but I'm presenting here the exact text of what I will relate to the Citywide Intelligence Task Force, should you require me to address them."

"Okay, go ahead but don't fuck around," the district attorney ordered, pleased.

O'Boyle obeyed. "Guido Insalata is known as the Admiral. He lives up in Throggs Neck and runs the Hudson River Trading Company. He's in the import-export business. He loves to fish and has a twenty-five-foot boat. When he goes out in his boat, he wears the hat from an admiral in the Italian navy. He's a mite eccentric but the shrewdest bad guy in New York. He's brilliant. He has only two numbers busts, and those are from when he was a kid. Nothing else. He's clean.

"Everyone figures that he's run things for the Cuzzi family in the Neck, Pelham Bay, and Morris Park for the last thirty years. He's sixty-four now and lives very simply. Every year he gets an audit from the IRS. The changes are minimal if anything, sometimes he even gets refunds. The Admiral is a smart survivor, and the feds think he's unsinkable. But he has one weakness, like we all do. In his case it's his daughter, Susan. Twenty-eight years old, magna cum laude from Barnard and has a master's in history and education from NYU. She teaches at St. Elizabeth's in Westchester County. She's an intelligent and well thought of woman. Now, her problem is that she is overly fond of the goodies that Pop imports. So she is shaped like a fire hydrant. And the poor girl has got a face that looks like she was in an ax fight and someone forgot to give her an ax."

There was a little chuckling as O'Boyle continued. "Now, some of New York's finest think the Admiral had his son-in-law hit. They think the Admiral knew Mickey liked a little on the side so the Admiral gave him a little something in the head, but I—I don't buy it. Susan loved Mickey too much. We spoke to her and she is really broken up. She knew that Mickey fucked around and she admits she didn't like it, but Mickey was always good to her."

"He was probably scared shit of his father-in-law," the DA broke in.

"Could be," O'Boyle replied. "But the Admiral treated him pretty good and they seemed to get along. Mickey was an officer of the Hudson River Trading Company and he drew a good salary. Along with his wife's teacher's salary, they had a nice life-style. Not grandiose, mind you, but nice."

O'Boyle paused and lit a cigarette. He took a drag and held the pack out to the assemblage. Brazberg took one, then O'Boyle inhaled and continued.

"Yesterday we brought in Mickey's girlfriend's brother. He is twenty-three years old. Tattoos on his arms and chest. Shirt opened to the waist and a gold chain with a big round pendant, I mean big, like one of those things the Chinese guy bangs on with the club to announce the presence of the warlord. The kid thinks he's Al Capone or something. A real asshole. But all he tells us is that he wants a lawyer. He was here for only an hour before we released him.

"We found him this morning in some bushes in the Botanical Gardens. The kid had two in the mouth, and he had been enoculated."

O'Boyle smiled at the detectives' bewildered expressions.

Brazberg explained, "His eyes had been removed."

Brazberg knew that O'Boyle loved to use such words. He remembered reading one of Johnny O'Boyle's homicide reports, which listed the cause of death as defenestration. Brazberg had to read the whole narrative before realizing that the victim had been thrown out the window.

"That's the whole case up to now," O'Boyle concluded.

The DA turned to Brazberg and the group of detectives. "Tell your bosses I am not going to let this thing die. Push them on it. I want them to give me a weekly briefing. In person."

He walked out of the room, and the group followed him. They had been dismissed.

In the eleven months following the assassination of Mickey Varino, Alcibiades LoConti subjected himself to the intense struggle of daily service in the New York City Criminal Court, Bronx County.

He told his uncle Peppy one night at dinner, "In the last eleven months I've done and seen it all. Arraignments are just tedious bullshit, no skill is involved, just speed. I did felony hearings for every felony in the Penal Law in the first six weeks. I prosecuted rapists, robbers, burglars, thieves, sodomites, child molesters, dog fuckers, and even a guy humpin' a deer in the Bronx Zoo."

"A deer?" his uncle asked.

"Yeah, a fuckin' deer. Guy had on big hip boots and he put the deer's back legs in the hip boots and slipped it to the deer from behind."

"I heard of guys fuckin' sheep and cows but never a deer," his uncle replied.

"Put a year in the Criminal Court and you see everything."

"But you just had the preliminary hearings on these things, Al. You didn't get to try the cases, did you?"

"Right, Unc. The Court has no felony jurisdiction except for the hearings. In ninety-nine percent of the cases, after the hearing the judge sends it over to the grand jury. Then they are indicted and tried by the senior bureaus across town."

"But you've had a lot of trials, right?"

"Just the misdemeanors Unc. That's all that this court has jurisdiction of for trial purposes. But I've done the drug cases of all kinds. You know, gamblers, prostitution, assaults, drunk drivers, dickie wavers, and flashers. Those guys only get charged with public lewdness. There are cock fights, dog fights, discon, harassment, menacing, bullshit, horseshit, and more shit. It never fuckin' ends and it never will. And we even get the fags in a bag."

"What's that?"

"Consensual sodomy. One thirty thirty Penal Law. Homosexuals in the public, usually subway, bathrooms. One guy puts his feet in a bag, the other guy sits on the bowl. Cop goes by and only sees one pair of legs. I don't have to draw pictures about what's goin' on. Last week I got twenty-two defendants. They were arrested in a sweep from Kingsbridge Road down to 149th Street and the Grand Concourse. Twenty of them were married and were stopping for some recreational sex before going home to the wife and kids uptown."

"Have any of your group been promoted?"

"One guy is goin' to the Grand Jury next month. I hope I can get out real soon. Even in Nam you went home after serving a year. This place is like shovelin' shit against the tide. All your efforts are meaningless."

"Well, Al, you've been playing the big leagues. I'm sure you've learned plenty."

Al nodded at his uncle, the man who had been a substitute for his father who had died in World War II.

"I've learned two things: that this city is a really dangerous place to live and that there is justice for no one."

"Nothing is easy, Al. You know the old saying—'There is no soft rock, no free lunch.'"

"I'm still years away from my goal."

"What's that, Al?"

"The epitome, Unc, the cream . . . you know . . . the fuckin' Homicide Bureau."

IT WAS A COOL October day this Columbus Day of 1971. Alcibiades, now in his fifteenth month on the job, had already tried three major felony drug sales and had been involved in two wiretap investigations. The work was exciting, but the witnesses were always professionals, policemen and chemists.

While the Columbus Day parade was proceeding in Manhattan, Al was anxiously waiting in the Bronx Supreme Court Part 12 for an arraignment. There had already been two indictments of the same individual for direct sales to Officer William Wotter of the elite 13th Narcotics Group. Members of the thirteenth included Pete DiCerrechia, recently transferred from the Four Seven, Wotter, and Rory O'Donnell. Lieutenant Bill Solwin was the CO.

DiCerrechia and O'Donnell sat in the back of the courtroom. After they had arrested the seller on a bench warrant, they had taken him for a friendly ride and asked him to cooperate—in other words, to "turn." Through the seller, they hoped to reach the goal of all narcotics officers, to climb the ladder to the holy grail, the ultimate source, the fictional, nonexistent, one and only, major supplier. But the seller, a kid named Fidel Vicun, had refused. O'Donnell didn't want to pursue the matter, but DiCerrechia did.

"I feel like this guy is a fuckin' fountain of information. Besides that, he's a fuckin' chameleon. He can go anywhere and make any fuckin' connection. He's bound to lead us to middle-level distribution or higher. Let's lodge him in the Bronx House of D instead of the Rikers Youth wing. After a few days there, his fuckin' asshole will be bigger than the Lincoln Tunnel."

"Then what?" Rory asked.

"Then we'll just ask him if he wants to fuckin' reconsider." Pete answered.

They were now awaiting their results.

Alcibiades sat in the jury box with other ADAs. The procession of cases was endless. Rapes, Robberies, Murders, Sodomy, Larceny, Burglary; Possessory crimes of Drugs, Guns and Stolen Property. Each section of the Penal law aired in the open Court of Part 12 on each and every day.

Bail, it seemed, was pleaded for incessantly with every case. Al could almost recite the arguments by memory. Each defendant always had roots in the community and a nonviolent past. Those with fifteen or twenty assaults were panned off as having been clean for six months or one year, as the case may be. There was always an excuse, there was always a story. Al was bored and disgusted with the whole system. Even bail here was low. People charged with murder had bail set at five or ten thousand dollars. This was the Supreme Court of the State of New York as Terry Hanratty had said and it was just another leak valve in a porous sewer.

The judge today was Samuel Flay. The DAs and defense lawyers called him "Mr. Judicial Notice." Now in his sixteenth year on the bench, Flay had been promoted to an acting Supreme Court judge, as a reward for having completed a clearing program in the criminal court. In the clearing program, known to the bench and bar as "Let's Make a Deal," Flay had seemingly given the courthouse away.

Flay was a short, prudish man of great pomposity. He was plump, wore horn-rimmed glasses, and had a pencil-thin mustache. His thin hair was parted down the middle and brushed neatly back, and he always wore a bow tie. He looked like a pimp disguised as a professor.

From time to time, in an effort to seem avuncular, he would lift his head and smile. When the outside light reflected from his horn-rimmed glasses, it made his eyes invisible. The effect was that of a demonic imp, sitting beneath the words "In God We Trust."

Flay said very little and cut lawyers off with a wave of his hand. As a result, his court was efficient.

Although he had caused Alcibiades his greatest embarrassment as a DA, Al had a grudging respect for the judge. Still, Flay's occasional erratic, irrational behavior and decisions made everyone in the courtroom fear him. You never knew what was up when old Sammy Flay was on the fuckin' bench, Al thought to himself.

The courtroom routine was always the same. The bridgeman announced the defendant's name and the charges in the indictment. "People versus Victor Moore, charged with Murder Second Degree, Possession of a Weapon as a Felony. Defendant represented by Mr. Myron Mercus under eighteen b of the County Law." Eighteen b meant the defendant couldn't afford a lawyer so the court appointed him one.

Flay would then say to the clerk in referring to the defense lawyer. "Tell him to file a Notice of Appearance."

The Notice of Appearance was a single-page preprinted legal form. The clerk kept a pad of these forms on his desk. Each Notice of Appearance contained the title of the case and informed the court of the name, address, and telephone number of the attorney appearing for the defendant. Though the notice was simple and easy to complete, it gave the judge total control over the lawyer the moment after it was filed. The lawyer could not even quit at that point and depended on the judge to relieve him. But judges seldom relieved lawyers, even when their retainers remained unpaid.

After Flay was satisfied that a Notice of Appearance had been filed, the DA would put in a pitch for bail. Naturally the defendant would ask for low bail or parole. Flay would make a decision, give a number, and then would call for the next case.

In the next case, lawyer "Fast" Frankie Hammon stepped up. He was a genuine comedian and all the judges and DAs got a kick out of him, yet Hammon was also very shrewd. Well dressed as always, today he wore a navy-blue suit, a powder-blue tie, and heavy silver-rimmed eyeglasses with tinted lenses. His silver hair was immaculately groomed.

"Good morning, Judge Flay. I already filed my Notice of Appearance."

Flay looked at the court file. "Why is this case still in this Part when the defendant was arraigned last month?"

"Judge, I worked out an excellent disposition with the District Attorney but before my man here takes a plea, I have to interview one more witness." Hammon paused, then he continued. "His name is Mr. Greene, Judge Flay."

The clerks chuckled and the stenographer smiled as she recorded the words. Alcibiades laughed to himself.

Hammon was just trying to tip off the judge that he still hadn't been paid in full. As he'd filed the Notice of Appearance he was on the case, and if the plea was taken without payment then he could kiss his fee good-bye.

The judge, to Al's dismay, understood the lawyer's plight. "How much time do you need, Mr. Hammon?"

Hammon turned to his client. "May I have a moment, Your Honor?"

Flay nodded.

Hammon and his client conferred. "Two weeks should be enough, Judge Flay."

"Very well. Next case."

Alcibiades had asked that his case be called during a recess so that he could make his application to parole the informer without the public viewing it.

It was almost 1 P.M. and the great rush of the morning arraignments was almost over. The courtroom had only a few spectators, and Alcibiades was expecting his case to be called next.

The cynical Terry Hanratty, now Al's close friend and a member of the Supreme Court Trial Bureau, was handling the calendar. Al heard a chant then a shout from behind the closed paneled door that led up a flight of stairs to the holding pens.

"Allah, Allah, Allah." All heads turned toward the door as it swung open. Four court officers accompanied a black man into the courtroom.

One look told Al that the man was deranged. His head jutted from a hole in a blanket that was draped over his shoulders and barely covered his front and back. He had nothing on underneath, was barefoot, and his feet and legs, face, neck, and arms were filthy. His face was bearded and the whites of his eyes shone iridescently in sharp contrast to the crusted grime of his face.

"Allah. Allah. Allah," he continued to chant.

"Roland Coleman aka Muhammad Aktwi charged with Sodomy and Endangering the Welfare of a Child. Arrested on a bench warrant for Failure to Appear on July 6, 1970," the bridgeman shouted.

The defendant grew quiet. He stared straight ahead and hummed. "AHOOOOOOOOOOOHM. AHOOOOOOOOO-OOOOOHM."

Flay was annoyed. "Do you have a lawyer?" he shouted above the chant.

"Allah, Allah, He be my lawyer," Aktwi stated and then resumed chanting. "AHOOOOOOOHM. AHOOOOOOHM."

"Tell him to file a Notice of Appearance," Flay came back, "and refer to Dr. Rehyn for immediate report." Flay finished and looked off in another direction as the defendant was taken out for an evaluation by Dr. Andrew Rehyn, the court psychiatrist. Rehyn usually found everyone competent to proceed. Alcibiades wondered what the doctor would do in this particular case.

Flay ordered a recess and motioned for Al to proceed into the robing room. The informer was then brought in with the stenographer. Al was surprised by not only Flay's courtesy but that the proceedings were over in a flash. The informer was paroled. After he was led back upstairs to be checked out, DiCerrechia and O'Donnell would join him and would start to put him to work on the street. Officer Wotter had finally got his man. The elusive Fidel Vicun turned out to be Chingo, who had been making his living selling drugs. Chingo had fucked up though, when he had sold to Officer William Wotter.

Al went back out into the courtroom of Part 12 just as Flay was taking the bench. As he was leaving, he paused at the sound of the chant and took a seat next to DiCerrechia and O'Donnell to watch.

"AHOOOOOOHM. AHOOOOOOOHM," chanted Aktwi as he was led back into the courtroom to stand in front of Judge Flay.

The bridgeman took a piece of paper from one of the court officers. "Judge, we have a report from Dr. Rehyn. He has found the defendant competent to proceed."

"Very well, assign a lawyer. Defendant remanded until tomorrow."

As Alcibiades was leaving Part 12, his cousin Allie Boy Spano, who had recently received his eighteenth citation for excellent police work and his twenty-seventh department award, was sitting in the recorder seat of an RMP.

Allie Boy had been assigned another clinker as a partner, another dud. This time it was worse because he had known this loser since childhood. They were the same age and came from the same block. Both had attended Our Lady of Solace School on Morris Park Avenue and Christopher Columbus High School. Allie Boy had graduated in four years, then entered the army. He stayed for four years and put in two tours in Nam.

Another big reason why Allie Boy didn't like his new partner Richie Zemberelli was that while Allie Boy was in I Corp in Vietnam putting his life on the line as a member of an elite LRPSE unit, (Long Range Reconnaissance Patrol), Richie had been baking pizzas and making "gabbagole" sandwiches for a bunch of guys in the National Guard back in New York.

Richie's second cousin Attilio "Otto" Palumbo, also made "gabbagole" sandwiches but at Jo-Jo's across from the rectory of Our Lady of Solace. Otto, who always bragged he could spell his nickname backward and forward, paid for the concession of selling sandwiches out of the small kitchen off the end of the bar at Jo-Jo's.

Otto's sandwich concession offered prime cold cuts and a daily special of roast pork, roast beef, sausages, or a special combination hero. The sandwiches were served on the freshest breads from the bakery near St. Dominic's Church on Victor Street. Soaked-in-oil red peppers, green olives, and fresh greens crowned each sandwich.

Even though the concession brought a lot of business to Jo-Jo's, Jo-Jo himself still received his generous monthly flat fee from Otto. The sandwich business was doomed to run at a loss, but Otto wasn't stupid. While selling sandwiches he was also taking all the Admiral's action between Bronxdale Avenue and 180th Street.

Someone, perhaps a person of religion or a disgruntled bettor or someone who had gotten heartburn from a copious sandwich, sent an anonymous letter to the mayor, who turned it over to the Police Commissioner. Cornelius "Connie" O'Toole, a Deputy Chief Inspector got the report from the police commissioner. Connie, who together with other brass had been involved with the Hat in an unspeakable felony while young policemen, picked up the telephone. Connie called the Admiral, and the Admiral called the Hat. He told the Hat he must arrest Attilio "Otto" Palumbo for gambling, but discreetly. Otto was to be a sacrificial lamb, a delicacy that alas had never been featured as a special at Jo-Jo's.

The Hat didn't bother to go through the Public Morals guys. He knew that they were on a pad and that they would tip Otto off, so he called in his two best detectives, Timmy Flanagan and Morrie Shapiro.

A young Spanish undercover officer named Valdez was selected as the pigeon. Clean cut and dressed as a construction worker, he placed a bet on two consecutive days.

Valdez walked to the back of the bar on the second day. As he faced the small kitchen counter, Otto stepped up. "Combination," Valdez said, leaving a small scrap of paper with three numbers on it.

As Valdez walked out Flanagan and Shapiro walked in. When Valdez signaled that he had placed the bet by nodding his head, the detectives took Otto from the kitchen and cuffed him. On the way out to their unmarked car they told him he was being locked up for policy. He claimed his absolute innocence. When they told him he had just laid off action for an undercover cop, Otto yelled, "Hey, this is a mistake. This is a big mistake. That fuckin' Puerto Rican guy when he said combination, I thought he meant 'gabbagole' and provolone. You know, today's fuckin' special."

The detectives both laughed.

That was two days ago. Fast Frankie Hammon had been standing in court waiting for Otto to arrive. Otto ended up pleading guilty. He was fined and was back in time to make sandwiches for the supper crowd at Jo-Jo's.

Allie Boy saw Zemberelli as really tainted by Otto. His family was corrupt, and that was enough for Allie Boy. For him the world existed in only two colors: black or white. No shades of gray, no in between.

Besides, for the last half hour Zemberelli had done nothing but talk about his brand-new girlfriend—a girl from England who had a cute accent and with whom Zemberelli was deeply infatuated. Much to Allie Boy's disgust, Zemberelli described in vivid detail all the sexual acts he had performed with the girl. Allie Boy felt that the sharing of such intimate information was unmanly, and yet he personally engaged in public suggestive acts with his women without shame. The paradox never struck him.

Allie Boy finally interrupted Zemberelli's narrative. "Richie, is this girl from London?"

"No, Allie, like I told you . . . she's from England."

Spano groaned. Richie continued to drive and to talk, talk, talk.

Allie Boy looked out his window. I'm really in fuckin' purgatory with this fuckin' guy," he thought.

RONALD DEPEW WALKED DOWN Tremont Avenue after coming off Third Avenue. A train rumbled overhead. He had no special destination and as he passed a construction site cordoned by yellow stanchions, he looked down into the excavation and spotted a large smooth stone. Ronald climbed down into the hole. He bent to pick it up and found that it was not heavy. He could hold it in one hand. He brushed the dirt from it, placed it inside his jacket, and held it there with one arm.

Ronald walked up the block and went into one of the small four-story apartment houses that lined the block. He climbed up to the roof quickly. On the top floor he passed the doorway of his only friend, Dewey Mulligan. Dewey's dog growled as Ronald went passed the door. Ronald hated Dewey's dog.

Ronald knew that Dewey was home alone. About twenty minutes before Ronald had seen Dewey's mother and father walk through the doors of the Tunes of Trallee Bar and Grill on Third Avenue. Ronald knew they'd be there for hours. Ronald opened the door onto the roof and walked out quietly. He was careful in placing his feet so that no noise would filter through the thin tarpaper into the apartment below.

When he got to the edge he opened his jacket and took out the smooth stone.

He looked up the block and smiled. Mrs. McNeill, the fifty-four-year-old widow of a transit motorman, was coming down the block, as he'd expected. Ronald didn't like Mrs. McNeill because when Foley the butcher had asked him to deliver a package of meat to her last month, Mrs. McNeill had only tipped him two cents. Then she had slammed her door in his face. She had screwed him and Ronald had not forgotten.

As Ronald waited for Mrs. McNeill to come near the roof, in his mind's eye he saw the stone descending slowly and striking her head. He then saw her lying in the gutter, her head smashed, blood gushing out like water from an open hydrant.

Mrs. McNeill suddenly stopped, turned around, and returned toward the Third Avenue El. She had forgotten to pick up a fifth of Fleishmann's blended whiskey for her friend Jimmy Shaughnessy. That memory lapse had probably saved her life.

DePew was angry at the loss of his prey.

As she walked toward Third Avenue, Ronald continued looking down from the roof as Allie Boy Spano and Richie Zemberelli turned their RMP onto Tremont Avenue.

Allie Boy Spano was attentive as always. He continued to treat each patrol as if he was still in Vietnam, always alert, always watchful, and ever mindful of the fact that police officers had been assassinated in the very seats of their cars. Zemberelli had finally quit talking and was now driving slowly.

Richie spotted the falling rock first, heading right for the windshield in front of Allie Boy. Realizing in a flash that someone could get hurt, Zemberelli gunned the car and cut the wheel hard to the right. The stone crashed into the side window next to him. The move had saved Allie Boy's life. Allie Boy Spano sat motionless. Glass shards had peppered his face and two large slivers had struck Zemberelli on the forehead and the cheek.

Allie Boy's eyes bugged out in fear as the RMP raced across Tremont Avenue in front of an oncoming bus. Luckily the bus struck only the rear of the RMP, sending it careening and spinning up on the sidewalk.

The RMP finally crashed through the front door of Foley's Butcher Shop and came to rest against the walk-in freezer at the rear of the store.

When Richie looked at Allie Boy and saw blood streaming from his face, he didn't realize that the wounds were not serious. He threw the car in neutral. It started immediately. Then he popped it in reverse and it shot back outside the butcher shop. Allie Boy sat frozen in horror. Richie shifted the gears into drive, floored the accelerator, and in three minutes they were both at the emergency room of the Thomas Jefferson Medical Center.

Both men were stitched up, but Zemberelli's cuts were deeper. Other detectives swarmed around the ER. When the two officers were ready to be released, Allie Boy put his arm around Zemberelli and said, "Thanks, Rich. I'm gonna put in for you as my partner permanently. You saved my fuckin' life."

Richie was moved but just nodded, not trusting himself to speak.

Uniformed police and detectives scoured the roofs in the Tremont area. Meanwhile Ronald DePew sat talking in Dewey Mulligan's apartment. Ronald was secretly pleased not only with himself but also with his perfect shot through the cops' window. After a couple of hours when Ronald looked out the window and saw that the street was quiet, he said good-bye to Dewey. As he passed the kitchen toward the outside door, Dewey's dog growled. Dewey could never understand why his dog just didn't like Ronald DePew.

It was Saturday night, October 16, 1971, and everything was in place at the Last Supper. Peppy Gennaro had rescheduled the Columbus Day dinner to tonight from last Tuesday after his nephew had been injured. As a surprise he had even added Richie Zemberelli and his English girlfriend to the guest list.

Tonight was to be a special occasion. Peppy wanted this evening to finally honor his favorite nephew, Alcibiades LoConti, for all of his achievements: his education, his war service, his decorations, and most recently his promotion in the District Attorney's office. If only his sister and her husband were here to see what had become of their boy.

Al's father had not survived World War II. He remained in a cemetery in the Philippine Islands where he had been killed in 1944. Peppy's sister, Al's mother, had died of a stroke in 1969, while her elder son was serving in Vietnam. She had become obsessed that he, like his father before him, would not return from the dreaded Far East.

Return he had. But lately Peppy had observed that Al had become just too serious, almost grim. He noticed that his new experiences as an ADA did sometimes spark him into the cheerful, witty youth of his past, but more often than not his nephew was just getting grimmer, more resigned, too serious, and too depressed.

Peppy had also received reports from Al's wife that he was not the same. She said that he brooded, he sulked, he wouldn't talk for hours at a time, he was obsessed with his work and in general was disheartened with the whole system he served.

Peppy hoped Al would soon be promoted to the Homicide Bureau, the boy's obsession. Perhaps a few more years after that he would really get smart and join a large law firm and try civil cases and make real money, not the pittance handed out to assistant district attorneys these days.

So tonight Alcibiades would be honored by his uncle at the Last Supper. A large banquet table was set up in the restaurant's semi-private rear room and extra waitresses had been hired to serve this table only. No expense was to be spared, and a special menu with the finest delicacies was available for all the special guests.

INSPECTOR ALOYSIOUS X. MCDANIEL, Assistant Borough Commander, to all known as the Hat, was riding in the recorder's seat of an RMP down Morris Park Avenue just as Peppy Gennaro was preparing for his nephew and guests.

The Hat directed his driver to drive past Our Lady of Solace

Church and to then to make a righthand turn onto Hunt Avenue. He then ordered the driver to park at the No Parking sign in front of St. Martha's Episcopal Church and to wait for him there.

The driver, who had chauffeured the Hat for the last four years, silently mused that the Hat was probably either going to glom a free case of booze or some other scag. Driving the Hat was like going to the movies every day, the best job in the world, except for the times when it got a little hairy, like yesterday. Yesterday afternoon the Hat, as always, was half shitfaced, and while riding on the Grand Concourse he had spotted a young black kid push another kid from his bicycle, then hop on and pedal furiously away. The Hat had screamed for his driver to give chase, which they did, even to the extent of going against traffic on a one-way street. It was a real Keystone Cops scene, cars and people going everywhere trying to avoid the RMP with the screaming Hat in the rear. Finally the driver pulled next to the bicycle. The Hat reached over the front seat, grabbed the steering wheel, and yanked it down, causing the RMP to swerve into the bike and spill the kid into the gutter. In a flash the Hat had pounced on the kid. After punching and kicking the boy, he screamed at him to drive the bike back to the kid he had stolen it from.

"Stole, shit," the black kid had yelled back. "This here is my fuckin' bike that motherfucker done stole it from me." The Hat dropped five bucks in the street then got back in the RMP and drove off.

The driver then drove through the Belmont and Arthur Avenue neighborhood, which was part of the Bronx's Little Italy. The Hat spotted four youths running from a tenement basement. "Stop," the Hat had ordered as he bounded from the car and retraced the fleeing youths' steps only to return within minutes and direct a call for both an ambulance and homicide. A man was hanging from pipes running along the basement ceiling. His hands had been tied behind his back. The four fleeing youths undoubtedly were the perpetrators.

Just another afternoon with the Hat, his driver thought.

The Hat got out of the car and walked down the sidewalk alongside the church to the rear. Rather than entering the church, he followed a path back to Morris Park. At the corner he walked through a rear cellar entrance to a candy store and entered. After knocking on a door, a peephole opened and closed and he was admitted by Santa Giacomo.

Giacomo ran a gaming establishment that consisted of four crap tables, eight blackjack tables, and one wheel of fortune. The Hat got wise to the operation when he noticed that Giacomo ran valet parking from the Cudahy Funeral Parlor over on Van Nest Avenue. On one of his routine patrols the Hat had observed that Cudahy's parking lot was always full. None of the other funeral parlors was ever as crammed with cars, and the Hat tended to doubt that so many Irish were dying in the Bronx. So he staked out the funeral parlor in his own vehicle and discovered the valet service shuttling from Van Nest Avenue to the intersection of Morris Park and Hunt. After a week of surveillance, watching the high rollers enter the candy store from the rear, the Hat was satisfied that there were only two officers making a score on the operation. Both were reassigned to Bronx Public Morals. They had been acting as entrepreneurs and acting alone. After having them reassigned, the Hat took their places.

Now he walked inside.

Each week a little ritual was played out. Santa Giacomo would disappear behind a concrete wall, then reappear with two cold glasses. One contained Heineken and one contained Hennessey brandy. The Hat would down each of them and hand them back to Santa Giacomo.

"Thank you, me lad, and now the envelope please. I must be going. . . ." Giacomo would then hand him an envelope with fifteen crisp one-hundred-dollar bills and a shopping bag containing three bottles of Remy Martin Cognac and three bottles of Bushmill's Irish Whiskey.

The Hat patted Santa Giacomo as one would a treasured pet, winked, and then left.

This time, though, the Hat's exit was being watched by a stickup team made up of DiDi O'Sullivan, Henry Quade, Ronnie Bucchiossi, Ira Silver, and LeRoy Joseph, all of whom had done hard time together at Attica State Prison. Prison overcrowding and a federal judge's concern with inmate rights had led to their recent early release.

LeRoy Joseph, the only black in the group, had heard about the high-roller game on Morris Park Avenue. He was also the only one of the stickup team who came from the Bronx. Except for DiDi O'Sullivan, the rest were from Long Island or Brooklyn. O'Sullivan, from Albany, was one of the reputed criminal geniuses of northern New York.

O'Sullivan had discovered through his own investigation that the gambling in the candy store basement was related to the gambling that went on in the rear of the Glory of Ulster Bar and Grill. There seemed to be a ferry of cars between the candy store and bar. The Glory of Ulster was located directly across the street from the Last Supper on Morris Park Avenue. O'Sullivan had been correct in guessing that a link existed between the two. In fact, Hugh O'Grady, the owner of the Glory of Ulster, and Santa Giacomo ran a joint operation. Hugh had three card games in the rear of his bar and also served whatever food his patrons desired. His messengers could deliver any food, no matter what the ethnic origin, within forty-five minutes at any time up to 5 A.M. Hugh was a real legend on Morris Park. Al's uncle Peppy refused to supply Hugh with any food, because Peppy knew Hugh O'Grady was engaged in illegal activities.

Yet many people loved Hughie. Members of the International Brotherhood of Lathers Local 199 and other alcoholics were never refused a drink at his bar when they were broke. Hughie was always there to help the fellow with a problem with the booze, but his kindness did not end there. He was a generous contributor to the Van Nest Little League and to the Morris Park chapter of Unity for Christians and Jews.

His wife, the former Heather Goldstein, had made him a genuine devotee for better Catholic and Jewish relationships. Hughie and Heather had married thirty years ago, just before Pearl Harbor. Since they could not satisfy both of their families, they had been married by a justice of the peace and had a magnificient reception at the recently opened Last Supper.

Al's uncle had given them the reception as a wedding gift but since that time had steadfastly refused to be involved in any of Hughie's gambling activities.

"I serve delicious, quality food at a reasonable price. I have a good honest business. I don't want to get involved in other things. I do not want to involve myself or my family in anything that could disgrace us."

Everyone respected Peppy's wishes. He had been a marine in World War II and had made five landings on islands garrisoned by Japanese. He was also the all-service light-heavyweight champ in early 1943. His marriage was childless and his youngest nephew Vince LoConti, Al's younger brother, now in Vietnam, had summed up the neighborhood's attitude: "No one fucks with Peppy Gennaro."

His nephews worshipped him.

After watching the Hat leave, DiDi O'Sullivan's masked stickup team robbed the gamblers at Santa Giacomo's casino at gunpoint and left them tied and gagged. They threw pillow cases filled with money, watches, and rings into the trunk of a '67 Buick, then jumped in the car and drove five blocks up Morris Park Avenue, passing the Last Supper, then made a U turn, and double-parked at a hydrant four stores up from the Glory of Ulster Bar and Grill.

Henry Quade entered first. He pointed his .45 at Hughie's head. A surprised Hughie raised his hands and . . .

THE GUESTS WERE BEING seated inside the Last Supper across Morris Park Avenue from the Glory of Ulster Bar and Grill where Hugh O'Grady stood with his hands in the air.

Alcibiades and his wife, Renee, sat at one end of a long banquet table. Al was flanked on one side by Pete DiCerrechia and his wife, Connie, and on the other side by William Wotter and Rory O'Donnell. Wotter and O'Donnell were the stags at the party.

O'Donnell was now divorced for the third time. "Three strikes and you're out," his friends had teased.

Wotter, before his release from the marines and while still recuperating from battle wounds, had terminated his marriage.

Balthazar "Bill" Solwin, the 13th Narcotics CO, was there with his wife, as were Detective First Grade Timothy Flanagan and Detective Second Grade Morrie Shapiro.

Ruella Watkins, the black policewoman now assigned to the 13th Narcotics, attended with her new boyfriend, Detective Elrod Harrison of the Bronx DA's squad.

A bandaged Allie Boy Spano and his current fling, a go-go dancer named Matarda, an illegal immigrant from the Dominican Republic, arrived late. Matarda wore a bright-orange dress with a kelly-green sash around her waist. The dress was trimmed with white bunting on the hemline, which was only inches below the delectable curve of Matarda's ass. Her figure stopped the entire party conversation in midsentence.

After all of the introductions had been made, Alcibiades exhaled loudly as he watched Matarda sit down. His wife Renee glanced at him angrily. Then she heard hard breathing from Wotter and O'Donnell. It sounded like they had just completed the decathalon. She stared daggers at them both. Wotter was oblivious but O'Donnell caught the displeasure.

In a conciliatory tone he turned his attention to Al's wife. "I was only thinkin'," he said in his thick Irish brogue, "that the colors of her dress are the same as the flag of Ireland."

"Bullshit," Connie DiCerrechia chimed in.

Then everyone laughed. The tension, which had been as tight as Matarda's orange dress, subsided and everyone settled down for a good time.

When Richie Zemberelli and his English girlfriend walked in, everyone cheered. Richie was delighted to be the center of attention. He savored the moment, then strolled up to the table slowly, like a marshall in the Old West entering a saloon.

Peppy Gennaro had champagne poured for all and toasted Alcibiades. After all the glasses were refilled, he gave a short speech on how the family and the neighborhood were proud of Al LoConti. As he spoke, Al blushed. Inwardly he was glad this toasting part was over because a six-course meal followed.

Renee LoConti, formerly Irene Prescott of Cardiff, Wales, watched her husband as he cut into his beefsteak pizziola. Though she had borne two children, heads still turned when Renee walked into a room. Her skin was soft and pale, her eyes were green, deep green, the color of pine trees against a summer sky. Her reddish-gold hair was lustrous and draped long and silken onto her white dress. After her parents' death in an automobile accident, Renee had come to America at the age of eighteen to live with her sister on Long Island. Her sister, eight years her senior, had arrived in New York in 1956.

Renee loved her husband. She was troubled that even now at this party he was still grim, still tense and still withdrawn. He was far different from the young officer she had met seven years before. The war and the job had transformed the smiling, caring, and loving man she knew into someone completely different. They had married while he was a law student, and ten days after the bar exam he had entered the army as a first lieutenant. She traveled with him to Fort Gordon, Georgia, for his first assignment and then waited faithfully for his return from overseas. Now when he had been awarded the job he had sought for years, he had become a different man. After all the years of scrimping and saving, when finally they had a decent living, he could not even enjoy it. She knew he could never understand her concerns. He had become a fly that was trapped in the web of his job. She was pleased when he turned and pecked her on the cheek. It was true that he was under a lot of strain, but maybe, just maybe, Al would return to his old self soon.

As if on cue after the last course was served and eaten, all of the women excused themselves to the powder room. They did not invite Matarda.

In the bathroom they gossiped about Allie Boy's latest tramp, whore, *putan*, slut. While they complained the men watched as Allie Boy and Matarda shamelessly caressed and fed each other from a bowl of hot tomato sauce filled with shrimp and other seafood.

Allie Boy boomed another order out to one of his uncle's waiters. "Hey, Guido! Bring my lady a rum and Coke and bring me an ice-cold Pabst."

Guido nodded and complied. The women returned to the table.

Pete wasn't pleased with his wife's scowl as she watched Allie Boy and Matarda feed each other, so as she began to sit down, he placed his upright thumb in a position to meet her descending ass. At contact Connie reflexively bolted upright. The speed of her actions loosened her blond wig, and it popped off her head right onto a platter of bread.

Connie was humiliated and furious. Her face became blood red and Pete knew trouble was coming. He froze and could only display what Allie Boy used to call his shit-eatin' grin.

Connie grabbed the assorted seafood bowl from under Matarda's descending fork and dumped the entire contents on her husband's lap. Though Pete was shocked, the only notice he gave was to widen his shit-eatin' grin.

Meanwhile Timmy Flanagan had just finished his seventh martini. He was in the midst of explaining to his partner, Morrie Shapiro, that Jack Nicklaus would never be surpassed as the greatest golfer of all time, but when he saw Pete with a lapful of seafood in red sauce he burst out laughing. This triggered the entire table, and everyone began to roar. Guido the waiter came over, but Guido was not laughing. Alcibiades jumped up and grabbed the bowl from Connie's hands because he was afraid she might break it over her husband's head. He held out the bowl as Pete brushed the seafood from his lap with a napkin. Pete was so humiliated he could not even relax the grin, which was frozen in place.

When Al's uncle came over and beckoned Pete to the front of the restaurant where he could clean up in the private employees' restroom, Rory O'Donnell signaled William Wotter to accompany him to the bar. Ruella Watkins and Elrod Harrison followed. As the four police officers placed their drink orders, Pete DiCerrechia left the room to clean himself up.

Across Morris Park Avenue inside the Glory of Ulster Bar and Grill, DiDi Sullivan was directing his team like a squad leader in combat. They were fluid and efficient.

Bucchiosi and Silver stood guard at the door. Bucchiosi trained a Colt Combat Commander automatic .45-caliber pistol on the patrons while Silver, armed with a 9-millimeter Beretta, stood watching the street. Quade meanwhile kept his .357 Smith & Wesson revolver trained on Hughie's head.

DiDi O'Sullivan and LeRoy Joseph directed the twelve card players to empty their pockets on the table and then to lie facedown on the floor. The players all obeyed.

As LeRoy Joseph stepped forward to place the wallets and money into a shopping bag, Bucchiosi ordered the bar patrons to put their wallets, rings, and watches on the bartop. Henry Quade handed Hughie a pillow case. "Open it and place the register contents inside," Quade ordered.

Bucchiosi placed his pistol inside his waistband and swept the top of the bar clean of wallets, cash, coins, rings, and watches into a large plastic shopping bag.

When Bucchiosi had cleaned the bar, he retreated toward the front. As he walked, he blocked Quade and Silver's view of one of the patrons at the bar's far end. One of them was a thirty-four-year-old police officer, Jimmy McLaren, who had been drinking heavily at the Glory of Ulster for the last three hours. Jimmy had placed both his feet on the wire rung of the bar stool and therefore did not have far to reach to withdraw his .38 Colt Detective Special revolver from his ankle holster.

Suddenly McLaren screamed, "FREEZE, POLICE."

Bucchiosi dropped his bag and reached for his gun as Quade turned toward the voice. Officer McLaren shot Bucchiosi in the temple, killing him instantly. Quade then fired and missed. McLaren's second shot got Quade in the throat. As Quade staggered, his head thrown back, his body jerked and the .357 went off. Hughie was still standing with his hands up when the .357 Magnum bullet entered his brain. Hughie O'Grady was dead before his hands came down.

DiDi Sullivan stepped forward two paces, braced his right gun hand, and pumped two shots from his Colt .45 into McLaren's head. The bullets were soft-shell dum-dums and they splattered McLaren's brains onto the mirror behind the bar.

LeRoy Joseph looked down at all of the prostrate gamblers.

Nineteen-year-old Lenny DeStefano, a member of Bricklayers Local 923, raised his head to look. Joseph put his gun to Lenny's forehead and pulled the trigger. The gun fired and the back of Lenny's head blew out.

After a shouted command from DiDi O'Sullivan, the remaining members of the stickup team bolted from the Glory of Ulster Bar and Grill. O'Sullivan paused to pick up the bag of loot next to the prostrate Bucchiosi. As the stickup team passed through the doorway, throat-shot Henry Quade dropped dead.

No one stopped to verify the fact that he wouldn't be joining them.

In the bathroom Pete DiCerrechia had done all he could to clean the red stains from the front of his pants. He left the bathroom and paused next to his friends drinking at the bar. He didn't feel like facing his wife yet. While he was standing there deciding what to order, the first shots echoed from across the street. Other shots followed. Pete bolted from the Last Supper with his gun in hand. All of the rest of the cops in the Last Supper ran out with weapons drawn seconds later. Timmy Flanagan drew his gun and walked quickly toward the exit door. Timmy was feeling no pain, and he knew that if he ran he might just collapse with a heart attack. Morrie Shapiro beat him to the exit and ran into the street.

Pete saw men armed with pistols fleeing the Glory of Ulster Bar and Grill across the street. When he saw one of them fall over, he pointed his revolver at him and screamed. "POLICE OFFICER, FREEZE."

O'Donnell, Wotter, and Ruella Watkins leveled their revolvers at the three standing members of the stickup team. Ira Silver fired a shot that nicked the side of Rory's left arm. Rory fired back twice, as did Pete and then William Wotter. Only Rory's first bullet missed. The others struck Silver in the head and chest.

Morrie Shapiro saw DiDi Sullivan and LeRoy Joseph running toward their getaway car that was double-parked up the block. Morrie and Ruella rushed toward the car and opened fire. Joseph and Sullivan could not stand still long enough even to get the doors of their car open. Police cars were screaming down Morris

Park from Bronxdale Avenue and up from White Plains Road, cutting off all avenues of retreat. Like cornered wolves, Joseph and Sullivan ran across the avenue trying to double back past the police officers.

They ran past Morrie and Ruella and they passed Rory, who was holding his bleeding arm. Timmy Flanagan saw exactly what they were doing and crouched behind a parked green Cadillac. As Joseph and Sullivan rushed by, they opened fire on Pete DiCerrechia, who was crossing the street diagonally, trying to cut off their escape route.

Two of Pete's bullets caught Sullivan, dropping him directly in front of the Last Supper. LeRoy Joseph ran as far as the parked green Cadillac where Flanagan was. There Flanagan stood up and shot LeRoy Joseph dead.

In the midst of all the gunfire and confusion, Alcibiades LoConti placed emergency calls to the police department. Then he stepped unarmed from the restaurant with the other police patrons of the party.

Police cars with sirens screaming and red lights revolving stood double-parked on both sides of the block when the police brass arrived. One of the first RMPs rushed Rory to Jacobi Hospital. When two uniformed policemen approached Pete DiCerrechia, they noticed the red stains on his lap.

"This guy is hit bad," the driver said to the recorder.

"Come on, fella, let's take you to Jacobi."

"I'm not hit," Pete responded.

"He's probably in shock," the driver said.

"Come on, fella." The driver put his arm around Pete, urging him toward the RMP.

"I tell you, I'm fuckin' okay," Pete exclaimed. The adrenaline was starting to wane and he felt like retching.

Timothy Flanagan walked up to the officers when he overheard their conversation. He understood the officers' concern over Pete's red-stained pants.

"I'm Detective Flanagan," he said. He had holstered his gun and had placed the leather back of his shield in his front suit breast pocket so that the gold detective shield was visible. The other officers had done the same with their shields.

"Don't worry about him. Those red stains are from before the shooting."

The driver looked at the stain. "Looks like blood to me," he said.

"Yeah, well, he ain't been shot." Flanagan said.

"Well, can you tell me where all that blood came from?" the driver asked the detective.

"Who knows?" Detective Flanagan grinned. Then because he couldn't resist, he said, "Maybe he just got his period a little too early."

The Hat was one of the first of the police brass to arrive on Morris Park Avenue. He got a briefing from Timmy Flanagan and Morrie Shapiro, then he inspected the inside of the Glory of Ulster Bar and Grill. When he saw the body of his buddy Hughie, he became even grimmer. "I'm glad ye got all of 'em, Timmy."

"You can thank Pete DiCerrechia and Rory O'Donnell and Ruella Watkins too, Inspector," Flanagan replied.

"I remember Hughie, God rest his soul, always havin' a nice word for one and all." The Hat paused, then continued. "I'm goin' to see that these boys all get a gold shield."

Just then ADA Johnny O'Boyle, now the chief of the Homicide Bureau, and Terry Hanratty arrived on the scene. Both men had stenographers with them. After inspecting the scene and having a short conversation with Alcibiades LoConti, they requested that all the officers involved report forthwith to the Four Three precinct, in whose area the shootout had taken place.

At the precinct station, Johnny O'Boyle took everyone's statement including that of Al LoConti and all the patrons of both bars. Alcibiades, coolly professional, impressed Johnny O'Boyle. On Monday O'Boyle decided to himself he would have Al begin felony duty. He wanted to start grooming him for Homicide. The kid was good. Really good, he thought.

Back on Morris Park, the Hat looked over Henry Quade's body and recognized a ring that looked like one that Santa Giacomo used to wear. After seeing the ring the Hat decided to retrace the route down Hunt Avenue that he had taken earlier that evening. He got in his car, and had his driver park in front of the Episcopal church. He got out of his car and walked through the churchyard to Holland Avenue. From there he trotted to the rear of the candy store and opened the door, where he quickly untied Santa Giacomo. After leaving the rest of the patrons tied and blindfolded, the Hat led Santa Giacomo behind the concrete wall.

"The guys that did this to you are all dead," he explained. "They killed three guys, including Hughie and a cop. The DA will question everyone and put this before the Grand Jury, and they'll rule that the bastids were killed justifiably. So maybe it would be better if you made good these guys' losses so that they don't say anythin' to anyone. *Capeesh?*"

The Hat put his arm around Santa Giacomo's neck and gave the gambler a sharp squeeze. Then he released him and patted him on the back.

"I'll take care of everythin', Inspector."

"That's me boy. That's me boy." The Hat gave Santa Giacomo a big grin as he left the back room.

Hours later, Al LoConti parked in front of his apartment house in the Inwood section of Manhattan. He walked into his building then took the elevator upstairs. Minutes before his sister-in-law, who had been babysitting, had left. He had sent his wife home by cab after the debacle at the Last Supper. When Renee opened the door, she was not grinning.

"What's the puss for?" Al asked.

"Nothing, nothing at all. It just seems that your job has taken over our life. Even tonight your job took over. A special night and look how it was ruined," Renee said.

"How can you blame the job?" Al asked rhetorically. "It's not the job. It's this city, it's this country, it's because everything has turned to shit. If these guys hadn't been released from jail because of concerns over their rights, then a lot of people wouldn't have died tonight, and your little world wouldn't have been upset."

Al grabbed a beer from the refrigerator and stalked into the living room to brood. His wife went to bed. Each was furious for failing to care about each other.

Al slept on the couch and gave his wife the cold shoulder in the morning. She was far from smiling herself. Just before he left for work, he got a call from Johnny O'Boyle.

"There's an awards ceremony down at police headquarters this afternoon and the DA wants both of us to be there. Put on a good suit. And I got some more good news. You're on the felony duty list now. In fact, I got a case that I just gave to Hanratty and I want you to work with him . . . it'll be good experience."

"Thanks, John." Al smiled to himself. "What's the case about?"

"Black guy found hangin' in a basement off Arthur Avenue. The Hat saw four Italian kids fleeing the scene when he drove up. The DOA was fifty-six years old and had over a hundred arrests. About seventy of them were for burglary. The kids probably caught him burglarizing a flat and brought him to the cellar, tied him up, and stood him on a chair and put a rope around his neck and then over a pipe. The chair had been knocked out from under his feet. There was adhesive tape over his mouth. Check in with Hanratty; see you at the ceremony. By the way, the DOA's name was Woodrow Johnson."

Later that day at police headquarters the Hat hosted his usual array of dignitaries and brass. The mayor was present, as were the DAs from all five counties of the City of New York, borough presidents, members of the Board of Estimate, the City Council, and congressmen. One section was roped off for State Senators and members of the New York State Assembly. Assemblyman Elias Baruba of Queens County led the state delegation. The Bronx DA looked over at it and whispered to the Queens DA standing beside him, "They should call that bunch Ali Baba and the forty thieves." The Queens DA didn't laugh.

The ceremony began with Rory O'Donnell receiving the highest award a police officer could achieve, the Medal of Honor. Pete DiCerrechia received a Meritorious Service and Wotter and Ruella both received EPDs, Excellent Police Duty citations. Rory was promoted from patrolman to Detective Second Grade and the other three were jumped to Detective Third Grade.

Despite the inequities in promotion, due to the Hat's fine hand, all of the newly promoted detectives were pleased for the others.

When the speeches were over and the assemblage started to disperse, Terry Hanratty, who was seated between Alcibiades and Johnny O'Boyle, stood and put his arm on Al's shoulder.

"Let's talk to the Hat about Woodrow Johnson," he said. They approached the Hat and Hanratty greeted him warmly. "You know Al LoConti, Inspector, don't you?" Hanratty asked.

"For sure. Since he was a tot, and I know his uncle Peppy even longer. Your uncle is a real credit to your people," the Hat said, shaking Al's hand warmly.

Al tried not to show his anger. I thought we were all Americans, he fumed to himself.

"Inspector, we're looking into this case of Woodrow Johnson, the guy you saw hangin' the other day."

"Yeah, well, read the DD fives, it's all there. I reviewed them myself and made additions, and so did my driver. Can't think of anything else to add except I want ya to know that anything you want or need just pick up the phone and call me." He smiled graciously.

"Did you know him, Inspector?" Hanratty asked. He had read all the reports and there was no mention of the Hat's recognizing the deceased.

"I recognized him down in the morgue when I made the ID and when they had taken the tape from his mouth. He was an old-time Bronx burglar. Sure, I knew him for many years." The Hat smiled again. "If you don't have nothin' else, I'd like to have a word with the mayor before he leaves." Without waiting for a response, the Hat turned and left.

After he shook the mayor's hand, the Hat stared after the two DAs. Smart kid, that Hanratty he thought, but a little too cocksure, thinks that God gave brains to no one but him. . . . Then the Hat replayed in his mind the events of the day before yesterday.

He had been feelin' no pain when he saw the four dagos run out from the basement. One of them musta been keepin' chiggee and warned the others when he spotted the RMP, they must've panicked. He ran down the stairs and spotted his old friend Woodrow—they used to call him Woodie back in the late forties after the war. You had a burglary in the Bronx or Manhattan north in those days and you had a 50 percent chance of solvin' it if you nabbed Woody. But Woody had a smart Jew lawyer. If he couldn't get him off, he'd get him a plea and a good plea at that. The Hat could never make a good case stick against Woody, and when the Hat's sister's apartment on University got burglarized and there was no arrest, the Hat swore he'd get Woody. And now Woody was staring at him. Relief flooded the black man's eyes when he saw the uniform. That expression of relief was replaced by utter shock and horror when the Hat gave the chair a kick and watched Woody swing. After a minute, satisfied that Woody had departed the land of the living, the Hat bounded upstairs to his driver.

As he walked away from the Hat with Hanratty, Alcibiades LoConti felt that something was wrong.
"Smell a rat, Al?" Hanratty asked.
"Something ain't right."
"The Hat knows a lot more than he's fuckin' tellin' us," Hanratty said. "But you got to have evidence, and all we got is suspicion, Al. In a court of law, suspicion ain't worth shit. This is just a small part of felony duty Al; welcome; this shit never gets to be routine, no matter how many years you got on this job."
Alcibiades just nodded. Nothing ever ended and nothing really changed.

7

NOTHIN' EVER FUCKIN' CHANGES, thought Rory O'Donnell, who was sitting in an unmarked car at the south end of the Four Three precinct. His car was parked across the street from the last known residence of Marlon "Cheech" Rodriguez. As a newly made detective, O'Donnell had been given the job of serving Rodriguez with a Grand Jury Subpoena to testify in the investigation into the death of Dominic "Mickey" Varino, the Admiral's son-in-law. A squeal from a reliable informant had identified Rodriguez as the felon who put two soft-nosed bullets into the hard bone behind Mickey's ear. This squeal was made into a report for the department's intelligence unit and was then promptly leaked to all the newspapers in the City of New York. When Rory parked his car in front of Rodriguez's tenement, he knew that the man had most likely fled the United States. Even if he had not and Rory did find him, serving him with the subpoena was like pissing in the wind. No lawyer in his right mind would ever permit Cheech Rodriguez to sign a Waiver of Immunity. And no assistant DA in his right mind would ever put a suspected perp before the Grand Jury without the perp's notarized signature on the bottom of the Waiver of Immunity. It was the Catch-22 for law enforcement in the State of New York. The greatest gift that the DA's office could make to Rodriguez would be to allow him to testify without signing that waiver. Rodriguez would then joyfully walk into a room of twenty-five grand jurors and honestly confess to killing Mickey and then walk out forever cloaked with the armor of immunity from any prosecution. No ADA would dare fuck up and permit such a catastrophe, Rory thought, so I'm just playin a fuckin' game.

It was eight in the morning and Rory was hungry, so he reached into the backpack on the passenger's seat and took out an army mess kit and a small box of Wheaties. After pouring the cereal into the mess kit, he turned and fished out a cold bottle of Löwenbrau dark from a cooler in the backseat. Rory poured the beer over the Wheaties and spooned a full portion into his mouth. Breakfast of Champions, Rory thought as he kept his eye on the street.

Feliciti Rodriguez, Cheech's stout fifty-one-year-old mother, passed in front of Rory's unmarked car and entered her tenement building carrying two bags of groceries from the twenty-four-hour Superette. Her son was hidden next door in her friend's apartment, and she kept constant vigil. She immediately identified Rory as the man. Reporters and police had hounded her since the newspaper had reported that her son was a murderer. The headlines had produced hundreds of crank phone calls and stressed her heart, already damaged by the trauma of raising her "Cheech."

Feliciti, gasping for breath, stopped on the third-floor landing and placed her two heavy shopping bags on the cold tile floor. Then she looked out the window to see whether or not the plainclothes officer had gotten out of the car to follow her. She had to lean over the sill and look left to see the unmarked car.

Suddenly she felt herself being pushed from behind out over the windowsill and into the black void below. Feliciti could only scream as she felt herself plunging headfirst down toward her concrete death. Ronald DePew, lured to this address by the news stories, looked out and watched as Feliciti splattered onto the sidewalk. He watched until Rory O'Donnell ran from his car, then he hurried up to the roof, crossed over two buildings, and came down the stairway into the street. As he passed the crowd gathered around Feliciti's body, he glanced at Rory O'Donnell and, for a split second, their eyes met. DePew moved on. Meanwhile Marlon "Cheech" Rodriguez sat laughing at the antics of Daffy Duck on television, unaware of his mother's fate.

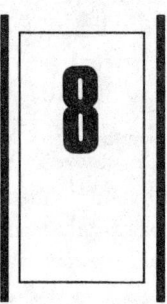

THEY FINALLY FOUND CHEECH Rodriguez on Christmas Eve of 1971, two months after Ronald DePew had sent his mother out the window. Al pulled felony duty that day and on his first call, he found out that Cheech had been hiding out with his old common-law wife on Simpson Street in the Four One precinct known as Fort Apache. Cheech had spiked the eggnog with overproof rum and as usual had gotten abusive. He screamed at his wife, calling her a whore and a cunt. Infuriated, she put a shotgun to his temple.

"Go ahead and pull the trigger," Cheech had taunted. Unfortunately for him, she obliged. As a result of his death, she was granted what was known to the police as "an instant Bronx divorce."

Later, around eleven-thirty that night, Al was getting out of his car in front of a four-story tenement on Alexander Avenue. He was tired and he still had ten more hours left until he went off duty at 9 A.M. on Christmas Day. Felony duty was a real killer.

Two uniformed police officers waited in front of the multi-family dwelling. Four RMPs and six unmarked cars were on the block as well. The forensic station wagon was double-parked in front of the building.

Al entered the lobby and noticed that all eight mailboxes showed signs of being jimmied open. The hallway reeked of urine and disinfectant, an empty wine bottle lay in a corner. The pale-yellow glow from one single light bulb barely pierced the gloom.

Al walked down the hallway and then climbed the empty stairway. After four flights he reached the top floor and saw two uniformed officers outside an open apartment door. He walked up to them, and they challenged him with their looks.

"DA," Al said.

Randy LaTourde, a detective, came to the door. Randy was six feet three inches tall weighed three hundred and sixty pounds but he could move like a cat. Al had heard that each morning he had a dozen Dunkin' Donuts and four cups of coffee just for a warmup. He was one-half of a highly respected detective team. His partner, Augie DiFillipo, came up behind him. Augie was six one and weighed two twenty. Augie did one-arm chins on fire escapes. Eight on each arm. Augie and Randy were rough guys. They both nodded at Al.

The apartment looked like someone had been trying to clean up; there was a mop and pail in the middle of the floor just inside the door. The detectives ushered Al into the living room, where the floor had been mopped but there still was blood on the walls. Al followed them down a short foyer that led to the kitchen. There was blood on the walls of the kitchen too. The floor was still damp from the mop. On the far side of the kitchen a door led to a bedroom. Behind the bedroom was a bathroom. Al walked through the bedroom. There was only a little blood in the bedroom, but the bathroom was a mess. The tub was three-quarters full of pink, soapy water; the sides above the waterline were speckled with blood. Blood spattered the walls in red goblets but the floor was mopped clean. After a preliminary inspection, the detectives led Al back into the living room.

Al noticed an artificial, small, white Christmas tree on a table in the living room. There were a few balls hung on the tree but there were no presents beneath it. A large pool of blood was on the floor in front of the tree and a cello, violin, and a music stand lay off to one corner.

The sickly sweet smell of blood was everywhere. Detective LaTourde puffed smoke from a fat Macanudo cigar to dissipate it. Al lit a Parodi cigar. The odor of the Parodi was a blessing.

Al looked at all the blood. He thought of all the blood that had been cleaned away.

"How many people died here?" Al asked.

"Only one," Randy said.

Augie motioned to Al with his head and he followed. The two detectives led Al out of the apartment, down four flights of stairs, and out a rear doorway. They entered a back alley surrounded by attached tenement houses. The alley was covered with bags of garbage, empty cans, and broken bottles thrown from the windows of the surrounding houses.

Three klieg floodlights on stands had been placed in the center of the litter-clogged alley. Detectives in overcoats, hands in their pockets, stood beneath the lights watching the Medical Examiner when Al walked up.

The ME was squatted next to a naked body of a black man. The man was lying faceup on a pile of garbage. The klieg lights shone down. Al took a long look at his body. He had never seen so many stab wounds. The man was literally perforated. His face, however, was unmarked.

The dead man seemed to be staring at a point past the klieg lights, into the winter sky above. The intensity of his stare caused Al to look above, to see what the fixation of the dead man had been.

The eyes, Al thought. They're still alive.

The ME got up and spoke with the detective lieutenant next to him. LaTourde came up to Al. "Eyes kind of get to you?" he asked.

"They look like they're still alive," Al answered.

"That's 'cause this motherfucker didn't die till after he hit the ground. He really wanted to live. You can see the fuckin' horror in his face. He was fightin' what was happenin' before that big switch got flicked."

Al was shocked by LaTourde's report.

"This guy ever do anything to you?" Al asked.

"Not to me," LaTourde answered, smiling.

Augie DiFillipo explained. "Randy knew the guy, Al. He locked him up twice. Once for rape. That got tossed for no corroboration. Second time was for puttin' his common-law wife on the critical list. He used to beat the fuckin' shit out of her. She was in the hospital for two months once and when she came out, she went right to the DA to withdraw the charges. DA says no way." Augie motioned toward the dead man and continued.

"He was indicted for Assault One. Used a pipe on his girl. So the DA gets the case ready for trial. Notifies us, and we bring the girl in. She is cooperative then. Starts living with friends and not him. Next day the DA picks a jury. Jury pickin' goes on for two whole days. She was to testify on day three. We call her the night before to check on her. She says she's fine. Next day we go to get her to take her to court and she's gone. That was two years ago. We never did find her. End of story." Al looked at the corpse.

"You seen a lot of dead guys before you were a DA, right, Al?" LaTourde questioned matter-of-factly. Al nodded.

"Those eyes bother you, Al, and you don't know why," LaTourde stated again.

Al was annoyed and didn't answer. LaTourde was macabre. He was so obviously delighted that this poor guy was dead that Al was shocked. Al had always had pleasant dealings with this team, so rather than speak his piece he remained silent.

Undeterred, LaTourde went on to explain. "A guy who's been killed suddenly goes into shock. And then his eyes get filmy, like those of a dead fish. In the army where you seen dead guys they close the eyes, right? You know, for morale's sake. But here in this kind of war sometimes a guy don't go into shock and sometimes he fights goin' out. And that's exactly what happened to old Claude here. See, old Claude was starin' up at that half moon up there"—LaTourde pointed to the sky—"and he didn't want to stop seein' it."

"Leave the DA alone," the detective lieutenant muttered. The police loved to shock new DAs. They love to gross and psych them out. Tales of DAs vomiting from seeing corpses were recounted with glee throughout the precincts of the police department in Bronx county.

"I ain't tryin to shock him, Loo. This is fuckin' Al LoConti. He was an MP captain and a war vet. He didn't teach school or run off to fuckin' Canada. Nobody's gonna shock him," Randy said. He looked at Al with a twinkle. He knew he had psyched Al out.

"Cut the shit. Who can say whether this guy died before or after he landed here?" the lieutenant asked.

"He died after he landed here," the ME stated. "See, there are claw marks in the ground and cinders under his nails. His heels are dug in. He died here looking up like the detective said. I'll put it all in my report," the ME said to Al as he left.

LaTourde smiled.

"I'm leavin'," the lieutenant said. Then, turning to DiFillipo, he ordered, "Fill the DA in." As they walked back into the building, forensic was still photographing the body.

"Randy reconstructed the whole thing," DiFillipo said. "I can't take credit for shit. Guy went off the roof. You want to go back up?"

Al nodded.

By the time they climbed back to the apartment DiFillipo had told Al that the deceased was Claude Temoles and that he had a sheet of over forty arrests, mostly for crimes of violence. LaTourde had kept track of Claude. Claude was going with a woman from LaTourde's neighborhood on Gun Hill Road. Claude beat that woman up just as he beat up all his women.

When LaTourde "caught" the homicide and got Claude's name, he immediately phoned Claude's girlfriend. Her daughter answered and said that her mother was in Montefiore Hospital; she'd been there since the night before. LaTourde called a nurse he knew at Montefiore, who related that the woman had been beaten severely and her cheekbones fractured. Though the woman knew her assailant, she had refused to name him.

When the body had been discovered, detectives had canvassed

the neighborhood. They found one witness across the street who had spotted three teenage boys running from the apartment house. They ran when they heard the sirens, she said.

LaTourde knew that the battered woman in Montefiore had a teenage son, so right after he had seen that Claude was dead he raced up to Gun Hill Road and found the boy. He talked with him alone and the son had made a full confession. LaTourde then had returned to the scene of the crime.

At the doorway to the apartment, LaTourde pointed out a trail of blood going up a stairway to the flat-topped roof. Al had not noticed it before.

Detective Timmy Flanagan arrived then and greeted Al. It was not his case but he had been assigned to it. Working with six detectives, he had canvassed the neighborhood earlier. No door remained unknocked. They were still at work when LaTourde solved the case. "Not one of these fuckin' people saw or heard a fuckin' thing," Timmy said. "I mean, I listened to the 911 tape before I came out. The lady who made the call on the tape said they are taking him up to the roof. You could hear the poor fuck screamin' for help on the phone. I mean, the fuckin' screams were inhuman, like a fuckin' animal bein' ripped apart. You would think it was an animal except you could hear *'Help, please, Jesus, God.'* The lady was yellin' come quick, they're takin' him up to the roof. She gives the address, then hangs up."

"We got a perp," DiFillipo said. Flanagan nodded; he knew.

LaTourde explained, "Perp is a kid named Leon Brastock. Sixteen. Perp finds that Claude, who is thirty-seven, beat the shit out of his mother, so he gets two of his friends, Kelvin and Maynard, and they come up here and force their way into Claude's apartment. They back him into his bedroom and then his bathroom. They put him in the tub and the three of them start stabbing him with their knives. When he passes out, they think he's dead so they run the water. He wakes up while they're in another room and tries to run out of the house. They catch him in the kitchen. As they're wrestling with him, one guy is stabbing him. Claude then breaks away and makes it to the living room. Then he passes out again. Then the kids start to clean up. They clean up everything on the floors until they get to him. They try to put him in a garbage bag. Then he comes to again so they figure the guy has to die some way. So they drag him naked up to the roof. He is screaming bloody murder. Someone calls 911. Timmy told you what's on the tape. They drag the fuck screamin' all the way to the roof and fling him over the wall. And the fuck is still alive after he hits."

LaTourde then led Al up to the roof.

"Forensic photograph this route?" Al asked.

"Every which way," LaTourde exclaimed emphatically.

Al walked over to the bloodstained wall and looked down into the rear of the building below. Claude's eyes were still looking up through the brightness of the klieg lights.

Al left the roof and, on the way down, asked, "This kid Leon . . . has he made a full confession?"

"Complete, total, full and signed," LaTourde answered.

"What about the other two friends?"

"They're in the wind. But the lady that called 911 . . . well, Morrie Shapiro found her. She gave us the names of the other two kids. She's known them for years. So I got a Christmas present tonight."

They went downstairs and Al walked to his car.

He started the Dodge, then drove to the Four Eight. He quickly took the confession of the teenager with a stenographer from the DA's office. Then the kid was taken back to the cells. Al got up to leave, said good-bye to LaTourde and DiFillipo, then as an afterthought, he asked, "I saw a violin and a cello or bass fiddle in the apartment. Was this guy Claude a musician?"

"Yep, he played them all," LaTourde answered. "Wasn't much good but I guess he's famous now."

"How's that?" Al asked, walking right into Randy's trap.

"Well, tonight he became the fiddler off the roof."

Al almost smiled.

"Merry Christmas, Mr. LoConti."

Al waved and went home. When he entered his sparsely furnished apartment in the Inwood section of Manhattan, his wife and children were all asleep. He got a beer from the refrigerator, then sat in front of the unplugged Christmas tree. His dog, a German short-haired pointer, sat next to him and he petted it as he sipped his beer. It was 4 A.M. He still had five hours to go before he was off duty.

9

ON THIS FIRST DAY of the year in 1972, Chingo, now an informer for the elite 13 Narcotics Group, knocked on the door to apartment C46, on the fourth floor of the tenement on Southern Boulevard in the South Bronx. Hearing the *click* as the peephole opened, he looked at it and smiled.

"It's me, man. Chingo. I got someone here who wants to cop." He nodded in the direction of the black woman who stood behind him. The door opened, revealing a horribly scar-faced man clad in an undershirt and black pants.

Chingo beckoned the woman forward and made the introductions. "Mary, this is Mr. Ferro." The man stared and then nodded to her.

"How much you wanna spend?" he asked her.

"Fifty dollars," she answered, holding out the folded bills.

Chingo walked to the top of the landing and looked down the stairwell.

Ferro took the money and disappeared inside the apartment. After a few moments the door reopened and he handed Mary a package of glassine envelopes. She grabbed the heroin, paused, then thanked Ferro and ran after Chingo down the stairs.

They ran past two telephone repairmen next to a pole on the corner of Southern Boulevard and 163rd Street, turned there, and got into a car. The two repairmen, William Wotter and Pete DiCerrechia, watched as they drove off.

The drugs were vouchered in a ceremony called "Sign and Seal" by the New York courts. The final signature on the evidence voucher was that of the undercover officer "Mary," and after her signature was affixed, the drugs were taken to the police lab in Manhattan for analysis.

Lieutenant Bill Solwin, the commanding officer of the elite 13th Narcotics Group, had his men watch Ferro's tenement building for ten straight days. The officers saw countless junkies, men and women, black, white, and Hispanic, enter and leave the building during that time. They relied on Chingo's information that Ferro was the only seller in the building. Confident that due to the amount of traffic Ferro would never be able to recall which woman he sold to, Solwin had Pete DiCerrechia file an affidavit and obtain a search warrant. Armed with a no-knock warrant, the officers broke down the door of apartment C46 and arrested the forty-eight-year-old Ferro. When the officers entered Ferro's wife unleashed her pet, a ferocious pit bull. When the pit bull's teeth bit through his calf muscle, Rory O'Donnell momentarily forgot his alimony problems. He screamed, then collapsed.

Solwin, who was handcuffing Ferro, turned at the sound of gunfire, and saw DiCerrechia standing with his service revolver above the prostrate dog. While officers hurried to tend to the writhing O'Donnell, DiCerrechia turned on Mrs. Ferro and raised his gun to point at her face. Terrified, she raised her arms.

"Don't you fuckin' move, bitch," Pete ordered. "I don't want to have to shoot another fuckin' dog tonight." Solwin then cuffed Mrs. Ferro, and a search of the apartment netted over three hundred glassine envelopes filled with heroin. Other narcotics paraphernalia, including mannita, a mixer, was recovered. Two thousand glassine envelopes were found in another drawer but they were all empty.

Lieutenant Solwin was pissed. He had had an intuition that Ferro was going to get a large shipment for New Year's and he wanted to find it here.

Mr. and Mrs. Ferro were arraigned on New Year's Day. The undercover policewoman was identified only as Jane Doe "Mary." No police report revealed her true name. The Ferros were the

155th and 156th persons in Bronx County arrested in less than one year as a result of her undercover work.

As the Ferros were being taken to jail, Mary and her boyfriend were enjoying a day off. They sipped a glass of wine in her apartment in Co-op City overlooking the Hutchinson River Parkway.

Mary mused reflectively and almost seemed to be brooding over her white wine. "I hope seventy-two is my good year. I've had a lifetime of bad ones."

"I know you have, hun, and I've a feelin' it will be. I've a feelin' that seventy-two will be a great year for both of us. I think you've left bad times behind, Ruella."

Detective Ruella Watkins sipped more of her wine. "You've been the start of good luck for me, Elrod. Thanks for bein' you."

Detective Elrod Harrison just nodded and smiled.

DESPITE PRESSURE FROM HIS lawyer to take a plea and cooperate, Ferro refused to reveal his connections. He would not budge. Al began the trial of the indictment charging Ferro for his drug sales to Ruella Watkins. The case took one week, and the jury returned with a guilty verdict on Thursday, May 11, 1972.

Al told Ferro's lawyer that if he cooperated, he could still get a break at sentencing, but Ferro still hung tough.

The trial against both Mr. and Mrs. Ferro on the indictment charging them with acting in concert in possession of heroin started May 15. Ferro took the stand and claimed the drugs were his and that his wife knew nothing about them. Al ripped Ferro a new asshole on cross examination. Mrs. Ferro did not testify. The case took eight days and the jury returned with a guilty verdict against both defendants.

Mrs. Ferro cried, screamed, and shrieked like a paid mourner at an old-time funeral.

"Yo soy innocente, Yo soy innocente," she cried, proclaiming her innocence, although her English was as good as Al's.

Al told both lawyers if either defendant cooperated before sentencing, he would recommend some years off the maximum sentence.

For a time the Ferros wouldn't budge. But on the date of sentencing, Mrs. Ferro finally broke. She provided the police with a wealth of information and confessed that it was totally her operation. Her husband was just a flunky.

Mrs. Ferro disclosed another exciting new tidbit of intelligence. A new and exotic drug hit the street from the Orient. It's name, Chinese Rock #3—heroin.

Mrs. Ferro drew one to five. Her husband, who maintained his silence to the end, maxed out and got five to fifteen. Mrs. Ferro never asked for any favors for her husband in return for her cooperation.

Because Ruella's cover was blown when she testified at the Ferro trial, Solwin began substituting William Wotter as his undercover. Wotter was in on the investigation resulting from Mrs. Ferro's information.

In the past, Wotter had made four undercover buys of pure heroin from a hood named Jimmy Nofrio. All of the buys happened near or in Nofrio's home on City Island. When the 13th Narcotics Group had applied to the Bronx district attorney for a wiretap order on Nofrio, they ran into problems. The officers had to show that they couldn't use ordinary means of investigation to learn Nofrio's source. The 13th documented the number of times that they had followed Nofrio's circuitous routes from Connecticut, doubling back to New York, then heading toward Jersey. For three weeks the team had followed Nofrio and had always lost the trail.

Al grinned at DiCerrechia and Wotter, pleased to have been

assigned the job of preparing the wiretap application. He questioned the entire investigating team, including Rory O'Donnell, Wotter, and Lieutenant Bill Solwin.

The state's Criminal Procedure Law required that the county district attorney file an affidavit with the court before an eavesdropping or wire-tap order was signed.

The Bronx DA's office customarily prepared three affidavits: one from the police officer in command of the operation, one from the assistant DA assigned to supervise the investigation and one from the chief of the Narcotics Bureau. All three would then be signed and reviewed by the Chief Assistant DA who then would approve or disapprove. If approved, an appointment would be made with the DA himself. He would then question his Chief Assistant, his Bureau Chief, the supervising assistant, and the police, and only then if fully satisfied would he sign the affidavit. From the DA's office the ADA would present the application to one of the two judges assigned to the Narcotics Parts. The judge and his law assistant would review the application and invariably sign the order authorizing the wiretapping and or eavesdropping.

Al gathered all the police reports and read them, then prepared the affidavits necessary for the order. It took him four days just to prepare the paperwork, get it typed, signed, and presented to the court. The order was good for thirty days. Twenty days after the wire was in place, several officers came to Al's office one morning to discuss their results.

Lieutenant Solwin briefed Al on the status of the investigation. "Nofrio calls only two suppliers. When he calls he uses the name Jimbo. One guy calls him and tells him to call him right back. The number is always a different pay phone, and the phones are all over the city of New York. The guy always introduces himself as Mr. P. We have nothing else on him. So far just a dead end. But the other supplier he speaks to is named Teach. We thought that maybe the guy might be a teacher or working for the Board of Ed or something. Anyway we get the number and Rory calls our contact at the phone company and we find the number is listed to a Miles Macomber at 339 Boston Road.

"We went over there and found a two-family house but only one family lives there, and the name on the doorbell is Dano. We find a different telephone number listed to Dano at this address so we checked the City Register and found out the deed is in the name of a Richard and Marguerite Dano. The deed is dated 1971.

"Neither Dano nor his wife have any priors. He's a bus driver, and on Friday and Saturday nights he sings in a couple of nightclubs and cabarets in the Boston Road area. The guy has tomato plants and fuckin' zucchini growing in his backyard.

"Detective DiCerrechia's father-in-law works for MABSTOA in the dispatcher's office. He knows Dano and says the guy has a very good rep but he's a little on the slow side. You know, like his elevator don't quite make it to the top floor.

"We followed Dano last Friday night. He was all dressed up in a tux. He went to the Peartree Lounge and he's a guest singer. Well, the guy has a great voice, believe me, and he is real good-lookin'. He was singin' 'San Francisco' in Tony Bennett's league except midway through the song he kind of forgets the words. The guy playin' guitar in the band comes over to him and whispers a couple of things to him and then he finished the song. In the next song the same thing happens. When the audience started to laugh, I felt sorry for the guy. But you should see the way this guy scores with the broads, Al, he's a real swordsman, a fuckin' Valentino.

"But he don't seem to fit the bill for a big dealer so I ask O'Donnell to check on the address again. O'Donnell comes back with the same answer. So I begin to think that a bus driver is a pretty good cover for gettin' around. And if one of the times Nofrio slips us and boards a bus, you know an exchange could easily be made. Like a lunch pail, thermos, there's a thousand ways.

"So Willie Wotter puts an order in for a key of heroin to Nofrio two nights ago. Nofrio calls Teach, we of course intercept the call, and Teach says he'll have it at his home by Friday, which is tonight. Nofrio is all set to meet Teach at Teach's house at eleven tonight."

Solwin's story was interrupted by the phone ringing on Al's desk. "ADA LoConti here," Al answered. It was his wife, Renee. She was calling to tell him that she was going to her sister's house on the Island for the weekend and if he wanted to join her there, he could. Pissed off at the interruption, Al slammed the phone down.

Solwin continued. "So today we feel we got enough for a warrant on Teach based on the wire. What we figured was we take

Nofrio at his house and we get a search warrant for his apartment. Tonight half the team will hit Nofrio and the other half will take Teach. Do you think you can get us the search warrants, Al?"

"You certainly have enough to show probable cause to get the warrants. There's no question as to Nofrio, based on the four sales to Wotter and the wire, but as to this guy—Teach or Dano or whoever the fuck he is—he . . . he . . . sounds like a "shrudule," a dope. It bothers me."

Solwin came back, "It bothered me too, Al. That's why I laid it all out for you. But if you think about it, the guy might be smarter than the rest of us. I mean, the guy keeps his nose clean, acts like a chooch, and no one suspects him. Meanwhile he's dealin' in real heavy weight and secretly thumbing his nose at the system. O'Donnell checked out the address of the telephone twice, and there is no doubt that the instrument recorded the right telephone number. We tested the instrument before, during and after the calls. And we got a safety factor built in. This guy always sings in clubs on Fridays and he is always out from ten P.M. to four A.M. If he's home tonight, we know it's him."

"How do you know that? The wire has only been in place for three weeks," Al asked.

"We asked the bartender in the Peartree. O'Donnell knows him. Served together with him in Nam. When he asked him who the singer was with the great voice, the bartender told him the guy's name was Rick Dano and that he sang in one of three clubs in the area every Friday night. The guy is booked solid. Girls love him. Guys get a kick out of him when he starts forgettin' the words.

"And another thing, Al," Solwin continued. "There is no record of any mortgage. Mr. and Mrs. Richard Dano paid cash for their house."

"Okay," Al said. "Look, I'll prepare the affidavits and the warrants. I'll try to get the judge before lunch, so stick around so you can sign the affidavit as soon as it's typed."

Al got the judge and the judge signed the warrants.

Friday was the worst day in Jimmy Nofrio's life. His yellow sheet showed arrests for petty larceny, grand larceny auto, and warehouse burglaries. The arrests totaled thirteen. On his last burglary in 1968 Jimmy was caught inside a warehouse by two officers of the Four Oh precinct. Jimmy was locked up for the D felony and faced up to seven years, but he copped out to a Class E felony and drew zip to three on a plea bargain. He did fourteen months and hit the streets in February of '70. Raul Alquerido, an Argentinean who had been his cellmate, put him in the drug business. Alquerido set up all the deals and used Jimmy as a cut out, a blind alley, a shield. In March of '72 the Argentinean was walking his dog in Bronx Park behind the motorcycle precinct. In the early morning the park was always full of joggers in running clothes. A jogger approached the Argentinean, his breath puffing smokelike from his mouth in the crisp March air. The jogger nodded to the Argentinean. The Argentinean nodded back. The jogger passed, then paused, and took a silenced .22 pistol from underneath his zippered jacket, and pumped five rounds into the Argentinean's back. After the Argentinean fell, the jogger walked up to him and put the sixth round in his temple. Then he jogged away out of the park and crossed White Plains Road. Jimmy was suddenly out of business. He couldn't reach the Argentinean anymore and then he read in the paper that the police had found the body of Raul Alquerido, his former cellmate, the Argentinean. Jimmy was depressed. He had to go back to burglaries or else get a job.

Mysteriously Jimmy Nofrio was then contacted by Mr. P, who put him in touch with Teach. Jimmy thought Mr. P's contact had been a gift from God. He failed to make any other connection.

Now seated in his rented apartment in a house on City Island Avenue, Jimmy thought about how much he was going to make on this deal. He just knew that Teach would take good care of him for a deal involving a key, a whole kilo of heroin.

His dreams of riches were shattered when his front door flew inward, wrenched from its hinges by a battering ram operated by men of the 13th Narcotics. The officers were also armed with a no-knock warrant, which gave them the legal authority to enter unannounced so that Nofrio could not flush narcotic evidence down the toilet.

Jimmy was handcuffed and placed under arrest. He was advised of his rights and shown the search warrant. As he sat on a chair in his living room, he watched as his apartment was searched and destroyed before him. No drugs were found, and Nofrio denied ever selling drugs. He told the police that he wanted a lawyer, that he would not answer any questions, and that he would not cooperate with them.

Later that night as Rick Dano escorted his wife home from Fratello Brothers Funeral Home just off Bronx Park East, he had no idea that this somber and dismal evening would evolve into an even greater horror.

His father-in-law, Vincent La Magna, had died suddenly the night before. Rick Dano made all the funeral arrangements with his childhood buddy Jackie "Graves" Fratello, one of five brothers who owned a chain of funeral parlors throughout the city.

Rick had sat out this first night of the wake, at his wife's side as a dutiful husband. He would sorely miss his singing and catting around this evening, but he could not leave his wife alone. And, Rick Dano thought, the old man, a retired contractor, had taken good care of him and had given him forty big ones in cash to buy his house. The old man had even arranged for his own lawyer to do the closing. Rick Dano didn't have to do a thing.

Rick had to show respect. It was the least he could do.

He put up with the wailing and the crying on this first night of the wake and was glad that Fratello's closed at nine-thirty. By the time all the mourners said good night, it was after ten. Rick and his wife lingered outside for a few more minutes and then drove home. They stopped at Rick's sister's house and picked up their children.

When he pulled up in front of his house, Rick noticed a Dynahoe excavating machine parked in the street with its big shovel raised only inches from the ground. Rick thought it odd, since he was not aware of any construction in the neighborhood.

The Danos all went in the house. The children were put to bed and Rick mixed his wife a strong highball before he took his miniature Schnauzer out for a walk. The Schnauzer, Meatballs, loved to be walked and even seemed to respond to Rick's singing during their walks. As Rick walked Meatballs up the block to an empty lot, the men from the 13th were in place and watching.

Jimmy Nofrio sat in an empty room of the Four Seven precinct. Sergeant Denny Driscoll was doing his best to intimidate him. Driscoll showed him the arrest warrant and promised he would do sixty years in jail for the four sales. Jimmy said nothing. Finally Driscoll brought in Wotter, who had his shield displayed over his shirt pocket.

Jimmy was good at hiding his surprise.

"Hi, Jimbo," Wotter said. "Remember me?"

"I want to see my fuckin' lawyer," Jimmy responded.

After the walk Rick Dano went into his house and took the leash off the Schnauzer. The little dog scampered into the kitchen, ready for his little doggie treat. Rick put a biscuit into the dog's mouth and smiled as the animal ran into the bedroom to eat it.

At that very moment the men of the 13th ramrodded Rick's outside door off its hinges and flooded into his home. They grabbed him and his wife and handcuffed them to chairs. Rick almost had a heart attack, and his wife fainted but came to after a few minutes. Solwin read the warrant out loud to the Danos. He ignored their pleas that a mistake was being made.

One team ripped open the walls of the house and removed pipes, while another cut open all upholstery and mattresses, removing moldings and destroying the interior. A third team set up arc lights in the backyard. Then Pete DiCerrechia drove the Dynahoe excavator into the backyard. The tomato, cucumber, zucchini, and lettuce plants were the first casualties, and after four hours the entire backyard was excavated to a depth of four feet. Nothing was found.

Pete DiCerrechia drove the Dynahoe back out onto the street and the arc lights were shut off. He conferred with Solwin. Nothing had been found in the house. Solwin also could not find a phone with the number that belonged to Teach. Solwin called a friend of his with the Four Seven squad and asked if he could roust a contact with the phone company at this hour and check a number for him. He asked the detective to call him back one way or another.

During all of this Dano and his wife had been removed to the kitchen where they were seated and handcuffed. The children were in a bedroom attended by a policewoman.

After the phone rang, Pete DiCerrechia and Rory O'Donnell watched as Solwin's face went bloodless white.

"What!" he yelled. "I never fuckin' heard of it."

Then after a pause he mumbled thanks and hung up.

"We've fucked up," he told Pete and Rory.

"How?" Rory asked, puzzled.

"The phone is registered to this street number but the street is wrong. It's not Boston Road, it's Boston *Close*." Solwin grimaced, almost in tears from humiliation. I never should have trusted that fuckin' drunk O'Donnell, he thought to himself.

Pete knew what he was thinking.

"Listen, Loo, I spent my whole life in the fuckin' Bronx and I never heard of no fuckin' Boston Close."

"It's a small street inside the Boston-Secor Housing project. I never heard of it either, but I just found out what it means from the detective in the Four Seven that called, "close" means a passage to a courtyard and houses inside the courtyard."

After a few minutes the team was gathered and the Danos released. Solwin was too honest to just leave. He turned to the Danos, apologized, and told them a mistake had been made. They were too shocked to respond.

Pete DiCerrechia was the last to leave. As he paused in the doorway, surveying the wreck, he shook his head. "I can only say we're sorry, Mr. Dano. That's all I can say. Good luck with your singin'—you got a real great voice."

Dano, flattered, just nodded to Pete DiCerrechia. As Pete stepped outside, almost as an afterthought Dano called out, "Hey, where are you guys from?"

Pete paused, then turned back and faced Rick Dano. "We're the Federal Bureau of Investigation, Mr. Dano. We're the FBI."

After the officers left, Solwin, by prearrangement, called Al LoConti at his home to make his report. Al immediately notified the chief assistant DA who after a gasp followed by a sharp intake of air directed Al to be in his office Monday morning with a full written report.

Al hung up and opened another cold beer. The window air conditioner in the bedroom hardly displaced the humidity of this hot August night. Al reached down and patted his dog. He thought of his wife and kids out in Long Island and how he would probably spend the rest of the weekend writing up the report for Monday morning.

By December 1972 all efforts to get Jimmy Nofrio to turn failed, so he was tried and pulled the maximum sentence. Even if he wanted to, Jimmy couldn't turn. He was an effective cut out, a blind alley in the dead Argentinean's operation. And "Teach" could not be found.

After the Rick Dano fiasco, the district attorney, to Al's surprise, put him in charge over the elite 13th Narcotics Group in this investigation. Solwin of course remained in control, reporting to Al when wiretaps and search warrants would be needed.

Chingo and Wotter were sent into the field to make buys, and they soon found the new Chinese Rock #3, the purest form of heroin from the East found in the U.S.

Chinese Rock #3 came in solid irregular form. It looked like a brownish crystal of rock candy. It was prepared for consumption by grinding it between two panes of glass. Then the granulated substance was cut with mannita and packaged for distribution.

Al was excited about his new investigation. He thought he finally had something he could put his teeth into and hoped that this investigation would progress "up the ladder" to put a major narcotics supplier away for life.

Al was impatient. He waited daily for the men of the 13th to arrive with sufficient evidence to obtain search warrants or wire-tap orders. He didn't know it at the time, but he would have a long wait.

By April 1973 Al had a string of unbroken convictions in the Narcotics Bureau. He began working himself tirelessly. He became even more obsessed with his job. He paid little attention to his wife, and she in turn became hostile and sarcastic. Her remarks only drove him further and further into the refuge of his work.

He plodded straight ahead like a horse wearing blinders. As soon as one jury would retire, he would have the Detective Coordinator assign the officers for the next case to his office. Then after a week he would commence another trial.

I'm knockin' them dead, he naively thought to himself.

He was convinced that his efforts were starting to make a difference. He was a rising star in the office and felt his reputation growing. He was hoping to be promoted to the Supreme Court Bureau and wanted to get a year of seasoning with his friend Hanratty. With luck he would make the Homicide Bureau.

Later that month Al was summoned into Johnny O'Boyle's office. O'Boyle sat smoking a Lucky Strike so Al lit a Camel. O'Boyle wore his usual Jimmy Cagney sneer.

"Welcome to the Homicide Bureau, Al. You've been promoted. Just you and Terry Hanratty. You're the first guy to come over direct from Narcotics. Congratulations. Drop down the hall and see the Coordinator. He's got a drawer full of cases for you. Mostly old pieces of shit but don't worry if you lose a few. Most of the shit you'll get has been around for at least three years. So give them a good shot but don't jump off the Washington Bridge if these guys walk. Hey, and . . . good luck."

Al got up to leave and they shook hands. He left O'Boyle's office and went down to get his new cases. It was going to be the happiest day of his life, he thought. Wait until Renee and his uncle Peppy found out about this.

WHEN ALCIBIADES LOCONTI BURST into his living room that evening with an enormous grin and a bottle of Dom Perignon champagne, his wife Renee was shocked to recognize the man she had married. He reminded her of the man she used to know, the one who went to Vietnam with his shoes spit-shined and officer's insignia brightly polished to a dazzle and with his Airborne Ranger wings and patches proudly displayed. He even walked with that jaunty, self-assured grace of an elite army officer.

He doesn't have a clue, she thought, not even a little teeny clue that our marriage is on the rocks.

The kids were sleeping soundly as she watched Al pop the cork and then pour champagne into two glasses. He gave her a glass with a grandiose gesture and kissed her on the cheek.

"To our family," he toasted, thrusting his glass forward.

"Cheers," she toasted back in her Welsh accent.

After the toast, Al changed into a T-shirt and blue jeans and then came back and sat down on the couch and sipped more champagne. Renee noticed that his once board-flat, hard-muscled stomach had now been replaced by a soft spare tire that bulged over the top of his jeans. He caught her look, sat up straight, and took a deep breath, sucking his stomach in as he petted Sport, the pointer at his feet. Inspired, he jumped up and ran into the kitchen, returning with the dog's bowl. He started to pour some champagne into it.

"Don't you dare," Renee said. This time she couldn't stop herself from smiling.

Al smiled back. "C'mon, he's part of the family. He should celebrate too. Besides, when I get my raise we'll buy him steak instead of dog food."

"He eats better than any dog I ever heard of," Renee said.

Al poured a little champagne into the bowl and placed it at the dog's feet. Sport got up, put his snout into the bowl, and licked only once, then sat staring at the bubbles. Then he turned, smacking his lips, and walked away.

"I guess he only likes the hundred-buck-a-bottle brand," Alcibiades joked.

Renee found herself laughing. She was watching the old Al, the man with the quick joke and smile, the gentle, kind man who was the caring and wonderful, beautiful—Alcibiades LoConti.

She was still smiling as she turned her attention to the barking dog. He was indeed a comedian, oafish and very, very clumsy and not even half as smart as his owner thought he was. Yet there was some strange link between the man and the dog. Renee just endured the German Short-Haired Pointer.

Al left and came back with another bottle of champagne. It was only nine o'clock, he thought to himself as he poured. He was relaxed so he joked and smiled. After a while Renee went into the second bedroom to check on the children. They were sleeping soundly. She returned to the living room, where she walked over to her husband and bent down and kissed him on the mouth. He put his glass down on the table and pulled her next to him on the couch. His eyes were closed as he felt the familiar touch of her warmth. After a while they pulled apart.

"Congratulations, Mr. LoConti, on your promotion," Renee said with her arms still around him.

Al smiled. "Thanks, kid," he said, and then kissed her again. She rose and walked into the bedroom as Al followed.

Al threw his pants and T-shirt on a chair next to the bed as Renee folded her clothes on top of the dresser. She locked the bedroom door and joined her husband under the sheets. He was anxiously waiting and ready.

Al rolled on top of her. Their lovemaking began slowly; each knew the other's every move. There were no startling discoveries, no new throes of passion, no soaring to breathtaking heights, yet there was a tenderness, a caring, a compassionate sharing, a non-selfish joining where each satisfied fully the other's wants. The rhythm grew in intensity and the bed squeaked with the bouncing of their bodies. Finally Al, spent, flopped beside her. In the pleasance of the afterglow, Al caressed his wife's breast. She stared at the ceiling and then kissed him again. Then to his displeasure she lit a cigarette and blew the smoke upward.

"More champagne?" he asked.

"I'd love a glass." She smiled.

Al got up, put on his bathrobe, and tied the cord. He unlocked the door and walked out into the living room where he picked up the glasses and the champagne bottle. When he started to pour, his dog got up and wagged his tail furiously. His mouth was opened and Al thought the dog was smiling, but when he looked down into the dog's bowl, it was empty. Sport obviously wanted more champagne. Al laughed. "Smartest dog in the world," he said out loud as he returned to the bedroom and told his wife. Renee was happy that the dog did not get another glass, but she was even more delighted to see Alcibiades laughing and joking. It was as if the hammering of the last seven hard years had not crushed the joy and humor from him. It was as if he was again the man she had loved once, the young man she had married. She intuitively knew that tonight was just a remission, and although she was happy, she was scared by the cancer of his work that would flare anew to consume him and eventually even the children and her.

Al sipped his champagne, then put his glass down and got into bed. His thoughts were now far from his wife and home. Tomorrow he had felony duty again.

THE STENOGRAPHER WAS IMPATIENT by the time that Al arrived at the Four Six precinct and he mashed out his cigarette as Al sat down across the table from the defendant. When Al started to speak, the steno's fingers flew.

"Mr. O'Brien, I'm Al LoConti. I'm an assistant DA in the Bronx DA's Homicide Bureau and I'm here to ask you certain questions concerning the death of your wife, Angela. Before I say anything else I'd like to advise you of you rights."

"The fuckin' detectives tol' me what my rights are and I tol' them what happened. I don't want to say anything more to you or to anyone else. I want a fuckin' lawyer. Don't ask me any more fuckin' questions. I ain't gonna say a thing to you or to any other fuckin' guinea scumbag," O'Brien blurted out.

"Fine, Mr. O'Brien, that is your right. Statement concluded."

Al was angry as he stormed out of the interview room.

Rory came out apologizing. "He's a fuckin' alky, Al, and he's needin' a drink. Pay him no mind, Al, no fuckin' mind at all."

"Just give me the facts for my report, Rory," Al said.

"Bronx divorce, Al," Rory said. "Blew the old lady away with a shotgun. Over and under. One barrel had a deer slug and the other was double-ought buck. His bride looked like a raw hamburger."

"You find any motive?" Al asked.

"He claims his wife beat the shit out of him. She was five three. He's six four. He claims she was messin aroun' with other guys. She called him scumbag, fucko, and dickhead and she was always playin' one of these home organs—a small one like a baby piano—and it drove him crazy. So last night he was watchin' a ball game. She started to play the organ. She began singin' out so loud that the neighbors were knockin' on the pipes. He claims this went on all the time. Well . . . he must've had his load on because when she goes to the shithouse, he tells her to cut out the fuckin' racket.

"She takes a leak then comes into the living room, pulls the TV plug from the wall, and then yanks the cord from the back of the TV and wacks him over the head with it and calls him fucko. When she starts to sing and play again he takes out the Bronx divorce kit, the over and under, and blasts away. The first shot is the slug. It goes right through her and into the organ. The second is the buckshot. He must have pushed it tight to her head. Fuckin' mess."

"Was the plug ripped out from the TV?" Al asked.

"Just like he says," Rory answered.

"Anyone else at home?" Al asked.

"No, they have no kids. They've been married fifteen years, she was thirty-seven and he's forty-one," Rory reported.

"Where did they live?" Al asked.

"Baychester Avenue, a few blocks from the Thruway. Twenty-family apartment house."

"What's he do for a living besides huntin' down his wife?"

"He's an ironworker. Made a big deal about bein' Irish, that's why he talked to me. Wouldn't say shit to anyone else," Rory said.

"What do you mean by a big deal?" Al asked.

"He says everyone thinks that ironworkers are Mohawk Indians. Says most of them are Irish and that he was Irish. Says two things pissed him off in life. One was people askin' him if he was an Indian when he said he was an ironworker."

"What was the other thing?" Al asked.

"His wife," Rory answered.

Al dictated his report to the steno, said good-bye, and went back to his office. O'Brien won't be paying alimony, Al joked to himself.

At 3 p.m. O'Boyle called Al to tell him that an RMP had been flagged down on Shore Road just south of the city line from Pelham. The officers were led into a wooded area to a body of a female. It had no legs.

O'Boyle proceeded to review the legs case and told Al that a pair of female legs had been found in August of 1970 at Split Rock Golf Course. The Hat had directed that the case not be classified a homicide, which caused O'Boyle to raise hell with the commissioner to get it reclassified.

"There's been a lot of effort in this case, Al, there's been a constant review of missing person files, countless pleas to the public for any information regarding a missing female, Caucasian, approximately forty-five to fifty-five who was anywhere from five two to five six in height. All the efforts proved negative, a dead end for almost three years. Now I guess we finally found the body. And it looks like it was only a short distance from where the legs turned up. Al . . . this is your case now."

"Okay, John, I'm on my way." Al said.

Thirty-five minutes later Al arrived at the scene and parked his car behind a group of RMPs and unmarked official vehicles. He walked two hundred feet inside the woods and saw a crowd. Al walked towards the crowd. A large area was roped off. Signs hung from the ropes. They read CRIME SCENE DO NOT ENTER.

Uniformed police stood on the outside of the roped area, keeping the public back from the crime scene. Al picked up the rope, ducked underneath, and approached a group of detectives that included Rory and Pete DiCerrechia. They both showed signs of being awake all night and just nodded to Al.

In the middle of the roped-off area between two large bushes was a plastic bag wrapped with sash cord. Allie Boy Spano stood ten feet from the bag smoking a cigar. Standing next to him was his partner, Richie Zemberelli. As Al walked up to Allie Boy he was joined by Jimmy Farrell, the Narcotics Felony DA. The Narcotics Bureau had six female missing witnesses on major drug prosecutions, and the DA had directed that a Narcotics DA respond to the scene of every murdered female found in the Bronx until the missing witnesses surfaced.

Allie Boy told Al that two fishermen had found the green garbage bag that contained the legless, hairless cadaver of a female. Al was led to the plastic bag. A fold in the plastic formed a crevice and a watery substance oozed slowly from it. When the smell hit Al in the face like a baseball bat, he turned and puked. The police were all breathing through their mouths. Jimmy Farrell lit two cigars and handed one to Al.

Jimmy puffed furiously so that the stench from his cigar would mask the odor from the bag. A forensic detective arrived wearing surgical gloves, and pulled the bag all the way open. Al looked down and saw the exposed hairless head and shoulders. The body was wrapped in clear freezer wrap, and the color and texture of the skin reminded Al of something . . . something which he could not quite remember.

The horror of the corpse had a fixation all its own, and against his will Al looked down again. Then it clicked. The color and the texture of the skin looked like that of a leg of lamb, the dark-textured, semishiny appearance of a leg of lamb trussed in a supermarket showcase.

"What're you starin' at, Al?" Jimmy Farrell asked.

"Christ, Jimmy, she looks like a fuckin' leg of lamb."

Farrell looked thoughtfully at Al and took a long drag on his cigar. "Yep, in a way she does. . . . You like lamb, Al?"

"I used to," Al said. "Never seen a body like this before Jimmy. Can't make out her features, she's got no hair."

"She's got no legs either, Al," Farrell quipped.

"I know, Jimmy, I know about the legs."

"I hear from Pete DiCerrechia that this case is almost three years old," Farrell said.

"Yeah, they had a special number at one time trying to find out from the public any information regarding a missing woman. It started when the legs were found in 1970."

"Well, looks like you finally found the rest."

"That's right, Jimmy."

Farrell continued to smoke and look at the body. After a while he bent down and pulled back the green plastic. "Pussy hair is all gone too," he observed.

"Very interesting," Al remarked sarcastically. Jimmy Farrell had been in the office for a year longer than Al. Like Al, Farrell had been a soldier, having gone through OCS and been Airborne and Ranger qualified before his tour in Vietnam. Farrell, however, was never promoted beyond first lieutenant. He had loved Nam and Al now recalled Farrell's telling him of his flight in a chopper when Farrell had assumed the door gunner's position. He had flown over rice paddies and along tree lines. No fire had been drawn and nothing suspicious observed. After a while the chopper flew over an old man in a field behind a water buffalo. Al knew that the Vietnamese valued a water buffalo more than Americans did cars. Farrell knew this too. Farrell directed the chopper pilot to swing back to the old man. When he passed in range he opened up. He told Al that he had shot the living shit out of the water buffalo and ended by saying he was sorry he only killed the animal. The *papasan* was probably VC too.

Farrell had brought an expression home from Vietnam, and he applied it to his plea negotiations.

"You gotta grab 'em by the balls," he would say. "And then when you got 'em real tight, you can bet that their hearts and minds will follow."

At times Al was fond of Farrell, but at other times he felt that the man was an embarrassment to the office. Farrell, a bachelor, just loved felony duty.

"I eat this shit up," he would say repeatedly.

Now Al looked down at the body in the plastic garbage bag. "I wonder if we'll ever find out who this poor thing is."

"She's probably some goddamn fuckin' hooker pulled out of Hunt's Point. Or maybe she's some fuckin' derelict, a bag lady, cut up by the kids for laughs. She could even be a victim of one of these cults, you know, Al, these fucks that worship the devil, fuckin' covens of witches."

Al said nothing.

"Well, what do you think, Al? I know you think she looks like a fuckin' pot roast or leg of lamb or whatever, but how do you think she got here?"

Al puffed the cigar, looked at Farrell, and just shook his head slowly and sadly.

Forensic was finishing up, taking a few final pictures at DiCerrechia's request, when the ME arrived. Al had never seen her before. She was a tall blue-eyed blonde with a beautiful and voluptuous body.

No one would take her for an ME, Al thought as he watched her walk over to the corpse and then kneel to begin her examination. He watched her as she ran her hands slowly over the head and then poke and probe. Al looked at the ME's face, watching for a grimace, a flinch, a flicker, or even the smallest sign. There was none. Al stepped back and turned as the odor struck him, causing him to again gag and wretch. When his stomach spasms stopped, Al was humiliated.

Even Jimmy Farrell grimaced at the odor that penetrated the thick smoke from the cigar in his mouth.

After Al straightened up and recovered, he motioned to the ME kneeling next to the body.

"Nice ass," he said in an effort to divert attention from his puking.

"Which one, Al, the one in the bag?" Farrell asked.

Al just shook his head. "You know fuckin' well I was talking about the doc, Jimmy."

The ME continued her examination for another ten minutes.

"What the fuck she tryin' to find out, Al?" Farrell asked.

"Beats me, Jim—never saw one take so long at a crime scene," Al answered.

"She's probably ambitious, wants to do a good job."

"Maybe she eats this shit up," Al said.

Finally finished, the ME removed her surgical gloves, then walked over to the two assistant DAs.

Al watched her gorgeous face, her pert nose, her clear blue eyes. The eyes were cold . . . cold like a high mountain lake in the dead of winter.

The doctor snapped, "Which one of you guys is the DA?"

"I'm the Narcotics DA," Jimmy Farrell said. "Mr. LoConti here is the homicide DA."

"Yes, well, I'm Dr. Cristen from the office of the Chief Medical Examiner of the City of New York," she announced imperiously.

"I'm Al LoConti and this is Jimmy Farrell," Al said as pleasantly as he possibly could.

Farrell just waved and leered at the ME, causing her to glare back in scorn and revulsion, a look that was not lost on Farrell. Realizing that he had struck out and knowing that he could never score, he decided to have a little fun.

Farrell motioned with his head toward the corpse.

"Is she really dead, Doc?" he asked seriously and with a deadpan look. Al became angry.

Dr. Christen did not answer and thought, The contents of that plastic bag have more personality than these two vaginal sprays.

Al tried to retrieve the situation. "Doctor, would you please tell us what your findings were?"

Dr. Cristen thought that this one was a smug prick and the other just a Neanderthal. She began her recitation in a monotone. "Well, I can tell you she has been dead—"

Farrell interrupted. "We figured that out for ourselves, didn't we, Al?" Farrell said, guffawing at himself.

Al cringed and the doctor continued without pause.

"For a period of years. The body has been frozen, but the freezing process still shows signs of what you would call freezer burn. Based on my initial observation, it is probably close to three years."

Al thought, She damn well knows about the legs case to make a guess like that.

"I'll have to post her, of course, but she has been frozen and the odor stems from the defrosting process. That's why it seems to intensify. I'm aware of the legs found some years ago in this area. I read that file before coming here today, and I'd venture to guess that this is the remainder of the deceased. Anything else, Mr. LoConti?"

"No, thank you, Doctor, but if it's okay with you, I'd like to call you sometime tomorrow after the autopsy is completed to discuss your findings. Since tomorrow is the weekend, I'd like to know a convenient time and number to call."

Dr. Cristen thought he was making a pass. "You may call the medical examiner's office by eleven A.M. If the autopsy is complete, I'll discuss it with you. If it is incomplete, I will not."

There was no disputing the logic, so Al politely thanked the doctor and she nodded and walked away. Both DAs looked after her.

"She's a real professional, Jim," Al said admiringly.

"She shows a great bedside manner, Al," Jimmy Farrell said. "I'd be scared shit to have her hold my balls and tell me to cough."

"Yeah, that would be frightening, Jim. Fuckin' woman has got to be a ghoul to do a job like this. She is a real fuckin' ghoul. But again she's a pro. Never seen an ME take so much time to do an exam. She's a pro."

"She's very insensitive, Al," Farrell chastised.

Al looked at him, shocked. "That's like Hitler callin' someone nasty, Jimmy," he said.

They watched as the ME walked out of the park. She never turned and looked back.

Al and Pete DiCerrechia talked and agreed that they would have to return to the media with this one. Perhaps the publicity would uncover a lead.

Jimmy Farrell watched them confer. He knew them both. They were dedicated. They'll get the perp, he thought. He looked at the corpse in the garbage bag. Since his return from Vietnam, Jimmy couldn't feel anything. He walked up to the corpse, trying to position himself upwind, but the odor now saturated the entire area. He smoked his cigar furiously.

Jimmy was through fuckin' around for the day.

AL HOPED THAT THE scene of the legless cadaver would be his last call for the day. Of course he had no way of knowing that his day was far from over.

He entered his apartment and was greeted by Sport, who rubbed against his leg affectionately as Al reached down and petted him. Then he walked into the kitchen and saw Renee cooking dinner. His mind was still on Dr. Cristen as she kissed him, and he did not respond. He then sat down and watched her pour him a beer. Nodding his thanks, he sipped slowly and then rubbed his children's heads after they came to greet him. They went back into the living room to watch the flickering cartoons.

"You pet them, just like you pet the dog," Renee said.

"Come on, lighten up," Al said. "I got a lot on my mind."

"Your wife and your kids should be on your mind," Renee answered.

"Come on, it's not easy. Give me a break," Al said.

"Do you even remember how you used to be . . . Alcibiades?" Renee asked.

She never never called him Alcibiades. He detested the name. Something was wrong. Really wrong.

He looked up at her and opened his hands outward, palms flat up. "What do you want from me?" he asked.

"I want you to pay more attention. I want you to realize that your life should not be wound up playing cops and robbers. I want you to come home and be here and not be ten thousand miles away. I want a husband and a father and not someone who is here only in body. Your heart is never home. Your heart is always on the job."

"Hey, look," Al LoConti said. "I got a job to do and I'm gonna do it. I bring home all my money and I don't cat around. It's a tough life and you got no complaints. Don't break my balls. They get broke enough every day."

He opened a can of soup and made himself a ham sandwich. Then he fed the dog and put fresh water in the bowl. Man and dog dined together.

Al placed a leash over the head of his eager friend and they walked together in Inwood Park. Twenty minutes later they returned. Al flipped on the news on and then a Yankee game. After a while he fell asleep on the couch.

The beeper woke him up. He shook his head and shut it off. It was 2:35 A.M. He picked up the phone and dialed. The police had found a dead Puerto Rican female inside her locked apartment on Sedgwick Avenue in the Four Four. Al got the address.

As he drove to the scene, he thought perhaps it was just another Bronx divorce. He never dreamed that he was about to discover a mystery that would baffle him and the police for years and that he would recount to his son Ray, along with the DePew murders and the legs case, some fifteen years later in 1988.

He drove south on Sedgwick Avenue parallel to the Harlem River. After stopping behind a row of double-parked police cars, he went into the building and took an old elevator up to the fourth floor. As he expected two uniformed cops were outside the door. Al identified himself and went inside.

There he was met by a tall thin officer wearing a black trench coat. The officer wore his hair close cropped and his head was shaved around his ears in the military style known as "whitewalls."

"Sergeant Talbot, Four Four IU," he said in a clipped military manner.

"LoConti, ADA," Al replied. They did not shake hands.

Sergeant Talbot didn't waste any time. "We've got a female inside—twenty-four years old; hairdresser; family lives in 6C upstairs. They haven't heard from her since yesterday, so tonight around midnight her brother, he's twenty-one, comes down with the father and they use their key and open the door, come in and find her inside . . . then they call us. We then wake up her boss and he tells us that the last he saw her was the day before yesterday and she hadn't come to work since then. You wanna go inside, Mr. DA?" Al nodded.

They walked down the hall to a bedroom at the rear of the apartment, passing a living room and kitchen on their left. Once inside the bedroom, Al saw Martha Valles on the bed. She was lying facedown, eyes shut, and her head was turned to the left. Al noticed that her features were contorted in a slight grimace. He could tell that she had died in pain. It seemed strange that there were no signs of blood or of struggle, no bulletholes and no stab wounds. Al looked at her neck and could see no signs of strangulation.

Al's eyes then swept the room. There was no note, no pill bottles, no set of works. He went back and looked closely at her arms and legs to see if there were any of the tracks, the telltale signs of a junkie. She was clean.

Timmy Flanagan and Morrie Shapiro came in exchanging warm greetings with Al. Flanagan began to talk, totally ignoring the sergeant from the Four Four.

"Al, the windows were all locked except one that had a four-story drop behind it. No pills, no note, no junk, nothin' in the whole apartment. No signs of force on the door. It has a bolt lock and it was locked from the inside."

"I already spoke to Sergeant Talbot," Al said.

"Al, as far as we are concerned, this is investigate DOA, it's Sergeant Talbot's case and not Homicide's," Shapiro said.

Talbot flushed bright red and for a moment Al thought that he might actually punch Shapiro, but the sergeant regained his composure and said, "As far as I'm concerned it's clearly a homicide case and it's in your ballpark." Talbot then turned to Al. "No one has touched her, Mr. DA. We've followed department procedures and we're waiting on the ME and forensic. We've no idea what's underneath her."

"What's the verdict, Al?" Flanagan asked, smiling warmly. His eyes twinkled. "I guess you need another homicide like Custer needed another Indian," Flanagan quipped.

"Let's wait on forensic and the ME," Al said matter-of-factly, not willing to be drawn into police jurisdictional squabble.

Al looked at a portrait picture of Martha on the dresser and then looked back at the naked corpse. His mind registered the sight of a beautiful girl smiling out from the frame, eyes radiating with the joy of life, and his next glance took in the obscenity of her naked death. What a beauty, what a difference when the spark is smothered, he thought while shaking his head sadly. "What a terrible sin," he muttered.

"Hey, Al, don't grieve, it ain't a fuckin' homicide," Flanagan said. Al didn't answer. He knew that Flanagan was full of shit and the girl had been murdered. Talbot knew it too. Al looked back at the photo and saw a handsome blond police officer smiling at Martha's side. The picture was clear enough to show his badge number. Al pointed at the picture.

"I assume you fellows know who this cop is?" he asked.

"Yeah," Talbot responded. "He's a kid works over in the One Fourteen in Queens. Used to be here in the Four Four. Name is Carleton. He was doing a four to twelve. Went home to Rockland County. He's bein' brought down to the Four Four right now," Talbot answered.

The door opened and the ME came in. It was Dr. Cristen. Al nodded to her. Ignoring him, she went immediately to the body and performed a thorough visual examination. Al watched as she probed the neck and the back and then pushed the left shoulder to rotate the corpse slightly onto its right side. "There it is," she said. "Looks like a thirty-eight but I can't be positive."

Al looked and saw a reddish-purple hole slightly above the left breast and blood on the sheet below. Then the ME released the corpse, causing it to flop back on its stomach.

"Good night," Talbot said, leaving with two detectives from the Four Four IU.

Forensic arrived and started to dust for prints. When they finished they photographed the entire apartment. One forensic detective put on plastic gloves and rolled Martha over on her back and the other detective took pictures of the gunshot wound.

Al could see that they were doing a good job. They took multi-angled shots of every room. Al called Flanagan over.

"Call the Four Four and have them bring Carleton over to the Seventh. Call the DA's office and have the steno meet me there." Timmy Flanagan nodded and obeyed.

"There's petroleum jelly here," Dr. Cristen stated while examining the corpse's rectal area. "Looks like she's been sodomized," she concluded matter-of-factly, looking at Al. He was beet red.

After she examined further she said, "There are no visible signs of vaginal penetration."

She finished her examination and before leaving spoke to Flanagan and Shapiro. "I'll do a complete post and toxicological study tomorrow. If there's any semen found, I'll be able to tell you the perpetrator's blood type." After taking a final look at Martha, Dr. Cristen turned and left.

She never even blinked, Al thought to himself.

As the door closed behind her, Morrie Shapiro came up to Al and Flanagan. "Ten to one it's the cop boyfriend. We'll have this one over before breakfast," Shapiro said. Al wondered.

"I can't wait to try the fuck," Al said, thinking of the beautiful, violated, lifeless young thing.

Al got into his car and drove south to the Cross Bronx Expressway, took it to Webster Avenue, and then got off and drove through local streets until he reached the parking lot of the Four Eight precinct. He parked his care and went upstairs to the offices of the Seventh Homicide Zone. It was 3:40 A.M.

He was not surprised to find the PBA attorney, who was obviously very nervous.

"Al LoConti, ADA," Al introduced himself.

"Paul Neumann of the Patrolmen's Benevolent Association."

They shook hands. "I thought you were great in *The Hustler*," Al said.

Neumann shook his head. "You don't know how old that joke is." He smiled and Al smiled back.

"Mr. Neumann, have you had an opportunity to confer with your client?"

"I have. Is he a suspect?"

"All I can say, Mr. Neumann, is this. I've just come from a crime scene. There is a picture of the victim in the room. Your client is in the picture with her. No one else is." Al didn't wait for a response. "I'd like to question your client about his relationship with the deceased as well as his most recent whereabouts."

Al and Neumann had now squared off in their adversarial roles.

"Well, Mr. LoConti, my client is aware of his rights. He has elected to answer questions posed by you provided that I have the right to be present with him at all times and to advise him not to answer questions that I find inappropriate for whatever reason."

"That's the jist of the Miranda decision, Mr. Neumann. You know that those are your client's rights and those terms are agreeable because that is the law."

The steno arrived and they set up in the interview room. For the first time since he had become a DA, Al felt outright hostility from the police. He was on one side and they were on the other. Even his friend Timmy Flanagan kept his distance.

"Okay, on the record. My name is Al LoConti and I'm an assistant DA in Bronx County. The time is now three fifty-five A.M., June 30, 1973. We are in the interview room of the Seventh Homicide Zone in the Four Eight precinct. Present are Bob Livgrum, the stenographer, police officer Roy Carleton of the One Fourteen precinct, and his attorney Mr. Paul Neumann, Esquire, of the PBA. Also present are Detective Timothy Flanagan, shield 36752986, Seventh Homicide, and Lieutenant Richard Drelko, Deputy Commander, Seventh Homicide Zone.

"Officer Carleton, I am investigating the murder of Martha Valles. Before I say anything else I must advise you of your constitutional rights. After each right is pronounced to you, please indicate to me whether you understand it."

Al advised Carleton of the Miranda warnings. Carleton indicated that he understood them and that he was willing to answer questions.

Al paused and lit a cigarillo. He inhaled, then blew the smoke out slowly. As he stared at Carleton, he saw a very worried young man, twenty-five or twenty-six years of age, and red-eyed from crying. Al was too professional to be sympathetic.

"Did you know the deceased, Martha Valles?" he began.

"Yes, sir, I did."

"Ever been to her apartment?"

"Yes, sir, I have."

"How long have you known her?"

"About eight months."

"Where did you meet her?"

"When I was in the Four Four, I used to stop the RMP to get smokes at the candy store next to the beauty parlor where she works."

"Did you date her?"

"We went out."

"Were you intimate?"

"You mean were we close? Yeah, we were close."

"I mean, did you have sex with her? Did you have sexual intercourse with her?"

"Yes."

"Now, Officer, I don't want to be offensive, but I have to ask you whether or not you ever engaged in anal intercourse with Martha Valles?"

Neumann tried to cut off the answer.

"Yes," Carleton said.

Neumann exploded. "Now, Mr. LoConti, what can that possibly have to do with a girl being shot to death? I strenuously object to that question and I want it stricken from the record."

"I can't strike anything, Counselor. In any event the deceased was sodomized. She may have consented. I don't know . . ." Al paused. ". . . whether force or compulsion was used."

Carleton interjected apologetically. "I already told the detectives when they asked me, Mr. Neumann."

"May I continue, Counselor?" Al asked softly.

"I have no objection," Neumann replied.
"Did you shoot her, Carleton?"
"No, sir, I didn't shoot her."
"When did you see her last?"
"Two nights ago."
"When did you leave her?"
"Eight in the morning."
"Where did you go after you left her?"
"Home."
"And did you have sex with her at any time that evening that you last saw her?"
"Yes, but it was regular sex. The other thing was only a couple of times in all the time I knew her."

Al softened his tone. "Roy, could you tell me how you felt about her?"

"I loved her very much. I have a wife and an eighteen-month-old kid. If it wasn't for the kid I would've gotten divorced and married her. I didn't know what to do. I've really screwed up so I asked for a transfer out of the borough. I figured I could get away from her and forget—you know what I mean, Mr. DA."

"Yeah. When were you transferred?"
"Two weeks ago."
"When you left her at eight where did she go?"
"She was getting ready to go to work."
"Did you leave together?"
"No, I had coffee and toast and left. We kissed at the door. She closed it and locked it, and I heard her put on the chain."
"The chain?"
"Yeah, the bolt chain. She always chained the door."
"Did you have a key?"
"Yeah, I still have it. But if she was home I couldn't get in. She always put on the bolt chain."
"But if she wasn't home you could get in, right?"
"That's right, I could."
"How many firearms do you have Carleton?"
"Duty revolver, off-duty revolver, and a shotgun."
"What type of revolvers?"
"Both S and W thirty-eights."
"When did you last fire them?"

"At the range up in Rodman's Neck about four months ago."
"When did you last clean them."
"About a week ago."
"What about the shotgun?"
"Twelve gauge, single shot. My old man gave it to me when I was a kid."
"Do you have any objection to the detectives obtaining your revolvers and the shotgun to run ballistics tests?"
"No, I have no objection."
"Counsel, do you object?"
"No, he could be ordered to surrender them in any event and he has no objection. So go right ahead."
"Very well then, we will stipulate that when we are concluded here the lieutenant will arrange to have detectives escort Officer Carleton to his home. There the officer will surrender all his firearms to the detectives for testing purposes. Is that so stipulated?"
"So stipulated," Neumann said.
"Agreed, Carleton?"
"Yes, sir."
"Did you ever quarrel with Martha?"
"Never."
"Did she know that you were married?"
"Yes, she did."
"She ever ask you if you were going to leave your wife?"
"She understood the problem."
"Tell me what the problem was."
"I told you—my kid."
"What did she say to you when you told her you had transferred?"
"I hadn't told her."
"Did you intend to tell her?"
"Sooner or later."
"Well, you transferred so you could get away from her, isn't that correct?"
"That's right. I couldn't work near where she lived, I needed time to think."
"You want to go back to the Four Four now?"
"I don't know what's going to happen now."
"By the way, did she keep all the windows locked?"

"I think she did. They were always closed. There were bars in front of the ones that faced the fire escape."

"The apartment is four floors from the ground. There is one window in the bedroom. Was that locked?"

"I don't know. It probably was. I never saw it open."

"Well, I've just about finished my questions. Mr. Neumann, do you have anything to add?" Al asked.

"Well, the only thing that I could observe is that I'm sure that you would agree that the officer has been most cooperative and has made a statement despite my advising him to say nothing. I think he has been totally responsive to all of the questions that you posed and that his cooperation was exemplary."

"Your observations are noted for the record, Counselor. The statement is now concluded. Time is four fifteen A.M."

Al walked out of the room. You could smell the fuckin' hostility, he thought as he turned to Drelko. "I would appreciate receiving the ballistics reports by Monday morning at nine sharp."

"You'll get them, Mr. DA." Drelko said officiously.

Al started to leave with Flanagan. Just then the Hat burst in and everyone froze.

"Evenin', Inspector." Detective Timmy Flanagan saluted.

"Who'd the cop kill?" the Hat barked.

NOVEMBER 13, 1973, DAWNED cold and bleak. In the intervening months there had been no movement in either the legs case or in the investigation into Martha Valles's death. All of Officer Roy Carleton's guns had been ruled out as the murder weapons, and although he was a prime suspect there was not enough evidence to even suspend him from the job.

Life went on and Ronald DePew continued to hunt, a dangerous predator still undetected by the authorities in the City of New York.

Alcibiades LoConti left for work on this Tuesday morning thinking of the summation he would deliver today. Renee was fuming.

The bastard didn't even notice me. He couldn't even say goodbye, she thought as she looked out the window and down four stories to watch him get into his blue Dodge and drive to work. It was 8 A.M. and Renee had caught only fitful minutes of sleep last night. She was tired and irritable and certainly in no mood to attend to her young children's demands. It's okay for Alcibiades, she thought. He could keep everyone awake all night with his pacing and rehearsing. Then he could escape to his precious job, oblivious to her and the children.

She sighed, stubbed her cigarette out, and finished her coffee. The children were playing together in their room after she had washed, clothed, and fed them. Renee LoConti decided to take them to the park.

I have to escape this jail, she thought. After she dressed the children warmly, they walked down to the playground two blocks away. She went over to the sliding pond and watched the children climb up then slide down and then climb again. The boy and girl giggled together in that warm and special world reserved for children.

Renee was divorced from that world today, disgusted with her life. At one time just watching the children so happy together would snap her back from disenchantment. Today nothing seemed to help. After a while she took her children to the swings. After securing them behind the bars, she pushed them back and forth. As they swung with their hands holding tightly she thought back to her childhood in Wales. Her family had been poor, her father a bus driver in Cardiff, yet though their possessions were few their family life was rich. She had only fond and warm memories of those days. Then her emigration to America at age eighteen to live with her older sister after her parents' death. An emigration filled with the hopes and fantasies of the millions who preceded her. She sighed, thinking of Al.

They had met in late 1964 at a military wedding in the Bronx.

Al was the best man for his friend Denny Watkins, who like Al had been commissioned a second lieutenant in the Army ROTC program.

By this time Renee had been in America one year and was working for an insurance company. She and Ruella Johnson, the black girl who sat next to her, had become friends, and Renee was pleasantly surprised that Ruella had asked her to be a bridesmaid at her wedding. Renee was even more surprised at the rehearsal to find that the entire bridal party, with the exception of the bride and groom, were white. America was indeed a strange and different land, she had thought.

The wedding had been picture perfect, a living fairy tale. How handsome Al had been in his dress blue uniform lined with the yellow and green piping of the Military Police Corps. Lightning had truly struck. Al had asked Renee out, and they were married fourteen months later. A true-life fairy tale, except that Cinderella's magic coach had long since changed into an ugly pumpkin. Renee had kept her job in the insurance company while Al finished law school. Al had worked odd jobs in his uncle's restaurant and at construction to help with the bills. Yet it was her work and her support that was the mainstay of their economic life. They had nothing. It was just work and work, with not even a honeymoon or a vacation. Yet she had always been there. Then came the army. Ten days after the bar exam and Al was in Fort Gordon, Georgia. Then the long year while he was in Vietnam. The constant turmoil, the addiction of the evening news with bulletins of the deaths of others and the horrors wrought by imagination and waiting. The terrible bitterness of the memory of her son's birth with his father so very far away.

She had shared these times of absence with Ruella Watkins, whose husband, then an army aviator and a captain, had been completing his second tour in Vietnam.

Then came the day of shock, the horrible news of Denny's death. A fiery death in a crashed helicopter, shot down by a Chinese heavy machine gun. It was a memory that still caused Renee guilt even today, after so many years. Guilt that the body of Captain Denny Watkins had been escorted home to America by his childhood friend, Captain Al LoConti.

She could never forget the funeral. The crashing shots of the rifle's volley, which caused her to flinch as if she herself was stabbed in her innermost psyche with an electric cattle prod. The long, slow, so-sad notes of the bugle playing Taps for Denny. The muted cries and sobs followed by the snap fast-folding of the flag from the coffin top; the placing of the spent shells inside the folds of the flag and then with stars only showing its presentation to Ruella by Al, and the snapped salute of a final farewell.

And then the DA's office. Renee had been through it all, one struggle after another, and they still lived like Spartans. They had told her that America was paved with streets of gold. She smiled at the naïveté of the thought. America was a real tough place, and nothing could possibly be tougher than New York City.

She was very tired today. Tired in body because she had not slept and tired in mind, worn down by the lean and so tough years. The thoughts of her marriage were not pleasant. Time did not soften the edges for Renee LoConti. She was disillusioned and angry. Her husband could not even bring himself to say good-bye.

Renee walked back toward the building on Seaman Avenue with her children. Two of her neighbors stood on the stoop in front. Both women were from Ireland, and Renee had paused to chat when a taxicab pulled up. Renee paid no attention and turned her back. Then after a few moments she heard her name shouted.

She turned and saw a young paratrooper in full uniform, cordovan boots spit-shined and bloused. Two sets of ribbons topped by a Combat Infantryman's badge and paratrooper wings.

"Renee," the young man said as he grabbed and kissed her. She was still startled. Then she grabbed him and hugged him tight. He was not due home for another week. Renee cried. She was glad he was back home, safe and alive. She had a special love for this young soldier, a special love for her brother-in-law Vincent LoConti.

Vincent would sleep on a cot in the children's room. As he drank a cup of coffee, he promised Renee that he would have a place of his own in a week. The children were shy in his presence, but after he talked softly and laughed with them they began to respond. Sport remembered him and nuzzled Vince's hand, his tail whipping ferociously with glee.

"Your brother is summing up today, Vinnie," Renee said. "And then the judge will give the case to the jury, and if there is no verdict you probably won't see him until after midnight."

"What kind of case, Renee?" Vinnie asked.

"I don't know, Vinnie, he never tells me," she answered.

"You ever watch him sum up, Renee?" Vinnie asked.

"I've never been to the court. I've asked him but he says he doesn't want to be distracted."

"Hey, Renee," Vinnie said, "let's go see him this morning. Just you, me, and the kids. Come on."

"He wouldn't like it at all." Renee did not want to go. And then again, she did not want to disappoint Vince.

"I'll leave the children with Mrs. Owen across the hall. She's like a grandmother to them and a mother to me," Renee said. "But I don't want to go for more than an hour or two."

"Sure, Renee. Sure. Let me change into civvies and I'll get a cab. Jesus Christ, is my brother gonna be surprised."

It was to be a day full of surprises for Alcibiades LoConti. The very first surprise was that the van from the Bronx House of Detention, known as the Men's House as opposed to the Women's House on Rikers Island, broke down on Jerome Avenue. The second surprise was that it took the department of correction until eleven thirty in the morning to move the prisoners on the van some five blocks to the Bronx County Courthouse. The prison van, of course, held the two defendants in Al's murder trial. Since Al had been at a peak after rehearsing his summation the entire night before, he was like a prizefighter in a dressing room awaiting the call to the arena. The inexcusable civil service delay stretched his tautly strung nerves even further.

When the van finally arrived, Al went from his office to the courtroom flanked by the detectives assigned to this case, Morrie Shapiro and Timmy Flanagan.

The defendants on trial were two animals who preyed on homosexual men who flocked to Hunt's Point from all of New York, New Jersey, and Connecticut in search of quick sex. Many of these men were married and many were affluent. The pickin's were good.

The younger defendant, a handsome, blond, effeminate twenty-year-old, was the bait. His name was Ricky McNaughton. The codefendant was a heavily tattooed and ugly sadistic ex-con named Marvis Qualkeeve. Marvis had emigrated to New York from the hills of West Virginia and had done eight hard years in New York for manslaughter. When Ricky McNaughton got two and a half to five for a reduced Robbery Three charge, he shared a cell with Marvis. After both were paroled they continued to live together and decided to moonlight at the Hunt's Point Market.

Last year Trevor Cunard, a comptroller of a brokerage house, took a detour on his way home to Connecticut from Wall Street. Trevor wasn't thinking of his wife or his kids when he exited the Bruckner Expressway ramp and drove onto the roadway below leading to Hunt's Point Avenue. It was six-thirty on a cold and damp November evening. Cunard passed lines of parked trucks filled with produce and meats for the enormous market. The drivers were in the trucks being serviced by the legions of hookers who surrounded the market.

Cunard turned up a side street reserved for those who had different preferences. Some trucks were double-parked. Handsome youths, both black and white, were trolling the street for fish such as Trevor Cunard. Cunard pulled up next to a quite handsome blond youth just off the corner, lowered the electric window on his Mercedes, and flashed a fifty-dollar bill and Ricky McNaughton got in the car. Trevor became excited. Throwing caution to the winds, he readily followed Ricky's suggestion that they go to Ricky's place.

Ira Schmorkler, a shrewd twenty-four-year-old undercover officer, was walking from the market in his pose as a rabbi inspecting the kosher meat industry. Ira noticed the youth get into a Mercedes with Connecticut plates. Ira took a hard look at the youth and noted the time and the plate number in his memo book.

Ricky directed Cunard three short blocks to a small rooming house just off Hunt's Point Avenue. Upon their arrival they proceeded to the second floor where Ricky held out his hand and accepted the fifty-dollar bill.

It was an offshoot of the old Murphy game. When Cunard started to mount Ricky, he didn't even hear the opening of the closet behind him. Marvis crushed the back of Trevor Cunard's skull with a three-pound solid steel bar. Cunard was dead before his head hit the mattress. Marvis wrapped a towel around Trevor's head and took the money and credit cards from his wallet. The towel served to prevent the spilling of brains from his crushed skull. Many hours later, at one-fifteen in the morning, Ricky and Marvis each placed one of Cunard's arms around their necks and hustled him outside as if he was a drunk. They put him in the backseat of his car and then drove the car six blocks away where they parked and left it.

The next morning after both Cunard and the car were found, word spread throughout the department and eventually reached Ira Schmorkler, who proceeded directly to the offices of Morrie Shapiro and Timmy Flanagan. Ira went through mug shots and in fifteen minutes identified the youth he had spotted with the deceased. It was an incredible piece of luck. The parole board furnished Flanagan with an address and Al LoConti quickly got a judge to sign a search warrant.

Ten cops broke down the rooming-house door and grabbed Ricky and Marvis in the midst of making love. The steel rod with pieces of Cunard's skull still on it was recovered as were credit cards bearing his name. Neither defendant would make a statement to ADA Al LoConti. No fingerprints from inside the Mercedes could be identified.

The case was a lock. Alcibiades offered no plea. The trial, which should have been a DA's pleasure cruise, was turned into stomach-churning pilgrimage by the antics of the two radical defense attorneys. They yelled frame and flake. They claimed that Schmorkler, Flanagan, and Shapiro framed the ex-cons and that the evidence—the credit cards and the steel rod—were planted by the police.

The lawyers, although radicals, were extremely bright and talented. Had they chosen Wall Street rather than a political agenda, they would have been millionaires. They put both Alcibiades and the police on trial. It was an old tactic and it often worked, but the law provided that he who had the burden of proof would have the final say, the last word and this was the summation that Alcibiades LoConti intended to deliver today.

And so he had stayed up all night polishing up the final punch, the last word and the last laugh. It would be payback time for the two radical lawyers, and Al wanted the payback to be a fuckin' bitch.

Renee entered the packed courtroom with Vincent LoConti. They took seats in the last row. Al, intent on the task before him, did not even notice them. The jury was brought in and seated. The judge nodded to the first defense lawyer. He thanked the judge and rose and delivered a thirty-five-minute summation—relatively short. But for thirty-five minutes he was a roving cannon shooting down the police department and blasting the personal integrity of Alcibiades LoConti. Renee watched her husband's neck go red. Once he turned his face toward the defense attorney, and Renee saw that his face was as red as his neck. She knew that Al was furious. The second defense attorney was even more dramatic. He was a skilled actor, and his lines flowed without miscue. The audience in Part 25 hung on his every word. He was so good that even Renee and Vince wondered whether the police had framed the defendants and whether Al was an unwitting accessory. Renee knew her husband would never do anything unethical let alone illegal. Why does he take this abuse? she wondered. Why doesn't he follow his uncle Peppy's advice and get a job with an insurance defense firm and make some big money? Why does he stay in this meat grinder? Renee had no answers as she watched her husband, still red in the face, rise for his summation.

"Boy, is he pissed off," Vince LoConti whispered to her. She nodded.

"I hope he can think," Vince whispered again. Renee made no response. She was only mildly interested. She was surprised that she wasn't even rooting for her husband.

Al started his summation off slow and low. He reviewed the evidence in scrupulous detail. He went over the background of each police officer, giving the dates and times of each one's various decorations and awards. Then his voice grew a little louder.

"There's an old saying in law school, ladies and gentlemen of the jury. And that saying is that when you are on trial and the facts are against you—well, in that case you must argue the law. And in the case where the law—that is, the legal precedent—is against your position—well, then in that case you must argue the facts. And, ladies and gentlemen, finally in a case such as this, where both the facts and the law are totally against the defendants—" Al turned and pointed with disdain, then continued. "When the facts and the law are against a pair of murderers and robbers such as these two . . . well, then, there is nothing left for their lawyers to do except the third thing and that is to just argue. And that is all they have done. Argue. Argue and argue. They yell frame and flake. Well, let me tell you. . . ." Al paused and his voice rose to a loud boom. "If you feel that either or both the DA's office and/or the police framed these two, then walk them right out that door." Al pointed. "But I know that you were selected in this case to use your God-given common sense, and that God-given common sense will tell you that the defense arguments are red herrings, smokescreens designed to distort the evidence and to hide the truth. The overwhelming truth, which is simply that these two predators are guilty of Murder in the Second Degree and Robbery in the First Degree and Possession of Stolen Property and a Weapon all as charged in indictment number 2287 of 1972, and I ask you to return a verdict of guilty to each and every count. Thank you." Al sat down. He had received another surprise—how well he had done. He was surprised that he did not lose his temper. He sensed victory.

Renee watched him. "Boy, was he good," Vinnie said to her. She just nodded. She had been surprised also. She was surprised to realize why her husband kept at this work. He loves it, she thought. He really loves it. Loves it even though it keeps him from his family and even though it tears him apart. He loves it and won't leave it. Renee considered Al's relationship with his job as if the job was a jealous mistress. And she vowed right then in Part 25 with Vince LoConti next to her that since Alcibiades would not leave the jealous mistress, then she by God would leave him. The audience filed out just before the judge charged the jury. No one was permitted to enter or leave during the charge, which lasted over an hour. As Renee walked out with Vince, Al raised his eyes. Renee thought he had seen her. In fact he had not.

The bastard refused to even notice me, Renee thought. He couldn't even nod good-bye.

NOVEMBER 19, 1973, WAS a bad Monday for Al's boss, Johnny O'Boyle. It was a cardinal sin for a bureau chief to have a courtroom without a trial going on, which is known in the criminal justice system as having a Part go down.

Today Johnny O'Boyle had two Parts down. One was Judge Flay's and the other, Judge Finch's. O'Boyle had sent Al into Flay's part with the Roosevelt Greg case and had sent Dave Hornbein into Finch's part. In less than half an hour Hornbein came back to say the judge had adjourned for the day because he had stomach cramps. O'Boyle knew Finch had probably knocked off a quart of gin Sunday and needed the time to crawl home and nurse his hangover before having to perform before a jury.

Flay, however, was vying for the party nomination for New York State Supreme Court. The people of the Bronx always voted for the same party, so the nomination meant the job. Flay was using the time-old formula for a good judicial report card, disposing of cases, and he was now leaning hard on DAs to give good pleas. Flay only wanted to try felony murders so that he could whack defendants with the maximum sentence and make headlines. There were no such cases before him today.

Al was called before Flay with the Greg case. In a few minutes he briefed the judge. Greg and the deceased, Lee, had done time together for a botched burglary years ago. They had managed to stay out of serious trouble and both found work with the Transit Authority cleaning graffiti from subway cars.

Lee had invited Greg to his rooming house on a Friday night for a party, a bring-your-own-booze affair. So Greg had stopped after work and picked up a bucket of Kansas Fried Chicken and found a crowded party when he arrived. He had a quart of Mr. Berry's six-month-old scotch with him but did not remember to buy a couple of six-packs, so he asked Lee for some beer to wash down his chicken. Lee refused.

Greg asked Lee to watch the chicken while he went downstairs to the Superette to get some malt liquor. Lee told him not to sweat and Greg left, but when he came back ten minutes later he found the chicken bucket full of clean bones. Then he noticed that some people were still eating chicken, and everyone now seemed to be laughing at him. He turned to demand an explanation, but Lee couldn't answer because he was too busy munching on a leg. When he finally swallowed he looked up and smiled, saying that this was his second piece, and after eating his first piece, which was so good he wanted to please everyone so he "Done gave it all away." Lee then went back to eating. People all around heard him and started to laugh and snicker at the defendant. The defendant yelled at Lee, but Lee just chewed on the chicken and said, "My, my, is this goooood."

Just as Lee was taking another bite, Greg pulled out a switchblade and stabbed him once in the heart. Lee got up and staggered toward the bathroom, where he died.

Greg was picked up at his rooming house and promptly confessed all to an assistant DA. He stated that he saw Lee reach into his pocket and thought Lee was going to pull a knife on him. The police found nothing on Lee.

"What plea did you offer, Mr. LoConti?" Flay asked.

"Man One, no promises," Al said, signifying that the defendant could plead guilty and in return could not be sentenced to more than eight and a third to twenty-five years. "No promises" meant that the DA would take no position on sentence and the court could sentence as it liked.

Sy Gold, an old-time seasoned 18b lawyer, put in a pitch for Greg but Flay held up his hand. He and Sy both belonged to the Iroquois Club, a political club in Riverdale.

"Spare me, Sy. Take the plea and I'll give him zip to ten."

Al started to protest but Flay held up his hand again.

"Even if you convicted him I would only give zip to ten. So save your breath and your time," Flay said in a snotty, condescending tone. Al and Flay got into a heated argument for five minutes while Gold conferred with his client. Then Greg took the plea. The judge promised him the sentence on the record.

Al was disgusted and the Part went down.

THE NEXT DAY WHEN Fast Frankie Hammon, one of the slickest criminal defense attorneys, stood in front of Finch's bench beside his cocounsel Jim Fisher, his brain was working in overdrive figuring escape routes from the trial looming ahead of him. Fast Frankie had two tickets for a flight to the Bahamas this afternoon and a full comp at a casino hotel. Imelda, the sexy barmaid who could suck the bark off a tree, was eagerly waiting for him. Trials in Bronx County had no place in Fast Frankie Hammon's schemes. Finch took the bench and Frankie started to talk.

Five minutes later Alcibiades walked into court with the backup case of Poquay and Bix ready for trial. Only once before had Al tried a case in front of Finch, whom everyone knew was a contract man. Finch's decisions were subject to financial consideration received prior to the trial. Yet he was invariably polite to all.

O'Boyle had summed up the attitude of the assistant DAs toward Finch. "He's a corrupt fuck but that don't make him a bad person."

Al had asked O'Boyle how on earth could a guy like Finch ever become a judge and O'Boyle told him. "His old man was big in real estate and he guessed the right number of seats in Yankee stadium."

Al didn't understand.

The case Al brought before Finch had been thoroughly prepared. It was a "lock"—a cinch to try because it could be proven by one civilian witness and two police officers, the ME, and a relative of the deceased.

Poquay and Bix had been in jail for eighteen months awaiting trial. At their arraignment they had been offered a Man Two plea, which they refused. When Al inherited the case he withdrew the offer and raised the ante. Now the plea offer was Manslaughter in the First Degree, known as Man One.

The case was conferenced before Finch by Frankie Hammon, Poquay's lawyer, and Jim Fisher, representing Bix. Frankie was a funny guy, always with a smile and a story that could split your sides. All the judges loved him. Frankie, thinking of Imelda's talents and the crap table on Paradise Island, was really pushing for a Man Two Plea.

"Come on, Al, give me the Man Two, take the Judge off the hook," Frankie cajoled.

"Man One, Frank, eight and a third to twenty-five. I'm ready for trial today," Al said.

"Judge, Al here thinks the whole Bronx is another province in Vietnam. Come on, Al, I don't want to try this case. I got plane tickets to the Bahamas this afternoon. Two tickets. One for me and one for the new barmaid in the Justice A Go Go across the street. This is Eighteen b, the state pays me shit for this case, but I filed a notice of appearance and I know Judge Finch isn't gonna let me out. At least give me an adjournment."

"I can't let the Part go down, Frank. This is the only case we have for Judge Finch. His Part went down yesterday."

Finch nodded. The administrative judge had called him this morning warning him not to let the Part go down.

"I can't give you an adjournment, Frank. Either you plead him out or go to trial," Finch said.

Finch did not want to work today. He turned to Al. "I don't think your plea offer is very realistic, Mr. LoConti."

"It sure isn't," Frankie Hammon echoed.

Jim Fisher had been silent throughout this exchange. He liked Al but thought him inflexible and not realistic in not accepting the system for what it was.

Fisher said, "Al, a Man Two will give Judge Finch plenty of scope to deal with this case. Why don't you reconsider?"

Finch chimed in. "I really think Man Two would be justice in this matter, Mr. LoConti. Man One, on the other hand, is a trifle too severe.

"Judge, for four months I've had this case and I offered Man Two one time. That was because the nineteen times this case was called in court before I got assigned to it that plea was offered. Now I upped the ante. If I lower it to Man Two, the whole inmate population gets a signal that if they string the case down to trial they get a better plea. And in that case this system, which is held together with spit and bubble gum, is going to burst and pop like the intestines of a rotted corpse, and the stink is going to attract some attention from the poor slobs that pay taxes to support it."

Frankie Hammon smiled. He was slicker than shit on ice and would never lose sight of his goal—sun and fun with Imelda.

"Come on, Al, this is no murder, these guys couldn't do anything right. Hey, Judge, these two are the Keystone Cops of the crooks in the Bronx. They can't tell their asses from third base. This case is an *unarmed* robbery and an auto accident. These guys were deliberately unarmed. They wouldn't hurt a fly. Why crucify them? Come on, Man Two is plenty. Get rid of the case, it's a piece of you-know-what, Judge. Come on, Al, move the goddamn calendar. We don't want any promises, Judge Finch can give them up to fifteen years. We got all the faith in the world in Judge Finch. I know the Judge will be fair, and I told my client that."

"May I recite the facts of the case, Your Honor?" Al asked.

"Well, Mr. Hammon and Mr. Fisher here filled me in this morning just before you arrived. But if you want to state your version, please proceed."

"Thank you, Your Honor." Al began. "Poquay and Bix entered Mercado's Bodega on Tremont Avenue. Bix then went back out and started the car they arrived in. The car was double-parked. Poquay makes out he has a gun in his pocket and tells Mercado to empty the till. Mercado gives him all the cash. Poquay ran out the door, looked up Tremont, and saw an RMP comin' down the street and so he dove headfirst into the car and Bix took off with Poquay's legs hangin' out the window."

Finch nodded politely.

"Mercado runs out after Poquay, yelling bloody murder. Mercado's got a white apron on. The cops in the RMP get the picture, they put on the light and siren and pursue."

Finch nodded again.

"They pursue for three blocks up Tremont, and at Third Avenue Bix hangs a sharp left and loses control. The car goes up on the sidewalk and pins Mrs. Blanchard against the building and crushes the life out of her. She is sixty-six years old and still working as a cleaning lady."

Finch interjected, "I know, I know, Al." He shook his head sadly. "It's a terrible tragedy but, like Frankie says, it's really a Robbery Two and a traffic accident. These guys were unarmed."

"Judge, this is Felony murder. They were fleeing the commission of a felony and in the course of the flight a nonparticipant is killed. It is irrelevant whether they were armed and it is irrelevant whether or not they intended to kill her. Felony murder. It's plain and simple, Judge, we have all that the law requires: Kill someone in the course of a felony and whether you intend it or not you go for Felony murder."

"I'm fully aware of the law, Mr. LoConti, what I am trying to achieve here is some semblance of justice," Finch shot back.

"So am I, Judge. Mrs. Blanchard was a sixty-six-year-old black lady who lived and worked here all her life. She had meager savings and her funeral was attended by few people. These defendants are hardened recidivists. They should have no plea at all."

Al saw a look of surprise cross Finch's face. Realizing that the judge might not have all the facts, Al continued. "Did anyone tell you of their criminal records before I arrived here today?"

"Well, we discussed waiving a jury," Frankie Hammon put in. "So it would not have been proper for the Judge to be told about their records."

"Well, if you are discussing a plea it would be unfair to keep the length of their yellow sheets from the Court," Al replied.

The cat was out of the bag and Finch turned angrily to Hammon.

"Do they in fact have criminal records?" he asked. Bad headlines loomed in front of Finch, but Frankie Hammon could charm his way through a sea of sharks and not just with professional courtesy. Smiling, he adjusted the knot on his white silk tie.

"Judge, these guys got records so long, so long, I'm tellin' ya, you could read *Gone With the Wind* faster than their yellow sheets."

Everyone chuckled except Judge Finch; he just howled.

"I love this fuckin' Hammon," he said to Fisher and Al.

Al was fed up and interrupted the festivities. "Judge, it's got to be Man One and I want the court to commit to a sentence of eight and a third to twenty-five. Otherwise I want to start to pick a jury right now." The chuckling immediately ceased.

"Come on, Al, why insist on the maximum sentence?" Hammon pleaded.

"Because career guys have to get it. There's been too many adjournments, too much screwing around, they had plenty of opportunity. No more."

Finch injected. "I think we can abide by your feelings as to an Open Man One. You can make your recommendation but you can't bind the court."

"Judge, I would appreciate it if you would promise to sentence these two as I recommend. I have no backup case and the Part will go down, so frankly I hope that they don't take the plea," Al responded.

Fisher then exploded. "Because of your goddamn calendar congestion my client has got to do eight and a third to twenty-five. Some goddamn justice. I'm shocked and disappointed in you, LoConti. I had you pegged as a square shooter."

"You had nineteen adjournments, Jim. You were before seven different judges. That's plenty of time to take a Man Two. I don't blame you for using the system's congestion to help your client. I know that you're just doing your job. But everyone got too greedy and conveniently forgot the length of these guys' yellow sheets," Al said, opening his case folder.

"Poquay has thirty-five arrests, twenty-seven of which are felonies. He's spent a grand total of three years in jail and he is twenty-eight years old. Bix has thirty-nine arrests, twenty-four felonies, he's done four years. He's thirty-three. And they crunch a grandmother on our streets like a grape." Al closed the folder.

"No Bronx jury will convict these guys of murder, Al," Hammon said.

"Okay, then, take your chances, gentlemen, and go to bat, I'm ready for trial," Al said.

Finch's attitude had changed and he turned to the two lawyers. "Gentlemen, I suggest you confer with your clients. If they dispose of this case I will abide by Mr. LoConti's recommendation as to sentence."

The lawyers retreated to the bench where their clients sat surrounded by court officers. As the lawyers spoke to them, they shook their heads vehemently and postured, pouted, and grimaced.

Finally fed up, Finch sent for a panel of jurors.

Hammon looked at Poquay and thought how ugly he was compared to Imelda the barmaid.

"You stand a good chance of being convicted for murder, Otis," he said. "And you will max out with your sheet. You won't see the parole board for twenty-five years. By then people will be drivin' around Tremont Avenue in little spaceships, and pussy for you, my friend, will be a distant memory. You understand. Hey, Otis, eight and a third is a lot shorter than twenty-five. But it's your decision. This DA's got a hard-on for you. And if you take the stand, he is going to ask you about all your convictions and the jury is going to convict your ass."

Al noticed a look of resignation on Poquay's face. They're going to fold, he said to himself.

Hammon stood up. He began the soliloquy that resulted in both defendants pleading guilty to Manslaughter in the First Degree and eventually being sentenced to eight and a third to twenty-five years.

Later that afternoon when Poquay and Bix arrived at the Bronx House of Detention, Frankie Hammon looked out the window of the 707 jet somewhere over Maryland. He sipped his drink, and turned and smiled at Imelda, and Imelda smiled back.

17

"ALCIBIADES IS A VERY strange first name. Is there a story behind it?" lawyer Reynard Foxworth asked while watching Renee LoConti blow a smoke ring up toward the ceiling. Renee had been asked this question many times before, so her answer was a set speech, which she now told to her lawyer.

"Alcibiades, the Greek general, was the nephew of the famous Greek statesman Pericles, and he went to live with Pericles when his father died. Pericles restored temples ravaged by the Persians and was prominent in the Golden Age of Athens. Alcibiades married into great wealth. He was a great general but got himself involved in intrigue. Some even called him a traitor, so he was banished from Athens but after many victories was recalled to the city and honored. But in the end his enemies conspired and burned his house, and when he tried to escape he was killed with a volley of arrows. In the movie *Patton* when Patton is standing in North Africa he mentions Alcibiades. Patton studied all of his campaigns."

"How did your husband get the name?" Foxworth asked while thinking that he would give up ten fees to climb into the sack with this beauty.

"His grandmother's favorite neighbor was a Greek woman whose husband was named Pericles, so she named her son Pericles. Before Al was born someone told his mother that the famous Greek Pericles after whom her favorite brother was named had a nephew named Alcibiades. So she named my husband Alcibiades."

"In a way it's nice to have such unusual classical names," Foxworth said in his sickly sweet manner.

"He hates being called Alcibiades, and his uncle Peppy, who is a very wonderful guy, hates being called Pericles."

Renee had been in the office for almost an hour. Her sister had told her that this guy was a great divorce lawyer, but Renee couldn't stand him. He had asked her every personal question imaginable, even grilling her for details on her sex life.

At the end of the interview Foxworth knew that the LoContis were two decent young people. What they needed was counseling and not lawyers, and though he liked this young pretty Welsh girl, he didn't like her enough to lose a fee. Foxworth knew he would have to sue for divorce in New York County and that no judge in Manhattan would hurt a young DA from the next borough. So goaded by the prospect of an uphill battle and forearmed with the knowledge that these people had nothing and that the husband was not a part owner of his uncle's restaurant, Reynard P. Foxworth was forced to do the right thing.

"You should go to counseling with your husband," Foxworth said.

"You don't understand. He will never go anywhere. I want out," Renee replied.

"Okay," Foxworth said. "My retainer will be twenty-five hundred dollars. When you pay me I'll go to work and sue your husband for divorce."

"I'll need some time," Renee said.

"Fine," Foxworth replied. "Too bad you can't move in with someone in the Bronx," he added.

"Why?"

"Because if I could sue him in the Bronx it could embarrass him with his job and with that at stake he would settle quick. Do you have any friends or relatives in the Bronx?" he asked.

"No, my only relative is my sister on Long Island."

"That's no good at all. There would be no leverage to bringing a suit on Long Island, and in any event I would have to refer you to another attorney on the Island."

"You mean if I lived with my sister and I sued in Long Island my husband's job would not be affected by the divorce?"

"Precisely. The divorce action would have little if any effect."

"Thank you, Mr. Foxworth," Renee said as she stood up and left.

While the elevator was descending she made a decision that freed her from her feelings of guilt. She would move in with her sister on Long Island, and then his precious job would be saved. It was truly worth the fifty bucks that the horrible horny old lawyer had charged.

RONALD DEPEW, NOW SEVENTEEN years old, was a psychiatric patient at Bronx State Hospital. His parents had committed him because of his violent tantrums and erratic behavior, but after only three days he was diagnosed as having no violent propensities and was discharged to an outpatient status.

But Ron was a paranoid schizophrenic. He wanted to join the US Army, but his father refused to sign him in. "Finish high school, learn a trade," the older DePew, a sheet metal worker, had pleaded over dinner, but Ron ignored him, storming from the house with his hamburger. He ran up onto the roof. It was a very dark night, but he was able to see Dewey Mulligan's dog on the roof. The Mulligans always left the dog on the roof so that they didn't have to walk him. The dog growled at Ronald, who sat down next to the parapet overlooking the street. He held out the hamburger and coaxed the dog forward. Smelling the meat, the dog cautiously walked toward DePew, who broke off a piece. The dog grabbed it and quickly swallowed and then came back for more. Ronald gave the rest of the burger to the dog and petted the animal affectionately. The dog licked his hand. Then Ronald picked the dog up over his head and flung him over the parapet, four stories down into the street. The dog did not survive.

There was a witness to this murder, a Mrs. Grimaldi who lived across the avenue. Mrs. Grimaldi was married to a local banker in the neighborhood and she was the chief teller. Every day the numbers' runners in the area would deposit action in the "Grimaldi" bank. Her husband James, known as "Jimmy Clams," worked for the Admiral, Guido Insalata.

Of course the odds of Mrs. Grimaldi reporting what she had witnessed were the same as the odds of her reporting her husband's weekly lunches with Judge Marty Honig at the Ristorante degli Amici on 189th Street.

Mrs. Grimaldi accompanied her husband to this restaurant each week, where they would happen to bump into the judge. Grimaldi would then invite the judge to lunch. Judge Marty Honig always had a long thin cigar in his mouth—in fact, the only times that he didn't have a long thin cigar in his mouth was when he ate and when he sat on the bench. Judge Honig always smiled while he ate. When he was doing his job, which was judging, he would frown because he couldn't wait to get off the bench so that he could put another long thin cigar in his mouth.

During these lunches Mrs. Grimaldi would listen to her husband discuss foreign policy and political matters for a while until she had to go to the ladies' room, whether or not she really had to go. When she came back Judge Honig would have a real big smile on his face and would be smoking a long thin cigar. And then Mr. and Mrs. Grimaldi would leave the restaurant.

Mrs. Grimaldi told her husband about the DePew boy, and he in turn had asked for a free opinion from the judge.

"Let his old man deal with it," Judge Honig had said. Mr. Grimaldi saw to it that when Mr. Depew, Sr., placed his gambling action he was informed of his son's deed. The DePews discussed the matter, and two weeks later Ronald was at Fort Benning, Georgia.

DePew Senior never even thought about what trade the army would teach his son.

* * *

Ronald DePew loved the army but he hated his drill instructor, Sergeant Feldman. Feldman, who was born in the Bronx and a veteran of two combat tours in Vietnam, felt that DePew was strange but couldn't put his finger on any specific peculiarity. He just didn't like the kid even though DePew followed orders, was above average in the training battalion, and always kept his gear in tiptop shape.

Supersensitive, DePew knew that Feldman disliked him, so he vowed to pay Feldman back just as he had paid back Dewey Mulligan's dog.

One morning Feldman was inspecting the barracks in anticipation of an inspection from the assistant deputy post commander. He was pleased to find the toilet bowls in the latrine spotless, the floors clean enough to eat from, and the shower handles polished and all aligned. Feldman was only too aware that the colonel loved to check the handles of showers for proper alignment.

After his inspection of the showers, Feldman went to inspect the four-foot-long trough that served as a urinal for the platoon but instead of the usual gleaming white surface, he found a brown mound in the middle. It took him a second to realize that someone had defecated in the urinal.

Feldman immediately made the platoon fall out and put the urinal off limits. The platoon was instructed to shave, dress, and go to chow, after which they would clean the urinal. He threatened the wrath of hell should there ever be a repeat performance.

Afterward some of the trainees discussed watching the urinal to catch the perpetrator, but others were too amused. Word of the mound spread and soon the battalion was joking about Feldman's Phantom Shitter. The mounds reappeared from time to time.

It stopped being funny when Feldman discovered a cat's head in the shower, and it was even less of a joke when the head was identified as belonging to Flutzie, the colonel's wife's cat.

Feldman called the platoon leader, who called the company commander, who called the MPs. They brought in CID, who took fingerprints and statements from the whole platoon. No leads were found.

Feldman then posted a twenty-four-hour guard at the latrine. It prevented further incidents but failed to catch the malefactor. Obsessed, after much pondering Feldman went to the 106th Military Intelligence detachment to speak with his old friend, the detachment NCOK (Noncommissioned Officer In Charge), Sergeant Danforth.

The next day when the platoon was at the range, Danforth and Sergeant Brutti, a photographic expert, rigged up a miniature state-of-the-art radio-controlled intelligence camera under the sink across from the urinal. The camera was undetectable.

By arrangement, the CQ came through the squad bay at 3 A.M. the next morning with a flashlight and went up to the guard outside the latrine door. The CQ flashed the light over the eyes of the sleeping DePew and told the guard in a loud voice that he had been granted emergency leave. The guard and the CQ left. No relief was posted.

Feldman was outside and across the company street on a slight rise with binoculars. He was able to detect shadows in the latrine when someone entered. When he spotted the movement of a shadow, he activated the camera.

Hours later Danforth extracted the film and developed it. He gave the prints to Feldman, who showed the company commander six shots of DePew in living color defecating into the urinal of the 1st Platoon. CID came and advised DePew of his rights under the Uniform Code of Military Justice, but DePew denied everything.

Reports went to the General and the Staff Judge Advocate, and DePew was ordered to see a psychiatrist. After the examination had been concluded, the psychiatrist, the Staff Judge Advocate, the General and everyone involved agreed that DePew should stop being an army problem as soon as possible. DePew and his assigned attorney did not agree.

But when the attorney was shown a duplicate set of Feldman's photos, his legal opinion underwent a quick reversal. During a long conversation with his client, he advised DePew that he would surely be court-martialed and thrown out of the army. DePew shouted angrily that he loved the army and wanted to make it his career. The lawyer told him promotions would be hard to come by with color photos on the front of his 201 file that showed him shitting in a urinal and DePew finally got the picture.

He was granted a 212 discharge, the rough equivalent of a World War Two Section 8, and his parents were alerted to pick him up. They conferred with the attorney and the psychiatrist, and soon after Private DePew left the army to become an outpatient at Bronx State Hospital for the Insane, multiple murders of elderly women began to occur in Bronx County.

IT WAS A FOUL February day in 1974, a day when snow, sleet, and rain came down without letup, a day that made you crave for the solace and warmth of your home and the pleasure of playing with your children, free from the many horrors of your daily work. But Alcibiades LoConti would not be granted such sanctuary.

The bodies of eight women had been found in Bronx County since the army expelled Ronald DePew, and on this day a felony call reported number nine.

Hanratty was the felony DA but since he was in court, O'Boyle and Al took the call. They drove ten minutes from the courthouse to an apartment house on University Avenue just south of Fordham Road. When they arrived they saw three RMPs and five unmarked police cars. They entered the building and went to the elevator. A sign over the button read OUT OF ODOR.

Al pointed a finger at the misspelling and started for the stairs, and O'Boyle just shook his head. They walked up three flights brushing snow from their coats and stamping their cold feet. When they got to the third floor they identified themselves to a policeman who was guarding an apartment, then entered to be met by a captain from the borough command. He was the Hat's personal representative and only one of many detectives and police brass milling around inside the crowded apartment. He acted extremely nervous, constantly flitting in and out among the detectives, picking up tidbits of information and then obsequiously relaying them to the deputy inspector. Al knew the captain and knew that he would never be far from his flute, a Coke bottle filled with whiskey, because this captain was a quart-a-day man.

Petey DiCerrechia had caught the case along with Detective Rory O'Donnell. Solwin had finally had O'Donnell transferred from Narcotics due to the Dano fiasco, and Petey had lucked out and got a permanent transfer with him.

"The deceased is in the kitchen," Captain Quart-a-Day told Al and O'Boyle. The two ADAs walked down the hall to a doorway blocked by a chair and a uniformed officer. Forensic and the ME had come and gone, but the morgue wagon had been delayed by a triple homicide in Manhattan.

Al and O'Boyle looked into the kitchen from behind the chair and saw a woman lying faceup. She was apparently very old. Her facial skin was chicken-textured loose and she had thin gray hair bunned at the back. A large cut ran across her throat from behind one ear to the other, nearly severing her head. Al looked at the kitchen floor, which was covered with her blood, and then stared at her face. It was contorted and the skin was drawn crisp and tight with the pain and the terror she felt while dying. Al saw footprints in the blood.

"ME's?" he asked DiCerrechia. Pete nodded yes. Then Al heard talking and female laughter from a room farther up the hallway. He walked toward the voices and looked into a room to see a well-dressed woman pouring tea into fine china cups. Each and every cup without exception was held by a very uncomfortable police officer.

"Oh . . . Petey, Rory," she called, as if greeting long-lost friends. "Tea is ready." DiCerrechia and O'Donnell looked sheepishly at Al as Pete made the introductions.

"Mr. O'Boyle, Al, this is Mrs. Underwood. She was a roommate of the deceased lady, Mrs. Farquier."

"Gentlemen, how do you do," she said with a smile. "Would either of you care for a cup of tea? It's fresh brewed and nice and hot."

"Uh, no, thank you." Al smiled.

O'Boyle shook his head and muttered, "No thanks, Mrs. Farquier."

"Mrs. Farquier is inside, young man, I'm Mrs. Underwood," she snapped in an angry tone.

O'Boyle turned red at the rebuke and Al tried to cut short his embarrassment. "We are both very sorry for your loss, Mrs. Underwood," he said.

"Thank you. It's terrible." She smiled at Al. "Dorothy was eighty-two last week."

Pete started to brief the DAs. "Mrs. Underwood had been out shopping and came back and found the door closed but unlocked. When she came in she found Mrs. Farquier. Isn't that right, Mrs. Underwood?"

"Rose, Rose, Petey, please call me Rose. And yes, that is correct." She smiled. "There are four deadbolt locks on that door and all the windows have iron grates, as you can see. All the grates are always locked, and Dorothy would never let anyone in. In fact, we didn't even open the door for each other for safety reasons," she said, still smiling.

Al looked at the false teeth in her smiling mouth and he tried to smile back but noticed that Mrs. Underwood's eyes were not smiling. Al felt a chill dampness that ran from his neck all the way down his spine. She gave him the creeps.

"Your name, young man?" she commanded.

"My name is LoConti, and this is Mr. O'Boyle."

"First names please, Mr. LoConti."

"I'm Al and this is John."

"Mrs. Underwood, did Dorothy let in delivery boys or Western Union or anyone that you could think of?" O'Boyle asked, trying very hard to smile but only managing to grimace.

"No one, Jim, no one at all," she said, deliberately addressing him with the wrong name to repay him for his confusing her name with that of her dead friend. "We were quite cognizant that elderly women are being slain all over Bronx County and we have been quite aware that we are past the flower of our youth. So our door would not be opened for anyone. I had been out shopping and I picked up her prescription, which of course she knew. There was nothing else that was to be delivered. She was very alert and would not succumb to a ruse."

"How about the mail?" Al asked.

"Carmine, the dear man, he is our mailman, brings it up, and on his day off the substitute carrier does also. They always knock at the door and ask how we are and then slip the mail under the door. We open the door for Carmine once in a while and of course always at Christmas to give him his present. Sometimes he even has a cup of tea with us. He's such a fine man, divorced now, and his wife lives with another man without benefit of marriage. Poor Carmine." She stopped smiling momentarily and then smiled again.

"What time did Carmine come today?" O'Boyle asked.

"It wasn't Carmine, it was the substitute, and he came about ten-thirty this morning, before I had left," she replied, anticipating O'Boyle's follow-up question.

"Does the deceased have any relatives?" O'Boyle asked.

"She had three sons. Two died in the Second World War, and the third one died in the Korean police action. She has a grandson and a granddaughter who are about the same age as you gentlemen are." She nodded to Al and O'Boyle and then, reading O'Boyle's mind, she continued. "Everything she had was left to these two grandchildren."

"Then I assume she had a will." O'Boyle's interrogation was so crude it caused Pete and Rory to shift their feet in embarrassment.

"She had a will. I suppose you would like to see it?" the woman answered angrily.

"I would like that very much," O'Boyle said.

"Please follow me."

The two detectives and two ADAs followed her into a bedroom. In doing so, they passed the outside door, where the press were standing blocked from admittance by uniformed police officers. A TV camera outside the door was trying to gain shots of the apartment interior, and the deputy chief inspector walked outside into the hallway and started to ham it up. The Hat then arrived and peremptorily dismissed him so that only he would appear on the six o'clock news.

Mrs. Underwood opened a dresser drawer, withdrew a green leather pouch with a small lock on the flap, and then, taking a key from another drawer, she opened the lock. Inside was a deed to a cemetery plot, an old insurance policy, a bank book, and the will. There was also a packet of old black-and-white photos.

O'Boyle reached for the will, insurance policy, and the bank book, while Al asked politely for the photos.

Mrs. Underwood smiled at Al and said of course. Al looked at the pictures. One of them portrayed a young, very pretty girl with a soldier dressed in the doughboy uniform of World War I. He wore the old-style campaign hat now worn by army drill instructors. The photo was encased in a glass frame and on its reverse side it had a yellowed piece of paper with transparent tape over it and an inscription reading "February 2, 1919."

"That is Dorothy and Albert, her husband. Albert fought in the Meusse-Argonne, and that photograph was taken on the day that he finally came back home."

Al looked at the picture. "They were a lovely couple," he said awkwardly, and then looked at the other three glass-encased photos. One of them was the smiling face of a marine in dress uniform. A date on the back read "9/27/42." Another photo showed an aviator in the Army Air Corps wearing pilot wings and lieutenant's bars.

Rose Underwood looked on. "The marine was her oldest, Eddy. He died on Guadalcanal. The pilot was Joseph. He died over Germany."

Al looked at the last photo. It showed an unsmiling face, the mirror image of the corpse in the kitchen except the features in the photograph were not contorted.

"That's Albert Junior. He died in Korea. Either fifty-two or fifty-three. She had great hopes for all her boys. Eddy has one daughter who is married and lives in Throggs Neck. We have her address and phone number. We never saw very much of her. Joseph had a son, Paul. He's a fireman in Queens. He used to call his grandmother twice a week, but if we saw him twice a year it was a lot."

O'Boyle passed the will to Al, who opened and read it. The attestation clause showed it to be only two months old. It had been prepared by Joey Cassossa, a very good lawyer, and everything was in perfect order. The executor was the grandson, and the grandchildren split the estate. Al opened the insurance policy. The face amount was $1,500 and the two grandchildren were the sole beneficiaries. The bank book was a trust account, and the grandchildren got the deposit upon the deceased's death. She had been well advised, and her wishes would be carried out. There was seventy-five grand in the account and no recent withdrawals.

Al handed the papers and the photos back to Mrs. Underwood. "Thank you very much." He smiled.

She smiled back. "You are very welcome."

"Well, we have to get back. Good-bye," O'Boyle said, abruptly nodding to Mrs. Underwood who was just coldly civil in response.

"Our sincere condolences, Mrs. Underwood, and thank you for your kind assistance," Al said, and was met with her beaming smile in return.

Rory escorted the ADAs out while Pete DiCerrechia stayed with the woman. As they passed the Hat talking and fielding questions from the TV reporters, Al turned to O'Boyle. "She really loved you."

"Yeah, well, I fell in love with her too," O'Boyle said. Rory walked down the stairs behind them.

O'Boyle resumed the conversation. "She's just too cool, just too composed, I mean, her roommate and friend is nearly decapitated and she serves tea. All that's missing is the fucking crumpets. What do you guys think?"

"We thought at first she could of done it, Mr. O'Boyle, but I don't think so. These are old-time people, they're different. Almost like aristocrats. They take a lot of pride in putting on a good face in tough times. I just think she's a fine old lady doing a good job dealing with this fuckin' massacre. She could also be in shock. It does funny things to people. Al, you was in the army, you know what I'm talking about, right?" Rory said, looking for support for his thesis.

Al nodded without any conviction.

O'Boyle looked at his watch. The conversation was over, and

the two ADAs got in their car and drove back to the courthouse. Then on University Avenue going southbound O'Boyle turned to Al. "What do you think?"

"I doubt that she had the strength to almost sever a head with a kitchen knife. Nothing was taken," Al answered, and then he said the last thing that O'Boyle wanted to hear. "This is the same pattern as the other old ladies, John. Like it or not, we got a fuckin' mass murderer on our hands."

"This is one fuckin' time I wish to God you were wrong," the Homicide Bureau Chief answered.

PERICLES "PEPPY" GENNARO WATCHED his nephew Vincent LoConti standing outside Part V of the Supreme Court of the State of New York, Suffolk County, in Hauppauge, New York. Peppy lit a Lucky Strike and inhaled the smoke deep into his lungs.

It was nine in the morning outside the divorce section of the court, as Peppy watched Vince plead earnestly with Renee LoConti. Peppy had always said that Vince had more heart than anyone in the neighborhood. Vince was generous and brave beyond belief. Peppy's prayers had been answered when his nephew returned alive from his second tour in Vietnam. And it was these traits of recklessness and foolhardiness that led Vince, Vince with his big, kind heart, here this morning on a desperate mission to rescue the marriage of his older and shrewder brother, Alcibiades.

Peppy Gennaro had arranged with Al's lawyer, Marty Guildern, to keep Al away until nine-thirty. Vince was convinced that he could pull a last-minute miracle. But as Peppy watched the fixed set of Renee LoConti's jaw, he knew that Vince's efforts were being repulsed.

Peppy watched Vince's final surrender as he just shrugged his shoulders and then kissed Renee. Peppy was surprised by the intensity of Renee's reaction to Vinnie although he knew that she truly loved her brother-in-law. Renee surprised him by blowing a kiss at him too as she walked back to her lawyer.

Vince lit a Camel and stood next to his uncle. Neither man spoke. Vince was deep in thought. He knew that his brother feared his wife and children being left alone and unprotected. The fears were made more intense by the carnage his brother saw every day, the dead men, women, and children, the victims of life in the City of New York. And now Vince had failed to make things right for his brother.

Finally Al arrived with his lawyer. He was shocked to see his uncle and his brother. They clasped each other fiercely in greeting. The lawyer held the door open and they walked inside.

Renee nodded to her husband but Al ignored her. Once she had left their apartment and sought the lawyer, things had escalated quickly. Each had sued the other for divorce. Neither would retreat. The pent-up anxieties of their tough lean years together had erupted. Renee had wanted out and when Al finally knew that she would not return, he spurned her and sued first.

They had torn at each other's innards, each using the knowledge gained by years of intimacy as a sword, to stab and slash the other into submission. And as in all such battles, it was forgone that each would lose. Only the lawyers would profit from the encounter.

Al thought briefly of the dead old woman lying on the floor in the apartment on University Avenue where he had been only yesterday. He thought of her three sons, all victims of war. He thought of his own father, who had died in World War II, and all the sadness, and all the death.

He looked at the woman next to him and she looked back. Though he felt like strangling her, he turned and watched the judge mounting the bench. The lawyers had finally reached an agreement last night, trading visitation for money. As in all such matters the children had become pawns, objects to be sacrificed and ransomed to satisfy their parents' furies.

It was over in five minutes. Al and Renee recited the divorce litany, known as the Good-Bye Chant, and as they left the courtroom, they hurried past Vince and Peppy. They did not speak. Renee entered her sister's car and drove off, and Al got into his blue Dodge and pulled away.

Vince LoConti had seen tears in both of their eyes. He wished he could cry.

"How could they have been so stupid as to let this happen?" he asked his Uncle Peppy.

"The pressure of living, hopes not realized, endless struggles cause people to strike at those nearest them. And that's what happened to your brother," Peppy answered. They got into Peppy's Cadillac and drove toward the Bronx.

"She should have thought of her kids," Vince said.

"She's disillusioned, Vince. She's had a tough time. Remember, she came to this country when she was eighteen. She thought the streets were paved with gold and that all Americans were rich. My father—your grandfather—like millions of Italians also thought the same thing. And he told me that he was shocked to find out that not only were the streets not paved with gold, but that they were not paved. And they were covered with shit. And what was even worse, the ultimate disillusionment, the final straw, was that the only work he could find was cleaning the shit and paving the streets."

Vince didn't laugh. He could not understand Peppy's excuse for Renee, whom he truly loved as the sister he never had. Vince grieved more today than he had done for any fallen comrade. Vince LoConti, the gutsy vet, the man of heart, shook his head. His heart had been broken today at Special Term Part V. His brother Alcibiades's marriage was as dead as any Bronx DOA.

AL LOCONTI DROVE OVER the Throgs Neck Bridge linking Queens County and Long Island with the Bronx mainland. When he crested the top of the span, snow flurries began to brush his windshield. Minutes later they changed into a storm. By the time he crossed through the Bronx to his home on the northern border of Manhattan Island, a full-force blizzard had arrived.

The snow filled the chill air and covered the city's sin and grime with pristine whiteness.

Al was still shivering from his two-block walk in the ice-cold, snow-filled air when he put the key in the apartment door. He entered and shut the door behind him.

The divorce settlement had left him with a bed, a table, two chairs, and a dresser. His uncle had given him an old couch, which stood next to the window in the living room facing a small black-and-white TV.

His dog, Sport, ran in circles and then lowered his front legs on the floor and shook his head from side to side. Al knew the drill. He had to fake running after the dog, who would then shoot into all of the four rooms of the apartment. But today he just grabbed the leash and took the pointer for a walk. The storm had grown in intensity. Al's car was totally covered by a mound of snow. Al, pleased that he didn't have felony duty tonight, was very happy to return to the warmth of the apartment lobby. He dreaded the one remaining trip with the dog before going to bed.

It was very lonely in the apartment on this snowy night. Thank God for Sport, he thought while heating up some canned soup and making two sandwiches. He plopped one sandwich into the dog's bowl and poured some of the soup from the pan over it. He ate the remaining soup from the saucepan and munched the sandwich.

Al walked into the children's empty bedroom. He kept their beds and toys there for the visitation periods. He wanted them to have a sense of continuity, a sense of home.

He smoked a cigarette and shook his head. He still didn't know why his marriage had been murdered and his fatherhood imprisoned by the bars of fixed visitation.

Then he walked to the window and looked up at the snow falling from the heavens.

Maybe it was preordained, maybe everything was predetermined and life was just the acting out of a script written down before one was born. Maybe the ancient Greeks were right, he thought. Then, turning from the window, he thought of his wife and kids alone tonight with no idea of the horror outside, no idea how randomly injury and death might strike. They were just as oblivious as the populace at large to the real peril of life in the Big Apple in the year 1974.

So Al sat alone, safe and warm yet suffering with guilt and despondency. The dog nuzzled his leg and sensed the man's sadness. Al rubbed Sport's head, thinking how he would give anything—and everything—just to hug his kids firmly to him on this frigid night.

22

WHILE ALCIBIADES LOCONTI WAS mourning in his apartment, his cousin Allie Boy Spano sat in the recorder's seat of an RMP that was being driven by his partner Richie Zemberelli.

The snow pelting down turned into slush upon hitting the heated windshield, then was brushed aside by the wipers sliding back and forth.

The officers were approaching West Farms. Being Zemberelli's partner made the job even tougher for Allie Boy. Yet, instinctively following some ancient and unknown code of honor, he felt an eternal allegiance to the man who had saved his life. Despite whatever anybody said, Richie Zemberelli always repaid loyalty with even more devotion. You always got back triple when you did the right thing by Rich.

Yet strangely enough, despite having been assigned as the partner of the city's most decorated officer, the Zemberelli tales, known as classics, continued.

Now, looking out the window through the snow that turned to slush on impact, Allie Boy thought that it had been only a month since he had to intercede with the Hat to prevent Zemberelli's banishment to the far outer regions of Staten Island.

Unlike today, that day had been very mild, almost springlike and only two degrees short of the record for warmth in January. On that day the President of the United States had addressed the United Nations and then traveled to a groundbreaking ceremony for a federal housing project in the South Bronx.

Security was the strictest that Allie Boy had ever seen. Fifteen special squads of hand-picked officers were concealed in unmarked vans along the route, each squad comprised of twenty men sent to fortify the riot police and the many other special units on duty that day. Allie Boy Spano, although only a patrolman, was asked by the Hat to lead a special squad. After accepting, Allie Boy personally appealed to the Hat to get Zemberelli assigned to Mounted for the day so that Richie, an excellent horseman who rode horses every weekend on Pelham Parkway, could achieve his lifelong dream. Richie would be a Mountie.

And so on that day Richie cantered up Brook Avenue helmeted and dressed in blue, daydreaming of pursuing bandits in the wilds of Canada and seeing himself as Sergeant Preston, resplendent in scarlet tunic and astride a powerful stallion.

Richie and fifty-five other mounted officers rode easily along both sides of the presidential cavalcade.

Due to the unusual warmth the limousine tops were down. The President sat in the back seat next to the governor of New York, waving at the crowds thronging the sidewalks.

The Mayor of New York and the Bronx political boss Milberg Greenway rode in the limousine directly in front of the President's. They too were having a very nice day.

When the party arrived at the site of the groundbreaking ceremony, a huge empty lot, Richie's detail dismounted and shielded the VIPs during the brief proceedings, and after their conclusion the entire presidential party climbed back into their limousines ready to depart.

The Hat had also detailed Pete DiCerrechia to Mounted. Unknown to Zemberelli, Pete slipped a burr under Richie's saddle. When the troop commander barked, Richie obediently saddled up.

No member of General Custer's famed 7th Cavalry, no member of the brigades of Jeb Stuart had greater pride than Mounted Officer Richie Zemberelli on that day . . . but as soon as his ass hit the saddle, the horse took off like a bat scorched by hell.

Witnesses, their sides splitting with laughter, would later recount the scene of Zemberelli's huge brown horse running flat out up Brook Avenue and after two blocks being finally turned around by Zemberelli's frantic yanking on the reins, and then the horse galloping back, running at full tilt smack at the President's limousine. The mouth of Captain Dreygould, the mounted commander, had been gaping open wide beneath his flowing handlebar mustache, then bolted up in his stirrups, screaming as loud as he could in utter and complete panic causing laundry stains to mushroom in his drawers.

Finally Zemberelli pulled up next to the President and the horse reared in the air, whinnying and blowing hard. Its front legs flayed the air over the President's head and when they hit the ground the horse started to buck, first on its front legs then and then on the rear ones.

The President, who always appreciated a horse show, smiled.

"Quite a demonstration of horsemanship," he said to the Governor. The astounded Governor just nodded, and then the President stood up and applauded, which caused everyone to begin clapping their hands and cheering. The horse continued to buck and to turn in circles while Richie hung on the saddle's pommel for dear life. Finally the horse bucked next to the limousine with the Mayor and the Bronx politico Greenway. Greenway, a political powerhouse, was a very rare individual because he was disliked even by his own mother.

Following the President's lead, Milberg and the Mayor politely stood up, clapping and smiling politicians' waxlike grins.

The horse continued to spin around, trying to dislodge Zemberelli, as the burr beneath the saddle became excruciating. Then raising its tail and bucking, it voided its bowels, shooting a semisolid mass of excrement over the limousine door and onto the white-on-white shirt of the Bronx political boss, Milberg Greenway. The sound of the clapping then rose to a crescendo.

When the burr was finally found on the horse, Pete DiCerrechia confessed to Allie Boy and begged him to speak to the Hat. Allie Boy had never revealed Pete's role.

Allie Boy's thoughts turned to a good meal at the Last Supper, hoping that this tour would be uneventful. There was too much snow tonight for him to drive to Greenpoint in Brooklyn where his latest girlfriend, Sadie Gracowski, lived, and he wondered if Millie, one of his uncle's attractive waitresses, would be working tonight. What a great pinch hitter she would make, he thought, but he was jolted from his fantasy by a blast from the radio, it was a woman's voice transmitting. . . .

"Rape in progress inside a 1970 Blue Buick, license plate number New York 425 UZK. Acknowledge, Sector Adam."

"Sector Adam here. You say rape is going down inside subject auto?" Allie Boy asked.

"Affirmative, Adam."

"Ten four," Allie Boy signed off.

Richie floored the RMP, turning it from under the El and passing a Strauss Auto supply store, and then after slowing up he spotted a parked car with the called-in license plates. He stopped the RMP some seventy feet behind the suspect vehicle and began to get very nervous, finally breaking into a cold sweat. His misfortunes had shattered his confidence, and he greeted every job with high anxiety, washing away years of training in a deluge of fear. Not wanting to fuck up, he turned all of his concentration on Allie Boy because while Richie was one frazzled nerve, Allie Boy was the total opposite. He was slow, calculating, and icy calm as he opened the glove compartment, took out a car mirror on an adjustable stand, and then placed it on the dashboard to his left. Once satisfied with the alignment he ordered Richie to proceed slowly down the block.

Allie Boy then took off his hat and leaned his head against the passenger window. To the casual observer he appeared to be just another lazy cop almost asleep on duty.

Richie put the RMP in drive and pulled out into the street.

"Don't do more than fifteen," Allie Boy said, staring into the mirror. As the RMP passed the parked car Richie sensed Allie Boy's highly charged state. He glanced at his partner and saw that his nostrils were flared, his eyes staring, a true hunter with his prey in sight.

"What did you see?" Richie asked.

Allie Boy responded mechanically. "White dude gettin' blowed by a black chick. He's got a revolver to her head and he's no kid, about fifty-five to sixty, looks like a mick. Go aroun' the block, Rich, and pull up right behind the car."

The Hat—Inspector McDaniel—whose revolver was at the head of the black prostitute he had picked up at West Farms, noticed the RMP and saw the Recorder almost asleep. He would fix those pricks later, he thought.

The Hat always acted out the same fantasy every week with the same girl, but unlike many other members of the force, he paid in full and even gave tips. Tonight had cost him fifty dollars. Unfortunately a passing motorist had noticed him pull a gun on the girl, march her to the car, and then usher her into the backseat. The motorist had called 911. Allie Boy and Richie had responded. They did not know that the Borough Commander was the blowee and that a sexual script was being performed.

McDaniel was seated in the rear of the car on the passenger side.

"When you stop the car, flip on the light. Don't touch the siren and cover me. Keep your head down," Allie Boy commanded.

Richie pulled the RMP right behind the parked car, and Allie Boy rolled down the window. When the RMP came to a complete halt, Allie Boy threw open the door, kneeled behind it, and aimed his revolver through the open window. His sights were right on the Hat's brain.

"POLICE," Allie Boy screamed. "Drop the fuckin' gun or I'll blow the top off your fuckin' head."

Richie drew his gun. He was shaking and his gun snaked as if it were alive.

"Get the fuck outta that car with your fuckin' hands up," Allie Boy screamed.

LouAnn Wilson, who was ministering to the Hat, would later relate to her girlfriends that when . . .

"The honky cop heard that voice, well, he didn't know whether to shit or go blind."

The Hat immediately dropped the revolver, becoming instantly limp. He himself had killed three men during his career who did not instantly obey such an order, and so he quickly snapped both hands sharply above his head.

"Get out of the fuckin' car and put your hands way up high," Allie Boy called, leaning forward, arms outstretched and gun pointing straight.

Richie Zemberelli trained his revolver on the emerging inspector who was not in uniform.

The Hat got out onto the street and stood in the snow with his hands half raised. Allie Boy recognized him.

"OOOO-shit" he said, then turning, he screamed at Richie, "Cancel the call for backup."

Now even more unnerved by Allie Boy's sudden change of mood, Richie reached down with his left hand and picked up the radio microphone. He brought it to his lips and placed a finger alongside the transmit button while keeping his eye on the white dude standing with his penis exposed and his hands half raised. In his right hand he kept his revolver trained through the windshield.

"Come on, Rich, hurry up," Allie Boy yelled, and then, to the Hat, for effect." "Get those fuckin' hands up."

Anxiety caused a short circuit in Richie's brain that sent an erroneous signal to his hand. So instead of pressing the transmit button on the radio, Zemberelli jerked the trigger and the windshield shattered and the bullet flew out, grazing the Hat's earlobe.

The Hat's hands and arms shot straight up, extending to their longest reach. The Hat yelled, "How fuckin' high do you want em!"

When the backup arrived they found Allie Boy still laughing. The Hat was cuffed, there was no complainant, and Allie Boy did not disclose the inspector's identity except to his partner. There was no gun arrest, and after the backup had left Allie Boy released the inspector.

"You were never here, Inspector," Allie Boy said.

Later that night when he took Millie home from the Last Supper he was content. The Hat owin' me one is gonna be even better than having money in the bank, Allie Boy Spano thought, still chuckling to himself.

23

VINNIE LOCONTI, SITTING IN the passenger seat of the blue '68 Dodge Coronet, listened to the radio playing softly while his brother drove. Vinnie turned and smiled at his nephew and niece in the backseat and they smiled back. He made small talk with the children as Al left the Long Island Expressway at exit 50 and drove through local streets half a mile to his children's home, where he stopped and parked. It was the same old sad Sunday night routine.

As always, Al arrived right on time at six-thirty and the two brothers got out of the car. Renee came out on the porch waiting for the children to walk up the driveway. Al hugged his son and his daughter and they kissed him. Then they hugged and kissed their uncle Vinnie. Al glared as Vinnie waved to Renee and she waved back. The brothers then got into the car and drove back to the City of New York.

Vinnie talked about the Yankees' prospects for the coming season—both brothers were avid fans—but Al said nothing. He was quiet all the way back until they entered their uncle's restaurant and ordered drinks at the bar. Later, when Millie the waitress went off duty, Al LoConti went with her. They drove to Al's apartment where they had one drink and went to bed.

Just before Al LoConti put Millie in a cab at 11 P.M. Ronald DePew slit the throat of a grandmother walking her dog next to Bronx Park. As the gray-haired woman slumped gurgling in her death throes, Ronald grabbed the dog's leash.

The dog was a small poodle. It whimpered in fright. DePew put his hand over the dog's snout and snapped its neck. He threw it on top of the woman. Dying, she clutched at her pet.

Two days later, February 26, 1974, Johnny O'Boyle walked to Al LoConti's office.

"I got something else for your list," Johnny said. He walked over to Al's list of pending investigations and stopped in front of a piece of white cardboard tacked to the wall. It was two feet square and covered with clear acetate. A grease pencil hung down from a nail driven into the cardboard's top left corner. Johnny grabbed the pencil while his eyes scanned the board. There were two lists; one, titled "Cases," had the fifty-four names of the Homicide indictments assigned to Al for trial. The other list was "Investigation." Johnny scanned this list of unsolved crimes:

1. Legs case—legs found Split Rock Golf Course 8/23/70. Female torso found June 29, 1973. No ID. Homicide/Strangulation. File DA-Bx 2768/70.

2. DOA Martha Valles, beautician. Found DOA, own apartment, June 29, 1973. Homicide/Shot—.38 Caliber. Sodomy/Burglary-1st Degree. File DA-Bx 3191/73.

3. Assist DA Jimmy Farrell—narcotics investigation—Wiretaps. 13th Narcotics Group.

Johnny handed Al a piece of paper and the grease pencil and told Al to copy the information on the board. Al scanned the paper and then wrote.

4. Serial killer—senior citizens—female, Bronx County. See cases grouped under 2178/74—Bronx County Homicides.

"Al, I can't spare you for the narcotics cases any more," O'Boyle said.

"I'm just bein' kept informed, John," Al replied.

O'Boyle shook his head but Al was equally emphatic. "Look, John, I put a lot of work in it. One of the main cops on the case is an ex-marine named Wotter whom I grew up with. I'd like to stay with it. It really doesn't take much time, Farrell is doin' everything."

"Farrell is a fuckin' head case and Tommy Finley, the Narcotics Bureau Chief, is keepin' you involved because he trusts your judgment. After Farrell's last caper Tommy needs someone to play nursemaid, and by usin' you he frees up his own manpower in the Narcotics Bureau and crimps me."

Al knew the caper that O'Boyle was referring to.

"Nobody proved that Farrell did it," Al said.

"Yeah, but everyone knows he did," O'Boyle retorted.

The incident had occurred just last week. Farrell was on trial with an A-1 felony drug case against four defendants. The police had seized six pounds of heroin from a car that had been occupied by the four then on trial.

The stage was set and the stakes were very high. If convicted, Judge O'Neill was sure to max them out with life sentences. They were all tried together in Part 26 on the seventh floor where the defense attorneys' table had a long fluorescent lamp supported by two brass rods on its front. The brass rods were two feet apart.

The most dramatic of the defense lawyers was the ever-obnoxious Quiet Marvin Pollard. Pollard was set to cross examine the last and most damaging witness for the prosecution. Farrell had watched Pollard carefully and knew he would dramatically pounce to the front of the defense table and grab the first brass rod, then thunder and tirade against the witness. His face would flood red in indignation and rage, and his shaved head would even glow pink before he finished. Quiet Marvin was a class-A prick who always put on a good show.

After Jimmy Farrell finished the direct examination of Detective Marty Doolan, Pollard stood up, smiling with pleasure. He paused dramatically, then he sprang forward three short steps and grasped the brass rod. But instead of swinging on it like a door on a hinge, to enable him to pounce on Doolan, he stopped abruptly and stared down at his hand. It was covered in Vaseline.

Someone had greased up the rod during the luncheon recess. Quiet Marvin took out his handkerchief and started to wipe his hand frantically. Everyone knew what happened and Jimmy Farrell, trying not to lose his composure while sitting next to the jury, was forced to put his face in his hands. His shoulders shook as he tried without success to smother his laughter and the jury started to snicker.

"Please proceed," O'Neill commanded. Judge O'Neill really hated Quiet Marvin.

"Yes, your honor." Pollard walked to the far side of the well of the court away from the witness, and the court clerk handed him some tissues. Pollard wiped his hands, threw the tissues in a wastebasket, retrieved his notes, and advanced on Doolan. He did not grasp any rod. He played with Doolan, but the detective was too sharp, fielding each question just like a routine grounder. Quiet Marvin wanted to lull Doolan into complacency. Using only two fingers, he felt the other brass rod. It was clean. He retreated behind the defense table. Marvin had thought he had set a trap for Doolan so he threw a few more routine grounders from behind the defense table, and Marty Doolan shot back the answers without effort.

Then Quiet Marvin paused for effect, ready to spring the trap. He ran three steps forward, stopped suddenly, and dramatically clasped the far brass rod while facing the jury so that they might behold the rage and indignation flooding his face. Then after a split second of clenching the clean brass rod even tighter in his left hand, he used it as a fulcrum to twist vehemently to his right to confront the witness.

The rage on his face turned to disbelief as he staggered uncontrollably and finally fell beneath the Judge's raised bench. O'Neill rose and looked down. Pollard still held the brass rod in his hand. Someone had loosened it during the recess. The jury began to howl.

The next day the jurors could not even look at Quiet Marvin, who sported a large gauze bandage on his shaved head. They snickered all during his summation and then convicted all four defendants.

In the big flap that followed, Jimmy Farrell swore on his mother's eyes that he did nothing.

Now O'Boyle ordered Al to give up the narcotics case.

"Come on, John," Al implored. "It's my fuckin' case."

"Yeah," O'Boyle shot back, "but you're in my fuckin' bureau. Give it up," he said, walking out.

Al rubbed out number 3 on the list and replaced it with a new number three—the case involving serial murders in Bronx County.

THAT NIGHT WHEN JIMMY Farrell slid onto a bar stool inside the Silver Shillelagh on 207th Street in the Inwood section of Manhattan, he was very pissed off. Rumors that he was responsible for Quiet Marvin's mishaps with the brass rods had blackened his reputation. Jimmy had spotted Fast Frankie Hammon fuckin' around with the brass rods, and he now knew that the shrewd lawyer had been trying to inject some levity into the proceedings in an effort at helping his client, who was in the backseat when the car was stopped and the drugs were found. Jimmy, always a stand-up guy, never squealed on the lawyer.

"Bat and a ball, Mike," Jimmy ordered.

"Do ya want Fleishmann's or Three Feathers, Jimmy?" the bartender asked.

"Fuck it, I'm working tonight, give me VO."

"Oh, yer have the duty tonight, do yer?" Mike asked in his County Cork brogue.

"That I do, Mike, that I do."

Mike placed the shot glass in front of Farrell then poured a shot and quickly drew a small beer from the tap.

Farrell downed the shot and the beer then rapped the beer glass on the bar two times quickly for a refill. After Farrell drained the shot and half of the beer, he pointed at the empty shot glass as he walked to the phone booth.

He dialed the number for the 13th Narcotics and asked for Lieutenant Solwin. Farrell wanted to be brought up to date on (what was now called) the Chaparral investigation so he might inform his friend Al LoConti, but Solwin was out. Jimmy went back to the booze and reflected on the investigation he had inherited from Alcibiades LoConti.

When Nofrio became a dead end, Solwin had resorted to the buy-and-bust routine. After a series of street buys over several months, Officers Ruella Watkins and William Wotter had uncovered and busted the source of Chinese Rock #3. They turned the source and were sent up the ladder to one rung below "John Doe Chaparral." They had been shocked to discover this "rung" was none other than their treacherous informer Chingo.

Chingo had gone astray with a nice little side business selling Chinese Rock #3. Of course he never informed the men of the 13th Narcotics Group of his new enterprise. He'd buy from Chaparral and sell only in Manhattan and then only to the same six individuals. One day one of the six came to Chingo on Riverside Drive with a very effeminate white man. Afterward Chingo sold Chinese Rock #3 four separate times to the "white faggot," as Chingo called him. The "faggot" turned out to be Officer Marty Doolan of the Commissioner's undercover squad. Marty told a Manhattan Grand Jury all about Chingo, and they proceeded to indict him immediately. Marty's backup team, armed with arrest warrants, picked Chingo up and for the second time he was taken for a nice ride, this time around Manhattan Island, and by the time he reached Central Booking it dawned on him that he was facing seventy-five years. Realizing that seventy-five years might be tough to do constrained him into revealing that he was an informant working for the 13th. Solwin and Farrell were immediately notified. After Farrell made a deal with the Manhattan DA, Chingo was paroled and given only six months to make some very big cases or else he would be tossed right back inside.

Farrell reflected on what Wotter had screamed into Chingo's face. "When you're in Attica your ass is goin' to be wider than the eight lanes of the fuckin' Long Island Expressway." Chingo promptly gave up Chaparral.

But after they investigated him, Chaparral still remained a mystery. He had rented an apartment on Jackson Avenue under the name F. Chaparral, but the telephone company had no record of any line to the apartment and the Con Ed meter was in the super's name. Disguised as a Con Ed representative, Solwin had interviewed the super. Chaparral was described as male white or Hispanic, twenty-five to thirty years of age, five nine, 130 to 150 pounds, with brown hair and eyes. The chatty super, a Con Ed retiree, had told Solwin that Chaparral paid him a thousand bucks in cash for the apartment plus two months rent. There of course was no lease, no credit check, and no references, and Chaparral paid the rent in cash promptly on the first of the month. No one was ever seen visiting him, and Chaparral always wore dark glasses and a large-brimmed hat.

Chingo had in fact made good-faith efforts to nab Chaparral. He took William Wotter up to Chaparrel's apartment to try to set up an undercover sale. But after Chingo rang the bell, Chaparral looked through the peephole. When he spotted Chingo with a blue-eyed guy, Chaparral promptly ran into his bedroom. Peering out from the fire escape, he observed that the streets were empty, and so were all the parked cars.

Chaparral continued to look out on the street as Chingo rang again and again. Finally, fifteen minutes later, he watched Chingo and Wotter exit the building.

Farrell went back to the telephone booth, redialed, and finally spoke to Solwin. Then he hung up and walked back to the bar where he downed the shot and beer waiting for him. Solwin had informed him that they had gotten nowhere. Farrell thought, Nothin' to do . . . might as well drink." He signaled again for Mike.

Chingo went back alone the next day—March 2, 1974—in compliance with Solwin's orders. Again Chaparral just looked through the peephole without opening the door. As Chingo left, Chaparral looked out the window and watched him walk up the street alone.

One hour later Chaparral, dressed in a conservative gray pinstriped suit with white shirt and blue tie, hailed a cab on Jackson

Avenue. He drove to the Criminal Court at 161st Street and went into the clerk's office. There he searched the index book of pending cases and checked all the new arraignments, looking for any entry that had the name of Fidel Vicun. After checking the records for the past year and discovering nothing, he walked outside and hailed a cab, which took him to the courthouse at 161st Street and the Grand Concourse. A check of the indictment files there also failed to reveal the name of Fidel Vicun. With a sigh of relief Chaparral hailed a cab and returned home. Fortunately for Chingo and the men of the 13th, Chaparral never thought to check any official records in Manhattan.

Solwin decided to play it ballsy.

"Let's just take the approach that Chingo has people that want to buy directly from the source and not through him. Chaparral undoubtedly saw Willie Wotter and shied away from dealing with a white guy. Let's send Ruella in."

Wotter objected; it would be too risky, and besides, he had promised his friend Detective Elrod Harrison that he would take care of Ruella.

"Butt out, Willie," Ruella said, "I want to do the job."

So she got it. Afterward she came over to Wotter and kissed him on the cheek. "You're sweet to worry about me, but you and Elrod should remember I'm a big girl now."

Half an hour later when Ruella and Chingo knocked at Chaparral's door, the woman had a bad premonition. Butterflies flew in her stomach and she became nauseous. She grasped the .32 snub-nose revolver inside the pocket of her loose-fitting dress.

From any outward appearance she was a narcotics user but not quite a street junkie. Although she played the role to perfection, Chaparral still felt something was very wrong as he looked at her through the peephole. Chingo rang again.

On the landing above, leading to the roof, Officer William Wotter and Lieutenant Solwin stood watch. They had entered a building down the block and crossed the roofs to their present vantage point. They wore white hard hats identifying them as employees of the New York telephone company. The large toolbox Wotter carried contained a loaded pump-action shotgun and a tear gas dispenser with grenades. Wotter and Solwin had removed the weapons from the toolbox and waited while Ruella and Chingo knocked on Chaparral's door.

Chingo could really put on a great act appearing impatient and annoyed and knowing that Chaparral could hear him, he turned to Ruella. "Show me the cash."

Ruella handed over her pocketbook. It contained nothing but fifty-dollar bills—$5,000 in buy money. Chingo took the purse and, just as he was about to hold it to the peephole, he reconsidered and handed it back.

"If my man inside could only see this five G's he would open up and do business with you, Dolly. But I guess he's not home."

"Knock on the door again. Maybe he's takin' a shit," Ruella said.

Chingo rang and knocked and repeated the ringing for ten more minutes, but Chaparral would not answer the door.

Later he watched as Chingo and Ruella walked from his house into the street, but he never spotted Wotter or Solwin. Somethin' just ain't right, Chaparral thought. Somethin' just ain't right.

An hour later Chingo came back alone and knocked on Chaparral's door. After one knock the door opened and Chingo was yanked inside. Chaparral placed the tip of a fish fillet knife under Chingo's right eye and applied pressure, causing it to dig into the soft tissue and press on the covered portion of the eyeball.

"Why'd you bring the fuckin' man up here for?" Chaparral spat, through clenched teeth.

Chingo froze dead still. "I didn't bring the man here. I brought a white dude from Scarsdale and a black chick from Riverdale. I deal to both of them many times before."

The knife dug deeper into the tissue beneath the lower eyelashes. "Why the fuck did you bring them here?"

"They had big money, man, the guy had six fuckin' grand and he wanted Chinese Rock. I didn't have enough for him and he showed me the money. . . . I wanted it, man. . . . It was all there in fifties and hundreds. He had the fuckin' green in a motherfuckin' money belt, man. . . . He say he need a quarter key and would give me the six grand for it and if I couldn't get it for him he would go to someone else. I figure I bring him to you. I figure you a businessman and, like, I know you gonna give me my commission. Same thing with the black chick. She wants to buy right then and there. I don't take them nowhere else. I do the right thing by you. I show you fuckin' good faith and you do this shit to me. I know these people and they fuckin' A-okay."

Chaparral, still skeptical, removed the knife. "Get the fuck outta here, Chingo. I don't want to see you again."

"Hey, Chaparral, I thought we in business to make money together, we got a good thing. Why fuck it up?"

"Fuck you, Chingo. I told you a million fuckin' times. I sell to you and only you. Don't you know how the fuckin' man buys drugs? Someone introduces the man and you sell to your customer. The man is standing there, lookin' like a street person, and later in court he says he bought it from you. And what are you gonna do then? You gonna get up and say, No, that is not true, I sell it to my customer and not to this police officer. You gonna say that shit, man? Come on." Chaparral continued, "You can't cave in to greed. There are no exceptions. I deal only with you. What you do is your business. If you introduce the man to me and I get burned, then you will no longer be with the living. But you don't listen, so fuck you. Get fuckin' lost."

Chingo listened while trying his best to look crestfallen and contrite. "Man, I'm sorry, Chaparral. I didn't know that you feel so strong. I leave now. I'm sorry. I still tell you that I would not take anyone here I did not know."

Chingo, looking Chaparral square in the eyes, didn't even blink. "These two people, they good people. We threw eleven big ones down the toilet."

"Get fuckin' lost," Chaparral said.

Chingo left and went back and told Lieutenant Solwin, "You can't have me bring no one to this guy because he ain't gonna sell to no one but me."

Solwin looked sideways at Chingo. He would never trust him again.

For the next two weeks the members of the 13th Narcotics tried in vain to plan a strategy to nab Chaparral. It would be a terrible waste of effort if the climb up the ladder were stopped now.

"How about a controlled buy?" Solwin suggested.

Sergeant Denny Driscoll shot down the idea. Driscoll explained that a controlled buy from an apartment was a defense counsel's dream. The police would have to strip-search their informant and release him as near as possible to the apartment where the drugs were being sold, to ensure that he wasn't carrying drugs prior to making the buy. Then the police would lose sight of their informant as he entered the apartment house to purchase the drugs. When the informer returned, he would have the drugs and no money. But generally it would be the word of this addict with a criminal record against that of the drug seller's. Even the use of marked money would not provide leverage, since the seller could always claim that the informer was just repaying a loan.

Without leverage to turn the seller, the ascent up the ladder would cease. Officer Blatt, another team member, had suggested the use of a body mike and transmitter followed by a voice analysis at trial.

"Can't admit voice analysis in New York into evidence," Farrell had said. And surveillance of Chaparral from a vacant apartment across the street was just another dead end.

The officers discussed having Chingo order narcotics from Chaparral and then getting a search warrant but decided against it—Chaparral was much too paranoid to take the bait. He had no rap sheet and the 13th Narcotics didn't even have a fingerprint, and so he remained a total phantom.

Finally, on Sunday, March 24, 1974, Ruella Watkins had a brainstorm. "Let's get Chingo to buy him a drink, tell him to try to patch things up to get back into business. It would be the natural thing for Chingo to do. Then afterward we can get the glass and get a print. It's gonna be just sweet findin' out who the fuck this dude Chaparral really is."

That afternoon Chingo rang Chaparral's doorbell, but there was no answer. The next day he went to talk to Chaparral again, but there was still no answer. For four consecutive days Chingo tried with the same result. No answer and no sign of Chaparral.

On the sixth day Chaparral opened the door. "Hey, man, where you been?" Chingo said warmly, smiling at Chaparral's expressionless face.

"I've been right here," Chaparral said.

"Shit, man, I been comin' here for days and ringin' your bell and no one answers," Chingo said, still smiling warmly.

"We missed each other," Chaparral said. His voice was flat and without any emotion. "What do you want, Chingo?"

"I want to do business. You know, we had a nice thing goin'. I don't want it to get fucked up so I figure let me go up and say to Mr. Chaparral that I am sorry and let me take him out and buy him a drink, just like businessmen do."

Chaparral nodded. "Okay, Chingo, I want the business too. But I don't drink so let me give you something instead."

He reached into his pocket and took out one glassine envelope with white powder inside. "You got a set of works on you, Chingo?"

"Yeah, man, I got a set of works."

"Well, then, why don't you shoot this right now?"

"No, man, I want to save it," Chingo said.

He watched as Chaparral's eyes became bright with anger.

"Okay, okay, I'll shoot it right now if it's gonna make you happy."

So he heated the heroin in a bottle cap until it melted. Then, after tightly wrapping a piece of rubber from an old car fan belt around his arm, he took out his set of works, a syringe used by diabetics, and drew up the clear liquid heroin in the syringe, and then ramming the plunger down hard, he forced the drug into his popped out vein. He undid the apparatus and after a few more minutes shook hands with Chaparral and left. Chaparral was pleased. He knew now that Chingo could never be a cop.

Although Chingo had apparently been restored to Chaparral's good graces, the problem still remained of getting Chaparral to sell to an undercover officer.

Ruella Watkins provided the solution. "He'll sell to a queer," she said. "We have Chingo set it up, tell him he's got a rich queer with plenty of cash who will only deal direct. Tell him the queer has ten big ones."

"Great idea, except where do we get the queer?" Solwin asked.

"Ever see Marty Doolan do his quiff imitation?" Ruella asked.

"That's right, Ruella, you and Marty worked together on the Ricky Matthews case. I forgot all about it," Solwin said.

"I spoke to him and he spoke to his CO. You gotta call his CO, Loo."

"Who's the CO?"

"Berghaus."

"Oh, shit, not BB Balls Berghaus."

"The one and only," Ruella answered. "Just don't give BB Balls any more info than necessary."

"He'll never help anyone out," Solwin answered.

"Mention Wotter to him and he'll help you out real quick."

"How come?" Solwin asked.

"Don't ask questions, Loo. He owes Wotter a big one."

Solwin called BB Balls Berghaus and requested the temporary transfer of Marty Doolan. BB Balls told Solwin to go fuck himself. When Solwin said that it would be a personal favor to Willy Wotter, BB Balls told him that Doolan would report the following morning at 8 A.M.

Solwin decided to do one buy and then get Chaparral indicted by the Grand Jury. Following the indictment he would get both search and arrest warrants and then arrange for a second buy and bust fuckin' John Doe Chaparral. This would give them plenty of leverage to turn Chaparral and enable the 13th to climb even farther up the ladder.

"That is," Wotter had said, "if no one gets fuckin' killed."

On April 2, 1974, Chaparral opened his door as soon as Chingo knocked and nodded to him.

"I wouldn't bring anyone here without your permission, Chaparral, but I got a real rich fag with a lot of green and he wants to spend five G's on Chinese Rock. I made him no promises until you first said okay."

Chaparral was immediately interested. "Chingo, you tell this queer to give you the money. Then you come here and I give you the shit and then you can take it back to him. And you can take one-quarter of his stuff off the top. This shit can stand five hits. So, my man, you make a real nice commission."

"Chaparral, I like the deal but this guy may be queer but he is not stupid. He gives me the money he wants his stuff right there. So, maybe you give me the stuff, I make the sale, and bring back your money."

Chaparral smiled. "And suppose, my friend, that this queer only lives in your head?"

"Hey, Chaparral, this guy has five G's for openers. He is so fuckin' queer he can't be a cop. I don't know what you want to do. You want to lose the money, fine, that's up to you. But I thought that we are in this business to make it, man, not to throw it away. Chaparral, we can do real well with this dude. He says if this is okay he'll be back in a week with another five G's." This remark set the hook. Chaparral swallowed the bait.

"That means he's buying for someone and not for himself," Chaparral said.

"That's what I thought, Chaparral, but I find out that this guy is buying for five guys in Jersey. No one has this Chinese shit, Chaparral. You're in big demand, man; you got a real fuckin' commodity."

Suddenly Chaparral made a decision. "You bring him in here, go up to the next landing. It's a dead end before the roof. After you pass my door I'll see you. Before you bring him near this building make sure the fuck has the bread. You understand, Chingo?"

"I dig, Chaparral. I dig it, man."

"When will you bring him?"

"Tomorrow."

"Make it the next day," Chaparral ordered.

Two days later Marty Doolan got all made up in drag. He put on bright-orange lipstick and dark-blue eyeshadow. He wore a shocking-pink hat and a pair of white gloves that reached halfway to his elbow. The palms and fingertips of the gloves had been specially treated by forensic with a material that preserved fingerprints, and today Marty would definitely get a print from Chaparral.

Marty had to concentrate real hard to swing his ass while walking up the stairs in Chaparral's building in case Chaparral was watching. It's real rough police work, Marty thought, swingin' your ass with two-inch spike heels on your flat feet, always scared shitless that you'd trip any second and break your fuckin' ass.

Marty and Chingo walked past Chaparral's apartment up to the landing, one flight from the roof. Marty had a .25 automatic in his purse and $5,000 in a money belt under his blouse. After a wait of ten minutes they heard Chaparral's door open and close and then heard him coming up the stairs.

Marty swung forward a few steps and proferred his arm with wrist broken. "Hi, there," he bleated in a modified falsetto, "I'm Cheryl."

Chaparral looked at him with distaste and nodded, ignoring the limp hand. "Where's the fuckin' money?"

"Oh, don't you fret, I've got it, handsome, but first I want to see your merchandise," Marty replied, batting his eyelashes.

Chingo chuckled until Chaparral glared at him and then he stopped and dropped his eyes.

Chaparral then took out a large plastic bag containing premixed, precut, Chinese Rock #3. Marty noticed that Chaparral had tight black leather gloves on. No prints today, he thought. "How do I know how pure it is, honey?" Marty Doolan asked, hoping that Chaparral would remove his gloves to open the package.

"Chingo will show you," Chaparral said, taking a miniature coke spoon from a chain around his neck. He dipped the spoon into the plastic bag then withdraw some of the premixed, once-cut heroin. He then offered the spoon to Chingo. Chingo smiled; he loved the high he got from Chinese Rock #3.

Chaparral gestured toward Chingo. "My man here says you want to do another five if this stuff is okay. Is that right, Cheryl?"

Marty was at ease now, the script was playing perfectly. "That's right, sweetie," he purred.

"Well," Chaparral said, not even trying to disguise his scorn, "my man here is goin' to give you a little test demonstration."

Chingo placed the white powder into a bottle cap and held the edges of the cap on the end of a step. He lighted a match and held it to the bottom side of the cap. The powder melted. Chingo took out a set of works and drew the liquid up into the syringe. And then tied a piece of rubber tubing around his arm. He twisted it tight but this time the veins didn't pop. He undid the rubber tubing and twisted it tighter until the veins swelled. Chingo paused with the needle above the popped-up vein, then he depressed the lever hard and shot the liquid narcotic into his bloodstream. He withdrew the needle after all the clear liquid had been injected. He paused momentarily and smiled, relishing the first rush of the narcotic to his brain, and then turned and smiled at Marty Doolan. Still smiling, he dropped stone dead at Marty Doolan's feet.

Marty knew instantly what had just happened. His mouth fell open, and it took a physical effort not to vomit. He felt lightheaded and then very dizzy, and he leaned against the wall for support.

Chaparral smiled. "Is this shit pure enough for you, Cheryl?"

Marty couldn't trust himself to speak so he just nodded. His shocked, glazed eyes stared wildly from his painted face, making him look even more bizarre.

Chaparral held out his hand and Marty just stared.

"The fucking money, Cheryl." Chaparral snorted.

Marty hurriedly undid the money belt and handed it over to Chaparral. It had never dawned on him that he might be in real danger. Now, recovering, he took the plastic bag from Chaparral, put it into his purse, and placed his hand inside on the .25 automatic with the five-shot clip. Chaparral motioned for him to go down the stairs first. Marty, still not trusting himself to speak, made a halfhearted attempt to sashay.

"Don't walk around with your hand in your purse like that, Cheryl. You'll be ripped off in this neighborhood. I'll meet you on the corner of Jackson and Westchester avenues in four days at three o'clock, should you want more. Be sure to have the money with you."

Marty Doolan nodded, the hair on the back of his neck bristling beneath his wig. He walked slowly down the stairs, trying oh-so-hard not to give in to the panic urging him to jump down the steps four at a time and telling him not to give a fuck for the high heels he was wearing. He just couldn't help thinking that Chaparral was trying to con him before putting a slug right through the wig and into the back of his head.

Marty never even got a print.

Marty Doolan exited the building and went up to the corner. His backup team from the 13th Narcotics was blocks away when he got into his car with New Jersey plates and drove off.

Once safely in the office of the 13th, Doolan changed in the locker room and at the same time went through the "sign and seal" ritual with the backup team.

During this time Doolan in a subdued manner and in a monotone related the events of the last half hour, including the death of Chingo. Ruella and Wotter wanted to bust Chaparral immediately but Solwin said no. He was concerned with continuing the investigation and wanted to retrieve Chingo's body without alerting Chaparral. Calling the police was ruled out. He decided to request the assistance of the fire department but changed his mind.

The men of the 13th went to the Four Oh precinct, which took in the area. They knew many police and detectives in the Four Oh, and by the time they arrived the problem had been solved. Kids coming over the roof had found Chingo. They had told the super and he had summoned the police.

The homicide detectives responded but they didn't notify the DA, since it was an apparent overdose. Solwin spoke with the homicide detectives to make certain that they understood the facts. He also called the ME's office. Solwin knew the system and wanted to ensure that this death would not be treated as just another junkie overdosing—just another "Hot Shot."

Four days later Marty Doolan met Chaparral at the corner of Jackson and Westchester avenues. Solwin had sixteen officers in the area. They stood on the elevated subway station, on the tops of buildings, and even next to a Con Ed truck dressed in blue and white hard hats. They were omnipresent yet unobtrusive.

Chaparral had left his apartment three hours before the scheduled meet and followed a long and tortuous series of evasive maneuvers. He took the entire three hours to travel a distance he could have walked in less than five minutes. He spotted Marty Doolan dressed in conservative drag, easily passing for a classy woman and not a queer. Chaparral thought that no one was paying any attention to Cheryl. He quickly crossed the street, and Marty Doolan acted surprised to see him.

"Do you have the money?" Chaparral asked, and Marty nodded. Chaparral then guided Marty into the doorway of an abandoned store where they counted the money, their backs toward the street. Satisfied, Chaparral tucked the money in his waist and handed Marty a package. Marty opened it and withdrew some of the powder, and after tasting it placed the package into his carry bag.

"Is there a number where I can reach you for more business?" Marty asked.

"Give me a number where I can reach you when I have the product," Chaparral answered.

"I live with a friend, you know, and I don't want him to know what I'm doing," Marty answered coquettishly. "My friend is very wealthy but also very jealous."

"I'll be outside my apartment house in two weeks at four P.M. You want to deal, be there," Chaparral said.

"That's the same place I came to before with Chingo?" Marty asked.

Chaparral nodded yes.

"What's the address?" Marty asked. Chaparral gave it to him, took a final look around, and left. Doolan blew his nose, signaling that the buy had gone down and that all was okay.

Chaparral returned home, traveling through four of the five boroughs before reaching his apartment. He opened the door and walked inside. Then he took a screwdriver from a toolbox and went into the bathroom, where he wrapped the five thousand dollars in a plastic bag. After removing the shower curtain rods and some wall tile, he placed the money in the hole. Afterward he replaced the rod and tiles. Then while removing a .357 Magnum from his shoulder holster and a .22 pistol from an ankle holster, he made a decision . . . he was never to meet the queer again.

Chingo's homicide put the investigation right back on the acetate-covered cardboard list on Al LoConti's office wall. It was written there personally by none other than Johnny O'Boyle, who had forced Al to remove it when it was just a drug case.

On April 9, 1974, Al went to the Grand Jury with Marty Doolan, the ME, and the first officer who arrived at the roof landing where Chingo lay dead and who "IDed" his body at the morgue.

The Grand Jury indicted John Doe Chaparral for murder and for sale and possession of heroin. A judge then issued a bench warrant for his arrest and a warrant authorizing the search of his home.

Two days later on April 11, 1974, Chaparral spotted the officers entering his apartment house. He took the small amount of heroin he had and flushed it down the toilet and took a can of beer from the refrigerator. When all the officers had entered the building, he tossed his two pistols out the window.

A four-man battering ram took his door off its hinges. The police rushed in behind the falling door. A .38 was placed against Chaparral's head and the search and arrest warrants were shoved in his face. Although the police shouted at him that he was under arrest for murder and sale of drugs, he remained quiet, almost aloof, standing firm in his belief that there could be no case against him.

While he sat handcuffed to a radiator his apartment was searched and destroyed. Pictures were torn from walls. Every book on his bookshelf was ripped apart, the drainage pipes under the sinks were disconnected, and the floorboards pried up. His mattress was shredded into little pieces and dresser drawers were pulled out and emptied on the floor. Cabinets were stripped bare and the back of the TV set removed. The toilet tank was examined and the clothes hamper emptied. After two hours nothing was found, and Chaparral was taken from his apartment still handcuffed behind his back.

While the police padlocked the door, Chaparral laughed to himself, the $5,000 remained untouched in the bathroom wall.

Inside the Four Oh precinct on Alexander Avenue, Chaparral identified himself as Mervin Greene and gave his place of birth as St. John's, New Brunswick, Canada.

His fingerprints were taken and assistance from the Royal Canadian Mounted Police, the provincial police of New Brunswick, and the city police of St. John's was requested.

Solwin called the head of the intelligence and liaison office, Captain Arthur Thornwood. Thornwood, a true fountain of information, told Solwin that St. John's was situated on the Bay of Fundy and was a major seaport. The Bay of Fundy was well known for its tremendous tides, which sometimes rose to sixty feet, but Thornwood had no intelligence leads that St. John's was a transshipment point for narcotics.

However, since Canada enjoyed trade relations with Communist China, it would be logical to assume that St. John's could be an entry point to tap the affluent drug market in America.

The men of the 13th envisioned a Chinese–Canadian connection, and they imagined extraordinary promotions and honors.

Chaparral's prints, faxed back from Albany, proved negative. Then the FBI reported no record, and all the Canadian authorities were prompt in their cooperation but also had no record. Finally the city police of St. John's found no birth certificate for a Mervin Greene born on June 20, 1940.

The detectives decided to talk to Chaparral using all the skills and cajolery at their command. But it would be to no avail. Finally, even when graphic illustrations of sex life in prison were painted and photos of homosexual rape victims in Rikers Island were held in front of his face, he wouldn't even blink. He just quietly and respectfully requested the presence of his attorney, Fast Frankie Hammon.

The officers ignored the request and would not even call the DA. Finally, when Chaparral requested to speak to the officer in charge, the men of the 13th thought they had a breakthrough.

Solwin came up to Chaparral. "Lieutenant, I will repeat what I have said over and over, I am innocent. . . . There is a mistake here, and I want my lawyer. There can be no case against me because I have committed no crime. And I want you to know that once I have the opportunity to speak with my lawyer, I am going to sue you and all of these officers and the City of New York."

"You sold drugs, Chaparral." Solwin sneered. "You sold to an undercover cop and we got you by the fuckin' short hairs. You want to play hardball, it's okay by me."

"I never sold drugs, Lieutenant. I can't assist you as to any supplier like your men want me to, because, quite simply, I have no supplier; I've sold no drugs; I've committed no crime. Get me my lawyer. Get him now, Lieutenant. Now."

Solwin left the interrogation room and conferred with his men. They left Mervin Greene a.k.a. Chaparral alone . . . alone to brood and worry and to stew.

Chaparral stewed for another three hours, knowing that the cops were fucking with his mind, so he made his mind a blank and concentrated on enjoying the pleasures of the cigarettes they let him smoke. He took long drags, holding the smoke in his lungs, and then puffed out smoke rings. Suddenly he heard a female voice, a high falsetto voice. It sounded vaguely familiar but he couldn't quite place it so he just took another long drag.

The door opened and Chaparral looked up and gasped. Marty Doolan came in dressed in drag, and Chaparral stared at him. Then his eyes bugged out when he looked at Marty Doolan's left falsie. The bustline did not excite him but the object pinned to the false breast did. It was a gold detective's shield.

Marty Doolan minced up to Chaparral. A pocketbook dangled from his right arm. He waved the pocketbook in greeting, then smiling and in his best falsetto voice, Marty Doolan sang out, "Hi, bitch."

Chaparral moved his bowels. Marty's nose twisted at the sudden stench, and he continued speaking in his falsetto voice. "I think the bitch just did poo poo. Come on, guys, let him get clean, clean. I think he is going to be nice."

Then turning to Chaparral and continuing in his falsetto, he said, "Make the boys happy, dickie, they got you by your wee wee."

Marty minced out.

Chaparral cleaned himself and changed. A freight train called Reality had just arrived, running him down and crushing his will.

"I don't think I will need a lawyer just yet," he told Lieutenant Solwin in a subdued tone. Solwin turned to him expectantly. "What would you gentlemen like to know?" Chaparral said.

AFTER CHAPARRAL HAD BEEN arraigned and paroled on May 3, 1974, Al LoConti recommended a deal for him to Johnny O'Boyle.

"Man One, no promises. It will cover both the drug sales and Chingo's murder."

Johnny O'Boyle nodded approvingly. "You've arrived, Al." "At one time you would have objected to this arrangement, but now you deal with the facts. I think you finally lost your cherry."

Al replied, "I still hate dealing with scumbags like Chaparral but I've gotta be practical. I'm never gonna get the rats out of the sewer without sendin' down another fuckin' rat to flush 'em out."

"Yeah, Al, but even if we send a hundred million rats down the sewer, there's still gonna be a billion left. It's a shithole without a bottom, too fuckin' much money involved. It's never gonna fuckin' end."

"I'm just gonna take it one case at a time, Johnny. I'm gonna see what happens to Mr. Chaparral. If he don't produce he gets eight and a third to twenty-five. If he produces he can walk right out the fuckin' door and I'll have some big rat skins up on the wall. I'll adjourn his sentence for two months after the plea and give him a chance to make some cases. Then if he's working out I'll put it off again; it's up to him. I think he's gonna do the right thing because Marty Doolan really scared him shitless."

Chaparral did, in fact, go right to work and revealed that he had two sources of supply, a Jamaican who dealed drugs from his home on 161st Street, two blocks from Yankee Stadium, and a suave white man named Biagio Squerente who sold heroin from his home in Riverdale.

Solwin decided to conduct a double undercover operation, dispatching Ruella to buy from the Jamaican and William Wotter to buy from Squerente. The team would be ascending the rungs of two separate ladders.

Chaparral, following the script, introduced Ruella to the Jamaican. When he answered their knock Ruella was immediately intimidated by a heavily muscled giant of a man. At six feet five he was as lean as a top contender. His hair was worn in the long braids of the Rastafarians called dreadlocks, and his appearance was definitely fearsome. Chaparral had been thorough in making the arrangements, and Ruella gave the Jamaican $2,000 in exchange for a bag of Chinese Rock #3. After tasting the contents, she nodded to Chaparral and they left.

Later that same night he introduced Wotter to Squerente. Wotter purchased $2,000 worth of Chinese Rock #3, tested it with a kit, and said good-bye. Chaparral hung around to get his commission from Squerente. After being paid he went back to the Jamaican to collect his money. The Jamaican ushered him into his apartment, but when he only wanted to pay 5 percent instead of 20 an argument began.

In the midst of the argument there was a knock at the door. The fearless Jamaican just opened it, admitting three heavily armed men wearing ski masks who pointed guns to the heads of Chaparral and the Jamaican then pushed them into a bedroom where the Jamaican's wife and daughter sat watching TV.

The men had large silencers on their pistols and directed the Jamaican and Chaparral to kneel next to a steampipe that ran from the floor up through the ceiling of the bedroom. They then handcuffed the Jamaican to the pipe and Chaparral watched him kneeling with both hands cuffed behind him around the steampipe.

Next they gagged the wife and the daughter and cuffed them together and when they were done they hit Chaparral with the butt of a pistol behind the ear, knocking him unconscious.

The leader took off his mask. He was a Colombian dealer who

had warned the Jamaican time and again not to intrude on his territory, but the Jamaican had told him to go fuck himself. The Colombian knew that the Jamaican was just too tough and would just not scare.

"You make a fuckin' peep and we blow your wife and daughter away," the Colombian said, and then half nodded to one of his underlings who without any hesitation shot Chaparral twice in the heart. Only dull thumps were heard as Chaparral's body twitched violently. Then the man shot Chaparral behind the ear and the twitching stopped. The wife and daughter, gagged tightly, could only moan in terror while their eyes bugged out.

"I'll leave the country, mon, I'll leave tonight," the Jamaican said. "I won't pack. I'll get a cab to Kennedy and I'll be down in Kingston before the sun comes up. Just please don't hurt my family. I'll be gone, mon."

The Colombian just smiled and shot him from five feet away, hitting him in the chest. The bullet, a .357 Magnum hollowpoint, sent the Jamaican into shock instantly, but he was tough and didn't die until the Colombian put the second bullet into his eye.

The moans of the wife and daughter became muted shrieks as they watched their man being shot. Mercifully they did not notice the other two Colombians walk behind them, and they never heard the six small thumps as they were each shot three times in the back of the head.

The assassins' gloved hands left no fingerprints. They did not pause to take any money from the corpses but quickly left, entered their Lincoln, and drove to New Jersey. In the middle of the George Washington Bridge one of them asked the boss who the white guy was.

"Who the fuck knows?" he had said. "I only know one thing."

"What's that?" he was asked.

"That motherfucker was sure in the wrong place at the wrong time." The three started to chuckle and then burst out laughing.

Al, Jimmy Farrell, and John O'Boyle met at the Jamaican's apartment in the morning of May 4, 1974. Quirel, the homicide DA, was already there along with Timmy Flanagan, Lieutenant Solwin, Ruella Watkins, and William Wotter.

Al was truly horrified at the execution of the thirteen-year-old girl. Looking at her bullet-shattered body brought on visions of his own young daughter. All of the ADAs were subdued at the execution of their informer. Forensic and the ME had arrived and soon the Hat was on hand. He called for another forensic team to render assistance, and extensive canvassing of the apartment house followed, producing, as expected, not even a shred of evidence.

The Hat, strangely quiet and subdued, spoke to everyone assembled and turning to Ruella said, "Hadn't you better get downtown?"

Ruella looked at her watch. It was nine-forty-five. She would be late. "I'd better leave right now," she said.

"How will you get there?" the Hat asked.

"I'll take her, Inspector," Wotter answered.

"Move it," the Hat ordered.

Today the department had a special present for Ruella: She would be decorated and promoted to detective third grade as a result of her undercover work. In addition, Ruella had been informed that following the ceremony she would be transferred to the 7th Homicide Zone and teamed with Pete DiCerrechia. The Hat gave the impression that Ruella's advancement was a result of his intervention, but she knew that nothing could be farther from the truth. It was Solwin, Wotter, and her fellow officers who had lobbied long and hard for her.

As Ruella was leaving, Al LoConti, sick at heart, looked at Chaparral's body. O'Boyle, acutely aware of the strain on his assistant, walked up to him. "It's fate, Al . . . fate. If you didn't give him the plea and parole him, someone would have killed him in jail. It was just his time."

"I don't believe in fate, Johnny," Al said, still staring at the body of Chaparral.

In the next twelve days the team had turned their energies toward the remaining link to Chaparral, Biagio Squerente.

Squerente had been indicted by the Bronx Grand Jury for nine sales of heroin to William Wotter. There had been no problem obtaining buy money from the department, since they thought they had an "Italian connection," a made man, a soldier in some crime family. Solwin had visions of having penetrated the Mafia and the entire membership of the 13th was euphoric, except William Wotter. Wotter, whose mother was born on the outskirts of Palermo, had sincere doubts about Squerente's nationality but he kept them to himself. By buying nine relatively small amounts, he'd gained Squerente's confidence and had become a very good customer.

Solwin and the 13th Narcotics felt they could never get Squerente to turn and become an informer, because the "made guys," the members of La Cosa Nostra, could never be expected to become rats. So the 13th obtained an eavesdropping order to tap the phone in Squerente's luxurious Riverdale apartment.

Jimmy Farrell prepared the voluminous paperwork for the order. He hoped they would get a lead on the murder of Chaparral and the Jamaican family.

After the DA himself questioned Farrell, he signed his personal affidavit in support of the order and Farrell took the paperwork to Judge Termi, who spent the better part of three hours reviewing the application.

The Judge, a former member of the Colombian lawyers' association, didn't ignore the reference to organized criminal activity in Farrell's affidavit and didn't like veiled references to Italians being members of organized crime. Although Farrell's papers were legally sufficient as a matter of law, the objectionable ethnic innuendo was unsupported so Termi decided to question Farrell.

"Have the officers in this investigation discussed it thoroughly with you, Mr. Farrell?" he asked.

"Yes, Your Honor," Farrell answered respectfully.

"Have they described the appearance of this Mr. Squerente to you, Mr. Farrell?"

"They have, Your Honor, and at considerable length."

"I'll bet this guy wears a pinkie ring and talks with his hands," Termi said empatically and Farrell fell right into the trap.

"He certainly does, Your Honor, he certainly does."

Termi signed the order and gave the papers to Farrell. "Good luck, Mr. Farrell," he said. Farrell thanked him and left.

After the door closed Termi turned to his law secretary and just shook his head.

As soon as the tap was in place, Wotter picked up the phone and dialed. When Squerente answered, Wotter placed an order ten times greater than all of the previous drugs combined.

By the time that the wiretap was in effect for twenty-four hours, only one call had been intercepted: that of a female who spoke about the health of "Mother." Denny Driscoll, who would have been happy in the Gestapo, felt that "Mother" was some secret code, but it was obvious to everyone else that the caller was Squerente's sister. It was even more disappointing to hear the woman's distinctive New England accent.

At 4:47 P.M. Squerente made a call and the police apparatus automatically recorded the number and traced it.

The voice of a male, thought to be white and sounding mature, answered. "Hello."

"Tom?"

"Yeah, who is this?"

"Tom, baby, this is Blaze."

"Hey, Blaze, what's happenin', man?"

"Tom, you know that thing we did?"

"Yeah, Blaze."

"I'm talkin' about those dresses you sold me."

"I know, Blaze."

"Well, the guy likes them so much he wants to buy ten times the amount of dresses."

"Holy shit, Blaze . . . that's a big order. It's gonna cost him . . . forty . . . forty big ones."

"Well, Tommy, he's a good customer but you know he likes to see the dresses before he pays for them."

"Fine, Blaze, he's your customer, you give me your money and I give you the dresses and you can sell to your customer. I don' give a fuck what you charge."

"Listen, Tommy, you know I can't come up with that kind of bread, man. The only way I can do this deal is on consignment."

"Hey, Blaze, you want me to hang up?" There's no fuckin' credit in the dress business."

"No, no, Tom, hey, don't get pissed off. I'm just tryin' to put this thing together."

"Blaze, I like you. You're a good customer, man. But I don't make the fuckin' dresses. The guy that sells 'em to me ain't gonna give them to me without the fuckin' bread. Man's in business, ain't a fuckin' hobby."

"Just talk to him, Tom. Find out how we can make this thing go down, man. Okay?"

"Okay, Blaze, but he won't be back in town until next Tuesday."

"Okay, Tom, I'll call you then. So long, Tommy baby."

"*Ciao*, Blaze."

Farrell had received the news of the call at home and he stayed up all night typing the affidavits to secure an amendment to the order. At 9 A.M. he saw his Bureau Chief. By 11:30 he had secured the DA's signature, and Judge Termi signed the amendment authorizing the interception of telephone communications over the telephone line and instrument registered to Thomas Jassy at 4722 Cleton Avenue Bronx, New York.

Late that afternoon the equipment was set up in the basement of the precinct located one half block from the Jassy apartment. The basement of the precinct also had another wire going at the same time, manned by homicide and intelligence detectives investigating the murder of Mickey Varino, the Admiral's son-in-law. Neither team discussed any part of its investigation. The only common thread was that the investigation into Varino's death had produced conversations pertaining to dresses, and the homicide detectives correctly deduced that they were hearing drug talk. The identity of the persons whose conversations were intercepted on the two wiretaps were not the same.

At seven-thirty in the evening Wotter called Squerente.

"I'll be over in a half hour. I have business to discuss," Wotter said. At the appointed time he entered Squerente's lavish apartment, and Squerente put out a tray of cheddar and brie cheeses and tiny oyster crackers, then poured a glass of chilled Chablis for both Wotter and himself.

Wotter watched Squerente daintily eating the crackers and cheese tidbits. Squerente extended his wineglass. "Cheers," he said, holding the glass with his pinky extended.

Wotter, sipping the wine, said to himself, This guy is no more Italian than my old man, he's a fuckin' WASP.

Wotter emptied his glass and held it out for a refill. "Blaze, I want the full amount that we talked about."

"Okay, Billy, but it's gonna cost you eighty big ones."

"Listen, Blaze, don't try to put it up my ass. I'll give you forty-five, that's it."

Blaze shook his head. "Billy, you're a good customer but if I gotta offend you, then I gotta offend you. Forget forty-five, drive it out of your brain. Because you're a good customer you get it for sixty, and I'm takin' a beating. I swear on my mother's eyes I'm not makin' a fuckin' thing on this deal."

"Don't bullshit me, Blaze, fifty-five is all I'll go. Not one fuckin' cent more."

"You drive a hard bargain, Billy. Fifty-five it is. But on the day the deal goes down, you got to give me the money. You can wait here and I gotta go get the merchandise."

"So long, Blaze. No fuckin' deal." Wotter started to leave.

"Okay, okay, take it easy, Billy. The man I do business with is very cautious. Let me see what I can work out."

"Sure, Blaze. You work it out."

They emptied the glasses of Chablis and shook hands. Wotter walked down the stairs smiling all the way.

Following this meeting the 13th anxiously awaited Blaze's call to Tommy to order the drugs. All the detectives enjoyed the eavesdropping assignment; it was exciting and at times even hilarious to learn the innermost secrets of the people you were spying on.

The call went out from Blaze to Tommy at 8:30 P.M.—right after Wotter left the apartment.

"Hello," Tommy Jassy answered.

"Tom, my man."

"Blaze, how goes it?"

"Fine, did you talk to your man about those dresses?"

"No, but I know he's got the dresses. Do you have the bread?" Jassy answered.

"Tom, this has got to be consignment or else face to face. My guy ain't lettin' no money out of his sight."

"Forget fuckin' consignment, Blaze. I don't want to hear the fuckin' word consignment again. Understan'?"

"Okay, Tom, okay, but it's got to be face to face. Dresses have got to be there."

"I'll be back to you, Blaze." Tommy hung up.

The officers waited for Tommy's call to take them farther up the ladder. They were becoming very excited.

Tommy did nothing until the following Monday. The officers who had him under surveillance reported he had not left his apartment. Monday morning Tommy Jassy dialed out. The machinery picked up the phone number. Solwin called his liaison at the phone company. While Solwin waited for the information, Jassy's call was answered.

"Treus, may I help you?"

"Paulie there?"

"One second, please."

While waiting Solwin was informed the number belonged to the Treus Land Surveying Company on Fordham Road.

An intercom buzzed and a voice answered, "Carver here, may I help you?"

"Hey, Paulie, it's Tom."

"Tom, you can't call me here!" The man was enraged. "Where are you, Tom, I'll call you."

"I'm home, Paulie."

"Stay there." Paulie hung up.

Minutes later Tommy's phone rang. The men of the 13th listened as Tommy picked up the receiver and said hello.

"Tom, you stupid cocksucker, what the fuck is the matter with you calling me at work?"

"Hey, Paulie, I had to get hold of you, man. I got a guy wants to go for forty."

"Listen to me, Tom, you stupid fuck. I don't give a shit what you got, I don't ever want to talk about this shit on the phone. Don't ever call me at work. Did you ever stop to think, you dumb fuck, that the phone could be tapped?"

"Okay, okay I'm sorry, Paulie, I never thought. . . . By the way, where are you calling from now?"

"I'm not an asshole like you, I figure the angles, so I'm calling you from a pay phone and we don't have to worry about any fuckin' tap."

The eavesdroppers of the 13th chuckled silently, pointing their fingers at their temples and nodding, indicating to each other that Paulie was a real smart guy. Their antics stopped as the conversation continued.

"Paulie, this guy Blaze has a customer who he has already sold dresses to."

"Yeah, so who gives a fuck?"

"Blaze wants to go consignment."

"Fuck you, Tommy, fuck Blaze, and fuck the horse he rode in on."

"Hey, Paulie, let me finish. I tell him he's out of his mind, you know, no fuckin' way. So we got to figure a way to do this face to face—"

"This guy could be a cop or a fed, Tommy."

"Nah, Paulie, Blaze been sellin' to him right along. Guy never asks to meet no one, no questions, he just wants his shit, I mean his dresses, you know."

"Yeah, well, okay. We will meet Thursday at Split Rock."

"You want to golf with these guys, Paulie?"

"Yeah, we meet them on the golf course; the deal goes down on the fifth or the eleventh—whatever hole we want."

"Heeeey, Paulie, now I know why they call you the Brain," Tommy said admiringly.

"Okay Tommy keed, meet me at the clubhouse at ten-thirty Thursday morning."

The stage was set but before going on duty that Thursday morning, Officer Wotter met his friend Al LoConti at the Last Supper Restaurant for a cup of coffee and a briefing.

After finishing they shook hands and Wotter left to meet Biagio Squerente a.k.a. Blaze at the Split Rock Golf Course. Wotter was nervous and the coffee started to go through him. He had fifty-five thousand dollars on him, the property of the People of the State of New York. Before Wotter even set a foot in the clubhouse every man assigned to the 13th Narcotics Group had hit the greens, all exceptionally vigilant while playing at golf.

WHILE WILLIE WOTTER WAS getting ready to enter the clubhouse and begin the undercover operation against Blaze, Tommy and Paulie, Al LoConti, feeling great, sat in the Last Supper, basking in the glow of his sexual escapade from the night before. Unfuckin'-believable, he thought.

He had been involved with two back-to-back murders and worked until 10 P.M., so he was off today. The second murder had been a shooting over loaded dice in a Puerto Rican social club. Dr. Cristen had joined him at the scene, and even now he could not believe the fantastic turn of events.

Incredible as a matter of law. He smiled to himself. Un-fuckin'-believable.

The night had been so good that not even Renee's refusing his request to see the kids this afternoon could put a damper on his euphoria. Today he was scheduled to follow up on some of the cases on his list and he would follow it even though he was off. Just as he ordered another cup of coffee, his brother Vince walked into the Last Supper wearing the uniform of a milkman for Mother Nature's Farms. His route took in Morris Park all the way south to Castle Hill and north to the city line with Mount Vernon. Richie Zemberelli, who filled in for sick milkmen on his days off from the department, had got the job for Vinnie. They made real good money.

Vinnie sat down and greeted his brother warmly.

"You look tired, Vince. What happened? You get laid last night?" Al asked, smiling.

"Yeah, I got laid, but that ain't why I'm tired."

"You pissed off too, huh, Vince?" Al asked.

"Yeah, well, a little."

"You gonna tell me what happened?"

"Yeah, well, I took Helen out last night, you know, the Greek chick."

"You mean the blonde with the nice ass and three kids."

"Well, she ain't blonde this week," Vinnie said, and Al chuckled.

"She's redheaded and last night she tells me she wants to go to Astoria to one of these bazooki or kazooki joints."

"You mean where you do the Greek dances and break the fuckin' dishes?"

"You got it brother, well, I get there and she knows the owner and we have a couple of blasts and get a little lit and before you know it I'm doin' a fuckin' Greek dance and I'm drinkin' this white shit—"

"Ouzo?" Al interrupted.

"Yeah, that's it. And I'm hoppin' around breakin' these fuckin' plates and the owner is wavin' to the back for more plates, more plates, and they bring out more plates and I keep breakin' the fuckin' things—I mean, I even broke a couple of fuckin' plates on Helen's head. But they ain't real plates, Al, they're like plaster of Paris. The Greek song must've gone on for two fuckin' hours and I musta smashed a fuckin' million plates. All the Greeks are cheerin' and clappin' and Helen is havin' a ball. Then I pay up and leave and take her to my place where I proceed to hit a home run, and then I called a cab for her."

"Why didn't you drive her home—you know, treat her right, she's a nice girl," his brother chided.

"I shoulda driven her home, you're right, but I didn't want to lose my parking space," Vinnie answered.

Al nodded in understanding, then said, "I know why you're tired now, but why are you so pissed off?"

"The fuckin' bill, Al. . . . It was five hundred dollars."

Al was shocked. "What are you, nuts?"

"Five hundred fuckin' big ones, Al, five fuckin' hundred."

"What the fuck did you eat?" Al asked.

"Eat shit, Al, it wasn't what we ate, it was the fuckin' plates. They charge you for the fuckin' plates in those Greek joints. Now I know why the fuckin' owner was wavin' with both hands to the back and screamin' 'More plates—bring more plates.'"

Al started to guffaw. His face turned beet red and he started to cough. Then Vinnie started to laugh and soon the two brothers were roaring together. Their uncle came out with a fresh pot of coffee. After Al told him the story, the three howled together.

Al wanted to tell Vinnie about his great evening, but because his brother was so close to Renee he kept quiet.

Last night Dr. Linda Cristen had arrived at the Puerto Rican social club where a crap shooter had caught two thirty-eights in the forehead. The cause of death was no mystery and Pete DiCerrechia, fluent in Spanish, caught the case and had detained the club's twenty occupants, interviewing them all while Dr. Cristen looked at the DOA. Al spoke to other detectives and issued Grand Jury subpoenas while DiCerrechia translated.

After only fifteen minutes Pete had nailed down the ID of the shooter and when Al walked over to speak with Dr. Cristen, Pete went with him.

"Well, it's good to see the best ME in the City of New York workin' with the very best and most dedicated young Homicide trial assistant," Pete said.

Alcibiades turned red and Dr. Cristen smiled. She really liked the affable, ball-breaking detective.

"My friend Al here and I grew up together," Pete continued.

"Cut it out, Pete, will you . . . please," Al said.

"Yep, we grew up together and my friend here is a legend in our neighborhood; he and his brother are certified war heroes. Both Airborne and Strac all the way. Al here was a captain. Right, Al?" Pete continued.

Dr. Cristen looked at Al differently. "You were in Vietnam?"

"He sure was," Pete said. "Al here didn't go to Canada or duck the old draft. Al here was a volunteer."

"Ignore him, Dr. Cristen, he is really psychotic. He loves to see people squirm. He is a very sick guy, he's been sick all his life, and in fact, he should be committed," Al said.

Pete laughed good-naturedly and Dr. Cristen smiled.

"So long, folks. Gotta get me a shooter," Pete said.

Just as Al was noticing how truly beautiful Dr. Cristen was, a dripping wet Sue Stein ran up to them. Sue was one of the ME drivers.

"I just got a call on the radio. The mother-in-law of a member of the Board of Estimate got killed in a mugging in Queens. Deputy ME Richardson himself wants to go to the scene. I have to pick him up in Riverdale immediately. You had better catch a ride home with the cops," Sue said.

Dr. Cristen nodded, annoyed at being stranded in the South Bronx.

"I can give you a lift, Doctor," Al volunteered.

"Thanks," she said.

They scrambled out into the ice-cold rain and into Al's blue Dodge. By the time Al arrived at her apartment in the East Fifties, Linda knew his whole story. Though she didn't own a car she leased a parking space, so at her insistence Al parked his car and accompanied her to her apartment. It was beautiful and commanded a breathtaking view of the New York skyline and the East River. Al had never been in such surroundings in his twenty-nine years.

She hung Al's wet jacket in the bathroom and changed into a pair of tight jeans and a blouse. She was truly magnificent. After pouring strong highballs over plenty of ice, she snuggled close to him on the couch. He sipped his drink in disbelief.

"Lighten up, Al, you're too tense," she said softly.

Al was trying to be cool, trying for a sophistication he did not have.

"Would you like some music?" Linda asked.

"Sure, why not?" Al answered.

"Any preference?" she asked.

"Dion and the Belmonts, the Drifters, Beach Boys, I'm not hard to please." Al smiled.

"Well, I can offer you Beethoven, Verdi, Chopin, even Wagner."

"It doesn't matter," Al answered, refusing to be embarrassed.

While she played a record, he fixed two more drinks.

He had no idea which classics were being played so he just sipped his drink, and after a while he kissed her hard and she opened her mouth. From then on it was just pleasure. She led him into the bedroom and they undressed, embracing on the bed. He rolled on top and entered her. Clasping his arms around her neck, he kissed her. Then using all of his skills and strengthened by the longing of months of abstinence, he sated himself and then rolled off, leaving her breathless and fulfilled.

Lighting a cigarette, she turned to him. "Well, I know one thing."

"What's that?" he asked.

"You're wife didn't leave because you were lacking in the sex department."

"Is that a professional opinion?" Al asked.

"No, just an honest observation," she answered. "You and one other guy I know are in a league by yourself."

Al refused to ask who the other guy was.

"So you mean I'm not gonna get a bill for your opinion?" he joked.

"No bill." Linda Cristen smiled.

After an hour they made love again, and when they finished Al got dressed.

"Aren't you going to stay the night?" Linda asked.

"Gotta get home," Al answered.

"Why? You live alone . . . . why not stay the night?"

"Gotta take care of my dog."

Linda was incredulous. "This is an absolute first. You are un-fuckin'-believable, un-fuckin'-believable."

Al kissed her hard. "So are you, Doc, so are you, but he's not just a dog, he's my best friend," Al LoConti said as he left the room.

After a while Linda Cristen picked up her phone and dialed the 7th Homicide Zone and asked to speak to Pete DiCerrechia.

"Detective DiCerrechia, may I help you?" he answered.

"You set the whole thing up, you bastard, didn't you?" Linda said. "I bet you even got Sue Stein in on it so he would offer me a lift home."

"What can I tell you?" Pete said.

"I knew it, you scheming bastard, I should have realized it."

"Come on Linda, Al is the greatest guy I know. He's good people, he'd do anything for anyone, and I'm sure you found him to be a quite a guy." Pete chuckled.

"Yeah, he screwed me twice and then went home to walk his dog."

"Really!" Pete was shocked.

"Yeah. He said the dog was his best friend."

"Well, I gotta admit, Linda, Al is a little fucked up and he still loves his wife," Pete said.

"He certainly didn't speak very highly of her. You would never think he still was hung up on her," Linda said.

"Well, he is, except he don't even know it," Pete said. "He's just a nice gentle, good guy, but a real tough DA. He's your kind of guy, Linda. One day you're gonna thank Uncle Pete for fixing you up. Al's gonna get over his wife and you two got a future. Believe me, I know this guy since we were five years old. And you gotta admit I know you too," Pete said softly.

She refused to respond.

"Good night, Pete, you bastard," she said fondly as she hung up on the only man who had stood in a league by himself until Alcibiades LoConti had arrived tonight.

This DA even beats you, Pete DiCerrechia, Dr. Linda Cristen reflected as she flicked off the light. Un-fuckin'-believable.

ON THE GOLF COURSE a foursome consisting of Blaze Squerente, Paulie Carver, Tommy Jassy, and Officer William Wotter were approaching the eighth hole. Wotter wanted the deal to go down on the nineth hole because he wanted to get into range of the preset video cameras.

Paulie, teamed together with Tommy, thought, This guy Billy is no cop. Blaze is a shithead just trying to act like a hood, and he certainly ain't no cop. Maybe one more hole to watch them just to be sure. Besides, nine holes is enough.

Tommy Jassy was pleased since he needed the commission money for his bills, including his girlfriend's abortion. While she was hanging around her mother's for a few days afterward as she always did, he would get away to Paradise Island with Inez the Cuban go-go dancer from the Maroon Room on Williamsbridge Road.

Tommy asked the foursome if anyone had ever been to the Maroon Room. Blaze Squerente, the perennial high roller and ladies' man, nodded and said, "Man, that Cuban go-go girl there, she is the best piece of ass on the East Coast."

"How do you know?" Tommy Jassy asked.

"Shit, I been bangin' her on and off for years."

Tommy Jassy felt sick. "How did you get to the Maroon Room, you livin' in Riverdale?"

"Well, my lawyer has an office across the street," Blaze replied.

Tommy said, "Your lawyer is Quiet Marvin?"

"Yeah, Marvin has an office right across the street from the Maroon Room. Didn't know anyone who called him Quiet though. I always thought he talked too fuckin' much," Blaze said.

"Yeah, well, everyone does, I don't know why they call him Quiet. All I know is that he used to be a real crackerjack, you know, the guy to get if you had a problem, but I hear he is second rate now. Hey, Paulie, do you know why they call him Quiet?" Tommy asked.

"No I don't," Paulie lied, smiling.

As the four golfers walked together toward the green, William Wotter reflected on the reason Marvin Pollard had received the nickname. Wotter knew that the Maroon Room had more police wires and bugs than the American embassy in Moscow. Wotter had been inside a Con Ed surveillance van parked in the street in front of the club and had photographed all of his present golfing partners. He knew that the files contained the identity of this guy Paulie.

Guy thinks he's so bad but he's just another asshole, William Wotter thought, then switched his concentration on to Quiet Marvin. Marvin was always buying drinks in the Maroon Room and handing out his business cards. In time Marvin had become very big, so big that he would take frequent vacations to South America, and although it was suspected that Marvin did a thriving drug business in partnership with some of his clients, it could never be proven. Marvin's bags were always searched thoroughly by customs but nothing had ever been found, and twice Marvin had even been strip-searched at Kennedy Airport. Wotter chuckled to himself as he recalled the story. All during the time when Marvin was being searched he would talk, talk, and talk. In fact, the customs agent had remarked to the officer who prepared the file for the Police Department that Marvin continued to talk while he was bent over and his cheeks were spread so that the customs officers could look up his ass. During this time of course Marvin was talking about the infringement on his constitutional rights and who he was going to sue as soon as he could stand up straight and put his pants back on.

Marvin had sent a lot of nasty letters to the Attorney General and to the President and even to his congressman.

Marvin was a yapper, all right. A real yenta, Wotter reflected as the foursome chipped up on the green.

Wotter watched the others putt out. His ball was about thirty-five feet from the hole and he made the long putt. Finally Wotter had enough of this maneuvering. Fuck this shit, he thought, all morning sizing each other up. So he walked off the green and placed the putter back into the bag of clubs on the golf cart. Then he grabbed the cart handle and pulled it right at Paulie. Gotta grab the bull by the horns, Wotter thought, facing Paulie.

"We gonna deal or fuck around all day playin' golf?" Wotter said in his best annoyed manner.

"Hey, man, fuckin' relax, will ya? I don' wan' every motha fucka to hear. This ain't too fuckin' cool, man," Paulie exclaimed. "You got some fuckin' pair a balls."

"Listen, man, I have had enough of this horseshit," Wotter said, patting the fifty-five thousand in the money belt around his waist. "This bread ain't gettin' any lighter and it's gettin real fuckin' hot, so either shit or get off the fuckin' pot. You don't wanna deal, I take my fuckin' business somewhere else."

"Hey, man . . . chill out." Tommy Jassy jumped in. "This gentleman here is a businessman, you know, he's got a special commodity. If you don't like the way—"

"Eat my ass," Wotter interrupted. Then, turning to Blaze, he said, "Fuck this. You guys finish the game, I'm leaving."

"Hey, hey, Billy, hoold it, come on, man . . . Easy, look." Paulie started to smile broadly. "I'm just trying to do business right. I never saw you, you never saw me, so we got to eyeball each other, you know. We don't have Dun and Bradstreet or credit references in this business so we got to rely on what we see. So I see you and I think everything is cool with you, so let's do the ninth hole so that we don't draw attention to ourselves and then we deal, okay? We just look like businessmen playing the front nine."

"Okay, Paulie, but only one more fuckin' hole," Wotter said.

As they walked toward the tee on the ninth hole, Tommy Jassy looked admiringly at Paulie. "What a fuckin' brain, what a fuckin' brain."

JUST TO THE RIGHT of the ninth hole stood a small white snack bar selling franks, hamburgers, beer, soda, potato chips, and other quick meals. Fifty feet up the path from the snack bar stood two outhouses. Today by prearrangement the short-order cook was Lieutenant Bill Solwin. The wall of the shack had an opening that served as the counter and four empty stools stood outside. A phone on the back wall provided Solwin with communications. It started to ring while he was preparing for lunch.

The caller, an Inspector from the Commissioner's office, informed him that the Manhattan DA and the FBI had just discovered that the custodian of the evidence tapes from all the wiretaps in the City of New York had been selling copies to organized crime and that Solwin's investigation was one of the ones compromised. For safety's sake Solwin was ordered to now change to a buy and bust. As Solwin hung up, thinking of how to get word to Wotter, the subject foursome came into view.

Officer Wotter and the others played the ninth hole without incident. After all the putts were completed, Paulie put his arm around Wotter.

"Okay, Billy, we are going to deal today." Wotter nodded. "Waddaya say we have a beer first?" Paulie said. Again Wotter just nodded, delighted that everything was going down perfectly. They walked to the snack bar.

"Four beers," Paulie ordered.

Tommy Jassy surveyed the handwritten menu thumbtacked up on the wall. "Gimme a chili dog with onion," he told Solwin.

"Anyone else?" Solwin asked.

"I'll have a burger," Paulie said.

"Make that two burgers," chimed in Blaze. "How about you, Billy?"

Knowing the cook, Wotter declined and watched Solwin snap open four beers, then slap two burgers on the grill. After passing out four plastic cups to the seated men, Solwin exited the shack through a side door, walked across a short path to an outhouse, and entered the men's room. The women's room was locked and had an out-of-order sign on the door.

Inside the men's room were two stalls with commodes and two urinals. After checking the stalls to make sure they were empty, Solwin then began to urinate. He had a miniature transmitter under his shirt and a receiver was installed in the eyeglass frame behind his ear. "Everything all set?" he asked.

"Beautiful, Loo, beautiful," Sergeant Driscoll answered from his vantage point in the ladies' room where he was stationed with two police technicians. A special camera was videotaping the foursome sipping beer, and miniature microphones under the stools were receiving and transmitting to equipment manned by Driscoll's team. The conversations were of course being recorded simultaneously.

"What's happenin' now?" Solwin asked while tucking himself in.

"Paulie just told Wotter he's got the shit in his golf bag and the exchange will take place in the parking lot. But first they're coming here to the shithouse to count the money. We got the shithouse bugged so we'll get it all down."

"Real fine," Solwin said, zipping his fly, "but we gotta change the plans. If everything is okay, Wotter will enter the far commode next to your wall to signal us. When he does that I want you to make sure that he has them play the back nine. Tell him to have the deal go down on the fourteenth green, then make sure that Blatt and his team set up the video in the thick woods behind the fourteenth." Solwin washed his hands and went back to the shack.

Paulie spotted him first. "Okay, guys here comes the flunky, watch it." Solwin entered the shack and turned the hamburgers. He took a frankfurter from the hot water tray and placed it on a bun, then he turned the heat up under the grill. Using a spatula, he pressed down hard on the burgers until fat droplets began to pop. After lowering the heat, he slid each burger onto an open bun and topped them with slices of tomato and onion. He passed the plates to Paulie and Blaze and from another heated metal tray Solwin spooned a generous portion of his own chili mixture onto the frank.

Cooking provided Solwin with the only escape from his job, and he truly loved it. The officers of his team had to reach new creative heights in inventing excuses not to attend the many invitations to Solwin's dinner parties and barbecues. Now, watching Solwin while sipping his beer, Wotter recalled Ruella Watkins, her face scrunched up in agony after biting into one of Solwin's special creations and crying, "Even shit's gotta taste better than this." But as bad as his cooking was, he couldn't fuck up the hamburgers. The chili, however, was another matter, since Solwin had mistaken a small jar of ground red Hungarian wax peppers combined with ground New Mexico chili peppers for paprika and not being satisfied with the canned chili available he made his own by mixing some tomato paste with water and all the dried red hot peppers.

Tommy Jassy took the chili dog from Lieutenant Solwin and gently blew away the smoke coming from the top of the onions. Paulie and Blaze took huge bites of their burgers and nodded to each other and to Solwin in appreciation. "Fuckin' delicious," Blaze said.

"Fuckin' ay." Paulie nodded.

Solwin smiled, loving the compliments. He watched Jassy, expecting even greater approbation for his chili creation. Tommy Jassy watched Paulie and Blaze smacking their lips and became even more famished. He stared at the steam and smelled the fragrance of the tomato, chili, and onions. Finally, unable to restrain himself, he took a huge bite, chewed once, and swallowed more than half the frank. Tommy Jassy was a real fast eater and in only a second he had consumed the remainder.

I might try one of those myself, Solwin thought as Wotter watched, amazed. Suddenly Tommy Jassy's face grew scarlet and rivulets of sweat began to pour down his face.

After screaming "Mother of God," he drained the cup of beer while motioning with his free hand for another. Solwin snapped open a can of beer and fitted it into his outstretched hand. Tommy Jassy gulped it down. Wotter, looking on, just sipped his beer. Fuckin' Solwin, he thought. An operation like this and he has to fuck it up with his cooking. Wotter recalled a barbecue at Solwin's house the summer the lieutenant had assumed command of the 13th. Solwin proudly served his specialty, marinated lamb shish kebob. Strangely enough, it wasn't too bad—actually it was delicious—Wotter recalled, but it had given him the worst case of the shits he'd had since Vietnam. With the exception of Pete DiCerrechia, everyone who attended the barbecue had become ill, even the lieutenant and his wife. Mrs. Solwin had become so sick that she couldn't teach at Columbus for a full two weeks. Solwin was still paying dearly for that creation.

Pete DiCerrechia, on the other hand, ate plenty of shish kebob and devoured huge portions of the tasty, fluffy rice that accompanied it. But Pete declined to wash down the repast with Solwin's special champagne punch, declining because he had added a special mystery ingredient: four ounces of a clear liquid that he had obtained from his brother-in-law who was a gamekeeper at the Bronx Zoo. Petey had added a deer laxative concentrate to the champagne punch.

A little extra zing, he had said to himself as he furtively poured it in, thinking of his brother-in-law's words: "Be careful, Pete, that stuff can dissolve bricks, and there's enough there to clean out an entire herd."

Wotter looked at Jassy whose gyrations were sufficient to even cause Paulie and Blaze to stop eating.

"What the fuck is the matter with you?" Paulie said.

Jassy, now unable to speak, just pointed to his mouth.

"What the fuck's the matter, Tom?" Blaze chimed in.

"Looks like he burned his mouth," Wotter said in a tone devoid of emotion.

Wotter couldn't trust himself to look at Solwin, so he watched his golf partners. When he saw Paulie and Blaze's puzzled looks, he almost burst out laughing.

Solwin pictured his entire investigation being blown and being reassigned to community relations in Bed Sty. He couldn't understand what had happened. Surely the frank was not hot enough to make Jassy apoplectic. Solwin, debating whether to call an ambulance, thought of the chili. He dipped a spoon into the mixture, turned, and tasted. Even Solwin, who had a high tolerance for hot spicy food, had never experienced anything like this. As he popped a beer then took a long pull, he thought, Lava couldn't be any hotter.

Sergeant Driscoll, who was videotaping the whole scene, took a good look at Solwin's sheepish face and figured out that the lieutenant had fucked up the chili.

After a few more minutes, when Jassy was able to breathe, he walked over and began to scream at Solwin. "What the fuck are you trying to do, kill me, you fuckin' rat bastid?"

Wotter walked over. Grabbing Paulie by the arm, he said, "Chill this, asshole, and let's get going."

Paulie, nodding, walked over to Tommy and put one of his hands on each side of the man's bulging neck and whispered, "Shut the fuck up."

Tommy became indignant and tried to explain, but Paulie cut him off and then walked with Wotter toward the men's outhouse.

Tommy and Blaze stood together watching the door.

Inside, one of the technicians whispered to Driscoll, "What's that all about?"

"Nothing," Driscoll whispered in reply, "just one of the skells bitching about his hamburger."

"Which reminds me," the technician whispered, "I'm gettin' hungry."

Sergeant Driscoll said reassuringly, "As soon as they leave, we'll get something to eat."

The technicians started picking up and recording the voice of Paulie counting the money. When he finished they heard him say, "Okay, Billy, let's get going."

"I'll catch you outside after I take a shit," Wotter said as he entered the far commode. When Paulie left, Driscoll, whispering through the wall, briefed Wotter on the change of plans and told him that Blatt was setting up near the fourteenth green.

Solwin watched Paulie come out of the outhouse and join Blaze and Tommy. In a few minutes Wotter came out and looked at him. The lieutenant could tell that Wotter was thinking, trying to come up with a plan.

When the four golfers started to leave, Tommy Jassy turned to Solwin and gave him the finger. Not getting any reaction, he grabbed his balls with his right fist and yelled, "Your mother eats here tonight."

Solwin reddened but held himself in check, and Wotter turned to Paulie, saying under his breath, "You'd better muzzle this asshole or I'm goin' straight home." Paulie, losing control, grabbed a three iron from his golf bag and charged Tommy when Blaze jumped in.

"Paul, we are going to attract attention," he said. "We ain't goin' to look like businessmen, ya know."

Paulie stopped short and Tommy, cowed by Paulie's actions, just stood meekly by and apologized. Wotter conferred with Paulie and they agreed to at least start the back nine.

As they walked over to the tenth tee, Solwin called for a replacement. Soon a sergeant from the Four Five in plain clothes arrived and Solwin left.

"All clear," the sergeant announced over the four empty stools in front of him, and the three policemen exited the ladies' room.

"I'm starvin'," one of the men announced. "Say, Sarge, did you say one the skells complained about the burgers?"

Driscoll, who had just locked the door, nodded yes.

The man looked at the menu. "Gimme a chili dog with onions," he said.

"Make that two," the other technician said.

"Beer here," Driscoll said, sitting down to watch the fun begin.

"Two chili dogs comin' right up," the retired sergeant said while the technicians smiled and relaxed.

Wotter had no trouble convincing the rest of the foursome to consummate the transaction just to the right of the fourteenth green. Just behind a large sand bunker Wotter exchanged his money belt for a plastic bag of Chinese Rock #3. Wotter opened the bag and tested the contents with a chemical kit. Satisfied with the color change, he stuffed the plastic bag into a zippered compartment of his golf bag. Paulie put the money belt into his golf bag and the smiling group walked back onto the green.

Just before Paulie the Brain putted, he looked up to see three golf carts with two golfers each searching for lost balls. He turned to Wotter, Blaze, and Tommy Jassy, cursing the intruders who destroyed his concentration.

"Hey, Paul, don't worry, concentrate," Jassy said.

"What the fuck do you think I'm trying to do?" Paulie said.

He grasped the putter and took a deep breath. Having read the green and anticipating a roll to his left, he drew back and putted with a smooth followthrough. The ball, which was squarely hit, followed the intended path and plopped into the hole. The putt had been just under thirty feet and Paulie was delighted. When he looked up after retrieving his ball, he noticed that the three golf carts with the six men were now at different points around the green.

"Nice putt," one of the men said.

"Thanks," Paulie replied.

Suddenly, as if on cue, the six men surrounding the green drew guns and yelled freeze.

Paulie, who carried a .25 automatic in his waistband in the small of his back, instinctively reached. He felt his hand grabbed and the hard barrel of a gun in his back.

He was disarmed, and soon police swarmed all over the green

from the woods at the side of the fairway. Paulie was handcuffed from behind, then turned around to face William Wotter, who advised him of his rights. At that Paulie had a coronary and fell face forward on the green.

Tommy Jassy had never felt so out of control in his life. While he was being handcuffed he saw Wotter reading the Miranda warnings to Paulie and realized Wotter was a cop. When Paulie fell, Tommy Jassy shit his pants.

Strangely enough, Blaze Squerente was the coolest of all, but when he was being led away he vomited on the fairway and standing there with his hands cuffed behind his back, he turned to Wotter, "I'm gonna get you, my friend," he said with a smile.

The police officers huddled around him and Solwin watched as Sergeant Driscoll lined up and kicked Blaze square in his balls. Blaze lay writhing on the golf course as an ambulance sped up to the clubhouse to take Paulie to the hospital. As Paulie was loaded on a stretcher and placed in the ambulance, the attendant shook his head. Paulie the Brain was no more.

An hour later Alcibiades LoConti, summoned from his home on his day off, met Jimmy Farrell and the men of the 13th outside Paulie's apartment. Jimmy was armed with a search warrant and the police broke down the door to the empty apartment. After three hours they left the apartment in a shambles, having found neither money nor drugs. While looking through Paulie's telephone book for the names of likely connections, Al yelled "Bingo!"

He recognized the name of one of the Admiral's soldiers, a name that had come up during the investigation into the death of Mickey Varino, the name of Carlo Ogdalente.

"I'll bet my dick that this is the fuckin' connection," Al said. "He's into every crooked fuckin' racket in the Bronx."

"I never even heard of him," Solwin said.

"He's known by the American version of his name," Al answered.

"What's that?"

"Charlie Oakdale," Al answered.

"Holy shit, not Charlie Oakdale . . . the Plant?"

"The one and only," Al said.

"Why do they call him the Plant?" Ruella asked.

"Because according to his friends, after you know him for a while . . . he starts to grow on ya," Solwin said. "And he is going to take us right up the ladder to the very top rung . . . to Mr. Guido Insalata, the Admiral himself."

THE VERY NEXT DAY as the men of the elite 13th Narcotics Group began an investigation into Charlie "the Plant" Oakdale. Al waited for a team of detectives who were scheduled to interview some witnesses in the Martha Valles's murder case. During the intervening months, despite enormous pressure from the Hat and even some members of the Homicide Bureau, Al had steadfastly refused to lock up Carleton, Martha's young police officer lover. Al just didn't think the evidence to date was legally sufficient. And the stalemate extended to his other cases.

Months after the discovery of the legless, defrosting body, the so-called legs case investigation had yielded little more than the fact that the trunk did indeed belong to the pair of legs previously found and that death was caused by asphyxiation due to strangulation. The deceased's age was placed between fifty and fifty-five, and her race Caucasian. She had died within hours of the time her legs were found. An extensive media blitz following the discovery of the body had produced hundreds of thousands of calls, but to date all those followed had always led to blind alleys. Still there was a weekly ad asking that anyone who knew of a white female, between fifty and fifty-five, last seen around September 1970, to please call the special police number, 999-1000.

Police monitors were required to fill out a call fact sheet for each and every call, regardless of their opinion of the caller's sanity. So even calls saying that people had been taken to the moon and Venus were duly recorded.

Pete DiCerrechia had monitored a stack of these calls to separate out all those regarding kidnappers from outer space. After assigning case numbers to all these calls, he routed them through the Mayor's office to the Commissioner of Investigation and the Housing police. "I love to break fuckin' balls," Pete said.

Rory O'Donnell, Pete DiCerrechia, and Timmy Flanagan gathered to assist in the investigation into the death of Martha Valles. Timmy and his partner, Morrie Shapiro, had the best informant network in the Bronx, yet they had turned up nothing. They were zeroing in on Carleton and thought they had enough to lock him up. The detectives walked into Al's office, greeted him and had coffee. The legs case was the first to be reviewed.

Pete showed Al that, of the thousands of calls received, there were only thirty-five left that he felt were viable. Of these, seven were from outside the City of New York and three of the seven were outside the state. Pete was in the process of personally following up on the thirty-five calls.

O'Donnell pulled out a flask, poured a shot into his coffee, and took a long sip. He seemed somewhat distant today, and Al sensed that something might be wrong.

Rory looked terrible. His face was broken out in red blotches. He's still got the ever-present war with his ex-wives, Al thought. He's killin' himself with the booze.

There were absolutely no leads on the old lady cases.

"Johnny O'Boyle feels that this guy has killed more than just the old ladies," Al said.

"Who knows?" Morrie Shapiro shrugged.

"Well, we got a list of old homicides. Maybe you guys should go through all the unsolved Bronx homicides say for five years and see if you spot any common threads."

"Hey, Al, that's a lifetime hobby." Timmy said. Timmy had been drinking too.

"Just do it, okay?" Al ordered. "Let's go see the witness in the Martha Valles's case."

Al and the detectives drove to a diner just off the Harlem River on the Bronx side. It was one of those old aluminum types that predated World War II. Al had never even noticed it before.

It had a long empty counter running down its length. Booths across from the counter were jammed with customers. More people came in and the counter started to fill up as Flanagan grabbed five stools at the end and motioned for Al to sit next to him. Behind the counter middle-age men cooked quickly at six large grills. All of them looked like heavy drinkers.

"This place is owned by two retired sergeants from the Four One. All the cooks are ex-cops. The trade is mostly breakfast. The cooks like the ice cubes a little too much," Flanagan said.

"Rory is gonna apply for a job here soon," Pete DiCerrechia said as he sat next to Al. O'Donnell grabbed the next stool.

A man walked down to where they sat and asked what they wanted. "Just send us Gladys, okay Bernie, it's too early in the mornin' to look at your ugly puss," Timmy said, chuckling.

The man walked back and a waitress came over. "Hey, Timmy, how are ya?"

"Fine, Gladys, yourself?"

"No complaints, Timmy, not that it would do any good if I did complain."

When Timmy introduced her to him, Al thought it seemed like she was expecting to see an ADA. Then they ordered breakfast, Gladys writing their orders on a scratch pad and putting the pad in front of the grill man on the end grill. He broke eggs, then fried and scrambled them while turning mounds of breakfast sausages and ham and bacon and flipping patties of corned beef hash.

Gladys went down the aisle serving other patrons at the counter. Soon she came back and placed four long breakfast dishes in front of Timmy's entourage and the men began to eat.

While Al sipped his coffee and chewed bacon and eggs, Flanagan motioned for Gladys. "Tell us what you know about the dead hairdresser that was the cop's girl."

"I told you all I know is what I hear."

"What do you hear?"

"I hear that the cop shot her."

"Why'd he shoot her?"

"Because they had a fight about his kid. Cop lost his temper and shot her."

"Who told you this?" Al asked.

Gladys leaned over the counter. "Like I told Timmy, I overhear the cops who come in hear. They talk, you know. I can't help but overhear it."

"Do you know which cops said this?"

"No, I don't know anyone's name. Heard a lot of guys say it though."

"Could you pick them out?" Al asked.

"No, I couldn't tell if I recognized them from sayin' this or just from bein' here. You know you hear things, you don't stare at the face of the guy whose talkin'."

Al stared at Flanagan. All Gladys could give them was useless hearsay.

"DA's gonna put you in the Grand Jury, Gladys, even though you got the most beautiful ass in the Bronx . . . unless of course you give us some names," Flanagan said, smiling.

"Do what you gotta do, Tim," she said angrily.

"We're gonna do just that, Gladys. You're bullshittin' me and you are gonna go for perjury or contempt," Timmy threatened.

Gladys turned around toward the counterman and bent over from the waist and let out a long raspy fart.

"Up your giggy with a meat hook, Timmy," she said, walking away, down the counter.

Flanagan, nonplussed, continued eating.

"I bet you hope she don't do that in the grand jury, Al," DiCerrechia said, laughing at Flanagan.

Al had stopped eating. The counter was noisy with the talk of the truck drivers and policemen.

A bag lady entered, her feet and legs swathed in rags. She was wearing a filthy brown cloth coat, her face was streaked with dirt, and her hair hung gray, greasy, and matted. Her body emitted terrible odors as she walked down the length of the counter, and the diners looked at her and then quickly looked away.

"Anyone got a dollar please?" she begged. "Anyone got a lousy fuckin' dollar?"

No one paid her any attention. She reached the end of the counter and started back up again. "Please someone let me have a dollar," she wailed, "just one little dollar."

The owner came out from the back. "Rosie, get the fuck outta here. Don't bother my customers."

"Just a dollar," she begged one more time.

Pete DiCerrechia, pissed off at Flanagan for using Al as a prop, noticed that Al had stopped eating and Rory was just drinking what remained of his flask. Only Flanagan was still munching away as Pete DiCerrecchia turned to the bag lady.

Taking a bill from his wallet and holding it aloft, he shouted, "Hey, Rosie, I got a twenty here for you."

All of the patrons stopped eating. Pete had everyone's attention as the bag lady turned and looked at the bill and started to run towards him.

Pete held his hand out palm first. "Not so fast, Rosie, first you gotta do something for me," he said loudly.

"What you want me to do, man?" Rosie asked.

Pete paused for dramatic effect while everyone waited. "Show us your pussy," Pete yelled.

Rosie dropped the shopping bag and hiked up her dress. She was wearing no underwear and the stench was overpowering. As she turned around and started to walk up the counter, Al ran out behind O'Donnell. There was a stampede to the exits as Pete DiCerrecchia handed the bag lady the twenty just before sprinting out the diner's front door.

30

IT WAS DEWEY MULLIGAN'S old man's gun and it was a real thing of beauty. Its owner, Dewey Mulligan's old man, who was in fact very old, was one of those unusually fascinating people that you would meet from time to time in Bronx County. His name was Sean Mulligan, and though any New Yorker listening to him would have thought that he had emigrated from Ireland, he had in fact been born in Queensland, Australia, in 1897, and he had acquired this gun when he was only eighteen years old, a member of the Australian forces fighting in the Dardanelles at Gallipoli in 1915.

When the Anzac forces and the British and French withdrew, Sean Mulligan had been posted to fight in France, and after the cessation of hostilities and because of his many decorations for valor, he was permitted to take his discharge in France and then emigrate to Liverpool, England.

From there he emigrated to America where he became a master machinist with the New York Central Railroad. In 1950, at the age of fifty-three, he married a twenty-year-old nurse from Ireland who would become the mother of three daughters and also a son, Dewey, the only friend of Ronald DePew.

Sean Mulligan had smuggled his .303 British Enfield rifle with him through France to England and to the United States. Over the years in his spare time he had customized the stock by stripping it down to the bare wood and then had built up fine layer upon fine layer of linspeed oil until the wooden grain stood out in a glistening brilliance. He had replaced the old 303 barrel with a custom-made .222 chromed beauty, embedded it in a fiberglass base, and sighted it in with a Redfield scope so that it was dead on at 250 yards.

Sean took both his son Dewey and Ronald DePew upstate New York to hunt woodchucks on a retired friend's farm. Sean couldn't believe how well the army had trained DePew, for Sean had never seen such a crack shot in all his military career.

On the same day that Dewey Mulligan's old man's gun went missing, Anselm the accountant from Burke Avenue on the IRT line was standing near the garbage pail on the subway platform waiting for the guys from the night shift to drop off the *Daily News*. Anselm always saved money by picking someone's paper from the garbage and everyone who knew cheap Anselm always had the same nice things to say about him, nice things like he was so tight that when he walked his ass squeaked, and that he wouldn't give a dying bird a drink of water.

Today after retrieving a *Daily News* from the garbage can, Anselm boarded an IRT downtown express and took the last empty seat in the car.

Margaret McPort, a petite blonde with long, dead straight hippie hair hanging down past her waist, boarded the IRT at Pelham Parkway enroute with her two children to her mother's house in Bay Ridge, Brooklyn. It was going to be a very long train ride for Margaret and the kids. Although she stood right in front of Cheap Anselm holding her two-year-old Ruth by one hand while the six-month-old baby Dolores lay sleeping in a papoose, backpack hanging between her shoulder blades, Anselm would not get up and give her his seat.

Dewey Mulligan's old man's Enfield lay cradled in the arms of Ronald DePew lying in the U.S. army prone shooting position on the roof of an apartment house only 150 yards from the back of Margaret McPort's head. Ronald sighted the long blond hair through the scope, then set the crosshairs on the forehead of the baby asleep in the papoose backpack as the train slowly started out of the station. Ronald had been waiting for just this target of opportunity.

Then abruptly the train stopped, due to a signal change and a backup from the next station, Bronx Park East, and Ronald relaxed.

While the train was stopped Ronald practiced snapping the rifle to his shoulder, centering the crosshairs on Margaret's head, and then on the baby's head. Ronald didn't know if he could kill both the mother and the child and decided that the first head that sat in the crosshairs was the one that would be blown off.

The safety was off as Ronald pictured the baby's head being blown into pieces like the skull of a woodchuck struck by the hot lead of the .222.

As the train started Ronald snapped the rifle's stock hard onto his shoulder and brought the crosshairs to bear on the neck of the sleeping child, and then while slowly tracking the target, began to squeeze the trigger.

The train lurched forward, halted, and started again and the jerk of the sudden second start sent two-year-old Ruth sprawling from her mother's hands onto the floor.

As Margaret McPort kneeled to pick up her daughter, the bullet cracked through the open window, through the top of her hair, through the purloined copy of the *Daily News*, and into the left eye of Anselm the accountant.

Even though Anselm was dead instantly, his body still jerked for a full thirty seconds, just like anyone who is head shot by a high-powered round. The twisting spasms that rocked the body made it jerk onto the seat and onto the floor while the blood poured from the open hole. The train jerked again and then pulled out, picking up speed while the car passengers shrieked.

Even before Anselm's body stopped twitching Ronald DePew had bolted from the roof, leaving standing next to the parapet in all its beauty, Dewey Mulligan's old man's gun.

IN THE INTERVENING MONTHS up to July 3, 1974, the reports in John O'Boyle's office from the police activities contained nothing new for Al LoConti, no connections to the legs case, the case involving Martha Valles, or the serial killer.

The cases against Chaparral had been abated by the filing of a death certificate. Then the court folder was sent to the catacombs of the filing room, just as a twist of fate had sent the defendant into the earth.

Al, thinking of the 13th's ascension up the ladder to Charlie Oakdale and then to the Admiral, entered the courtroom of Part 12 with eight case folders in his arms. Today Alicia Endicott and Octavio Rolezon would be sentenced and Adian Bard and the Serquez brothers, who were also charged with murder, were going to fold. It was going to be real sweet for Al to watch Bard finally go away.

Years ago it had been Bard's case, before Judge Samuel Flay— Mr. Judicial Notice—that had caused Al such humiliation and heartache. Today his spirits were lifted. He even forgot his bitterness toward his ex-wife, his hatred of the one hundred mile round trip to see his children, and the hypocrisy of the system he served, because today would be payback time. And as Al walked into the courtroom, he couldn't help smiling at the slogan running through his mind, a slogan born in the smell of flaming napalm, of obliterated villages, of rotting Vietnamese corpses: Payback is a bitch.

And for those victims, those dead souls whose names appeared on the autopsy reports in Al LoConti's case folders, perhaps today might be payback time. For he knew that the only one in Part 12 who would think of them, who would be conscious of the horror of their deaths, would be thirty-year-old Alcibiades LoConti.

He sat in the jury box next to Hanratty as Judge O'Neill took the bench. There were nine other DAs seated in the jury box, all with cases on today, and they watched Hornbein and Torres, assigned to the Part for the month, walking and pushing a cart with the bulk of the 130 cases on the calendar.

As the routine humdrum of the calendar call and the pro forma applications proceeded, Al thought back to the night he had been called on the case involving Alicia Endicott.

It had been almost nine months ago and one of those nights of routine horror ameliorated solely by the fact that there were no mysteries. All the loose ends had been tied up before the tour had ended, and so from a strictly professional point of view it had been a very good night.

It started with Al being called to a homicide at 174th Street and Boston Road.

"Bronx Divorce, they got the perp on the scene. Detectives Denny McVeigh and Elrod Harrison. That's all I got," the DA desk caller had relayed, giving Al the address and apartment number. Twenty minutes later he had arrived and walked into the apartment house and upstairs to the crime scene.

He remembered identifying himself just before walking into a foyer and seeing Detective Elrod Harrison, who motioned him down a long hallway.

Now seated in Part 12, Al relived that night as if he were there again, as if he had been returned to the last place, seen alive by Mr. Endicott.

Al remembered spotting McVeigh inside the living room seated on a red couch talking to an elegantly dressed black woman in her mid-forties. A young black male, about seventeen, sat next to the woman staring straight ahead. As Al was walking past the living room, his eye caught a curious piece of sculpture on top of the TV console. It truly was a grotesque work of art.

Harrison entered a bedroom at the end of the hall.

"This is Mr. Endicott, Al," he said pointing to the floor.

Al observed a body on the far side of the room lying on the floor next to the bed. Shoeless feet pointed towards Al as he walked into the room, stopping next to an enormous pool of blood. The entire chest of the deceased was blood-matted and his blue shirt was a tattered, blood-encrusted, shredded pulpy mass. A long-bladed carving knife, a meat cleaver, and a hacksaw blade lay arranged neatly side by side on the bed. Al shifted two steps to his right so as to see beyond the bed and above the dead man's chest.

What he saw caused his stomach to roll. It rolled again and he tasted the coffee and then the garlic and the oil from his supper. Suddenly feeling cold and clammy, he knew what the grotesque art object on top of the TV was, for Mr. Endicott's body had no head. Al quickly examined the body and then stared at the hands, then turned suddenly fighting not to retch. The fingers had been hacked off.

Harrison began to report. "Mr. Endicott was a hard-working stiff, track repairman. Mrs. Endicott, who's inside with Detective McVeigh, was married to Mr. Endicott's brother. The brother died about ten years ago. She's a sharp piece of work. Has a good job as a secretary with a big insurance outfit. She married Mr. Endicott here about nine years ago. Boy inside is his nephew." Harrison inclined his head. "The kid is eighteen, still in school. Seems like Mr. Endicott was a good guy, a good provider. Boy's a little bit of a sissy. Mr. Endicott kind of picked on the boy. Been pickin' on the boy for quite some time—at least that's what Mrs. Endicott says, and I have no reason to doubt her. Well, Mr. Endicott is workin' a night shift fixin' track on the IRT and he gets home early this mornin', around four A.M. Boy is up and readin' one of these weight-liftin' magazines—you know, with all the muscles showin'—and Mr. Endicott, well, he gets the wrong idea, or"—Harrison paused—"maybe the right idea, and he starts to yell at the boy, insulting him, calls him a fag and says he's a disgrace to his father and to the family and slaps the kid around. Mrs. Endicott wakes up and butts in and they get into it. It ends by him tellin' her to go fuck herself, and he goes into the bathroom to take a shower.

"She goes into the kitchen and makes a concoction of lye and

Vaseline in a saucepan, then goes into the bedroom with the saucepan in one hand and that knife in the other. When Mr. Endicott comes out of the shower wearing his pajamas, he sits on the bed and begins dryin' his feet with his back to her. She comes in the room and calls to him and when he turns she flings the shit in his eyes. He grabs his eyes and she stabs him in the chest. He falls on the floor and is screaming bloody murder from the pain of his eyes burning out. About ten or fifteen neighbors call 911. He's screaming and writhing on the floor, and she's stepping around him and bending down and stabbing and stabbing until he stops moving. She then gets the cleaver and starts to hack off his head, but it's tough work so she goes and gets the hacksaw to finish the job and after his head is off she saws and cleaves off the guy's fingers and makes the nice little arrangement on top of the TV."

"Yeah, I saw it. I thought it was a fuckin' sculpture or something," Al had said.

Harrison continued. "Anyway, when we got here the first officer and his partner had already arrived."

Harrison smiled. "The first officer was supposed to be the driver. But he was a little sick to his stomach at the start of the tour of duty so they switched, and when the poor kid gets here Mrs. Endicott lets him in and tells him she was just about to call. She is smiling and polite, a very cultured lady."

Al raised his eyes and Harrison went on. "She shows him the decor you saw in the living room and brings him in here and shows him the remains. The kid doesn't know whether to shit, go blind, or advise her of her rights, but he tries not to puke and reads her the rights and she tells him what happened. He doesn't ask any questions and after she finishes me and McVeigh get here. First officer tells me inside what happened and what she says, and we advise her of her rights and she tells me what I've told you."

Al had suspected the son but the police investigation had already cleared the boy. When they went back into the living room, Al averted his eyes from the TV. McVeigh introduced Al to Mrs. Endicott, and she was extremely formal in offering her hand outstretched and palm down. Al took it and shook it briefly.

I ain't gonna kiss it, he thought.

Al advised Mrs. Endicott of her rights. She nodded eagerly after being told each one. After he asked her if she would speak to him without a lawyer being present, Mrs. Endicott said, "I told these gentlemen what happened. I see no harm in telling you."

"Okay, Mrs. Endicott, I'll call a stenographer who will take down everything that is said between us. We will now go to the police station. Is that okay with you?" Al had asked.

"Yes, that will be fine. Are we departing now?"

"Yes."

"Before we depart, may I brew you gentlemen a pot of coffee or some other refreshment?" Her smile beamed.

The detectives, the uniformed officers, and Al all thought of the lye and Vaseline mixture in the saucepan.

"No, thanks," they said very loudly and in flawless unison.

Other detectives arrived to preserve the scene for the ME while Forensic still worked. Fifteen minutes later they had arrived at the Four Eight precinct and Al set up in front of the steno. Mrs. Endicott was again advised of her rights and was told she was under arrest for the murder of her husband. Then she related the events exactly as she told them to Harrison. When asked if she was afraid of her husband, she replied no. Al then established that she and her son could have fled the apartment while the deceased was taking a shower. Self-defense was now out the window.

Al asked her if she had bloodstains on her clothes. She replied that she was covered in blood, but she had put on her husband's wet gear before she started stabbing him and when he finally died she threw it into the closet then scoured her hands and arms.

"Did you think about killing your husband before tonight, Mrs. Endicott?" Al had asked.

"Very often."

"And did you formulate a plan to kill him?"

"Yes, I most certainly did."

"Did you actually follow that plan in killing him?"

"To the letter." She smiled.

Al had sat back in thought. There goes the defense of extreme emotional disturbance and reduction to Man One.

"Would you like to add anything to this statement, Mrs. Endicott?"

The steno, the detectives, and Al looked expectantly at the defendant while she was thinking and finally she answered.

"The only thing I have to add is that he picked on my son enough and his time had come." She smiled calmly and the statement was concluded. As Mrs. Endicott was led away for booking, Al couldn't help thinking that the case was a lock.

The clerk's Bronx accent snapped Al back to the present.

"*People* versus *Alicia Endicott*. Defendant represented by Joseph Casossa. ADA LoConti's case."

Al stepped up and nodded to Joey Casossa, who represented the bright end of the spectrum of attorneys in the Bronx. Joey was a well-respected lawyer. The ass end of the spectrum was represented by the lawyer for another of Al's cases on today's calendar, Octavio Rolezon. His lawyer was the one and only Quiet Marvin.

Court officers led Alicia Endicott out from the pens wearing a loose-fitting gray dress and sneakers. She had become totally institutionalized, Al thought.

Turning to Al, she smiled and gave out a cheery "Good morning, Mr. LoConti." Al smiled back and nodded. To himself he thought, What a fucking loony tune, but at least she's not offering me anything to drink. Imagine this one puttin' out her husband's fuckin' eyes and slicing the poor bastard up like some roast and then offerin' us a drink.

Al had given Mrs. Endicott a Manslaughter Two plea and recommended that the maximum sentence, five to fifteen years, be imposed.

Joey Casossa had put in a long pitch for leniency. Judge O'Neill had only made up his mind that morning.

"Do you have anything to say, Mrs. Endicott, before sentence is pronounced?" the clerk asked.

"No, sir," Mrs. Endicott answered softly, her eyes cast down.

O'Neill whacked her with five to fifteen and as she was led out, Joey Casossa left and the clerk called the next case.

Al sat back in the jury box waiting for the Rolezon case. Quiet Marvin was seated in the front row for attorneys, and he waved to Al like a long-lost friend. Al nodded back. He hated Quiet Marvin.

The clerk continued calling the cases while Al sat and watched the boring proceedings. He knew what the lawyers would say even before they opened their mouths.

He started to plan this weekend's activities with his children, then he glanced down at the Rolezon folder and his attention snapped back to it. Unlike the Endicott case, Rolezon was barely two months old, a rare unaged matter in the criminal justice system.

Quiet fuckin' Marvin probably got a small retainer, Al thought, so he's dumping it as fast as he can.

Al remembered the day of the Rolezon murder, a day of unusually heavy rain in the Bronx. Rain had flooded the streets, washing the city's grime and litter down the sewers, and a day where circumstances had flushed Octavio Rolezon into the sitting room of the Three Four in Manhattan after he killed the young mother in Bronx County.

The Clerk droned on and on, and Al's memory slipped back to the day he had arrived at the murder scene. . . .

He had pushed past the throng of detectives speaking Spanish to people on the third floor just outside the apartment, then he walked through the door to be met by Pete DiCerrechia. They walked down a long narrow foyer into a living room where Al spotted two altars on the far side of the room. One of them had the Virgin Mary surrounded by candles and the other a saint that Al did not recognize. Both altars had cigars and strange reedlike fronds that were not at all like the palms Al saw on Palm Sunday. DiCerrechia noticed the puzzled look on Al's face.

"That's some Caribbean goddess. They got a religion that's a mixture of pagan saints and Catholicism," Pete said.

"Is it fuckin' voodoo?" Al asked.

"Somethin' like it," Pete answered, "but it ain't got nothin' to do with this case."

The apartment reeked of incense, and right between the two altars stood an easy chair. There sat the woman with her head slumped onto her left shoulder and her eyes shut tight.

On Al's right was a kitchen where two little girls sat at a table tended by Ruella Watkins and Detective Carl Gutierrez. Ruella spoke softly to the little girls and Al guessed one to be about his daughter's age, no more than four, and the other was probably seven.

Standing next to Al, Pete inclined his head toward the chair and said, "Mom is there." Then he commenced to narrate the facts. "The deceased's husband is in the wind. Her brother lives in Patchogue and is coming in to pick up the kids. Brother is a hard-workin', stand-up guy. Stopped in twice a week to check on sis and the kids. Kids aren't witnesses."

Al's eyebrows went up.

"No shit, Al, they were upstairs with a neighbor."

"What else?"

"DOA worked as a barmaid over on 145th and St. Nick. We made an arrest. Older guy. Took her out a couple of times. He's got a clean sheet. Mid-fifties. Has a Superette in the barrio. Does a little numbers, boli pol, small fry. Anyway, a few hours ago he walks into the Three Four in Manhattan. No one is on the desk so he walks into the sitting room. Two cops are on meal." Pete checked his notes. "Mancuso and Morales. They're the only cops in sight. He walks up to them. It's six in the morning. They're doin' a twelve to eight. Perp takes out the gun. Mancuso is eatin' a sausage and egg hero, he sees the gun in the perp's hand, goes ga-ga, and inhales the hero." Pete chuckled.

"They had to rush him to Jewish Memorial to do a tracheotomy. He almost didn't make it. Morales is a sharp kid. He sees the guy is givin' up the gun, so he grabs the piece and searches the guy. Guy's name is Octavio Rolezon. Tells the cops there was an accident. His girlfriend was shot with the gun and is dead. He gives this address. Morales calls the Four Four. And here we are. We pick the guy up and he tells us that he took the gun out and it went off by accident. He says he was across the room when it went off. One shot. Hit the girl in the heart. Says he was confused and ran out. Then he thought about it and walked back to Manhattan and turned himself in."

"In this fuckin' rain?" Al whispered.

"I asked the same question," Pete responded, "but the guy was wetter than a bag of shit in the Bronx River."

The woman in the chair was naked from the waist up. She had a small hole in her chest on the left side, which forensic was photographing when the ME walked in. After looking at her for a few minutes, he pronounced, "One in the heart."

"Very perceptive," Pete whispered to Al. "When Rory needs a liver transplant, I'm goin' to refer him to this ME."

Al shook his head. Pete didn't know when to stop, he even joked at funerals.

Carl Gutierrez, a true legend in the department, had joined them. Carl had over twenty years on the job, had been a paratrooper in World War II, and had a degree in Criminal Justice and now taught ballistics and forensic science in the academy.

He quietly gave orders to the forensic team, which always used up all its film when Carl Gutierrez caught a case.

Gutierrez motioned towards the body and pointed to black dots on the chest near the wound. "See those marks, Al?" he asked.

"Yes, Carl. They're powder burns, right?"

"Not really. They're called stipling, and they're caused by the discharge of a weapon at close quarters. I'd guess that since the deceased was shot with a .357 Magnum, that this shot came from about three inches away. Since we have the gun, we'll be able to match it to the slug in her body. Then we'll test-fire that gun at ballistics and determine exactly how far it was from her when she was shot. I can tell you now that he's lying through his teeth when he says he shot her from across the room and I'll make sure you'll have the ballistic evidence for the grand jury."

A detective Al had never met came into the room and whispered something in Pete DiCerrechia's ear.

"I was just informed," Pete said, "that Rolezon's lawyer showed up at the Four Eight. It's Quiet Marvin. There'll be no more statements."

As Al got ready to leave, he looked in the kitchen at the older girl, who stared resentfully back. Al read in the child's eyes all the shock and horror at her mother's death. He started toward her to comfort her, but she just glared with such defiance that he paused. Although Ruella was speaking softly to her, the girl was staring with such hatred that Al realized there was nothing he could do. Turning, he left. As he went down the stairs and back into the rain, he knew that no matter what he did with this case, it would not matter to that child. She knew better than all the cops and the DAs who tried to console her, who tried to show her sympathy and understanding—she knew that nothing really mattered because she would never be held by her mother again.

And that was why when the case came up Al took a hard line. The case for murder was still very weak, and at a meeting the members of the Homicide Bureau had agreed that the case was no more than a manslaughter two. Some DAs had suggested taking a plea to the gun charge only.

But Al had said it was reckless murder, and he knew he had enough for a prima facie case. And after two haggling sessions, Marvin took a plea to man one with no promises, trusting that Judge O'Neill would not hit his client with eight and a third to twenty-five. After all, Rolezon was fifty-four years old and was clean except for a few misdemeanor gambling collars.

Now Rolezon, Quiet Marvin, and Al waited to see what the judge would do. This was one of the few pleas where the length of the sentence was actually unknown until pronounced.

The case was called. Al announced that the DA's office took no position and that the court had adequate scope to deal with Mr. Rolezon within the parameters of the plea he had taken.

Marvin bullshitted for ten full minutes—long even for him. Al looked straight ahead and then glanced at Rolezon. His lips were compressed tight, bloodless, and his hands were shaking as the clerk asked him if he had anything to say.

"I'm sorry, your honor," Rolezon said in accented English.

Judge O'Neill, who hated Quiet Marvin, stuck it up Rolezon's ass.

"Five to twenty," O'Neill said. "You have a right to appeal, next case."

Just before Rolezon exited the courtroom flanked by the court officers, he started to curse at Quiet Marvin.

"You fock, you told me I wouldn't do more than five years. You fock. . . ." The door opened and closed.

Marvin ran out before Al had even sat down again.

After another hour the clerk came over to Al. Because Serquez and Bard had not been produced from the Bronx House of Detention, their cases went over to next week. It was almost lunchtime when Al walked back to his office. He nodded to Judge Samuel Flay, Mr. Judicial Notice, who was hurrying past Al to beat the crowd to the kosher deli. Al wanted to tell Flay that Bard was going to take a plea but said nothing, thinking that the pompous judge wouldn't even care.

Too bad I can't indict that fuck Flay for murder. If there was justice he would be accountable, Al thought as he entered his office.

Dave Hornbein, who was on trial, had ordered Al a brisket on rye. After pausing to think, of how much weight he had put on, Al wolfed down the sandwich and turned his thoughts to Bard and Flay.

It had been so humiliating then, he thought, but now after almost four years he could almost laugh at it—as everyone else still did whenever the story was told. Don't take yourself too seriously, LoConti, he thought. You're just another pebble on the beach. Why should you be spared bad luck and humiliation? Be happy that you made it back in one piece and not in a body bag.

As he reflected for the millionth time on the Bard case, he recalled the words of his uncle Peppy Gennaro. "When you're walking around with two loaves under each arm, you got nothin to cry about."

AFTER AL HAD CHASED the brisket sandwich down with a Diet Coke, he was joined by Hornbein who had started a hearing before Judge Flay. Hornbein was a little nervous. Although he was a good book man, able to flick case citations in court like a sharp Golden Glover throwing jabs, many members of the Homicide Bureau still felt that he was not a heavy hitter, like Johnny O'Boyle, Terry Hanratty, or Alcibiades LoConti, and that he lacked the killer instinct.

The fact that he managed to get into the bureau was testimony to the powers O'Boyle had assumed upon the retirement of the former Bureau chief, Sy Brasberg. O'Boyle himself had been promoted to the Chief's job over the heads of two old veteran trial assistants, Carmine Riccaldo and Maurice Slefner. They had virtually been the Homicide Bureau until the late sixties and always enjoyed the veto power over any new member. Johnny O'Boyle decided to override their veto, and Hornbein got into the bureau.

The defense bar hated and feared Riccaldo and Slefner, who were known as the Grand Inquisitors. They were men with a mission, unique since the ravages of time had no effect on the fervor with which they pursued their prey. They were indeed notorious. When dealing with them Judges even altered long-standing traditions of courtesy between the bench and bar, such as the unwritten rule of Appellate Courts never to mention the name of the individual prosecutor whose actions were the reason for a conviction being overturned. But when the prosecutor became infamous for outrageous conduct and the judges so exasperated at his continued transgressions, then printing his name was the only means they had to vent their boiling rage. Federal judges had much higher boiling points. Only twice in the last sixty years had they mentioned the names of Bronx district attorneys in their opinions. Carmine Riccaldo had been the first name mentioned.

In 1954, when Carmine had returned home from Korea after winning a Silver Star with the 2nd Division, he resumed his job as a Bronx DA. Carmine, who was also a World War II vet, was then thirty-four years old. A month later he had responded to the Four Four, where a youth had been arrested for a particularly heinous rape-murder. The youth's uncle was a lieutenant in the One Thirteen in Queens so the young man had not been beaten before Carmine's arrival. On the advice of his uncle, the youth refused to make a statement.

When Carmine arrived at the stationhouse, he ordered the uncle out of the room. When the uncle refused, Carmine called the police commissioner and had the uncle arrested for obstruction of justice. The police lieutenant, in full uniform, screamed his lungs out when the cell door banged shut. Even though Carmine had treated the youth with kid gloves, he had still refused to talk. Carmine finally got around to asking the youth if he would like to speak with a priest. Having been in the stationhouse for fourteen hours, the boy asked if he could be taken to confession. Carmine agreed. Detectives took him over to St. Nicholas of Tolentine and ushered him handcuffed into a confessional. He was told in the sanctity of the confessional that his penance was to confess to the police. After arriving back at the Four Four, he confessed his crimes for the second time that night to Carmine. Carmine, pretending to be a priest, had entered the confessional moments before the youth's arrival. The deception would never have been discovered had not one of the detectives decided to blab on the QT to the defense attorney. The Court of Appeals commuted the death sentence to life imprisonment. The Federal Appellate Court had sustained the conviction, but one of the dissenting justices, Judge Tiernan, had castigated Carmine in his opinion, naming him some fourteen times in a twelve-page dissent. And although Carmine had established a record, he would always claim that the judge was related to the defendant, whose name was also Tiernan. Maurice Slefner had had an even greater honor—he had been named in an opinion by the Supreme Court of the United States.

Maurie had been a brilliant law student and had been drafted into the navy at the height of World War II. At the war's end Maurie finished law school, passed the bar, and became a DA in Bronx County. In 1949 another ex-sailor, Georgie Nastolden, threw a three-year-old girl off a five-story roof and told the cops to kiss his ass when they requested his version of the events. Georgie, a very tough cookie, still refused to talk after the cops beat him almost unconscious for two full days. Even the cops began to think that perhaps Georgie might be innocent, but Maurie Slefner thought otherwise. Maurie and a few cops, including the Hat, took ex-sailor Georgie for a voyage on a police launch out of City Island. As they cruised the Sound off Rodman's Neck, they handcuffed Georgie behind his back and tightly chained his legs together. As they chained Georgie to the anchor, he sneered and cursed them and called their bluff. It took two men to lift the anchor and hold it over the railing while Georgie still sat on the deck insulting the Hat's mother. When the Hat pushed the two men away from the rope holding the anchor, it descended very quickly into the depths below and a very surprised Georgie zipped right behind.

The men raised and lowered the anchor four times with Georgie attached. On the fourth time Georgie surfaced, gasped for air, and screamed that he did it. Events would prove that Georgie was in fact the real killer. Yet one of the Justices of the Supreme Court, again in a dissenting opinion, had equated Maurice's techniques to that of Torquemada.

It was said that Maurie claimed it was tough to convict the guilty, but convicting the innocent was a real challenge.

Maurie and Carmine, thinking Hornbein too soft-skinned, ignored him at Bureau meetings. But even though they truly liked Al LoConti, they never ceased to criticize him for being "a Hornbein" and not locking up the fucking cop who killed the hairdresser.

Now Hornbein, sitting across from Al LoConti, was very nervous and couldn't eat so he passed Al his pastrami on rye. Al took a bite.

"I like working with Flay," Hornbein said. "I had a hearing before him last week and now I have another one. Guy's a little eccentric but he's polite and I think that thing about taking Judicial Notice is just bullshit and a bum rap. Right, Al?"

Al sat back chewing. After swallowing he smiled and shook his head no. "I'll tell you all about Flay. Those two fucks, the Grand Inquisitors, should have clued you in a long time ago.

"Flay is being considered for Supreme Court." Al began. I ran into him four years ago in the Criminal Court where he had a bad rep. Terry Hanratty warned me about him, saying that Flay was a cheap fuck who would eat at Pete's—you know, the Ptomaine Room—until he got the shits for the fifth time. Then he switched to the other dump, Sid's Sandwich Center. Old Sam Flay had been out for three weeks and lost thirty pounds after a tongue on rye with cole slaw at Sid's. After checking samples of his various body fluids and stool samples, the lab technician at the Thomas Jefferson Medical Center had told the health commissioner that he felt that the bacteria in the mayonnaise in the cole slaw and in the tongue were probably enough to knock out all the police personnel in the entire Bronx. It was a miracle that Flay was still alive. Too bad the fuck didn't die."

Al took another bite and chewed. "Hanratty told me that it served Judge Flay, Mr. Judicial Notice, right. But you know, Terry, either he loves you or he has a hard-on for you, so I paid no attention. But I can tell you I found out the hard way how right he was. Judge Flay is a fuckin' live atom bomb."

"Why is he so dangerous?" Hornbein asked.

"There was a routine felony hearing on a rape case. It should have taken fifteen minutes and gone over to the Grand Jury."

"Yeah . . . so what happened?" Hornbein asked. Alcibiades Lo‑Conti told him. . . .

The story brought Al back to a day in November 1970, a day when he was still a believer in the system, still finding rewards in the work he performed, and a time when he still had his wife and children.

He had been in the backup hearing room known as Part 2A. This part had no daily calendar, and everyday cases were called in other Parts of the court and referred, that is sent into 2A when they were marked Ready. Part 2A was a real dream assignment.

Unfortunately some DAs used it for a dumping ground, and it was not unusual to receive a few uncorroborated rapes that had to be dismissed as a matter of law. Then you had to explain to a stricken, incredulous complainant that to sustain a prima facie, a bare bones, case of rape, each element—force, identity of the perpetrator and penetration—had to be corroborated by other than the complainant's testimony and while the force and penetration requirement could generally be supported by medical evidence, the identity requirement—that is, independent evidence to show that the rapist was in fact the person charged—could rarely be met. Simply speaking, rapes did not occur in public and hardened criminals did not make habits of confessing.

Judge DiGrande and Judge Conmy had both made Al's job easier by giving a little speech to the complainants explaining that in the current state of the law, Al had no choice but to dismiss based on the lack of corroboration. Al grew to hate the Assistant

DAs who used the dump method to avoid an unpleasant task. Yet Al never re-referred a case—he never sent a case back where it came from. On this day Al was unhappy to discover that the presiding jurist in Part 2A was none other than the eminent Samuel Flay. Al had never worked before Flay but he remembered hearing that the Judge was a cheap prick. Flay also had the reputation of treating all lawyers alike, whether they were DAs or defense attorneys. He was always rude, abrupt, and pompous. But Flay's fame and renown as a jurist stemmed from his taking judicial notice of things. Judicial Notice is a doctrine wherein proof does not have to be offered to show facts that are notorious. Thus the Judge by Judicially Noticing a fact dispenses with the obligation of one of the parties before him to prove that fact. It is a judicial short-cut.

Flay felt that because of his superior intellect he could judicially notice anything he thought he knew. Judicial Notice in New York is taken properly only of the laws of the state, the Federal and State Constitutions, and certain other notorious facts that either "everyone knows" or that can easily be ascertained by sources of indisputable accuracy. Examples of things Judicially Noticed are that day follows night; the time the sun rose and set on a particular day; the rotation of the seasons; that freezing stops decay; that dynamite is a dangerous substances; the use of telephones; that a sleigh has no wheels; and that hamburgers are popular menu items in the United States.

Defense lawyers were warned repeatedly by their brethren that old Sam would often use the Doctrine of Judicial Notice to supply a missing link in the DA's cases. And at the time he even took Judicial Notice of a fact which could never be proved.

Hanratty had told Al that old Sam was a loose cannon rolling around the deck and that many times he would hold cases for the Grand Jury that should have been tossed at the hearing stage for lack of evidence.

On this day Al stood in the well of the court alone with the court personnel and the stenographer. Old Sam, sitting in the robing room reading the *Daily News*, had sent word to the bridgeman to call him when the DA had two or three hearings ready to go.

The back door opened and Al was truly pleased to see his cousin Allie Boy Spano and Detective Elrod Harrison escorting an attractive young woman.

A court officer trailed the retinue and handed the bridgeman a yellow back. Detective Harrison gave Al the DA's case folder sent in from Part 1G. Opening the file, Al found that he had a particularly egregious rape case with the defendant having six prior rape and sodomy arrests. Al smiled, this time there was full corroboration. Allie Boy had made the arrest right at the scene. Detective Harrison, who was assigned later by the Detective Squad, ultimately took credit for the collar. Harrison had done his usual outstanding work, providing Al with certified copies of all the medical and laboratory reports. Al reviewed the facts with the complainant and after five minutes was ready to conduct the preliminary hearing.

He had only to show that a crime was committed and that there was a reasonable probability that the defendant did it.

This case would be followed by a pocketbook snatch from Part IF, which would require a felony hearing, and then a public lewdness trial from IC. The pocketbook snatch was routine; the anticrime officers had witnessed the event. The public lewdness trial involved a transit officer and Al wondering if he had another dump job, inquired. . . .

"Dicky waver at the IRT," the transit officer explained in response to Al's question.

"At the IRT?" Al asked.

"Yep, Mr. DA, we been having complaints that a guy was waving his dick from a room in the Simpson Street Hotel as the IRT downtown turns from Freeman Street to Simpson. So I was assigned to ride and observe, and I saw this guy with the window open waving his dick at the downtown express. So I get off at Simpson and me and my partner go right from the station to the hotel, find out the room and go in, recognize him, and make the collar."

"Okay, take a seat." Al said.

Allie Boy grabbed his cousin and took him aside.

"Listen, Al," he said, "I want you to use all your skills to make sure that this rapist goes to the Grand Jury without bail. I want to see him indicted, held without bail, and convicted and I want him to max out: eight and a third to twenty-five big ones. This guy is a fucking cruel predator." Al nodded; he was ready.

When Flay came out on the bench, everyone stood up and then

Flay ordered them to sit down. After he nodded the bridgeman called the case, yelling out the defendant's name and the charges, 130.30 Penal Law Rape First Degree; 140.25 Burglary 2nd Degree; 140.35 Possession of Burglar's Tools. Then, turning to Al, Flay asked, "Are the people ready?"

"The people are ready, your honor."

"Defense ready?"

"Defense ready, Your Honor," the Legal Aid lawyer responded.

"Call your first witness," the judge said.

"People call Mrs. Sybil Shields," Al boomed.

Allie Boy smiled proudly, he loved his cousin.

"Motion to exclude all witnesses," the Legal Aid lawyer said.

"Motion granted," Flay intoned.

Even though Al had no intention of calling Allie Boy or Harrison, he played it safe and asked them to step outside. Then the witness took the stand. She was young and very pretty—about twenty-five years old with blond hair and hazel eyes—and dressed in a conservative gray suit. She was all business when she answered "I do" after the oath was administered and smiled at the judge as she sat on the witness chair. Old Sam, quite taken with her, smiled right back.

"Please state your name and address for the record," he said, beaming.

"Mrs. Sybil Shields, 2472 General Sheridan Drive, Bronx New York, apartment C2," she answered.

"May I examine, Your Honor?" Al asked respectfully.

"Of course, of course," old Sam said, snapping back from his reverie.

"Now Mrs. Shields, do you live at your stated address alone?"

"No, sir, I live there with my husband," she replied.

"Do you have any children?"

"No, sir, we don't," she responded pleasantly.

"Now, Mrs. Shields, I am going to draw your attention to the evening of November 2, 1970. Were you at home that evening?"

"Yes, sir, I was at home."

Old Sam leaned back and stared at the defendant.

"Were you alone that evening?"

"Yes, I was." Her voice had grown softer, and Sam's stare had turned into a glare.

"Did there come a time when you retired for the evening?"

"Objection," the Legal Aid lawyer yelled, "he's leading the witness. I've been very patient in deference to the witness, Your Honor, but this leading is now amounting to the DA's testifying."

"Sustained, don't lead the witness," Sam remonstrated.

Al was temporarily flustered. He had not been leading and the Legal Aid lawyer's tactic to destroy his concentration had succeeded.

Al turned to the witness. "Would you please tell us what if anything happened after you retired for the evening."

"Well, my husband owns a bar in Throggs Neck, called Shields Pub and he generally gets home at odd hours—you know, mostly after two A.M."

Al nodded to the witness. "Mrs. Shields, can you recall for us what time you retired that evening?"

"I went to bed about eleven-thirty that night."

"And did you fall asleep immediately?" Al asked.

"Yes, I believe I did. I go to work and I was very tired."

"Did there come a time when something caused you to wake up?"

"Yes, something did cause me to wake up."

"Mrs. Shields, please tell us in your own words what that was."

"Well, I was sleeping on my side and I felt someone lie down, you know behind me—I didn't have any—any, uh, undergarments on—just a night slip, and well, I, uh—felt him—uh, entering me."

"Excuse me, Mrs. Shields," Al injected, "when you say 'entering' could you be more specific? The law requires more specificity," Al apologized.

"Well, he put his penis in my vagina."

"Did you resist, did you cry out?" Al asked softly, his face now a deep red.

"No, I didn't because I thought it was my husband," she answered flatly.

Al resumed the attack while old Sam continued glaring.

"When you say he, Mrs. Shields, are you referring to anyone in this courtroom?" Al asked.

"Yes, I am," she replied, beginning to grow indignant.

"Would you point him out for us please," Al asked, about to deliver the coup de grâce.

"Over there," she said, pointing to the defendant.

"Indicating the defendant," Al pronounced dramatically for the record.

"What happened then, Mrs. Shields?"

"Well, there was a pounding at the door. I was still half asleep, and my husband came in with the police. The neighbors had seen him," she said, pointing to the defendant, "coming in through the fire escape window, and they called my husband at the pub and he called the police and they arrested him."

"Objection." The Legal Aid lawyer was on his feet.

"Sustained," old Sam ruled. "Strike any reference to what the neighbors did."

"Now, Mrs. Shields," Al began confidently.

"Just a minute, just a minute," Sam shouted. "Am I correct in my belief that the charge here is rape?"

"Yes, your honor, the charge here is rape in the first degree," Al stated.

"So then the charge then is not sodomy? Is that correct?" Judge Flay asked.

"That's correct, Your Honor, the defendant now before the bar of justice is not charged with sodomy," Al replied.

"Did I perceive the testimony to be that the defendant entered the vagina of the witness from the—uh—posterior?" Judge Flay queried.

"Yes, Your Honor has correctly and cogently summarized the jist of the complainant's testimony," Al said.

"So that we are quite clear," the judge continued. "At the time of the admission of the male organ to the female organ the parties to this alleged forced union were not face to face."

The court officers and the stenographer were getting a little puzzled at Flay's persistence, but Al had no option except to respond: "That is correct." And hoping to forestall any further questions, he volunteered, "The defendant would at that time have his face facing the back of her head, which is the position Mrs. Shields has just testified to, Your Honor."

Everyone nodded. Everyone had understood as they waited for the start of cross examination by the Legal Aid lawyer.

"I see." Sam nodded wisely. "Case is dismissed, defendant is released."

"What!" Al screamed as Mrs. Shield's face became blood red and the Legal Aid lawyer's jaw almost dropped down to Part 1C on the floor below.

Al finally shouted, *"Would the court kindly state its reasons for dismissal?"*

Old Sam banged his gavel. "Be seated. Be seated. I will gladly state my reasons." Everyone sat down and quiet reigned. "Very simply, Mr. Assistant District Attorney. Despite what you think, you young fellows don't quite know it all. Many of you are just babes in the woods, still wet behind the ears. I have been married to one woman for over thirty-two years and I am going to take Judicial Notice—you hear me, Judicial Notice of the fact that what this woman complained of is a total physical impossibility. Accordingly, the case is dismissed, the bail if any is exonerated, and the defendant is discharged. So ordered. Court is in recess."

Flay arose and left the bench.

Al had a rough time explaining to Allie Boy and Harrison what had happened. He took them and the complainant up to the DA's offices on the fourth floor and called across town to the Indictment Bureau. Within a half hour Mrs. Shields, Allie Boy, and Harrison had told their stories to the Bronx Grand Jury and the defendant was indicted. An indictment was typed up and handed up that day in an extraordinary rush of procedure, and a warrant was issued for the defendant's arrest. But he had been released. Al didn't know what more to expect from Flay when he returned to try the felony hearing on the pocketbook snatch. However, even though that hearing proceeded without incident, with the matter being held for the Grand Jury, Al was still shaken up as he began the trial of the "dicky waver" arrested by the transit officer at the Simpson Street Hotel.

The defendant was represented by an 18b attorney, one appointed by the court for indigents. Legal Aid had been relieved since the defendant had spat at one of their female attorneys. The trial started with the arresting officer, whose testimony had been very clear and convincing. Responding to the complaints made to headquarters, he and his partner had taken the train and when it took the ninety-degree turn from Freeman to Simpson Street, passing within ten feet of the Simpson Street Hotel, he had observed the defendant standing naked in the window, vigorously waving his penis at the passengers. Exiting the train at the Simpson Street station, he and his partner entered the hotel, ascertained the room, and, accompanied by the clerk, knocked on the door. When the defendant answered clad only in his undershorts, they recognized him as the "Waver." The officer concluded by identifying the defendant for the record and the judge.

Just as the 18b attorney was about to commence his cross examination, Judge Flay, to everyone's dismay, dismissed the case. Flay stated that the public lewdness statute defined the offensive conduct as that committed in a public place, and the hotel room was not a public place. So the defendant walked out the door.

As Al drove home up the Major Degan Expressway that evening, the freed rapist touched down in a Tex Air Jet at the Dallas-Fort Worth airport. At the same time, from his window in the Simpson Street Hotel, Mervin Flohic waved at commuters going home on the IRT. Mervin wasn't just waving with his hands.

"Jesus," Hornbein said when Al had finished the story, "Flay is really dangerous."

"Yeah, but he's a little more cautious now," Al said. "He's cunning enough to know that his fuckin' antics will keep him from the nomination. But you gotta watch him, be on your toes. He won't dare fuck with the Grand Inquisitors but, Dave, you are certainly no Grand Inquisitor."

"I know," Hornbein answered. "By the way, Al, did they ever get the rapist?"

Al nodded. "He was in the wind for four years. They got him two months ago on another charge, and when they locked him up the rape warrant fell."

"Where's the other case?" Hornbein asked.

"Bronx case, a murder, and it's mine," Al answered, "It was on today. The guy's name is Bard, Adian Bard, and he's gonna fold next week." Al LoConti's mouth broke into a grin and Hornbein noticed that Al's eyes were like black pits.

"FUCKIN' FLAY SHOULD BE doin' twenty years," LoConti said while on his fourth brandy stinger on the evening that he took pleas on Adian Bard and the Serquez brothers. It was Friday night and Rory sat across the table from Al at the Last Supper refusing to meet Al's glance. Something had been wrong with Rory for some time now; he was strange, withdrawn.

Rory, Wotter, Allie Boy Spano, Richie Zemberelli, Pete DiCerrechia, and Ruella Watkins eagerly dipped in to the cauldron of steamed mussels in hot tomato sauce that sat in the middle of the enormous round table in the restaurant's back room. They were dipping crusty pieces of Italian bread into the fiery hot-pepper sauce and washing the bread down with glasses of cold red wine while Al and his brother Vinnie sat waiting for the main course. Vinnie sipped his second martini as he listened to his brother's speech starting to slur from the effect of the brandy stingers.

"The Guzman kid is something I'll never get to live with," Al said.

"Forget it," Allie Boy said through a mouthful of food.

Al, ignoring him, said, "It's worse than getting divorced, worse than the army or even your family dyin'."

"You did your job, shut the fuck up and eat," Allie Boy said.

Al watched the others eating while he sipped his brandy. Despite having disposed of Bard and the Serquez brothers today, he still was despondent. While the officers ate he reflected on the saga that had began many months before.

It had been an uneventful Thursday, January 11, 1973. Al wore the beeper and had been lucky, receiving only one call at 2 P.M. After getting into his car, he drove to the Four Eight precinct with a stenographer. It seemed that the night before a group belonging to the Young Sinners were in a doorway on Prospect Avenue near the El of the 241st Street line. When the elevated subway went by a shot rang out. Seventeen-year-old Raoul Ortiz dropped in the doorway; a bullet had entered his forehead and lodged in his brain. Two hours later he was pronounced dead at the Thomas Jefferson Medical Center.

As soon as Al walked into the Four Eight, Jimmy McDonough gave him the rundown.

"We got a breeze here, Al, a real easy grounder." McDonough began, "this kid Ortiz catches one in the forehead last night while standing in the doorway of 899 Prospect. Then he goes DOA at Jefferson. I figure word hits the street and today we get a squeal from a sixteen-year-old girl, Lucy Munoz. Lucy is clean, no sheet, not a user. She's a junior at Roosevelt. She says her boyfriend was standing across the street with her at 884 and he had a pistol. She don't know the caliber but she describes an automatic. She says her boyfriend waits for the train and shoots across the street at the Young Sinners. She sees Raoul fall. She says her boyfriend takes her upstairs to his apartment and later after all the commotion is over she walks home with him."

"You find a weapon?" Al asks.

"No, we toss the kid's apartment but we find bubkus. He probably ditched it down a manhole when he found out Raoul died." McDonough responded.

"What's the perp's name?" Al asked.

"Heriberto Guzman, age nineteen. Funny thing is, he's clean as a whistle, no priors, no track marks, and he works in Korvettes and goes to Bronx Community at nights."

"Does his girlfriend say he pointed the gun and fired at the Sinners, or was he fuckin' aroun' and the gun went off?" Al asked.

"She says he pointed it, sighted it, and pulled the trigger after first waiting for the train to come so that the sound would be deadened," McDonough answered.

"So you took him for murder?"

"Right, Al. It seems like a lock. You got no ID problem and she supplies the intent and knocks out the accident theory."

"Why did she give up her boyfriend?" Al asked.

"That's what I asked her. She said that Raoul was just a kid tryin' to be tough and she couldn't live with herself if she kept quiet. Besides, she knows Raoul's mother since she is a kid."

"What kind of bullet did they take from the dead kid's brain?"

"We don't have a definite 'cause it was splintered, but the best preliminary guess is .380 automatic."

"Perp say anything?"

"No."

"Did you tell him his girlfriend gave him up?"

"No, because she begs us not to tell him and we won't give her up because we want her at the trial. You never can tell what can happen to a witness."

"Okay, I won't give her up. Bring him in here."

The stenographer set up in the windowless "interview room."

The nineteen-year-old was brought in, and Al motioned him to a chair. Al had conducted many similar interviews and he was now skilled at getting confessions. He extended a package of Lucky Strikes to the youth who eagerly took one.

After lighting it for him, Al began, "Mr. Guzman, my name is LoConti. I am an assistant district attorney. I am a lawyer but I'm not your lawyer. Do you understand?"

The youth nodded.

"Now, I am here to investigate the death of Raoul Ortiz. I'd like to ask you some questions about Raoul's death, but before I can ask you anything, the law requires that I advise you of certain rights that the Supreme Court laid down in a case of *Miranda* versus *Arizona*. Do you understand?"

The youth nodded again.

"Please answer yes or no to my questions, Mr. Guzman, so that Mr. Livrum here can get your response down. Okay?"

"Yes, sir," Heriberto replied.

Al went through the constitutional rights, speaking quickly yet relaxed, his tone calm and his manner laidback. It was designed to obtain a voluntary waiver on the record so that he could question the youth. The last question Al posed was superfluous.

"Now, having been advised of all of these rights and having indicated to me that you understand them all, would you like to answer my questions without a lawyer being present?"

"Sure, I didn't do anything, I don't need a lawyer. I'm innocent, Mr. LoConti."

"Okay, maybe we can get something from you to help us straighten this out with the police," Al said. "Now, where do you live, Mr. Guzman?"

"Eight eighty-four Prospect Avenue."

"And how long have you lived there?"

"All my life."

"And how old are you?"

"I'm nineteen, sir."

"Now, Mr. Guzman, I'm going to draw your attention to last night about ten-thirty P.M. Were you in front of your house on Prospect Avenue at that time?"

"I was in front of my house until eight o'clock then I went upstairs."

"Did you go out any more that evening?"

"No, it was cold so I stayed home."

"Did you find out about Raoul being shot?"

"Yes, I found out this morning that he died."

"Now, when you were outside your house, were you with anyone?"

"Yes, I was with my girlfriend, Lucy."

"And did you bring your girlfriend upstairs with you?"

"No, we had an argument and she went home."

"What did you argue about?"

"She thinks that I'm going out with this girl Maureen from Bronx Community College."

"Are you?"

"Well, I study with her sometimes and Lucy gets mad."

"So you argue about this frequently."

"Yes, we always argue about Maureen."

"Was anyone home in your apartment when you went upstairs?"

"Just my mother, and she told the policemen here that I was home all night. But they don't believe her."

Al looked at McDonough and McDonough nodded.

"Besides your mother, anyone else know where you were last night?"

"Just Lucy . . . you can ask her."

"Do you own an automatic pistol, Heriberto?"

"No, sir."

"Will you tell me what you did with the pistol you had last night?"

"I don't have no pistol ever, Mr. DA. That's the truth."

"Anything else you want to add, Heriberto?"

"No."

"Okay, statement concluded."

Heriberto Guzman was arraigned for murder in the Bronx Criminal Court that evening. Despite a plea from his Legal Aid lawyer and his mother, the judge remanded him without bail. As he was led into the pens, eight members of the Young Sinners traipsed from the courtroom.

Now Al LoConti, seated in the Last Supper, reflected, I should have realized he was telling me the truth.

Millie served the main courses, plates of veal, chicken, steaks, and seafood accompanied by side orders of French fried potatoes, mounds of steaming pasta, and oil-soaked vegetables. Al nibbled at a piece of veal and ordered another drink.

Even though Willie Wotter knew the story, he asked Al to describe the background of the Serquez and Bard cases. After Al related the events leading up to the arrest of Heriberto Guzman he continued the story . . .

He could tell the story without even thinking. His mind played the scene back to him like a movie camera, powered by submerged currents of guilt.

"The beeper went off at six fifteen that Sunday morning of April 22, 1973. I picked up the phone and dialed the office.

"They sent me to Mosholu Parkway just off the Grand Concourse and I got there in ten minutes. Forensic, the ME, and detectives and police were there. A young Hispanic was dumped on the grass divider of the parkway. He had been shot execution-style once behind the left ear. When I arrived forensic was completing their photographs. Timmy Flanagan was on the scene. It was his case. When forensic was finished with the photos, the ME and Timmy flipped the DOA over.

"The kid's forehead was real bloody. Everyone looked closer. The initials 'YS' were carved into the forehead. I made no connection. A young detective I had never seen before searched the deceased's pockets. He took out a wallet. From the wallet he extracted an ID card. Flanagan asked him to read it. He did. It was a Bronx Community College ID card with a picture of Heriberto Guzman. The 'YS' carved in his forehead meant Young Sinners. I had paroled the kid just two days before. His girlfriend, Lucy, turned him in and then she recanted. She passed three polygraphs, which showed that she didn't witness a fucking thing. The Young Sinners executed this kid because they felt he beat the rap. This kid was a good kid."

"But was he innocent?" Zemberelli asked.

"Sure he was innocent. If I was a prick this kid would be alive," Al went on, "you try to do the right thing and you get fucked three ways to Sunday."

"How the fuck can you blame yourself?" Allie Boy asked loudly, annoyed and frustrated since his efforts to stop his cousin's bouts of depression were always futile. "You did your fuckin' job, that's it. Cut the shit and eat," he ordered.

Al just sat sipping his drink.

"Who killed the innocent kid?" Zemberelli asked.

"Two hit men for the Young Sinners, the Serquez brothers. They both plead guilty today." Al answered.

"Timmy Flanagan and Pete here got them," he went on as Pete nodded.

"And a guy I locked up for rape years ago turned out to be the guy who shot the kid Raoul," Allie Boy said. "Judge Flay turned him loose at a hearing. He's been out of New York for years. He came back with a gun and was driving around and just shot the kid. Did it for kicks."

"How did you get him?" Wotter asked.

"Girlfriend turned him in, she was scared of him. And we got the gun," Pete said.

"He folded today," Al said. "He pled to manslaughter and the rape, he'll be in for a while. O'Neill will give it to him."

"It's fuckin' Flay's fault, Al, not yours," Wotter said. Everyone murmured agreement, trying to cheer Al.

"Cut the shit, Al," Pete said. "Things could be worse." Pete almost prescribed a session with Dr. Christen but kept his mouth shut. Wotter decided to wait another week before telling Al why Rory was acting strange, especially now when all Al kept muttering was "Fuckin' Flay should be doin' twenty years."

34

RENEE LOCONTI, WAITING INSIDE the kitchen of her sister's house on Long Island, thought that she could set her clock by Alcibiades's arrival and sure enough, he rang at precisely the start of his court-ordered visitation. Renee, fed up with all of the bitterness, had decided she would be the first to start building bridges. If only for the sake of the children, she thought. But knowing that fierce Lo-Conti pride, she doubted her chances at success. Because she dreaded having to tell him that his daughter was too sick to leave the house and expected him to demand to have a doctor examine her, Renee had decided to invite him in to see for himself. Maybe after she might even offer him a cup of coffee. Since her sister and brother-in-law were away, there would be no interference.

The doorbell rang again, and Renee smiled warmly as she opened it. "Liz is sick but Ray is inside. Why don't you come in and see her? My sister and brother-in-law won't be back for hours."

After hesitating a moment, Al walked inside and was led into a bedroom where he bent down to kiss his daughter. He placed his palm on her forehead to feel the fever's heat.
"We already took her to the doctor twice and he said she has a virus. She needs rest and then she'll be okay," Renee said.
Al drew up a chair and sat down next to his daughter, motioning for his wife to leave the room. After fifteen minutes of small talk, he kissed Liz and left the bedroom.
"Would you care for a cup of coffee?" Renee offered.
"No," Al said. "Where's Ray-Ray?"
"He's playing with his trucks in the basement."
"Don't tell me you're not letting him come without his sister?" Al said.
"Oh, no, I just thought that we might talk, you know, try to get so that we are not at each other's throats every minute. Like it or not, we are going to be connected through our kids for many years so what I'm trying to say, can't we at least take a stab at being friends?" Renee asked softly.
"If all my friends were like you, Renee, I'd do a fuckin' swan dive off the Triboro Bridge at high tide," Al said. "Bring the kid up. I got fifty miles to drive before I get home . . . old friend. Fifty goddamn long miles."
Renee called for their son. The boy ran upstairs and, after hugging his mother, said good-bye and left.
One hour later Al pulled up in front of the Last Supper and walked inside. At the rear a large plate-glass window enabled the patrons to look through into the kitchen's spotless interior. Large stainless-steel cauldrons hung on pegs alongside huge frying pans. Two large commercial stoves with six burners each stood opposite the wall with two large pizza ovens. The pizza ovens were lined with fire brick and were heated by coals. The Last Supper was one of the few places left in New York where you could get pizza cooked in such an oven. It was packed seven days a week from lunch until midnight. Al and the boy sat down.
A dozen drinkers lined the bar, and two young men standing at the end of the bar were playing an Italian game called Mortada. They each threw out one hand and called out a number. If the number matched the total number of fingers extended, the caller

would win the pot. If no one called correctly, each put a dollar in the pot.

Al's uncle came out, shook his hand effusively, and kissed the boy on the cheek. The bartender was calling in orders for pizzas, and a new waitress was ushering patrons to booths and tables. "Al, I'll make the boy a nice veal cutlet with a little broccoli rabe and maybe a little spaghetti on the side, okay?" Peppy Gennaro said.

"Okay, Ray?" Al asked, knowing that Peppy knew the boy's taste exactly. The boy, hungry by now, nodded and smiled.

"For you, Al, I got nice tripe or you could have veal and peppers."

"What kinda soup you got, Unc?" Al asked.

"Pasta fagioli."

"Good. Give me a bowl of pasta fazool and a veal and pepper sandwich."

"And a little spaghetti on the side with the boy, right?"

"Right."

"Coca Cola for the boy and for you wine or beer today?"

"Glass of beer."

"I got some homemade red wine with the Cabernet Sauvignon grape from California," Peppy said, kissing the first two fingers of his hand.

"Just a glass of cold beer, Unc, please."

His uncle shook his head, Everyone was being Americanized. Beer instead of the best wine. Before you knew it they would be putting hot dogs on pizza.

Peppy went back to the kitchen shouting orders to his three cooks, and another waitress arrived. She waved to Al and he waved back. It was Millie, who was everyone's girlfriend.

Soon Millie came out with the food and patted Ray on the head.

When she left Al looked down at the steaming bowl of pasta and bean soup. It contained the white kidney beans called cannelloni in Italian and the American navy or pea beans. Chunks of fresh celery floated in the rich bean broth along with just the right amount of garlic, a touch of tomato, and three types of pasta. Al stirred a little red pepper and two teaspoons of grated cheese into the soup. While it cooled he cut Ray's veal cutlet. The veal was white and soft and covered with a golden crust, served in the style of the northern Italians, à la Milanese, with only lemon wedges. Al squeezed some lemon on the veal and Ray began to eat.

Al blew away the steam from a spoonful of soup and, sipping, closed his eyes in pure delight. This is a close second to fuckin', he thought. Then, after taking a bite of the veal and pepper sandwich, he closed his eyes in ecstasy. Maybe neck and neck, he thought, revising his estimate upward.

Pizzas were coming from the kitchen in flat white boxes and the cash register was ringing. The tables had all filled up and the waitresses were scurrying. A third bartender was bringing drinks from the bar to those seated.

Al got up and went to the bar, walked behind it and drew a glass of beer from the tap, and then went back to his chair and finished eating. Peppy brought out a fresh salad with two plates. People from Avellino always ate salad after the meal to aid the digestion. It had slices of fresh tomato, crisp cucumber, red onion, lettuce, and curly chicory, and was dressed with thick yellow Sicilian extra-virgin olive oil and red wine vinegar. Al had two plates of salad, Ray had one. Then Al drew himself another beer and drank it. After passing Millie a five-dollar bill and waving to his uncle, Al and Ray walked out of the Last Supper.

Al put some more coins in the parking meter and walked up the block toward Williamsbridge Road, passing a crowded candy store with only five candy bars in a rack and two magazines yellowed with age. Still, it was mobbed with people. They didn't go there to buy candy or magazines, but to bet on horse races in Florida and football, hockey and basketball games, and of course the numbers.

As Al and Ray walked farther up Morris Park Avenue, they spotted the bookie Santa Giacomo who, ever since the Arab oil embargo and in defiance of rising gasoline prices, had taken to traveling on a green delivery bicycle. Santa Giacomo, now seventy-three years old, had sixty arrests for policy and numbers running. Since Al had became a DA, Santa Giacomo barely nodded to him. Al was thankful that the old man had become distant and grateful for his shrewdness and consideration. Al had known Santa Giacomo since he was three years old.

After stopping on the next block, father and son walked into a toy store and wandered up and down its four aisles. One aisle was filled with trucks and boats. Al grinned as Ray chose a big Tonka dump truck costing fifteen dollars. The boy was laughing with delight, pulling the lever, raising and tilting the truck bed. Al walked down another aisle and grabbed a doll for his daughter. After paying they walked outside, back down the avenue toward 180th Street, which anchored the other end of Morris Park. On the far side of 180th Street was an area known as West Farms. Once, before it had been annexed to the City of New York in 1874, it had been a separate, quiet village. In the 1840s its area included all of Morrisania in the West Bronx and the greater part of the Fordham area. Now it marked the eastward extension of the South Bronx decay and was full of junkies, drug bars, and hookers. Al and Ray stopped at Matthews Avenue about a mile from West Farms. They were in the heart of the area where Al had grown up. They entered a park that had been built when he was a teenager. It was still a mild day and Al put his son on a swing, pushed hard, and watched the boy squeal a child's delight as he reached the top of the arc and felt the belly-drop sensation of the descent.

While Al pushed the boy on the swing, he thought of his pending cases. He mulled over the facts of the Martha Valles's case, considering every factor that supported arresting Carleton, the young cop. Eventually he concluded that he had been correct in his judgment. Not only could he never convince a jury of Carleton's guilt, but more important he still did not even have a prima facie, or legally sufficient case. Al was worried because Flanagan, the Hat, and the whole department were convinced that Carleton had killed Martha Valles. He knew their conclusions were fixed in stone, and the two Stone Age minds in the Homicide Bureau, "The Grand Inquisitors," still urged him every day to lock the cop up.

On the swing, the boy squealed and chuckled like a little old man, and Al laughed. The park visit was therapeutic. Al felt even better now, more convinced in his own mind that he had done the right thing in preventing Carleton's arrest.

But they had all made his life miserable. The Hat had called Bureau Chief O'Boyle and then DA Frank Caporosso himself, inquiring why Carleton's arrest was being prevented. Al knew the police brass were just covering their asses to show that the DA's office and more particularly he, Al LoConti, was the reason Carleton was at liberty. The Hat had even told the DA that experienced detectives were convinced that Carleton was guilty and they should prevail, not some junior divorced ADA who should be working for the Legal Aid Society. Frank Caporosso had thanked the Hat and told him if anyone locked up Carleton without his authorization, he would personally dismiss the charges and cooperate with Carleton's attorney in suing all the cops involved, including the Hat.

There were very few in law enforcement like Frank Caporosso who were not afraid of the Hat, who routinely terrified the police brass as well as the rank and file. No one seemed to know the source of his power. Erratic to the point of psychosis, it was indeed a wonder that he had not been demoted and retired years ago. To escape any retribution after some of his capers meant that you must have the rabbi of all rabbis, and it was rumored within the department that the Hat's rabbi was none other than God himself.

The Hat just loved to beat up bookmakers, and he had issued standing orders that he was to be summoned whenever one was arrested. He would go to the squad room and punch the shit out of the poor bookie. No one would dare testify against the Hat, and bookmakers, knowing what fate awaited them, paid off quick and plenty to avoid a collar.

Bookies were not the only ones to fall victim to his fists. He would frequently cuff his men about when impatient and, of course, they never dared complain. But he had a soft spot for detectives; he was very fond of Flanagan and respected Shapiro, whom he referred to as "that brainy Jew." Al had heard a million Hat stories, one more bizarre than the next. But Frank Caporosso scorned the Hat, and Al was pleased to work for Caporosso, a DA with a great big pair of balls.

The so-called legs case would have to await good luck or good police work. Although Pete DiCerrechia would always be a wacko, he was still a great detective. The serial killer of old ladies had many of the best detectives in the city assigned, and Al would just have to await events.

Ray's swing stopped and Al unfastened the holding bar from in front of his son and lifted him to the ground. He took Ray to the sliding pond, waiting while he climbed the ladder in the back and grinning as he watched Ray laughing and sliding down the smooth run. After a few slides and a turn on the seesaw, Al and Ray left the park. When Al got to his car, he noticed a ticket on the windshield; the meter had expired. It would cost him fifteen dollars. More than Flay had fined guys carrying loaded guns, he thought as he put Ray in the car and drove away. It was starting to get real cold again.

AFTER AL AND HIS son had arrived at his apartment, the boy put a leash on Sport and they walked the dog down into Inwood Park, passing the point where the East River Estuary flowed into the Hudson, an area Al explained was still known by its Dutch name "Spuyten Duyvil." They watched the boats passing back and forth, and Al pointed out the spot where Peter Minuit had purchased Manhattan Island from the Indians for a few shells and beads. After an hour's walk they returned to the apartment.

A few minutes later the doorbell rang. Al opened it to see his brother, Vinnie, and William Wotter. When they spotted young Ray LoConti, they changed their plans. They had come here today to tell Alcibiades all about Rory O'Donnell.

"Where you goin' tomorrow, Al?" Vinnie asked.

"I'm takin' Ray for a ride to City Island. Then I'll take him home," Al answered.

"Maybe I'll see you tomorrow," Vinnie replied as he and Wotter were leaving. "We just dropped by to say hello to Ray."

The next morning, after driving across the Bronx, Al and his son crossed the bridge over onto City Island. They drove down the main thoroughfare to the water's edge where two restaurants on opposite sides of the street anchored the roadway's end.

After parking in the restaurant lot on the left side of the road, Al put his son on a stand that had binoculars mounted in a rounded casing. He deposited a nickel then showed Ray how to rotate the casing to follow the boats as they passed by. You could see the small fishing skiffs and the sailboats tacking and yawing, the whites of their sails filling with breezes as they leaned into the waters of the sound. Some had sails furled and were making for shore, fleeing the black clouds appearing over the Throggs Neck Bridge.

The fishing skiffs bobbing out in the sound were seeking flounder and blackfish, but only too often hooked the hated bergalls, the scavenger fish that infested these waters.

Ray was entranced. He loved fishing, and his father had taken him ever since he could walk.

"No one is catching any fish, Dad," Ray said as the motor in the binoculars died down and the view went black. Al deposited another coin and, looking through, scanned the fishing skiffs, watching fishermen hunkered down against the wind, their poles extending over the sides of the boats. Al watched as they pulled up and replaced bait that had been stolen by crabs or bergalls. The flounder fishermen were using sand worms while the blackfish-tautog fishermen used fiddler crabs. A fisherman reached into a bait container and pulled out a crab. He inserted the blackfish hook into the crab's inch-wide body, causing the crab's legs to claw helplessly at the air as it descended into the black waters toward the scavengers below. The light flickered and Al could see no more.

Al led Ray into the seafood restaurant. It was just noon and two men behind a counter were swiftly shucking clams and depositing them into an enormous cauldron of Manhattan clam chowder while a woman tossed in chunks of fresh tomato, fresh peppers, carrots, potatoes, and celery. Another cauldron of soup steamed on the stovetop. Al ordered a bowl of soup for Ray and batter-fried shrimp for himself, then took the food on a tray to a table overlooking the water. He peeled open a packet of oyster crackers, poured them into Ray's soup, then dipped one of the crispy fried shrimp into a tomato and hot pepper sauce, popped it into his mouth, chewed quickly, and swallowed. Tears flowed down his cheeks while his sinuses drained and his palate burned. He put out the fire with a long pull from a cold container of Coke.

"Man, is that good," he exclaimed.

"Daddy, can I try?"

Al shook his head, telling Ray that the sauce would burn him, but he gave the boy a shrimp.

Ray imitated Al by dipping the shrimp into the soup and taking a long drink of soda, and echoing, "Man, is that good."

Al laughed and Ray smiled back. Al rubbed the boy's head. After leaving the restaurant they drove back up City Island Avenue to the bridge connecting the island with Rodman's Neck. "This bridge," Al said, "was built around 1901. It replaced an earlier wooden toll bridge that had been built in 1876. The best fishermen in the Bronx were the old-timers who had always fished off the City Island Bridge."

After parking, they crossed the street and walked onto the bridge where a dozen men ranging in age from mid-forties to early seventies were fishing. Father and son walked across the bridge and then walked back, hearing many different languages spoken by the fishermen. A black man with a gray fringe of hair around his bald head smiled broadly at the boy and held out his hand. Ray shook the man's hand and smiled back.

"Nice boy you got there, mister," the man said, baiting a hook and casting over the railing.

"Thank you," Al answered. "Any luck?"

"Not yet." The man smiled as they continued back across the bridge.

Al looked out across the water toward a rock jetty marking the end of Orchard Beach. The beach was on their left across the strait separating the mainland from City Island, and more men were fishing from the jetty. The beach next to the jetty, called Beach Number 13, had been a favorite summer hangout for teenage Alcibiades LoConti.

Fondly remembering those glorious times at Beach 13, he

entered his car to drive to his son's home. As they passed over the bridge through Rodman's Neck, he explained how a battle was fought right there during the Revolutionary War and how the Americans prevented the British from cutting off the retreat of Washington's army toward White Plains.

"Mommy's British, isn't she, Daddy?" Ray asked. Al nodded yes, and neither spoke again until Al pulled up into the driveway on Long Island. He hugged the boy and then led him up to the door and rang the bell. When Renee answered, he turned and went back to his car and drove to his uncle's restaurant. He really hated Sunday nights.

THE BAD NEWS HIT Al hard, real hard like the clubbing from a baseball bat across your face. He got up from the table leaving his brother, Willie Wotter, and Pete DiCerrechia.

He walked to the bar and ordered a shot of VO with a beer chaser. After downing the whiskey, he went back to the table sipping the beer. Pete motioned to Enzo the waiter, who brought more drinks.

"So he's been fuckin' my wife," Al said. Vince and Wotter shook their heads.

"I was afraid you'd react like that, Al," Vince said, "Rory and Renee are just goin' out, just for companionship, no sex involved."

"Bullshit," Al said.

"Listen to Vinnie, Al. That's all it is, it's only platonic," Wotter said.

"How the fuck can you possibly know that?" Al snapped. "The fuckin', drunken prick has gone through three wives. Why does he have to fuck with his friend's wife?" Al was getting close to tears. "I mean, I know Rory since I'm fifteen, and I wouldn't even dream of going near one of his ex-wives."

"Neither would most human beings," DiCerrechia quipped, and Vince chuckled.

"Listen to me, Al," Wotter went on. "He's so far gone with the booze he can't even get it up. I'm tellin' you, he knows Renee for years, he just needs some companionship and so does she."

"That's right, Al, and besides, you better get it in your thick head that she ain't your wife anymore, you divorced her. Remember?" Vince scolded. Al drank and didn't answer.

Wotter, relieved at finally telling his friend the bad news, got up and patted Al on the back. "Relax, Al, for your own sake, I tell you it's harmless . . . only platonic." He walked toward the doorway as Vince looked at his brother. Pete watched them and drank.

Al LoConti looked up at the retreating Wotter.

"Hey, Willie," Al called out. Wotter stopped and turned around.

"Do you know the name of the last guy who had a platonic relationship?" Al asked.

"No, I don't, Al," Wotter answered.

"It's fuckin' Plato," Alcibiades LoConti said.

37

"CAN HE TALK, NURSE?" Hanratty asked.

"He can barely talk," she answered in an Irish brogue.

The three DAs were standing outside the hospital room, breathing hard from their run from the police car through Jacobi Hospital and into the nightmare job every DA dreaded beyond all others. They were here to obtain a dying declaration.

No one in the office with the exception of the Grand Inquisitors, Johnny O'Boyle, and of course the DA, Frank Caporosso himself had ever obtained a dying declaration. Yet the infrequency of the demand only served to heighten its dread and mystique.

Obtaining a dying declaration required DAs to be as hard as flint within while displaying a soft caring exterior. Doing the job churned your bowels and broke your heart.

If neither Carmine Riccaldo nor Maurice Slefner showed up, it would be up to Hanratty to take the dying declaration. He was senior to Jimmy Farrell and Jonah Quoe.

Riccaldo and Slefner could get a dying declaration without emotion and with the ease of an undertaker embalming the dead.

For the first time in his career Hanratty hoped for the miraculous appearance of either of the Grand Inquisitors, but they didn't show.

Allie Boy Spano and Richie Zemberelli came out of the room. Allie Boy's eyes were wet.

"How is he?" Hanratty asked.

Allie Boy just shrugged and shook his head; he couldn't speak.

"I've got to try to get a dying declaration," Hanratty told the nurse.

"Why?" she asked.

"Because it can be used at trial even if he doesn't make it. He can in fact be heard at the trial of his killer," Hanratty answered. Then he reviewed what he had to do.

Under the law, he had to get the victim to acknowledge that he knew he was dying and that he really had no hope of survival. Then Hanratty would have to ask him about the person who shot him. Just then the stenographer came running from the open elevator.

"Let's go," Hanratty said, and they went into the room. Two nurses stood next to the bedridden victim whose head had been bandaged. Tubes ran from sacs of liquid into his arms.

"I'm Terry Hanratty," the ADA began. "Can you hear me?"

The victim nodded.

"I don't want to tell you this but I have to ask you. Do you know you are in extremis?"

The victim's brow furrowed. "What?" he whispered.

"Do you know you are about to die?" Hanratty blurted out.

It was enough to make Jimmy Farrell blanch, but the law required it and the steno got it down.

"Yes, I do," Vince LoConti said.

EARLIER THAT SAME DAY, May 30, 1974, Al LoConti had met Fast Frankie Hammon in the hallway after arraigning a motorcycle gang leader for the murder of a nine-year-old boy. Fast Frankie told Al to follow him to Special V where a divorce trial was being held before Judge Flay. The case had become notorious.

"The husband is a real crazy bookmaker from Throggs Neck. Everyone knows the guy. I represented him a coupla times. He's not a bad guy, name's Charlie Oakdale. I handled his name change petition and a couple of bookmakin' raps. Guy's a bad payer."

"I heard of him," Al said. "Isn't he the guy they call the Plant?"

"Yeah, the Plant. He's a whacked-out, crazy, cheap fuck but after a while he grows on ya—that's why they give him the name, you know."

Al chuckled. "Yeah, I heard he was real crazy and I also heard he is a pretty big guy in Throggs Neck."

"It's all relative," Fast Frankie went on. "It's all relative. I suppose he does okay, but he lives in the Neck and works in a dry cleaning store so how big can he be?"

"Come on, Frank—you're talking to me."

"Listen, Al, enough said. All I can tell you is that the trial is about to start and it should be a pisser and a half, especially with Fuckhead Flay." Al agreed and Fast Frankie went on. "It's between Ball-less Beltzer and Fucko Flay for the Supreme Court job. They both got big fuckin' rabbis. It's got to come down to which one of the rabbis can guess the number of seats in Yankee Stadium," Fast Frankie said with aplomb. Although Al had a good idea what Fast Frankie was really saying, not being positive he just ignored the remark.

Flay, who fancied himself an author, was known to accept advance royalties for his legal opinions.

Flay's courtroom was in recess when Al and Fast Frankie took seats in the front row. Al looked around and noticed that there were more cops and DAs in this court than in the rest of the building. Charlie Oakdale sat on the left side of the courtroom in the seat reserved for the defendant. His wife sat on the plaintiff's side. Two court officers had been placed strategically between them. Judge Flay was behind the chambers door speaking with the two lawyers in an effort to settle the case.

"Gentlemen, my law secretary informs me that this case must be tried." Both of the Manhattan attorneys nodded.

The attorneys chosen by the Oakdales represented a special breed of cat, the matrimonial specialist—the Bomber.

Mrs. Oakdale was represented by Reynard P. Foxworth and Mr. Oakdale was represented by Howard Caven. Both attorneys had reputations of being dirtbags. In appearance they were almost indistinguishable except that Caven had about ten years on Foxworth. Both were wearing three-hundred-dollar suits and were bedecked with expensive watches and rings. If they told a fellow lawyer that it was raining, the lawyer would be constrained to look out the window for verification. Their reputations were such that they had found themselves on opposite sides more often than not, and they truly deserved each other as opponents. Their fees, of course, were astronomical.

Knowing these piranhas, Flay thought, There will be nothing left in this case for me, all I can look forward to is a long, drawn-out divorce trial.

"Gentlemen, how long will this take?" he asked.

Caven smiled at Foxworth. "I guess my guy can call your gal names for about two hours."

Foxworth smiled back. "My client can call your client names and relate his actionable conduct for about four hours, so I guess we are talking about a two-day trial, your Honor."

"Any infant children?" Flay asked.

"No," both lawyers answered.

"Let's get on with it."

The two lawyers and the judge came into the courtroom. Charlie Oakdale turned around to look at the spectators, waved to Fast Frankie Hammon, then turned back to look at Judge Flay.

"May I have the pleadings?" the judge requested.

The complaint and answer and counterclaim were handed up to the judge who looked over Mildred Oakdales' complaint. This is strong, even for Reynard, he thought, glancing toward Charlie the Plant. The Plant stared back. Flay dropped his eyes and read the Plant's answer, denying the complaint, and his counterclaim for divorce against the wife. It contained the usual allegations that had become rote to the judge over the years. There was really nothing new here.

After brief introductory statements by both attorneys, Mildred Oakdale took the stand. Foxworth skillfully led her through the preliminaries; establishing the fact that there was a marriage, they were both over eighteen, and they lived in New York for more than two years.

As she continued to testify, Flay inscribed on his pad the facts that the parties had been married for twenty-three years; the wife was forty-four; and the husband, forty-seven. They had two daughters, twenty and twenty-two, both of whom were married and resided in Westchester County. The wife gave her occupation as hairdresser and her husband's as the owner of a dry cleaning store. Both lived and worked in Throggs Neck.

Flay looked up, observing the wife closely. She was extremely well preserved and attractive. Flay noted that she dressed carefully and wore an enormous diamond ring on her left hand. Her platinum blond hair was cut short in the fashion of the day. Turning his attention to the husband, Flay observed that he was physically fit and dressed in a coal-black suit with a dark blue shirt and a white silk tie. He was wearing tinted glasses, and his graying hair was combed in the style of the early fifties. A flattened nose provided what the lawyers called direct evidence of his heavy fistfighting past. Flay was miffed that the husband, with his flattened nose, refused obeisance to the majesty of the court.

Tough cookie, Flay thought, settling back as the court grew stone quiet in anticipation of the interesting parts. As Mildred Oakdale began to testify, two men entered the courtroom and walked with care to the rear. They took their seats next to Rory O'Donnell and leaned forward. Lieutenant Solwin and Detective Wotter wanted to find out why the wire on Charlie Oakdale, which had been in place ever since Paulie the Brain had died, was not producing. It was Rory, a veteran of three marriages and the department's expert on the domestic relations law of the State of New York, who whispered the answer.

"Your wire is dead because this guy isn't attending to business, he's going through a divorce. When you go through this shit you can't concentrate on anything. Take it from me, I oughta know."

Wotter rolled his eyes back in his head wondering if Rory was putting them on. Solwin, ignoring Rory, listened as Mildred Oakdale started to tell Judge Flay all of the good stuff.

39

THE COP-FILLED COURTROOM was dead quiet listening to Mildred Oakdale's testimony. When a detective coughed, dagger stares forced him to rise and leave. He continued coughing all the way out to the corridor.

Charlie Oakdale, the Plant, listening attentively while his wife testified, began to worry that he might be embarrassed. When he got hints of where the lawyer's questions were leading, he began to sweat.

Charlie's lawyer had decided to permit the public to enter the courtroom. A packed house would be a deterrent, the lawyer had said. Mildred would never dare to testify to what her lawyer had threatened. It will prove to be a dynamite strategy, Caven had promised.

But when Foxworth asked, "And when did these strange sexual problems commence?" Charlie began to think, This guy's dynamite strategy is going to blow my fuckin' ass off.

Whispering loudly to his lawyer, in a voice heard by the first row of spectators Charlie remarked, "Your strategy is goin' right up my fuckin' ass."

The remark rippled back as those seated relayed its contents to the rows behind. Flay observed laughter ripple from the front to the rear of the courtroom.

"Mr. Oakdale, please!" Flay intoned, and Mildred answered.

"About a year after we were married Charlie began wanting to do things which I felt were strange," Mrs. Oakdale answered.

"And prior to the time that Mr. Oakdale wanted to do these things that you describe as strange, had you ever heard of them before?"

"Yes, I had heard of them but I could never imagine doing such things."

"And did you communicate to your husband the fact that you didn't desire to engage in such sexual activity?"

"Yes, I constantly told him that I did not want to engage in such activity."

Flay listened and thought to himself, How come it's always the men that want to do it and the woman never want to? Nothing new in this case, but I think I'll wack this guinea fuck just because of the way he looks at me. Flay looked at Charlie sitting next to his lawyer and Charlie glared back. Flay thought, You are damn right, you guinea fuck, it's goin' right up your ass.

Not knowing that he had already won more for his client than the had hoped for, Reynard Foxworth, Esq., continued questioning.

"And would you please tell his honor what these disgraceful suggestions consisted of."

The audience all leaned as far forward in their seats as they could, and Flay thought he had a courtroom of hunchbacks.

"Well, he wanted to commit sardmy."

"Sardmy?" the lawyer questioned.

"Yes, sardmy."

"Sardmy?" Flay said, looking quizzically at the witness and then the lawyer.

"Er, could you tell his honor what you mean by sardmy?" Foxworth asked.

"Sure," Mildred said. "Basically there are two types of sardmy that Charlie wanted to do."

Charlie, shrugging, leaned over and whispered to his lawyer, "What the fuck is sardmy?"

Howard Caven turned his hands palms upward and shrugged.

Mrs. Oakdale then told everyone what sardmy meant.

"Either he wanted head, or he wanted to put it up my ass," she blurted out.

A roar of laughter arose from the entire courtroom. Flay banged his gavel. Charlie's face and neck turned bright scarlet.

"And did you do these things with your husband?"

"Yes, because he forced me to."

Charlie began to get up.

"Had you ever done these things before?"

"No, I never did."

"Bullshit," Charlie screamed, now fully on his feet.

Fast Frankie Hammon nudged Al. "I told you this would be good."

Al listened and nodded as Charlie continued the tirade.

"You didn't get those lips from sucking oranges, you cunt. You fuckin' barmaid, a fuckin' barmaid when I met ya, I give you respect, you *putan*, you whore fuck."

Flay rapped so hard that the head of his gavel broke and flew into the audience. Charlie ducked as it whizzed by.

Caught up in the spirit of the trial, Detective William Wotter signaled for a fair catch and scooped the gavel head into his two hands while the audience applauded.

Flay screamed, "Order, order" and the court officers turned and put their fingers on the lips as if to sssssshh children.

The laughter from the audience even grew louder as Flay stormed from the bench. The court officers followed him into the robing room, and after a minute their captain came back into the courtroom.

"Ladies and gentlemen, his honor has directed that if there is even one more sound this courtroom will be cleared. I trust that I make myself clear." The door was then opened to the robing room and Flay bounced back in.

Al thought, Pompous little fuck acts like someone stole his candy.

Mrs. Oakdale proceeded to narrate the precise details of each of the occurrences of sardmy between the defendant and herself. Howard Caven listened with one hand on the defendant's shoulder, holding him in place. Charlie really began to worry now. If she would say these things, what would she say about his non-dry cleaning business? Although Charlie had followed his old man's rule regarding women, he was still worried. Charlie recalled his father's words.

"Women are not the same as men, Charlie. They are not as smart. So you tell them nothing. It is better for them to tell them nothing for it does not give them anything to think about. When they have to think it is very hard for them, and the difficulty makes them cranky. If you tell them nothing they got nothing to be cranky about."

Charlie was sure that he had told his wife nothing. Certainly nothing about business. Yet he wondered how much she knew. And he wondered how smart she was. He wondered because he remembered his mother's words when his father had told him about women. His mother's words to his father were brief and to the point. His mother had said, "Go and fuck yourself."

Charlie began to worry even more after his wife ended the sexual depravity portion of the testimony.

Foxworth asked, "Have you reviewed your husband's Official Form Affidavit listing his assets, liabilities, and income and expenditures?"

"Yes, I have."

"And did you also fill out an Official Form Affidavit as required by the rules of the court?"

"Yes, I did."

"And does yours differ from your husband's?"

"Not really."

"However, do you know of any other business your husband might be in?"

"I don't know exactly if he is or not but I know he always talks to some guy."

"And do you know this individual's name, whom your husband always talks to?"

"No. All I know is that he is some guy in the navy."

"How do you know that?"

"Because my husband always calls him the Admiral."

"And of what . . ."

By now Charlie was really scared. He jumped up, his fright turning to rage. "You fuckin' lyin' cunt, accusing me of all this shit. Now you try to say I make more money, you barmaid whore."

Flay was frustrated looking for his gavel until he remembered so he pounded his fist onto the bench screaming "Silence . . . silence."

"Silence, my schlong," Charlie screamed back. "I gotta sit here and listen to what a virgin this cunt was. Let me tell you something, Judge, when I married her she had a hole so big you could drive a tractor trailer in it and make a U-turn without touching the walls. And as far as fuckin' blow jobs, everyone knew she could suck the chrome off a bumper."

Charlie started toward the door. "I ain't listenin' to no more of this shit."

Flay also rose and pointed at Charlie. "I warn you, Mr. Oakdale, if you leave this court I will instantly award your wife everything she asks for in her complaint."

Charlie had the door already opened as he turned to the judge. "She is askin' for four hundred a week, Judge. I take home three-fifty. Be my guest, give her five hundred," Charlie said, closing the door behind him.

Flay stalked off the bench. "I'll see counsel and the reporter in chambers."

The audience was still applauding when Charlie got to the elevator.

"I'd better go right to the Admiral myself before one of those fuckin' cops tells him what happened," he muttered to himself. The elevator arrived and Charlie got in. On the way down he thought, I should have never gone to trial. I didn't think she had the balls. Why didn't I listen to the Admiral and given her what she wanted and gotten rid of her, the fuckin cunt?"

Detective William Wotter and Lieutenant Solwin came out of the courtroom. Al LoConti had been dead right. The Admiral was the rung above Charlie "the Plant" Oakdale.

EARLIER ON THE SAME day that the Oakdale divorce trial was proceeding and on the same day that Vinnie LoConti would give a dying declaration, Ronald DePew entered an apartment house on Holland Avenue just south of Pelham Parkway. Ronald had been meandering, like a shark swimming the sea, scanning for whatever prey chance might supply.

Since his army discharge Ronald had been an unemployed outpatient at Bronx State Hospital. Today he had spotted an old man buying a newspaper on Lydig Avenue at seven-thirty in the morning, at the same time that people were going to work and leaving all the surrounding apartment houses for the downtown trip on the IRT. None of these many people paid any attention to Ronald DePew as he followed the old man to a bakery and then waited outside.

Nor did the old man notice Ronald walking behind him from the bakery back to his apartment house. The old man entered the outer door while a neighbor held the inner door open. He ran up two steps inside. As the door started to shut, DePew sprinted to stop it, but it closed and locked in his face. DePew became very angry. He had not liked the old man, who had given him that steamy feeling in his throat, which spread down into his chest and made his mouth half smile. He ran his finger over the linoleum knife in the large pocket of his work pants. With the large set of keys and the working clothes he wore, Ronald DePew looked like the superintendent of every apartment house in this Bronx neighborhood.

Ronald went back outside into the hot morning air. He swallowed hard while looking down the block toward Lydig Avenue. A heavyset blonde, her hair in curlers and dressed in a shocking pink housecoat, walked toward him. She stopped midway down the block and heaped praise on the miniature Chihuahua she was walking as the dog urinated against the tire of a car. Ronald smiled at the woman as she walked past him toward the vestibule. She smiled right back at the handsome young man. Still smiling, he looked at her hands. She wore no jewelry, and the absence of a wedding ring led him to conclude correctly that she was divorced.

She held open the outer door while reaching into the pockets of the housecoat for her keys.

"Waiting for someone?" she asked coyly.

"I'm supposed to work on the bell connections. The electrical circuits are out of whack and the bells sometimes don't open the door. I just called my boss to see where he was but I found out he won't be here until ten. So I gotta kill over two hours," DePew lied.

"What a shame," Sarah commiserated. "Would you like to come in for a cup of coffee or a cold drink?"

"Gee, that would be swell." DePew smiled with genuine enthusiasm.

What a morning this could be, Sarah Gorshbein thought as she opened the inner door. Sarah had struck out on the previous Saturday. She'd made her way from the Maroon Room on Williamsbridge Road to the Wah Wah Lounge in West Farms, but no one had even made a stab at picking her up. Things had gone so bad that she had toyed with the idea of going down to the Ferrocarril nightclub on Freeman Street to try to pick up one of those sexy Puerto Ricans. But she had refused to accept that things had deteriorated so far. Even Sol, whose books she kept on a part-time basis, had stopped screwing her. Maybe she shouldn't have been so quick to dump Marty. His checks were always on time and he always called up, ever willing to give it a go again. Fuck him, she thought. At forty-one, time was running out. She wasn't going to keep herself tied to a falling star like that loser Marty.

Just think of what you have in tow now, big girl. She smiled as she pressed the elevator button and turned and looked at the tall lean DePew. Can't be much more than nineteen, she thought. She admired his lean flat stomach, his muscular arms, his trim torso, and the bulge in his crotch.

The elevator arrived. They entered and she pressed the button for the fifth floor. The door shut and the car ascended. She smiled at DePew and he smiled back. At the fifth floor, the door slid open and they emerged into the hallway. Sarah walked to her left while DePew smiled and followed, pleased that the hallway was empty. The blonde opened the door to 5C and held it for DePew. The door shut behind him. Ronald stood with his thumbs hooked through the pants belt loops, keeping his fingers clasped. This way he was sure to avoid leaving fingerprints. He was not aware that the pose gave him a sauntering, insouciant gait, which drove Sarah Gorshbein right up the wall. DePew looked around and was surprised. Funny, he thought to himself, A sloppy cunt like this has such a neat pad. Sarah led him into the small kitchen set off to the left of the doorway. The enamel sink gleamed and the wheat-color refrigerator and stove were polished to a high sheen. The walls were covered by a light-brown wallpaper with pastoral scenes and darker brown curtains framed the window.

"Sit down while I make coffee, then I'll freshen up and join you."

Depew watched as she filled up a percolator and then scooped some coffee into the basket. She assembled it then put it on the gas stove. As she turned the stove on, she said, "Be back in a jiffy."

She went through her small neat living room into the bathroom at the end of her apartment where she took out her curlers and quickly blew her hair dry, then put powder and lipstick on. She sprayed on cologne then went into her bedroom where she replaced the housecoat with the sexy, frilly nightdress Sol had given her. She got back in the kitchen just in time to lower the flame under the coffee. Quickly she set up two cups and two saucers and in a minute poured coffee into the cups and set out milk and sugar. As an afterthought she asked if he would like a cold drink instead. DePew shook his head and sipped the hot coffee.

"I'll bet a good-looking young fellow like you has a lot of girlfriends?" she asked.

"Not anyone special," he replied shyly.

She leaned forward and looked into his eyes, putting her hand on his leg. He looked down, seemingly indifferent.

"You ever been real close with someone; you know what I mean?"

"Twice," he lied.

"Good things come in threes," she said, giggling.

"I just can't believe I am so lucky," he said.

"That makes two of us," she replied.

He continued to drink his coffee and she moved her hand up onto his thigh and rested it on the bulge in his pants.

"What's your name?" she asked.

"I'm Ronnie . . . what's yours?"

"I'm Sarah."

"Hello, Sarah."

"Hi . . . Ronnie. Come on, drink your coffee and come with me. I want to show you the best time you ever had. Did you know that the best sex a man can get is with a woman who is experienced?"

"I never heard that," Depew lied again.

"Well, it is the absolute truth. Come on."

DePew put down his cup and followed Sarah into the bedroom. As she entered the room, she turned and put her arms around his neck. "Kiss me," she said, shutting her eyes.

DePew put his arms around her and kissed her. She dropped her arms and started stroking him between his legs. Then while leading him to her bed she took off her nightdress. Naked, she sat down on the bed. DePew stood before her, taking off his shirt and dropping it on the floor. He undid his belt and his pants dropped too. Then, affecting embarrassment, he stepped out of his shorts. His body was ice, his throat like warm soft heat. He looked down at her as she grasped his penis and rubbed her hand softly up and down. He felt no emotion as she placed it in her mouth. He watched her head slide back and forth and then closed his eyes and moaned as the pleasure began to engulf him. After a while she stopped and then guided him down to the bed next to her. As he lay there looking up at the ceiling, she straddled him and inserted him into herself. She moaned from deep within as she slowly moved her hips up and down. DePew arched his hips upward to meet her downward thrusts. They moved faster, then even faster. She moaned and breathed harder and harder. Finally she groaned deeply and shuddered and stopped. She looked down at DePew who was still hard inside her.

"You are just great, honey, just great," she said. DePew smiled back and just nodded, pretending shyness.

Sarah got up and went to the bathroom. "Be right back," she said. "Don't go nowhere without me." She giggled.

She sat on the bowl and peed. Then after wiping herself she took a mouthful of mouthwash, swirled it around her mouth, and spat into the bowl and flushed. Turning, she was surprised to see him in the doorway. He had his drawers on but that was all. She still noticed the bulge in his crotch. "I'd love a steady diet of you, honey," she said.

"I'd like to come back if I could," he said, walking up behind her. She was dabbing at the corners of her mouth with a tissue as she looked at him in the mirror standing behind her.

"When would you like to stop by?" she said. "I could make some dinner for you or take you out to eat if you like."

"Maybe I could come by on Friday and I'll take you out to eat. A lady should not pay."

I can't believe this, she thought to herself, while nodding yes to him in the mirror. As she nodded she felt his penis against her buttocks then felt it outside his drawers and between her cheeks.

"Can I put it in there, Sarah?" he asked.

"You have the wrong place, honey," she said, bending over the sink.

"No, I don't, Sarah, I'd like to put it in your behind."

"You sure you want to do that, Ronnie? I never really like to do that."

"Come on, Sarah, please."

She straightened up and turned to him.

"Okay, Ronnie," she said, opening the mirror door to the medicine chest. She took out a jar of petroleum jelly and handed it to him.

"Can you do it for me, Sarah?" he asked.

She shrugged and took out a handful of the jelly and applied it to his penis. Then she put the top on the jar and wiped her hand.

While facing the mirror she felt him against her. "Don't you want to go inside?" she asked.

"I can't wait," he answered.

Grasping the ends of the sink and bending over, she thought, For once I'm going to enjoy getting fucked in the ass.

She reached back, guiding him in with one of her hands.

Then she almost lost her breath as he thrust into her bowels. For a moment it hurt, but just for a moment. As he thrust back and forth into her, his hand and fingers played with her clitoris and his other hand fondled her breasts. She looked down into the sink and felt pleasure throughout her body as she absorbed his pulsing thrusts.

As she started to climax she didn't notice that the strokes on her breasts had stopped. Feeling a hard blow to the side of her neck, she noticed splashes of red in the sink. She still did not realize it was her own blood as he raised her neck with his hand. Their faces were reflected in the mirror, and she watched hopelessly as he placed his hand over her mouth while the blood poured from the side of her neck as he slashed her throat with the linoleum knife. Her severed jugular sprayed blood over the mirror and into the sink as Ronald DePew, still inside her, swung her around. The last thing Sarah knew was that she was falling headfirst into the bathtub.

DEPEW JUMPED BACK AS the body slumped into the tub. Sarah had collapsed in her final seconds and her sightless eyes stared onto the enamel porcelain of the tub's bottom, her knees resting on the floor outside the tub. Blood still spurted from her neck into the bathtub and onto the shower curtain. As DePew stepped forward and grasped her head, it flopped back easily on the hinge caused by the gaping slashed throat. He stared into her eyes, hoping to find a flicker of life and craving to see some terror in her last moment on earth. He saw nothing but a gaze from eyes that did not move and did not flutter.

Blood had spurted all over his drawers and flinging her head downward, he cursed aloud. Her body, sagging from the momentum, slid down onto the floor. DePew reached into his pockets and withdrew a pair of vinyl gloves, a type used by hunters when gutting and cleaning deer. He put them on and then took his pants off. Naked, he grasped an arm and a leg of the naked Sarah and lifted Sarah to the top of the tub. Then kneeling, he pushed her over the ledge into the tub. She thumped onto the porcelain like a large codfish hitting the deck after being dragged up through ocean waters by a hook through its mouth. But unlike a fresh-caught cod, Sarah didn't even twitch, Ronald thought, smiling, as he entered the shower with his gloves still on. He drew the curtain and turned on the water. Soaping himself thoroughly, he washed all the blood from his body. He looked down and watched the blood swirl, its deep red mingling with the soapsuds and turning into a pinkish froth that bubbled down the drain. While blood still pulsed from the neck of the corpse straddled beneath his legs, he finished washing then stepped out of the tub and began drying himself.

Once dry, he placed a stopper in the tub drain then emptied two bottles of shampoo and two of hair conditioner on the corpse. As an afterthought he poured perfume and bubble bath liquid on top of Sarah and turned on the water. After a while the tub filled and then her body rested facedown in soapy bubbles floating on red-tinted water. With the gloves still on, DePew wiped the sink and the floor clean. Then, using the same towel, he wiped the bottom of his feet before leaving the bathroom.

He got dressed and entered the kitchen where he quickly washed the coffee cups and saucers, then placed them on the floor and ground them into tiny slivers under his workman's boots.

DePew carefully searched each draw of the dressers and vanity in the bedroom and after finding Sarah's purse removed thirty-five dollars.

His frustration at not discovering any more money turned to pleasure when he opened the vanity next to the bed and picked up an edition of *Romantic Interlude* magazine. A Japanese officer's automatic pistol and a snub-nosed Colt six-shot revolver lay before him. The pistol had been given to Sarah by her late father, who had taken it from the body of a Japanese officer who had died from American bullets on Iwo Jima. The Colt came from Marty, her ex-husband. Both father and husband, concerned with her safety, taught her to shoot. She had become a dead shot.

Ronald DePew carefully lifted both small handguns from the vanity. He placed them under his shirt and inside his belted waist. Then he walked to the door and looked through the peephole. Satisfied, he stepped into the empty hallway and shut the door behind him. He took off the gloves and placed them inside the used towel, then rolled it up and tucked it beneath his arm. Ronald did not leave a print.

Back inside the apartment, the sniffing miniature Chihuahua crawled out from beneath the bed. He had been frightened of the man who had come in with his mistress. Now missing her he sniffed and whined and pattered into the bathroom, sniffing and smelling only the soap, the perfume, and the bubble bath.

His were the only tracks the police would find.

AS DEPEW WAS SEARCHING Sarah's apartment, Vince LoConti pulled his milk truck up to the curb in front of the Shupinsky Supermarket on Holland Avenue a few feet from the corner of Holland and Brady. He opened the door, jumped down, and opened the back of the truck, scanning his manifest to see that Shupinsky had ordered twenty cases of milk, three cases of orange juice, and a case of mixed creams.

Vince LoConti had really loved this job until he'd been held up in Harlem at gunpoint. After two milkmen had been shot, although not critically, Vince and the other Manhattan milkmen took to wearing bulletproof vests. It had been Vince's idea, since flak vests had saved his life in Nam. After he was held up a second time and unknown to him, Uncle Peppy paid a visit to the union rep and Vince found himself with a route in the Bronx. Vince was grateful when the president of Mother Nature's Farms, Mr. Maheny, informed him of his new route, telling him that after all the danger Vince had lived through in Nam, they couldn't afford to have him shot in New York City.

Vince took his handtruck and went back and forth from the truck to the supermarket until all but three cases of milk were delivered. Then he chatted with Mike Shupinsky, the owner's son, who never counted the delivery but just spotchecked the case orders for freshness. After Mike paid Vince in cash for the full order, Vince said good-bye and walked outside. He held the cash in his hand and began to fold it into his wallet. Then he opened the truck and placed his handtruck inside. Turning around, he spotted a good-looking kid walking towards him with a towel under his arm. The kid was smiling at Vince and Vince smiled back. Fuckin' kid goin' to the beach, what a fuckin life, he thought. Vince walked toward the driver's door but stopped as he felt the cold barrel of the snub-nosed Colt on his neck and heard a voice demanding that he freeze. As a hand reached into his pocket and retrieved his wallet, Vince LoConti knew that he was facing his last moments on earth. There was a certain tone in this gunman's voice, and there had been something about the blond kid's smile that had not seemed right. The kid was a killer. Vince knew his look just as he knew that cold, flat-timbered voice. It was like many of the guys on the Learpse team that Vince had been with in Nam. It was like the ear collectors, the ones who had killed for excitement, guys just like Vince LoConti.

Vince, ducking quickly to his left, crouched and ran. As he moved, DePew fired a round which grazed the top of Vince's head and crashed into the truck's window. Vince, pumping adrenaline, zigzagged down the block with blood streaming down his neck from the crease in his scalp.

DePew pulled the trigger and sent two rounds into the bulletproof vest. Vince cut to his right at the corner just as a third bullet from the Colt entered his right cheek. Vince was still lucky because his labored breathing had forced his mouth wide open and the bullet passed right through, exiting from his left cheek. DePew charging after him, still firing, and finally discarded the empty Colt. Foaming with rage, DePew, still hunting Vince LoConti, reached into his belt for the Japanese pistol and fired a shot. It smashed Vinnie in the hip and ricocheted underneath the bulletproof vest up into his chest cavity.

Ronald DePew had just found a new line of work.

Back at the borough command, the Hat was informed that a milkman had been shot. He immediately dispatched all available personnel to the area while ordering two detectives to drive him to the scene.

Once safely inside the borough command car, the Hat directed the detectives to detour to the Isle of Sligo Pub on East Tremont where he entered alone and had four shots of Four Roses with beer chasers. "One for each rose, me lad," he had said to McTigue behind the bar. McTigue's father was the owner of the Isle of Sligo, and the Hat picked up his monthly tithe—a case of Seagrams Crown Royal for his personal use and a few bottles of Jamieson's Irish Whiskey and some Four Roses for company. The Hat liked Crown Royal so much that he made it a rule never to have any while he was on duty except on holidays.

When the whiskey was safely loaded into the trunk of the car, the Hat realized that all available officers from the Four Three were in the vicinity of Holland Avenue, and so he decided to stop on Morris Park and pick up his envelope from Santa Giacomo, the bicycle-riding bookie.

When the borough command car arrived on Morris Park Avenue, the Hat, who had a nice buzz from the Four Roses, directed the car to go up and down the avenue, looking for the delivery bicycle that Santa Giacomo always drove.

At the intersection of Morris Park and Bronxdale, he directed the driver to make a right and glanced wistfully at the former site of the world-class pizzeria and bemoaned the passing of the Old Bronx. The car traveled one long block down to Neill Avenue, made another right turn, and stopped in front of a delivery bike chained to the fence of a cute shingled house. The Hat charged briskly out of the car and jogged up the four steps to the door. Impatiently he rang the bell and banged the door until Santa Giacomo opened it. The Hat barged into the neat, old-world home of the bookie Giacomo, holding his hand extended while *La Donna Mobile* was playing from a record in the living room. Santa Giacomo listened attentively to the opera while trying not to show his hatred for the drunken obscenity that violated this sainted place.

"Inspector, the money is not due until tomorrow," Santa Giacomo said.

"Well . . . make it a day early then," the Hat replied. "Today there was a shooting up around Holland Avenue in the Jew area, you know. The younger brother of that DA LoConti, that worthless fuckin' DA, got shot. I think he'll die and I don't know if the family knows about it yet, and I wouldn't have even come out meself but the fuckin' buffalo is a fuckin' milkman, and the press will probably be buzzin' all around the fuckin' mayor's balls and the commissioner's asshole like the gang of fuckin' flies that they be. And besides me fuckin' envelope which I would appreciate without any fuckin' further delay, Mr. Santa Giacomo me lad, I want to tell you to keep your fuckin' ears to the pavement like the fuckin' Indian that ye be, to see if ya hear anything about the motherless fuck what did this shootin'. Do ya understan' me, bucko?"

Santa Giacomo nodded and, taking cash from his wallet, placed it into an envelope and handed it to the Hat. The Hat stuck the envelope inside his jacket and turned to leave.

"I don't know how a smart man like you can stan' that fuckin' racket," he said, indicating the opera.

Santa Giacomo, alone with his thoughts, watched the Hat drive away and then went to work to find out who had shot young Vinnie LoConti.

TWO YOUNG FIFTEEN-YEAR-olds, Davey Kirschenbaum and Fred Margolis, witnessed Ronald DePew shooting and chasing Vinnie LoConti. They saw him throw a gun to the ground and take another from inside his shirt, run up the block, shoot, then stop and return, and finally tuck the gun back inside his shirt. They ran into Davey's apartment house. Davey called the police while Fred looked out the third-floor window, saw the gunman pick up a towel, place it under his arm, and walk briskly out of sight.

Ronald DePew crossed Matthews and Brady avenues under the Dyre Avenue El. He climbed up the earthen embankments and onto the train track. Seeing the way was clear, he sprinted up the railroad ties toward the Morris Park station where he bounded up three short steps to the platform. He dropped the towel and its contents into a large blue garbage pail and after a few minutes boarded an uptown train. After he exited the train he caught a crosstown bus to the Bronx Zoo.

Ronald had decided to visit the House of Darkness before going home.

At about the time that DePew was riding on the train toward Pelham Parkway, a police car, sirens screaming and lights flashing, roared up Brady Avenue from White Plains Road while another car sped with the bloody body of Vince LoConti toward Jacobi Hospital.

Davey and Fred had run down into the street after Fred lost sight of DePew to show the police where the gun had been dropped. The boys were proud of themselves—they hadn't touched the gun, so their fingerprints would not smudge the shooter's. Davey was extra proud for he had noticed that the shooter was not wearing any gloves.

The next police car to arrive was driven by Allie Boy Spano. Upon discovering that the victim was his cousin, he left his partner Zemberelli and sped off to the hospital. Davey Kirshenbaum proudly pointed to the gun and told Richie that it was dropped by the gunman. To Davey's amazement, Richie picked up the gun, opened the cylinder, checked to see that all the casings represented spent shells, and then snapped the cylinder shut.

A few minutes later Davey's faith in the abilities of the police was partially restored when two unmarked police cars arrived. The first car contained four detectives from the Four Three squad. The second contained Timmy Flanagan, the DA's homicide coordinator, Detective Pete DiCerrechia, who had been assigned to the DA's office that day, and Assistant DA LoConti, who came as soon as he found out that his brother was shot. He was immediately whisked to the hospital.

Pete took the gun from Zemberelli and, cursing to himself, made a note of the make, model, and serial number. He called it in to the Four Three from the radio in his unmarked car. Timmy Flanagan was starting to direct other arriving officers to the group of police forming around Captain Bourke of the borough command. Bourke, a former detective, knew his stuff, and Flanagan was pleased to see that he was organizing a house-by-house search. Two of the detectives from the Four Three were interviewing Davey and Fred.

Suddenly there was a blurb from the radio responding to Pete's transmitting the gun's serial number.

"Pete, this is Mulvey. Do you read? Over."

"Go, Sarge," Pete responded.

"Subject weapon registered to a Martin Gorschbein of 1832 Cruger Avenue. Bronx, New York. Weapon has not been reported missing or stolen."

"That's a rodge, sarge. Thanks. Out."

Johnny O'Boyle arrived in the DA felony car driven by Hanratty. They spoke briefly with Pete and Flanagan and then the four of them sped off, arriving at 1832 Cruger Avenue in less than three minutes. Marty Gorshbein told them that he had given the gun to his ex-wife. "And where does she live, Mr. Gorschbein?" Pete said in a soft voice.

"She's on Holland at 1529, Apartment 5C."

"Is she home, Mr. Gorschbein?"

"Let's see, yes, she should be home today."

"You don't know if she gave the gun to anyone else?"

"I don't think she would without asking me. Say, what's the matter? Where did you find my gun? I assume that is what you are talking about."

"It was found in the street," the detectives said as they left. Minutes later they pulled up in front of Sarah Gorschbein's apartment house. As they hurried inside, they passed two men on the stoop. One of them was the elderly man who Ronald DePew had followed into this very building. He had absolutely no idea how lucky he was to still be living.

Inside while O'Boyle and the detectives waited nervously for the elevator, the Hat and his detective bodyguards roared onto Brady Avenue. It was now 10:40 A.M.

Charlie Oakdale made a beeline from the courtroom to the Admiral's import company located in a warehouse in the shadows of the Throggs Neck Bridge.

When Charlie entered the warehouse, his fears were dispelled in part by the smells familiar to him from his youth.

Taking a deep breath, he shook his head appreciatively as he gazed at rows of large Provolone cheeses hanging by thick cords from the ceiling. He nodded at their pale-yellow waxlike exterior while inhaling their pungent sharpness. Rows of dried sausage, both sweet and hot, also hung from the ceiling. Behind them hung the imported and U.S.-made Prosciutto hams hanging like stubby mandolins against the white backdrop of the warehouse wall. Next to them hung the Westphalian hams of Germany and Smithfield and other cured hams from the American South. On a wooden rack against the far wall stood row on row of cheeses for grating. There were the Romano, from the middle of Italy, blackened on the outside lying like the wheels of a child's toy. There were also the Parmesan cheeses and the pepper grating cheese from Sicily, called Incanestrato.

High above the cheeses reachable only by a ladder hung large clear plastic bags of dried boletus mushrooms from the north of Italy, which sold retail for forty dollars a pound. Next to them hung bags containing both white and black truffles from the north of Italy, which were literally worth more than their weight in gold. Charlie knew that special pigs were needed to smell the earth to locate where these fungi, cousins to the mushroom, grew.

Toward the rear of the warehouse Charlie spotted Guido Insalata, the Admiral, busy with two assistants checking gallons of olive oil recently arrived from Italy, Spain, Greece, and even the West Coast of the United States.

"Hey, Charlie what do you say?" the Admiral called out, smiling broadly.

"Hello, Mr. Insalata. How are you today?"

"I'm fine, Charlie, but how goes your trial?"

"Not too well, and that's what I am here about."

"Go ahead, Charlie, go sit in the office. Umberto and I will be finished in a moment."

Charlie entered a small paneled office in the corner of the warehouse. A large opulently padded armchair stood behind a long rosewood desk. Pictures of the Admiral with members of the New York congressional delegation and with leaders of all ethnic and racial groups adorned the walls. Above the pictures were plaques from charities and community groups attesting to the magnificent generosity and community dedication of Guido Insalata.

Charlie Oakdale nervously lit a cigarette. Even though the air conditioning in the office was much colder than that in the warehouse, Charlie started to sweat.

Guido Insalata entered the office.

"Spare me the bullshit, Charlie, I already got a call. You might have pulled it off with your fuckin' little act but your missus still mentioned my name."

Charlie started to protest.

"I don't want to hear anything, Charlie. I told you that it was not a good idea to go before the judge with this thing. And you hire that marriage-murderin' skunk, rat bastid lawyer who is stupid enough to let half the fucking cops and investigators in the city sit in the court. I hear you put on a real nice show for them, Charlie, a real nice show."

"I can only say I am truly sorry I did not listen to you, Mr. Insalata, truly sorry."

"Okay, Charlie, listen. You've been a good man for me, and I appreciate how you were a loyal assistant to my son-in-law, God rest his soul. Now go about your business, Charlie, and don't let your emotions with your wife affect business affairs. Because if you do, Charlie, you could wind up staring at the river. And, Charlie, I'm certain that you do not want to wind up like that."

Charlie agreed. In fact, Charlie was never more certain about anything in his life; he knew only too well what "staring at the river" meant.

The words grew out of the one and only burglary of this fortresslike warehouse. Despite the steel doors, secured by the finest locks, a state-of-the-art siren system tied right into the Four Five precinct, and the fiercest dogs money could buy patrolling within the perimeter fence, two burglars had actually gained entry.

They had thrown fresh bloody steaks generously laced with cyanide to the dogs, and they had been so skilled that they easily bypassed the alarm and picked the locks. Swinging the loading platform gates up on their rollers they loaded a panel truck with every morsel from within the Admiral's warehouse, leaving him only one boletus mushroom and a bottle of vinegar. Then they had driven a few short miles to the entrance to the Whitestone Bridge, where they delivered the truck and its contents to the man who owned it and he drove it to his warehouse in Queens. It was a flawless operation except that the license plate of the truck had been spotted by the Admiral's wife from their home next to the warehouse. And so the Admiral, shortly after calculating the extent of his losses, decided to forgo reporting the theft to the police. With full knowledge that such an action would prevent his taking a casualty loss on his income tax return, he nevertheless comforted himself with what he was about to do.

Four days later, Jimmy "Giraffe" Gerello told four men the identities of those who had helped him break into the Admiral's warehouse. Jimmy Giraffe was six feet five and a half inches tall and had a very long neck. He weighed only 175 pounds. He realized that revealing his accomplices' identities would not be enough to save his life, so he struggled desperately with the three smaller men who held him. Each time the men tried to force him into the fifty-five-gallon steel drum, he would manage to get up and nearly out. This was due to two factors, one that he was full of adrenaline, and two that he was far too tall for the drum. So while his legs were inside the drum, one man held him by the hips and the other two bent his torso parallel to the ground. It was then fairly easy for the Admiral to chain-saw him in half at the navel. His assassins marveled that his screams still continued while his torso flopped on the concrete floor and his blood spurted from both severed ends. Seconds later his torso was secured in another steel drum, and the Admiral and his assistants left.

A week later the Hat was summoned to a street in the shadows of the Throggs Neck Bridge. Police cars filled the area and the press was swarming. Flashbulbs were popping from cameras pointed upward at the gray suspension cables. The Hat saw something hanging from the middle of the bridge, dangling over the water. He snatched a pair of binoculars from a captain from the Four Five standing at his side. The binoculars were attached to a vinyl strap encircling the captain's neck. The captain was happy when the vinyl strap broke. The Hat, swiveling, snapped the binoculars smartly to his eyes like a veteran U boat commander, upping scope. Then he blanched and staggered. Through the lenses he saw two bodies hanging upside-down, secured by thick wire cable to the bridge span. As the bodies twisted in the wind, the Hat saw their faces. Their genitalia had been sewn to their cheeks and their sightless eyes stared at the river below. The Hat vomited. The captain from the Four Five stopped being happy because he could not get out of the way in time.

Charlie Oakdale, now standing in front of the Admiral, reflected on the meaning of the words "staring at the river." He hung his head in contrition and in fear.

"Okay enough, Charlie. Now I want you to do something for me."

"Anything at all, Mr. Insalata."

"Charlie, I just got a call from Morris Park Avenue. Someone shot the brother of that DA LoConti. The kid is a milkman, and I would appreciate knowing who shot him."

"I'll get on it right away, Mr. Insalata."

"Okay, Charlie, you do that. Now, Charlie, do you think that you and the wife will patch things up?"

"No, it's over, Mr. Insalata. Today I realize that she is capable of anything. She's dangerous."

The Admiral nodded. Then he put his arm around Charlie the Plant. "Give her what she wants, Charlie, and you will find that these matters subside like the worst storms. You know, when I sail my boat sometimes the wind is so high and the waves are strong and furious and then later all dies down and all is calm. Soon all will be calm for you too, Charlie. Calm and peaceful like a sea of glass." Smiling, he patted Charlie's back. "Grab a gallon of olive oil when you go, Charlie." Charlie smiled back, relieved and pleased with himself as if he had received absolution. In fact, he had.

After Charlie left the courtroom, he had been followed by Detective William Wotter and Lieutenant Solwin. They followed him across the Bronx all the way to Throggs Neck. Both Wotter and Solwin knew all about the Admiral. So when Charlie's Eldorado convertible pulled up in front of the warehouse at the end of the Neck, the officers felt they had received corroboration to Mildred Oakdale's statement regarding her husband's talking to an Admiral. The corroboration was sufficient to warrant an application for an extension to the existing eavesdropping order on Charlie Oakdale. The investigation and the wiretap application were further enhanced by the length of time Charlie remained in the premises and the fact that he returned outside without having any significant merchandise except something wrapped in a paper bag. The officers followed Charlie Oakdale home from the Admiral's warehouse and then went to their precinct to begin the reports needed to tap the telephone listed to the Admiral's business entity, the Hudson River Trading Company.

In Judge Flay's courtroom pandemonium and hysterical laughter followed Charlie's exit. No one had noticed Wotter, Solwin, and others leave. Frankie Hammon also left, and called the Admiral. He gave a full report while Judge Flay was granting Mildred Oakdale a divorce and everything else he could think of.

Fifteen minutes after the Admiral received the call from Frankie, two electricians arrived outside the courtroom and mingled with the crowds.

Frankie, who got a good part of the gambling business in the Bronx, had been told by the Admiral, his chief patron, to use his charm and get Foxworth, Caven, and whoever was with them to the Old Bailey Tavern around the corner from the courthouse and to buy them all a drink. Frankie knew better than to ask questions.

Inside the robing room Flay proceeded to administer a legal drubbing to the absent Charlie Oakdale. After the recital of the "Good-bye Chant," Flay pronounced the marriage at an end. Howard Caven made pro forma objections but without any real zest. The record was protected and his fee had been paid.

Mrs. Oakdale was relieved. She was finally rid of Charlie and free to do whatever she wanted with her dentist, Dr. Silver, who was eight years younger than she and never married. He was the exact opposite to coarse, crude Charlie. She certainly didn't mind having sardmy with Dr. Silver.

As she left the robing room with the two lawyers, Mildred Oakdale bumped into Frankie Hammon. Foxworth introduced Hammon to her and he greeted her warmly. Fuck you, prick, she thought to herself.

Chatting with the lawyers, Hammon learned that the divorce had just been granted. He told Mildred he wished her well. Phony bastard, she thought.

Hammon then suggested that he buy them all a drink at the Old Bailey to celebrate Mildred's recently liberated status.

The last thing in the world Mildred wanted was to be anywhere with this fuck Hammon, but she could really use a very stiff drink. She started to refuse but her lawyer sidled next to her and, giving her a big smile, said, "Please, Mildred, join us. It's customary to at least have one to celebrate the end of this long and arduous road." He pronounced the word arduous very slowly and his enormous Adam's apple bobbed up and down.

Mildred thought to herself, I bet this guy's Adam's apple sticks out farther than his schlong. Then aloud she said, "Okay," catching herself just before adding "what the fuck. . . ."

"Great." Hammon smiled broadly. "Great."

What the fuck is he so happy about? Mildred wondered.

The four exited the courtroom and got into the elevator. Two electricians carrying toolboxes entered right behind them.

When they walked into the Old Bailey three minutes later, the electricians stopped at the bar and watched the lawyers and Mildred take seats in a booth at the rear.

Mildred noticed that the bar had specials. Today's was a triple shot of Black Cross rye with a beer chaser for thirty cents. The former barmaid knew that this was a real rummy hangout, but even so she could use a good triple of something. She was glad that Charlie had finally got the message. She never would have dared to even mention the Admiral, but her lawyer assured her she would be safe. Now seated in the booth, she was content that tough-nut Charlie had finally been cracked.

Mildred didn't notice the two electricians follow her into the bar, nor did she notice that one of the three bartenders sidled down to the end of the bar to overhear the drink orders that Mildred's party of four gave to the waitress.

Mildred ordered an extra-dry martini straight up with a twist. The waitress left and gave the orders to the bartender, who looked toward the electricians. They nodded and ordered beers.

Drinking their beers slowly, the electricians spoke to the bartender, who had overheard the foursome's drink orders. Then quickly, beneath the bar, he mixed three highballs for the lawyers and a dry martini for Millie.

From under the bar he took a small plastic dispenser like those used for eyedrops and spiked the martini with a short squirt. The waitress picked up the drinks and served them.

The bartender, Paddy Fay, served a select clientele from the courthouse. Paddy had the ability to control a person's actions by the amount of this mixture he added to their drinks. He had discovered the mixture while he was a pharmacist's mate in the navy. One of the young doctors had told him that the amount of Dramamine or other seasickness medication that a person was given must be carefully watched. The doctor had forbidden dispensing more than two tablets at a time. Curious, Paddy gave certain individuals more than the prescribed dosage. Over the months, Paddy noticed that these individuals become so drowsy they were in fact knocked out. One apprentice seaman who had been given eight tablets as an experimental dose started to shadow box on the deck and then kicked an ensign in the balls.

When the man was unable to explain or recall what happened at his court-martial, Paddy Fay stopped giving out more than two tablets at a time. He knew he had something almost as valuable as the elixir sought by the alchemists of old. He had discovered an over-the-counter knockout drop.

While a sailor, Paddy had experimented with the chief pharmacist's mortar and pestle, kept in the pharmacy as symbols of the profession. He had developed his own formula, an extremely potent solution of ground and liquefied seasickness medication. One drop could make the average man drowsy. Two drops would suffice for even the biggest individual, and a short squirt produced erratic behavior, followed by deep sleep. A long squirt could induce a brief coma, preceded by a psychotic episode.

Paddy Fay's brother was a famous bail bondsman who also ran an investigating service for insurance companies. He investigated those who commenced lawsuits against people who carried insurance. The lawyers for the insurance company used Paddy's brother's service. If settlement failed in really big cases, such as those with permanent crippling or the loss of a limb, and trial ensued, Paddy could be relied on to administer his special formula to the plaintiff's lawyer. Most lawyers were friendly outside the courtroom, and during a trial they more often than not met during lunch at the Old Bailey. During this meeting the lawyer for the insurance company would pat his adversary on the back and order a drink. If the insurance company lawyer put a ten-dollar bill on the bar, his adversary would become drowsy that afternoon. This might be during final summation or during the examination of a key witness. If a twenty-dollar bill was put on the bar, the plaintiff's lawyer would act like a moron in front of the jury.

On this day Frankie Hammon waved to Paddy Fay, who waved back, and Frankie put a twenty on the bar.

They both watched Mildred Oakdale down her martini. Her second martini did not have any of Fay's formula in it. Neither did her third. After her third martini she suddenly complained of a terrible drowsiness and began to yawn uncontrollably. She shook her head and said in disbelief that she could not keep her eyes open. Turning to Foxworth, she said she was feeling ill and had to get home. The men commiserated with her and told her that it was the strain that she had been under which had suddenly taken its toll. Fast Frankie Hammon volunteered to get her a cab, and she smiled her gratitude at him.

Frankie went outside and signaled. A cab was parked near a meter next to the Old Bailey. The driver pulled up and the three lawyers helped Mildred Oakdale into the cab driven by one of the Admiral's men. She gave her address and fought the sleep that was engulfing her as the cab proceeded across 161st Street. She was dimly aware that the driver was traveling a different route, but she was too tired to protest as the cab passed West Farms and stopped next to a barge on Westchester Creek. She didn't even care that she was being wrapped into a blanket and carried on board the barge. She sunk into oblivion as the blanket was wrapped in canvas and weighted with lead. She would never wake up.

Johnny, Pete, and Timmy Flanagan entered Sarah Gorschbein's apartment after first obtaining a key from the superintendent. When they entered they found tracks of a small dog throughout the house. Hearing a whine from the bedroom, they discovered the Chihuahua cowering in a corner and then found Sarah, submerged in a frothy bubble bath. The room was still warm and Timmy inserted one finger into the tub to test the water's heat.

Flanagan, not wasting any time, conferred briefly with Johnny and Pete then left the apartment. He got into the unmarked car and drove to the command center a few blocks away. There Captain Bourke had been joined by the Hat and Flanagan saluted. You always had to kiss the Hat's ass, Timmy thought as he reported.

"Owner of the gun gave it to his ex-wife. She's dead in an apartment up the block. She was probably killed right before Vince LoConti was shot. I think that the same guy that is shooting these milkmen is also killing the old ladies."

Bourke, who knew all the tricks, asked how old this deceased was. "Early forties," Flanagan replied.

Bourke looked skeptically at Flanagan but didn't say anything while the Hat was present. Undaunted, Flanagan turned to the Hat.

"In fact, Inspector Sir, I have a theory that this guy is the same one that has killed that hairdresser over on Sedgwick and jammed up the young cop from the Four Four."

The Hat snapped around, truly surprised, for he had been convinced that the cop Carleton had in fact killed the hairdresser. Now the Hat immediately saw the possibility of getting the milkman shooter, the old lady killer, and the hairdresser's killer in one swoop. "Just think," he said, "how many cases we can clear just as soon as we get the bastid." Flanagan had him hooked solid.

"Inspector, if forensic and the ME can show that this one has been hit in the ass, then I think there is no question that one guy is responsible. But by the time those lazy bastards get here, the trail will be colder than the mayor's wife's tits."

"In a pig's ass," the Hat screamed.

He entered the captain's radio car and patched a message through the Four Three precinct to Police Headquarters in Manhattan. Many FCC regulations were broken as the Hat screamed imprecations, curses, and vilifications against sundry public and police officials and castigated every ethnic group. The Hat, priding his fairness, did not exclude the Irish.

Twenty-five minutes later—record time—the head of forensic arrived at the command center with a six-man team. They were joined shortly thereafter by a deputy assistant medical examiner. All proceeded with the Hat to the apartment of the deceased. No one had thought to notify her ex-husband.

AL LOCONTI WENT INTO the room at Jacobi Hospital just after Vinnie had given his dying declaration. Vince had described his assailant in great detail, and a police artist was busy sketching. Al was so angry at this insensitivity that he could not speak. Allie Boy Spano put his arm around his shoulders as Al walked toward the bed. Seeing him, Vince tried feebly to extend his hand, and Al clasped it, looking down into his brother's eyes. Someone walked from the back of the room and stood next to Al. Having been admitted to the room minutes before by Allie Boy Spano she touched Al gently to offer solace. Al turned around and looked at Renee. Unable to speak, he just nodded as she squeezed his arm tighter.

"He's going to make it, Al," she said, "I just know in my bones that he's going to make it."

Al LoConti didn't answer. He could never again have faith in what she said.

The doctors ordered everyone from Vinnie LoConti's room, and Al left with Renee.

Renee had parked outside the hospital on Morris Park Avenue, and neither of them spoke on the way. Then as Renee put her arms around his neck to kiss him on the cheek, Al stiffened.

With tears in her eyes, Renee asked, "Is there anything that you want me to do?"

Al started to say no but then had a thought. Reaching into his pocket, he took out all his money, seven singles and a five-dollar bill. "Go down the avenue to Our Lady of Solace, go back to the church that married us and use this money to light candles for my brother."

"I'll go right now but I won't take a cent from you for that," she answered.

As he started to leave, Al turned towards her.

"Thanks," he mumbled and Renee nodded. She would pray for them all.

After driving to the shooting scene, Al walked up to a crowd of police, which included the Hat and Timmy Flanagan. Knowing that work was the best therapy, Al joined the investigation.

The Hat shook his hand warmly in greeting.

"I want to thank you for not lockin' up that innocent cop accused of shootin' that girl hairdresser on Sedgwick Avenue—you know the young cop from the Four Four with the nice wife and kid in Rockland County. Yes, yes. And Timmy Flanagan here has solved all these cases. Yes sir, this bastid that shot yer brother is the same that has been killing these old ladies and the same that killed that poor unfortunate on Sedgwick Avenue."

"And how do we know that?" Al asked, turning to Flanagan.

"Tell him, Timmy, tell him," the Hat ordered, smiling.

"Well, Inspector, it's just a theory, but since Dr. Stein here of the ME's office has informed us that this victim was sodomized and since most of the other victims were similarly sodomized, it seems pretty clear that we are looking for one perpetrator. And of course if we match the bullet they took from your brother with the gun found on the street, which we now know came from the dead lady's apartment, well, then we have the milkman shooter tied in also."

Al turned to Dr. Stein. "Is it possible to extract any semen from her so that we can establish a blood type?"

"We'll try, of course, but that bath she was in will probably prevent it," Stein replied.

Al, ignoring the Hat, turned to Timmy Flanagan. "We're going to need a lot more than what you are telling me to establish that this is the guy that killed Martha."

Flanagan only nodded but the Hat cut right in.

"When we get him, Mr. LoConti, I am sure that his version of the events will give us sufficient evidence to clear up all of these pending cases." The Hat smiled in anticipation.

"Make sure you notify our office, Inspector. I want a DA notified. I don't want any confessions suppressed and any indictments dismissed for lack of evidence. When my brother dies I don't want his killer's conviction reversed on appeal."

Then turning to the doctor, Al asked if he had anything else to contribute.

The doctor shook his head. "I know he shot your brother, Mr. LoConti, and believe me, we'll do every test on this woman that we can. But I'm afraid we're dealing with an extremely clever individual. You see, by placing the deceased in that tub with the hot water and all of the various detergents and powders, he has seriously compromised anything that we'll be able to discover except the obvious . . . manner of death and the fact that she was sodomized. The FBI has recently come up with a method of obtaining fingerprints from a corpse, but in this case that method also would be seriously compromised. Nevertheless, I'll request their assistance."

The Hat's head was bobbing up and down in affirmation of every word the doctor said, and when the doctor finished the Hat's head bobbed two more times. "That's right, Doc. Please do all the tests because we must get this clever fellow and stop him from killin' and robbin' milkmen and what else God only knows. And, Doc, he has been killin' the Irish, the Spanish, the Protestants, and the Italians, and now he's killin' your people so give it an extra bit of attention, will ya?"

Stein was too angry to speak as he stared at the Hat. He opened his mouth but nothing came out. Then turning on his heel, he actually ran to the ME staff car. After getting into the driver's side, he slammed the door and peeled out.

Tim Flanagan, the Hat, Al LoConti, and the forensic men stared after him.

"What do you think got into him?" the Hat asked, flabbergasted.

"Ah, you know these fuckin' doctors, Inspector," Flanagan responded. "They get real pissed off when they have to make house calls."

The Hat guffawed as Al walked away.

The next day all of the newspapers in the city carried the composite sketch of Ronald DePew. The youngsters who had viewed the assailant gave a description strikingly different from that of the dying Vince LoConti. The artists had made two composite drawings, one from the youngsters' description and the other from Vinnie's. Detectives Timmy Flanagan and Morrie Shapiro correctly chose to release the sketch from Vinnie's description despite his critical condition. As Al viewed the different drawings, he was vividly reminded of the inherent unreliability of eyewitness identification. It would be difficult for the casual observer to tell that the two drawings were of the same perpetrator. Yet the series of events proved that there could be only one.

Mrs. Grimaldi, the banker's wife on Tremont Avenue, recognized the composite immediately. She would never forget DePew throwing the dog off the roof into the street. Mrs. Grimaldi picked up the telephone and almost committed the greatest sacrilege in her life; she almost dialed the telephone number listed beneath the composite drawing. Saved by her years of training, she replaced the receiver on the hook. Yet she was unhappy. Though she'd avoided a transgression, she was terrified at living across the street from a depraved mass murderer. She became restless, vowing action. I must do somethin' about this fuckin' nut, she thought.

Later that day she did. The minute her husband came home from his banking business, she thrust the tabloid page beneath his nose and announced that the picture was that of Ronald DePew.

Mr. Grimaldi looked skeptically at the newspaper rendition and replied that it did not appear to be the DePew boy. Mr. Grimaldi's observations were tainted by the thought of the amount of action Mr. DePew placed every week. Mrs. Grimaldi could not be dissuaded, insisting that it was DePew and that if her husband did not do something about it, she would be forced to call the police. Shocked, Mr. Grimaldi grabbed the table, shaking his head in disbelief. "Next thing you'll be voting for the Communist Party," he said.

"You better do somethin' 'cause I ain't gonna live across the street from that murderer. Remember what he did to the dog?"

Mr. Grimaldi changed his mind and, satisfied, his wife served their supper.

The very next day Mr. Grimaldi had his weekly luncheon with Judge Marty Honig at the Restorante degli Amici. Mr. Grimaldi presented his problem to the judge, who became very distressed at having to make a decision. In fact, Judge Honig hated to make decisions, especially if they involved the criminal justice system where he worked every day. Many defense lawyers knew this and advised their clients to waive the right to jury trials so that the decision would be left to Judge Honig. The lawyers knew that the indecisive Honig would find it extremely difficult to find someone guilty beyond a reasonable doubt. Moreover Judge Honig felt that finding people guilty was bad for business and might damage his stature with the Admiral and Mr. Grimaldi.

Honig had a bad rep with the DAs. Soon Honig's courtroom became a dumping ground for what the DAs called pieces of shit.

So when a girlfriend complained that her boyfriend of seven years had raped her, the Assistant in the Part would announce before the court that this was a matter requiring positive action and the judge would refer it to Honig. Honig would dismiss for lack of corroboration and everyone would be happy. And when a woman complained that her neighbor was having a sexual affair with alley cats, Honig dismissed on the ground of lack of corroboration. Sometimes, however, there was a slipup, and something serious would come before Honig. One such case involved a housing police officer who had arrested a man for fondling an eight-year-old. The officer, a very good cop, had observed the act himself. The case was airtight, and the DA made mincemeat of the defendant when he took the stand to testify. Honig was upset at the sea of blue in the courtroom—some thirty to forty uniformed housing police officers were observing the trial. After all the evidence was presented and counsel had given their summations, Honig announced, "decision reserved." This would clear the court and permit Honig to decide the matter without pressure. The next day Honig was surprised to take the bench and still see a sea of blue. He announced that the matter was still under consideration. This persisted for six consecutive days. Finally a reporter printed a headline that assisted Honig in arriving at a verdict. The headline read COURTROOM PHENOMENON—HUNG JURY . . . IN NONJURY TRIAL.

Honig was forced to convict, making almost everyone happy in the process. The judge always became very decisive when matters affected his relationship with his banker friend who now sat across the restaurant table. After Mr. Grimaldi finished talking about Ronald DePew, Judge Honig excused himself and walked to the phone booth. He dialed the number of the Hudson River Trading Company and asked to speak to Mr. Insalata. The judge, who identified himself only as Marty, said: "My friend here who I meet each week is upset. He knows the picture in the paper belongs to a kid named Ronald DePew who lives on Tremont Avenue. I figured I should inform you immediately."

"Thank you, do nothing else," the Admiral responded.

Satisfied, Honig went back to Mr. Grimaldi and told him that everything would be taken care of. Both men smiled and began to eat.

As she listened to the tap of the Admiral's phone, Ruella Watkins motioned for William Wotter to pick up an extension. She was about to replay the entire tape of the call when the apparatus indicated that the Admiral was making an outgoing call. The number dialed was printed out on the monitoring register, and Wotter recognized the number of the borough command. Ruella and Wotter were dumbstruck as they overheard the Admiral pass the DePew information directly to the Hat.

Wotter called Solwin, then Al LoConti and ADA Farrell.

"Don't tell anyone else about this. Bring the tape right over here and make no duplicates," Al said. "It is goin' to be real interesting to watch what the Hat does with the information."

Wotter hung up the phone. Something had been bothering him since he heard the taped conversation. He was certain that he had heard the voice of John Doe Marty before, but he couldn't for the life of him remember when.

45

THE DOCTORS CUT A lot out of Vinnie LoConti. They took a piece of his liver and another of his spleen, eight inches from his intestines, and half the lobe of his right lung. Everyone waited for him to die. Fifteen minutes after he gave the dying declaration, the operations had begun. While Vinnie was under the knife Ronald DePew stood fondling the lineoleum knife in his trouser pocket in the Bronx Zoo's House of Darkness. True to its name, one could hardly see inside as faint light barely penetrated the inky blackness from the glass-enclosed cages. The House of Darkness had become a place of frequent refuge for Ronald DePew. He felt a kinship with the creatures that flourished in the dark, particularly the vampire bats.

This morning there were only a few spectators inside, and Ronald followed the displays through the oval building.

On his left pretty Migdalia Torres stood gazing intently at the life inside an obscure cave. There was barely enough light radiating from the glass interior to illuminate her lovely features. She moved slowly onward, fascinated by the exhibits and forgetting for the moment that her husband, Hector, had been laid off from the assembly plant in New Jersey and that the rent on their apartment was two months late. She had arisen that morning and showered and decided to walk the short distance from her home on Crotona Avenue to the zoo entrance on Fordham Road and Southern Boulevard. She had paid the admission, walked through the turnstile, and then taken a ride on the car train that whisked the sightseers through the grounds. She had watched the children throwing frozen fish to the seals at the seal pool and wandered through exhibits until she arrived at the House of Darkness. Hector had left that morning at 5 A.M. to shape up at a construction site for a laborer's job that paid three dollars an hour. The money was off the books and would supplement his unemployment so that ends could almost be met. It had been ten o'clock when she had left her apartment and since Hector had not come home, she knew he had found work.

She was deep in her own thoughts as she passed the darkest part of the building just before the dim exit sign. Suddenly she felt a crushing pressure on her mouth and a sharp pain across her neck. Falling to her knees, blood pouring from her throat, she collapsed, feeling for the life within her swollen belly. Her final sensation was the faint quiver from the heart of the child she carried.

No one saw Ronald DePew wipe the blade of the linoleum knife on the back of Migdalia's coat, then place it back in his pants, and casually saunter outside the House of Darkness, wandering past the bear cages on his way home.

After receiving the news from the Admiral, the Hat schemed for three days. Having traced DePew's route, the detectives tied him in to the murder of Migdalia Torres. At this juncture it didn't take the Hat long to figure out two things. First, something real dramatic had to be done immediately, and second, he had no idea what that something was. So he called the homicide coordinator, Detective Flanagan, and ordered him to stop in his office that day when he came to the borough command.

Al LoConti and Johnny O'Boyle, who were keeping tabs on the Hat, were pleased that he called Flanagan. They were about to so themselves, since everyone knew that Flanagan had a technique for solving crimes whenever informers supplied him with the perpetrator's identity. Flanagan would always come up with independent probable cause for an arrest, which invariably was followed by a full confession. All this, without ever revealing the identity of the informer. The Hat had indeed heard many stories of Flanagan's methods. Once convinced of the reliability of a tip, Flanagan would go to any extreme to obtain a confession that would stand up in court. And the Hat knew that Flanagan, clever man that he was, would never use strong-arm tactics, such as rubber hoses or placing a defendant in a wall locker then throwing it down a flight of stairs, or hanging them outside the windows of the Four Two precinct while the El ran by drowning their screams—none of the conventional methods of interrogation that the Hat had so fondly employed.

The Hat recalled a brutal rape-murder of a ten-year-old girl in the Four Seven that had baffled the most talented detectives for five months. Once Flanagan had been assigned, the case was solved in twenty-four hours.

They called him on a Friday and he had spent that night driving around the Bronx speaking to his many informants. Early the next afternoon the phone rang in the squad office. Flanagan received a name and an address from a caller whom he knew to be absolutely reliable.

The name turned out to be that of the girl's uncle. The suspect, Elvo Dunis, was picked up at his home and taken to the Four Seven squad room by Flanagan and two of the original assigned detectives, McSherry and Daniels.

Flanagan, McSherry, and Daniels, were Olympic class drinkers and after hustling Dunis into the unmarked squad car, they began passing a fifth of Cutty around, even offering to hold the bottle for the handcuffed Dunis while he drank. By the time they got to the Four Seven, Dunis, guilty as hell, started to sweat. They took him upstairs to the detective squad room and told him they would wait there until he confessed to killing his niece. Dunis was scared but not stupid and steadfastly denied any wrongdoing, even going as far as swearing on his mother's eyes. The detectives sat alone with him in the room drinking from the bottle of Cutty and telling Dunis he had better confess. After two hours of questioning,

Timmy Flanagan cracked another bottle of Cutty, took a long gulp, and passed it to McSherry. Flanagan knew that he had his man, but Dunis would not crack. Flanagan checked his watch; it was getting late. There was a racket that night at the VFW hall on Bruckner Boulevard: corn beef and cabbage and a setup for every table. Tim had paid ten dollars for himself and the bride and didn't want to miss the fun. Taking a long pull of Cutty, he left the room for the squad commander's office and called Pete DiCerrechia's brother-in-law.

That evening Al LoConti, who was two weeks out of the army and a spanking new DA, was doing his first weekend arraignment duty in the Bronx Criminal Court. Hanratty, the DA who had run against an incumbent judge and was in the shithouse with the party, was assigned as the supervisor, in charge of Al and the two neophyte DAs in the complaint room. Flanagan, now at the VFW racket on Bruckner, had already consumed two platters of corned beef washed down by two pitchers of beer. He was about to attack a bottle of Cutty when Dunis appeared before Judge Ned Rothman for arraignment on the murder charge. The Legal Aid lawyer assigned to Dunis had asked to approach the bench.

"Judge, I've been served with the notice that the people intend to offer this man's alleged confession at trial."

Judge Rothman thought there was a presumption of guilt for anyone who was arrested and felt that anyone working for Legal Aid was part of the international Soviet conspiracy. Rothman just looked at the Legal Aid lawyer.

"Why don't you get a fuckin' haircut?" Judge Rothman said.

"Your Honor, I must tell you that my client has related a story to me that is most bizarre."

"You guys are full of shit. This guy is going to be remanded unless you produce the Pope who tells me that he was with him at the time of this murder."

"Judge, I'd like to be heard."

"Step back. On the record. On the record," the judge yelled.

The Legal Aid lawyer and Al stepped back from the bench.

"What do you have to relate to the court?" Rothman asked.

"Your honor, the defendant informs me that his confession was coerced, that he is innocent, and that the only reason he confessed is that after the officers took him into custody someone came up to him in a stable or a barn riding on a camel. This person pointed a gun at him and fired two shots."

Even Rothman was taken aback. Al guffawed.

"What was this person wearing?" Rothman asked, winking at Al.

Dunis burst out, "He had on Scottish kilts and a cowboy hat."

"Okay," Rothman said. "Very cute, you're trying to set up an insanity defense. So I'll play along. I'm going to order a 730 exam to see if you are competent to stand trial. Remand."

The results of the 730 exam showed that Dunis was competent to stand trial. As a jury was being sworn he took a plea and got fifteen to life. Flanagan, McSherry, Daniels or the informer never had to testify.

The Hat knew each and every detail, including how Dunis had been taken to the Bronx Zoo, because Daniels was his man in the Four Seven squad and Daniels had done his job.

Timmy Flanagan had a stack of DD5s and unusuals on his desk. He had made a chart earlier this morning that contained a list of all the unsolved homicides in the last five years. There was a large wall map of New York City in front of his desk, and he had stuck various colored pins into the map. The color of the pins were geared to the chart. Each pin had a number marking the sequence in time when each homicide had been committed. The pins of course marked the location of each crime. The chart contained the names of the victims in descending time order. In columns across the page were blocks set aside for location, cause of death, characteristics, and suspects. A block next to the chart listed the names of the detectives assigned and the first officer on the scene.

Timmy Flanagan made an entry on the chart and stuck two pins in the map. Both pins had the same color and were numbered with the suffix A and B. The first pin was stuck in Van Cortlandt Park just south of the Yonkers city line. The second pin was stuck west of the first and marked the location where the golfers had discovered the legs. The legs case and the others listed on Timmy's wall chart had only one thing in common—they were all unsolved.

Timmy Flanagan was engaged in the broom method of police work. By linking all these many unrelated murders to one perpetrator he could, with only one arrest, make a clean sweep of all these unsolved crimes.

Flanagan put on his coat and went to the borough command, knowing that he had linked every possible unsolved murder in the City of New York to the old-lady murders and the milkmen shooter.

At the borough command the Hat took Flanagan into his private office and told him that he had a reliable tip that the killer's name was Ronald DePew. When he gave the address that had been reported to him, Flanagan immediately knew that Grimaldi was the source of the tips..

As Flanagan was leaving, the Hat told him that their conversation had never taken place, and Flanagan, smiling, said, "Yes, sir."

Timmy Flanagan had the power to pick any detectives in the county for this case, but anticipating the unconventional methods he might be forced to resort to, he chose only those whom he could trust without reservation. Consequently when he arrived at the home of Ronald DePew he was accompanied by Pete DiCerrechia and Rory O'Donnell.

Before arriving they had stopped at the Four Eight squad and made some phone calls to determine the number of persons in the DePew household. At Flanagan's request a young policewoman dialed the DePew number and a woman's voice answered. The policewoman asked if Ronnie was home. The woman replied, "Hold on, I'll get him." When DePew took the phone from his mother, he heard a dial tone and asked who had called. His mother replied that it sounded like a nice young girl. DePew, alarmed, went back to the supper table to finish his port butt tenderloin and left the apartment after gulping down a large glass of orange juice. He walked up the stairs onto the roof then crawled across the roof to an open parapet and looking down . . . waited to see who was coming.

Detective William Wotter stopped by the basement of the public school in Throggs Neck that held the equipment eavesdropping on the telephone conversations of Guido "the Admiral" Insalata. The wiretap had been in place for some time now and nothing of any significance had been reported. Wotter decided to use his own time to review the transcripts of the calls. Perhaps something would lead him to remember the voice of John Doe Marty.

Solwin's investigation had been thorough. Each call had been traced. A follow-up report to each transcript in the file contained the location of the telephone traced, the name of the subscriber, and a brief synopsis of the individual or entity involved. Most of the calls were from wholesale or retail merchants with whom the Hudson River Trading Company did business. Despite federal secrecy laws, the detectives had gotten copies of IRS investigations involving the Admiral. Thus the detectives verified that most of the calls involved entities with whom the Admiral did substantial business. All were reputable concerns.

Wotter pulled out the recorded tape with the voice of John Doe Marty. After playing it for the third time, suddenly he realized that the voice was that of Judge Martin Honig.

How could I ever forget? Wotter scolded himself.

He called Al and arranged to meet him at the Last Supper.

DePew, looking down, studied the unmarked police car pulling up in front of his building and watched the three detectives rush inside. He reasoned that if the police knew who he was, they knew his habits and would definitely search the roof and basement.

DePew looked across the row of rooftops that stretched up Tremont Avenue toward the Third Avenue El, planning his route carefully. Just before he left his crouched position behind the parapet, Ronald DePew looked at the street below. Seeing nothing unusual, he stood up. Mrs. Grimaldi was framed in her window across the street. DePew saw that her attention was focused on the police car in front of his building, and he instantly understood that it was Mrs. Grimaldi who had called the police and also told his parents that he had thrown the dog off the roof. Thinking of all the embarrassing questions that the probing doctors at Bronx State had asked him, he stared at Mrs. Grimaldi and then while creeping across the rooftops began to formulate a plan.

Wotter observed Al LoConti as he entered the restaurant. It was now two weeks since Vince LoConti had been shot, and Al and his ex-wife had kept a constant vigil. Wotter had heard from Allie Boy Spano that some of the bitterness between the two was gone. It was rumored that Renee had been seen two days ago with Al in the Last Supper. They were celebrating the news they had received: Vince was given an even chance to make it.

Wotter watched as Al conferred with his uncle. Peppy ushered Al to the booth in the corner of the rear room where Wotter was seated beneath a large wall speaker. Al nodded to Wotter and, pausing at the jukebox, dropped in some coins and punched some selections. The music was playing loudly overhead as Al sat down and summoned a waitress. After a minute she brought back a Pilsener glass of beer for Wotter and a glass of red wine for Al. Al sipped the wine listening.

"Your uncle has the best restaurant in the whole city, Al. No doubt about it."

The waitress came and put a large bowl of mussels and a basket of Barese bread in front of Wotter. The bread was baked in a brick oven and the blackened portions of the underside made Wotter smack his lips.

Wotter took a piece of bread and dipped it into the tomato mussel sauce. He took a bite and savored the peppery flash of heat on his palate and tongue as he swallowed the fiery mixture. He took a long sip of beer, then, turning toward the waitress, he held up two fingers, indicating he wanted two more beers.

Al watched and sipped the wine. He knew that Wotter had inherited his love of beer from his Flemish father and his love of the hot Italian seafood dishes from his Sicilian mother. Wotter's old man had dropped into Sicily on July 9, 1943, with the 82nd Airborne as Part of the Anglo-American-Canadian invasion of that island. Wotter had been born the following year in New York, and no one knew how the old man had smuggled Wotter's old lady out of Sicily to the Bronx.

Wotter was busy digging out mussels with a small fork, dipping them into the hot sauce, and swallowing. His eyes were tearing. Al watched his friend enjoy the food and thought of how incongruous it was that this sandy-haired, freckled-faced, blue-eyed police officer spoke the Sicilian dialect impeccably and enjoyed this feast as Al did. Only in America, Al thought.

"Great, great," Wotter said, drinking more beer. Al lit a Parodi cigar and sipped his wine.

Wotter began. "Do you remember when you started as a DA in the Criminal Courts bureau?"

"Sure," Al responded.

"You remember the drug cases that came in?"

"Sure."

"What were they like?"

"What do you mean?"

"Well, would you call them good arrests, good police work? What did they mean to you, if anything?"

"Well, at first they were, like, you know, interesting, then they took on a pattern. After a while if you had any smarts you knew which were good and which were bullshit, and also a lot depended on the cop involved."

Wotter nodded. "Ever see any really big collars?"

"There were a few big arrests for possession, but generally anything big came through the Narcotics Bureau. Big sales generally resulted in direct presentment to the grand jury. The criminal court would be sidestepped, and everything would go right to Supreme. But what's this all about, Willy?"

"What was the biggest piece of shit you ever saw when it came to sale cases?"

"You mean in general terms?" Al asked.

"Yeah, generally."

"Observation sale, buyer got away," Al replied without hesitation. Al was referring to cases where the drug seller was arrested while the buyer got away. The police would observe an individual pass glassine envelopes on a South Bronx street to others who were apparent addicts. In some instances the police would see money exchange. The officers would grab the buyer and toss him and come up with a glassine envelope. Chemical analysis later would show the presence of heroin. In such cases the buyer would be charged with possession and the seller with sale. This was a good arrest.

In other cases that the police observed, they could not see glassine envelopes or money, due to the furtiveness of the criminals. Without such evidence, the police knew that the case would be thrown out of court for lack of probable cause. Even if they saw a glassine envelope, they had to testify that they saw a white powder inside, otherwise judges would heave the case. A glassine envelope could contain a stamp, and the junkies in the South Bronx exchanging currency for such envelopes could merely be numismatists.

Sometimes when the police chased a buyer, the contraband would be discarded. When retrieved and analyzed, it would be found to contain heroin. In other cases the officers would arrest the seller and charge him with possession with intent to sell—a lesser felony than sale. In still other cases the buyer got away script would be used. Hence the analyzed contraband from the fictional buyer would be that sold by the accused. It would not take a DA long to know that the buyer-got-away story was really a piece of shit that must be disposed of by a simple possession plea in Criminal Court. Likewise the possession-with-intent-to-sell cases invariably involved quantities that would not of themselves amount to felony weight, so they too were disposed of by misdemeanor pleas. The cops got credit for a felony arrest, the case was disposed of, and the narcotics trafficker received a bargain. Only the public got fucked, Al thought.

"Well," said Wotter, "once when I was a young street narcotics cop I made a few legit collars where the buyer did get away."

Al looked interested. He had always assumed that such cases were police perjury designed to sidestep the impenetrable probable cause barrier. Al knew that his friend would not be bullshitting.

"It's true, Al. I was with Solwin. He'd just passed the sergeant's exam. We were off Brook Avenue and I was in the second floor of a burned-out building with binoculars and Solwin was in a doorway around the corner. We had information from a stool that a guy was selling, and he gave us a location and description. So I looked at the area with the binoculars. Sure as shit I could see the passage of envelopes and the exchange of money. I saw a junkie come up, give a guy some money, and take two bags and put them into his right front pocket. I could even see the white powder in the bags. The street was deserted. I called Solwin on the radio and I saw him come around the corner and grab them. Then I came down and searched the buyer and the seller. The drugs were right where I had seen them, and Solwin could testify the guy had not moved from the time he grabbed him until I came downstairs. Well, we get to a hearing for the sale and the judge treats it like a real buyer-got-away job, lambasts me for lying, and heaves the case. Anyway, the DA in the Part sends me to the grand jury and we indict the seller for sale. I never forgot the judge's voice, though."

"So. . . ?" Al said.

"So . . . we just picked up the judge's voice on a wire."

"Go ahead, Willy. Who is the judge?"

"Marty Honig."

Al raised his eyebrows. "Who was he talking to?"

"The Admiral. Honig was the guy who gave the Admiral the information about DePew—the information Flanagan is pursuing right now."

"Let's take a ride, Willy." They paid and left. Al was in such a hurry that he forgot to say good-bye to his uncle Peppy.

Mrs. Grimaldi stood at her stove preparing the boned and skinned chicken breasts the way her husband loved. She and her neighbors had attended an evening course at Roosevelt High School that taught them the latest in diet and nutrition. Concerned with her own and her husband's cholesterol levels, she had promised to change their dietary habits. Gone were the two eggs and bacon breakfasts and the cold cuts beloved by Mr. Grimaldi, the sliced Prosciutto ham, the salami, the cappicollo. They had been replaced by slices of turkey breast, carrots, and cucumbers.

Subsisting on this diet for some six months now, Mr. Grimaldi had lost twenty-five pounds. Customers who regularly bet with him began to compliment him on his new appearance. This made Mr. Grimaldi vain.

After dropping fifteen pounds herself, Mrs. Grimaldi began to dress more fashionably and convinced her husband to take her to the Stelle Azurre Ballroom on Gun Hill Road, where they danced together to the sounds of the big bands of the forties. The old flame between them was rekindled and a bonfire erupted.

While Mrs. Grimaldi was placing the chicken breasts in the roasting pan and ladling fresh tomato sauce on them, Ronald De-

Pew was crossing over onto the roof of her house. After traversing the roof to its far side, he climbed down the ladder to the fire escape, then scrambled down to the level of the Grimaldi apartment.

Mrs. Grimaldi placed thin slices of skim-milk mozzarella on top of each chicken breast, sprinkled fresh oregano leaves from the market on Arthur Avenue on top, then spooned on more tomato sauce. She placed the roasting pan into the oven, closed the door, and set the temperature for 350 degrees. As the oven door closed the window to her bedroom opened. Ronald DePew slipped inside and crouched near the doorway. Outside the bedroom door on a small table sat the only telephone in the Grimaldi household. Mrs. Perrotta, who lived across the air shaft from the Grimaldis and who had also attended the nutrition class, recognized DePew as he climbed in the apartment window from the fire escape. Mrs. Perrotta made two telephone calls. The first was to 911. The 911 operator was a young female trainee hired by the city through the CETA program. She had just come from a break in the ladies' room where she had smoked a joint and taken a pill to mellow out. After dutifully taking all the information, she concluded that Mrs. Perrotta was a flake and, disregarding department policy, did nothing. The second call Mrs. Perrotta made was to Mrs. Grimaldi.

When the phone rang Mrs. Grimaldi left the salad she was preparing in the kitchen and walked down the foyer. As she was about to pick the phone up, a hand grasped her from behind and covered her mouth.

She suffered a massive coronary as her throat was being cut and died before DePew released her.

When the phone was not answered, Mrs. Perrotta watched surreptitiously for the arrival of the police or the departure of DePew. She never did see DePew leave the Grimaldi apartment house and exit the front door onto the street. Ronald sauntered up to Third Avenue and caught a bus going toward West Farms.

After a half hour had passed and no police had arrived, Mrs. Perrotta decided to call her husband, Mikey. Mikey was a foreman for the Department of Parks and worked in offices alongside the Bronx River Parkway, right next to the motorcycle precinct known as Highway One. Mikey knew all the cops.

After his hysterical wife hung up, Mikey dialed the private line of the commanding officer of Highway One.

The evening after the police had discovered the Grimaldi murder and after Mr. Grimaldi had weathered the first shock of his wife's death, he picked up the telephone. Staring at the bloodstains on the floorboards, he dialed the Admiral's number. The Admiral consoled him and told him that all would be well.

The conversation between the Admiral and Mr. Grimaldi was overheard by Detective William Wotter, who then brought a duplicate tape to Alcibiades LoConti.

"GET THAT FUCKIN' HAT," commanded Frank Caporosso, Bronx County DA, after Johnny O'Boyle and Al LoConti had played all the intercepted telephone conversations.

"I want him indicted and convicted, and I don't want him to collect one fuckin' penny of his pension. I want that bastard Judge Honig too. And let's wrap up this goddamn Jack the Ripper crap. Johnny, I want you to form a Homicide Task Force. Get the best people assigned, put Al here in charge, have him report direct to you. One of you brief me every morning. Al, I want you to keep on top of this investigation with Solwin and your friend Wotter. Keep pushing." The DA waved his hand and dismissed them. As they were leaving he called them back and closed the door.

"Get a separate wire on the Hat. Get his car, his office, and his home bugged. I want to know everything about him. I want to know why a flake like him can do whatever he wants. I want the sources of his power. Drag every skeleton out of every closet. If the brass are covering him, I want their asses."

"Right, Chief," Al and O'Boyle said in unison.

"One more thing, Johnny," Frank Caporosso said. "Be real sure which cops you assign to investigate the Hat. I don't want any reports going up into police channels—I want them for our eyes only."

While Johnny O'Boyle went to work on the Homicide Task Force Alcibiades LoConti tackled the apprehension of mass murderer Ronald DePew. He had interviewed the Perrotta woman and obtained search and arrest warrants for the DePew apartment. Twenty specially assigned cops burst in. It was empty, but they recovered a photograph of the murderer, which they gave to the department's public affairs officer. Only hours later newspapers and television screens throughout North America carried the picture of Ronald DePew. Sergeant Feldman of the U.S. Army as well as others who knew DePew as an outpatient came forward. Within two days Al had a thorough profile of Ronald DePew. The Homicide Task force received fifteen thousand telephone calls after the first publication of the photo. There were sightings as far away as Copenhagen, Denmark, and Barrow, Alaska. With the exception of Hawaii, all of the states of the Union contributed at least one DePew sighting.

By the end of the week even Hawaii had phoned in three reports. The detectives assigned to the task force sifted through these thousands of calls and followed up with calls to local police of the reporting municipalities. None of the reports proved fruitful. A milkman was shot in Queens and another in Staten Island, which sent detectives scurrying. In both cases the wounded milkmen had been shot in the legs, and neither could identify his assailant. Both milkmen wore bulletproof vests and had all their money taken.

In Brooklyn Pat Lawless, the local delegate for the lathers' union, reported to the police that someone had shot at a garbage truck operated by the City of New York. Furthermore, Lawless stated that he had seen this individual from a rooftop across the street and he looked like the guy in the paper.

The 69th squad sent out Detectives Mincione and Cozzella, both of whom had over twenty years' experience.

The shots had been fired at 2 A.M., narrowly missing two sanitation workers. The employees never worried whether the racket they made woke up the whole neighborhood, so citizens were not too concerned that someone had fired on them. In fact, most of the Irish-Americans who lived in Pat Lawless's neighborhood were very disappointed that the shots had missed. They were rather tired of having their sleep interrupted by the grinding of the sanitation truck and the yells of "Yooooo" at two in the morning.

Just before the start of work at 7 A.M. and after his second beer, Pat Lawless made the mistake of telling his fellow lathers that he had fired the shots at the Ginny garbagemen.

One of the lathers, Jimmy O'Shea, wanted Lawless's job. At nine-fifteen during his coffee break, Jimmy O'Shea popped open a Budweiser and dropped a dime on Pat. At nine-thirty Pat was locked up by Mincione and Cozzella for attempted murder and falsely reporting an incident.

Jimmy O'Shea did not give his real name when he called the police, so two weeks later the case against Pat Lawless was dismissed for lack of evidence.

Predicaments such as this were being repeated all over the City of New York as Ronald DePew still wandered the streets.

Two weeks later the homicide task force was meeting with Al, O'Boyle, and Flanagan. Hanratty and Hornbein had also been assigned, since Hornbein was an indefatigable worker and Hanratty was by far the best trial man in the office.

Hanratty, delighted with the new job, sat quietly watching in the office of homicide coordinator Flanagan. Hanratty knew that he would be responsible for Flanagan. He had to watch everything he did, otherwise Timmy would use DePew to clear every open case regardless of who the real perpetrator was.

The men had gathered in Flanagan's office for his presentation. A picture of Ronald DePew hung on the wall above the chart and the map of the City of New York. Deftly, like a clever trial lawyer,

Timmy discussed each case, pointing to the pins and explaining the common thread.

Al was shocked as Flanagan hung up other maps of the states of New York, Pennsylvania, and New Jersey. Timmy had already inserted pins into these maps color coded to police and sheriffs' reports. Some of the pins Al noticed were past Lake George in the north, Tonawanda in the west, and Toms River in the south.

"This fuckin' guy is going haywire," Al muttered to Hanratty.

Hanratty whispered back, "Flanagan will be the most popular cop in the world. Pretty soon you'll have a map of Russia and South America here, with little pins in them."

Al smiled. "Not if you're watching his ass."

The Hat was also standing by, watching and beaming at all the cases being solved. Flanagan again thanked Inspector McDaniel—the Hat—for his assistance in the investigation. "Without the inspector's insights and suggestions we could never have found De-Pew," Flanagan said.

He's got a fine line of shit, the Hat thought, soaking up the praise. Knowing that the DA would give a press conference at the conclusion of the meeting, the Hat had brought Sergeant Kelly McKnight from Public Affairs along. The blond beauty now stood next to him. She'd already memorized her speech and she was primed to upstage the DA, to deflect all the credit to Inspector McDaniel.

Al looked admiringly at Kelly. "You've got to hand it to the fuckin' Hat," he told Hanratty.

Hanratty waved at Kelly who waved back, smiling broadly for the first time since she came into the room.

"You know her?" Al asked amazed.

"Sure, I know her for many years. She's an old friend," Hanratty replied matter of factly.

After the meeting broke up, and while the press conference was being held, Hornbein, under the direction of Hanratty, was getting a list of all the cases so that he could read all the charts and the DD5s and Unusuals. After he read all the autopsy reports, he would make two charts. One chart would disprove Flanagan's contentions, and the second would chart common threads based on evidence and not bullshit.

After the press conference, Al was approached by Detective Pete DiCerrechia. Pete had been assigned to the task force at Al's request. Pete was still working on the legs case and agreed with Al that there was no connection to DePew. While Al spoke with Pete, Hanratty and the blond beauty Kelly got into Hanratty's ancient Cadillac.

Hanratty smiled as he went north on the Degan, paying no attention to the cloud of black smoke visible through his rearview mirror caused by burning motor oil. He tried to concentrate on the road ahead, as Kelly rubbed her hand up his leg.

Later, while Hanratty poured some Bell's whiskey into the motel's clear plastic glasses for Kelly, Al LoConti got some information from Ruella Watkins, who was now assigned to the team investigating the death of Mickey Varino, the Admiral's son-in-law. A lawyer had sold two keys of heroin to a federal agent. The lawyer, the legendary Quiet Marvin Pollard, had been turned, and told the police that he had represented Mickey Varino some years before.

Mickey had financed an independent, wild-card importing operation organized by Quiet Marvin. Opium had been smuggled from Turkey in plastic bags using an ancient method of forcing the bags with a ramrod into the stomachs of camels and herding the camels from Turkey into Syria and then to Lebanon. There they were slaughtered and the plastic bags removed. The opium was smuggled from the port of Beirut across the Atlantic and transshipped to a pleasure boat off the coast of New Jersey. Quiet Marvin employed chemists in a private home in Toms River where the opium was converted to heroin.

Over Quiet Marvin's objections the Admiral's son-in-law "Mickey" Varino had visited the chemical plant in the home in Tom's River. He blocked the next-door neighbor's driveway, and the police were called and he got a ticket. The Jersey cops made a routine ownership check and found out who Mickey was. They of course knew of the legendary Admiral. A routine notification to the New York Police Department had alerted the Hat, who immediately informed the Admiral that his son-in-law was up to something in New Jersey. The feds grabbed Mickey Varino and tried to hook him and the Admiral up with an illegal enterprise. Varino, interrogated for hours, told the feds to go and fuck themselves. Eventually he was released, but the feds put the word out that he was wearing a wire. A week later he had been found dead.

Quiet Marvin swore that he had never dealt with the Admiral nor had he ever met the Hat. But Mickey Varino had told him that the Hat had a very impressive rabbi. "He's four-star Chief Cornelius 'Connie' O'Toole," Quiet Marvin said. "I don't know what the Hat's got on him, but it goes way way back, for many, many years."

O'Boyle and Alcibiades LoConti immediately reported to the district attorney, Frank Caporosso.

"I want O'Toole's headquarters, home, and car bugged by tomorrow," the DA said. His assistants nodded and went right to work.

Four-star Chief Cornelius "Connie" O'Toole stood next to his window in One Police Plaza looking out over the East River. One of his informants in the Narcotics Bureau, Sergeant Denny Driscoll, had told him that the Solwin team had now tied in to Charlie Oakdale and could prove that Charlie was the supplier to Paulie of the Treus Surveying Company who in turn had sold down to Tommy and Biagio "Blaze" Squerente. Paulie, now dead, was no threat and Squerente was a hard case, but Driscoll said there had been talk of Tommy Jassy becoming cooperative although so far no deal had been struck. Four-star Chief Cornelius Connie O'Toole realized that the Hat was in jeopardy and that he himself could be exposed. The Hat must be protected at all costs.

Connie turned to his assistant, Captain "Mac" MacNamara. "Reorganize all the Narcotics commands, shake them up. There have been too many corruption allegations. The commissioner and the mayor are furious, so transfer all the personnel of every other narcotics group. Put the men of the third, fifth, eleventh, and thirteenth Narcotics back on precinct duty, and disband those units completely."

"What about their current investigations, Chief?" Mac asked.

"Give them thirty days to wind them up with arrests. The commissioner and the mayor have ordered that the elimination of corruption is the number-one priority. I will follow those orders with all the strength at my command."

As Mac MacNamara left the chief's office with the orders sealing the fate of Solwin's 13th Narcotics Group, Connie O'Toole, looking at the busy East River below, reflected on the events that forced him to such lengths to protect the Hat.

Many years ago while a young patrolman, the Hat had been assigned with a group of detectives to guard one Ipsy Mankevich, who had been the chief accountant for the boss who ran numbers in the Bronx and northern Manhattan. Ipsy had a list of every patrol officer and every precinct captain and plainclothes cop who were receiving monthly payoffs to ignore the flourishing numbers and prostitution rackets, and this list included the highest ranks in the department.

Upon discovering that Ipsy had trouble making a proper tally of receipts, the boss installed his own quality control and learned to his chagrin that Ipsy was skimming.

"He's not makin' the right count," the boss, stung by betrayal, had told an underling. "Take the little fuck for a ride."

And so it came to be that Ipsy Mankevich, all four feet eleven inches of him, had been hustled into a DeSoto and driven from under the Third Avenue El toward a construction site on Mosholu Parkway, where he was destined to become part of the foundation. Fate intervened for Ipsy at the corner of Third Avenue and Fordham Road. A car driven by a youth named Nevins rammed into the DeSoto with enough force to kill Nevins and to knock the three gorillas with Ipsy out cold. Ipsy, who had been in the backseat sandwiched between two sides of beef wearing hats, was merely stunned. After managing to crawl over the man on his left, he opened the door and climbed out before the police arrived. Ipsy weaved through the gathering crowd, crossed Fordham Road, and went down onto the New York Central train station where he caught the next northbound train. He got off in the City of White Plains in Westchester County and was directed to the police station. There he asked to speak with the state police. In due course he did, and the next day he was turned over directly to the Bronx district attorney. The DA got an order making Ipsy a material witness and put him in protective custody. Among his protectors was the Hat and others who would ultimately rise to the highest levels in the department.

Ipsy became an instant celebrity. Based on his testimony, scores of police officers and underworld figures were indicted for corruption and crimes against the morality of the day.

Ipsy was seen on the front pages of the tabloids in a gray fedora smoking an enormous cigar. The five DAs of New York City had so many press conferences involving indictments handed up as a result of Ipsy's testimony that their pictures became known to all, thus ensuring their reelections.

As for those indicted, their legal woes would vanish should fate make Ipsy disappear, and it didn't take long for those in higher places to reach the same conclusion.

Accordingly some of the best minds in New York were put to work to find a method to dispatch the singing Ipsy.

Ipsy was being guarded in a motel just off Westchester Square, a single-story affair, thoroughly sealed off by the police. The Bronx boss, who had a number of his main men indicted by Bronx Grand Juries because of Ipsy's testimony, ordered a full frontal assault on the motel. A dead Ipsy would be worth the casualties on both sides. The Boss reasoned that the police, who also wanted Ipsy out of the way, would not offer much resistance. So he sent in four men to do the job. Knowing Ipsy's room number they decided to pose as patrons and gain entrance through the main door.

However, the police brass, though sympathetic, had let it be known that they did not want to be holding the bag when inquiries as to the lack of security arose. Accordingly they were not consulted further in the assassination plan; they did not give their approval to the attempt and they were not even aware of its imminence.

THE BOSS SET IPSY'S execution for October 29, 1948. On that date four hit men entered the motel and rented two adjacent rooms near Ipsy's under assumed names. They remained in them until 3 A.M.

At 3 A.M. they left their rooms and walked down the hall up to the plainclothes guard in front of Ipsy's room and knocked him unconscious with the butt end of a Colt .45. As he slumped to the floor with a fractured skull, they thrust their shoulders against the door and burst into the room. Ipsy lay in bed on the far side of the room and the Hat was seated at a table on the right drinking from a bottle of Four Roses. The Hat dropped the bottle, drew his revolver, and shot five times. All five bullets struck the four men in front of him. Connie O'Toole, who was urinating in the bathroom, burst out with his fly unbuttoned and Ipsy ran right in to defecate. His innards had been liquefied by the barrage going off in front of his bed. Connie O'Toole, bending over the four figures, had his revolver snatched by the Hat, who put one round into the head of each of the dying prostrate figures. He then returned Connie's gun and took two long pulls from the bottle of Four Roses. He would be promoted to detective the very next day and ordered to listen to Connie O'Toole if he wanted good things in life.

As soon as the shooting was over, Ipsy became so sick that he was rushed to the hospital. After a thorough workup, it was discovered that Ipsy had sky-high blood pressure and possible coronary disease. They moved him to five-story apartment house in the Pelham Parkway section of the Bronx. The building did not have an elevator, and Ipsy was guarded in a two-bedroom apartment on the fourth floor. Ipsy had told the Hat that he was pleased at least that they were not on the top floor because he was terrified of heights.

The apartment had a dumbwaiter, an apparatus for garbage removal. The doorway to it in the kitchen led to a shaft running from the roof to the basement. At the top of the shaft a pulley was anchored to a beam from which a wooden box was hung. The building super or porter would raise the box to each floor and the occupant would open the door to the dumbwaiter and place garbage in the box. The dumbwaiter would then be lowered and emptied.

As the Hat was placing garbage in the dumbwaiter, he got a brainstorm. Knowing that important people wanted Ipsy dead and that a thorough investigation would follow, a flawless scheme was needed. He conferred with Connie O'Toole and on the next Friday night the guard detail included only the Hat, Connie, and two trusted officers.

The Hat opened the dumbwaiter door and grabbed the rope that lowered the box. Ipsy was relaxing in his pajamas in one of the bedrooms, reading. Connie O'Toole and the Hat went into the room and Connie put a gun against Ipsy's temple. The Hat told him to open his mouth and they shoved a gag into it and lifted him off the bed, onto a chair, while enclosing his torso with a special leather harness that was heavily padded on the inside so that Ipsy's body would not be bruised. The harness enclosed his torso, pinning his arms to his sides. Ipsy was then blindfolded and led into the kitchen. He could not see the officers attach a heavy wire cable to the harness, nor could he see the cable being threaded over a pulley and through a winch. When the blindfold was removed, Ipsy was hanging upside-down in the dumbwaiter shaft.

The Hat whispered in his ear in a thick brogue that Ipsy should pray, this was his last moment on earth. The Hat shined a flashlight down the shaft so that Ipsy could see just how far down he would be falling. The Hat snickered as he stared into the bulging, terrorized eyes of the man whose life he had saved. Ipsy, trying to scream, could hear only grunts coming from his throat. The Hat nodded and the officers holding Ipsy's ankles released them . . . and Ipsy fell straight down four stories into the shaft. Just before his body struck the bottom it was jerked sharply by the cable and the impact of the abrupt halt was cushioned by the harness. Ipsy bounced and dangled, hanging at the end of the long flexible cable. When he was winched back into the apartment, the detectives noticed that his eyes were like those of a fish. They removed the harness and found that he had no pulse and no heartbeat. He was carried back into his bed, his eyes closed and his body composed. The next morning the guard team reported that Ipsy had apparently died in his sleep, a finding supported by the very thorough autopsy that followed. When the death certificate reading cardiac arrest was signed, the Hat's future was born. Of the four members of the original guard detail, the Hat was the lowest in department rank when Solwin began to close in on the Admiral.

And today, almost thirty years after Ipsy had been executed, Connie O'Toole and the other members of the guard detail, now all senior chiefs, shuddered at every horrendous Hat episode. For they were prisoners of his whim and caprice, unable to thwart his madness and bound with him in a pact of silence concerning the coldblooded slaying of a man they had been sworn to shield, save, and protect.

MacNamara issued the orders directed by four-star Chief Cornelius "Connie" O'Toole. Solwin was to be reassigned to the Bureau of Criminal Identification and the remainder of the team split up among commands throughout the five boroughs.

The brass handled the shakeup so expertly that not even the perennially suspicious police ventured guesses. It was chalked up to another asshole move by the department hierarchy who were paranoid on the issue of corruption.

Solwin was directed to end any pending investigations with arrests, if possible.

At the time Solwin got his orders, Al LoConti and Johnny O'Boyle were reporting to District Attorney Frank Caporosso. The wires and bugs on Connie O'Toole produced no incriminating evidence. Yet it was perfectly clear that the departmental reorganization was designed to protect the Admiral and the Hat.

"Don't tell Solwin anything about the wires and bugs," the DA of Bronx County said. "But Al, I want you to do everything you can to help him bring his investigation to a successful ending. If he needs more time when he is due to report to BCI, then I'll have him and some of his men assigned to me."

"What happens if Chief O'Toole overrides you?" Johnny asked.

"I'm the chief law enforcement officer in this county. If he tries I'll put his ass before a Grand Jury so fast he won't have time to put his pants on. And then I'll ask him who he's covering up for."

"Yeah, but you run the risk of immunizing him. We should turn this over to the feds. The federal grand jury just gives him use immunity, not full transactional immunity. They have the tools. We don't," Johnny O'Boyle said.

"Too bad we ain't the feds," Al LoConti said.

The District Attorney smiled and said, "You gave me a brainstorm, Al, a brainstorm. We are going to become the feds."

And then the DA dialed the man who had fought with him as a paratrooper in the Second World War, the man who had been his close companion and fellow prosecutor in the office of the immortal Frank Hogan, District Attorney of New York County: the Honorable John Servetter, the United States Attorney for the Southern District of New York. After ten minutes an agreement had been reached and a joint investigation begun. Two assistant United States attorneys would be deputized as Bronx assistant DAs so as to permit them to present any aspects of the investigation to the state grand juries, and two Bronx DAs were to be sworn in as deputized assistant U.S. attorneys to grant them access to the Federal Grand Juries. The two were selected on the spot: Johnny O'Boyle and Alcibiades LoConti.

"So now we wear two hats to catch the Hat," Al quipped. Johnny groaned inwardly at his friend's corny sense of humor.

"That's right," Frank Caporosso said, pretending he did not get the joke.

Solwin was immediately called in. There was not enough evidence to arrest Charlie Oakdale except on federal conspiracy charges. Solwin told them that Tommy Jassy had cut a deal. He'd been paroled, and only the night before he had introduced Wotter to Charlie Oakdale.

"Let's try to get Oakdale and the Admiral," Al said. "Let's have Wotter place a big order. The DA will get the buy money from the feds. Who knows, we may get a big hit."

Solwin directed Wotter to order a large quantity of Chinese Rock #3 from Oakdale. Unknown to the members of the team, Oakdale had followed an old Yankee business practice, one utilized by all good businesses except the U.S. government. That is, Oakdale had not limited himself to one supplier, and had found another source of Chinese Rock #3. The officers already had Charlie Oakdale's phone tapped and had placed his house and the Admiral's Hudson River Trading Company under surveillance.

Wotter explained to the members of the team that when he had spoken to Oakdale, Charlie told him to use the word "shirts" when ordering the narcotics. Each shirt would equal a kilo, or 2.2 pounds of narcotics. Oakdale had told Wotter that if his phone was tapped and a conversation relating to shirts was overheard, then there would exist nothing to incriminate him.

"Fuck him," Al LoConti said. "Order a shirt and a half."

Wotter called up Oakdale and ordered a shirt and a half and Oakdale, nonplussed, arranged to deliver. After the call was made, Oakdale left his house. Team members followed him from his Bronx home down to Bruckner Boulevard, onto the Bruckner Expressway, over the Triboro Bridge, and down the FDR Drive to the Brooklyn Bridge exit. Charlie then turned onto the local streets in the vicinity of police headquarters and the Federal Penitentiary. From there they followed him through the winding streets of Chinatown. After he parked his car they followed him on foot. Oakdale was carrying a small attaché case, which the officers knew contained U.S. currency. At the corner of Bayard Street, Charlie "the Plant" Oakdale paused and waited. Fortunately for the surveillance team, the streets were crowded and the officers managed to blend into the crowd. A Chinese youth approached Oakdale and took the attaché case from him. Solwin and Blatt broke away from the team and hurried down the street. After observing the youth enter an alley, they rushed into the alley, but it was empty. Running down its length revealed nothing. Disgusted, they exited back onto Bayard Street. Oakdale had vanished. After a minute they spotted him again entering his car with a different attaché case. Not one member of the 13th Narcotics Group knew where it came from.

Each day the tides of Long Island Sound and the Hudson and Harlem rivers relentlessly deposited filth and debris on the shores of Bronx County, and every day just as relentlessly a new list of murder victims flowed into the offices of the Homicide Bureau.

O'Boyle had told Al that in 1963 there were less than seventy homicides in Bronx County. In 1973 there had been over four hundred. And the Bronx was only one of the five counties of the City of New York. The year 1975 already was proving to be another banner year. The resources of the police and all the District Attorneys' offices were totally inadequate to deal with the sheer volume.

Since the system was hopelessly overloaded, DAs were forced to decide which cases to try. The rest were routinely plea bargained down to manslaughter. Dispositions or pleas were the order of the day.

"If the public knew what went on in the court system, there would be a fuckin' revolution," Al told O'Boyle, who agreed.

Al had compiled a list of the cases Flanagan was trying to link to DePew. Many were in fact supported by substantial evidence. Al was impatient to use the weapon employed by Thomas Dewey when he prosecuted Lucky Luciano—evidence of other crimes to support the charges at bar—but it was a risky business. The longstanding rule in New York was that one started fresh when one was charged with a crime. Evidence of other criminal activity was not permitted on the theory that it would unduly prejudice the jury and deprive the defendant of a fair trial. In the celebrated case of *People* versus *Molineux*, the Court of Appeals announced the so-called Molineux rule, which set forth five categories when collateral criminal conduct may be introduced on the direct case. Such evidence may be presented when it is relevant to establish motive, intent, the absence of mistake or accident, a common scheme or plan, or the identity of the perpetrator charged. Al wanted to proceed on the motive and the identity exceptions.

O'Boyle argued against it. "Why fuck around?" he said. The Appellate Division was scrupulous in reviewing all criminal convictions, and O'Boyle wanted to try the strongest case, convict DePew, and ship him off for twenty-five to life. Al wanted either to use the Molineux rule and join many crimes in one indictment or alternatively to try DePew for three, four, or five murders and ship his ass out with multiple life sentences. The Supreme Court had put the cabosh on the death penalty. If ever a fuck should fry, Al thought, it should be this guy.

O'Boyle wanted an error-free trial. He had file cabinet draws full of hundreds of other murder indictments. If it was decided to prosecute DePew more than once, then O'Boyle wanted to lead off with the strongest case.

While the two of them argued, the report of DePew's latest escapade arrived. The crime had occurred in the South Bronx just yesterday. The victim was a milkman and full-time cop, none other than Allie Boy Spano's partner, the legendary Richie Zemberelli.

Yesterday Richie had gone on his milk route at 5 A.M. wearing a bulletproof vest. At seven-thirty in the morning he was delivering to a supermarket just off Freeman Street and as he exited the supermarket, a young man with blond hair had approached. Zemberelli knew that a blond young man was out of place in the area, yet he did not recognize DePew from his picture. So Ronald DePew had walked right up to Richie Zemberelli, and placed a pistol to Zemberelli's temple, demanding all of his money.

Unfortunately for Zemberelli, the bulletproof vest made him feel like Superman, invulnerable to any danger in the jungles of the South Bronx. And so feeling impregnable as if surrounded by a stone-wall fort and cocksure and confident, Richie Zemberelli with the gun at his temple taunted Ronald DePew.

"Go ahead, shoot—I'm wearing a bulletproof vest."

And DePew, too astounded to shoot, withdrew in shock.

The crime charged was attempted robbery and Richie Zemberelli was neither robbed nor injured—DePew's only victim who had not been brutalized.

And the search continued.

Solwin had Wotter testify before the Grand Jury. Charlie "the Plant" Oakdale was indicted for the sale of heroin. Since all his work was going down the drain, Solwin had ordered Charlie's arrest, hoping against hope to turn him and go up the ladder to the Admiral.

Solwin supervised the arrest and Jimmy Farrell requested $1 million dollars bail. The judge set the bail at $5 million. Charlie had had no warning of the impending arrest and neither did the Admiral. Charlie refused to even give his name and would of course never dream of mentioning the Admiral. Solwin and Farrell had been defeated. They were as high as they would ever climb.

Charlie's lawyers took out a writ of habeas corpus to the Appellate Division. Jimmy Farrell went to argue the writ and at the suggestion of the Grand Inquisitors consented to having the bail reduced. "Fuck him if he don't cooperate. Let him out. The other humps will think he's helping us. Justice will be done," they said. The Admiral sent Fast Frankie Hammon to observe the appellate proceedings and he and the Admiral were shocked at the consent to the bail reduction and even more shocked that Charlie made the bail.

Although he was dead wrong, the Admiral concluded that Charlie had cooperated and agreed to become an informer.

"It's time he visited his wife," the Admiral said.

Three days later Charlie Oakdale followed a 100-pound concrete block into the waters under the Throggs Neck Bridge. Five chains from the block led to iron bracelets around Charlie's wrists, ankles, and neck. Unlike his wife, he was wide awake as he entered the water.

Detectives Ruella Watkins and Pete DiCerrechia had checked out over 1,200 dead end leads in the legs case. After every lead they meticulously prepared a DD5, and now two enormous file cabinets were filled with these reports. On this Friday morning—March 14, 1975—Ruella was reviewing a stack of hundreds of old leads. Again she sought the cooperation of the media, and like a trusted ally again it came through.

Over the weekend and on Monday, St. Patrick's Day, the media would blitz the citizens, requesting information about a middle-age female who had been missing for almost five years. Ruella and Pete wondered if there would be any bites.

Detective Second Grade Rory O'Donnell walked into the offices of the Four Six Precinct. Rory had fallen out of grace with his fellow officers due to his persistent attention to Alcibiades's former wife. Although Rory's impotence was legendary, the detectives felt he was an obstacle, an irritation to the renewing relationship between Al and Renee.

Renee LoConti had been a constant and loving presence during the long recovery of her brother-in-law, Vince LoConti. Her former husband grudgingly admitted to himself that Renee alone probably was the single greatest contributor to Vince's remarkable recovery. Her selfless, complete, and utter devotion to Vince had gradually brought about a change in Al's attitude. He realized that there was nothing on earth that he desired more than to put his family together again, to reclaim his lost son and to bask in the adoration of his daughter, and he began realizing that the job must take second place. The system was corrupt from top to bottom, and justice was an illusion. Still, some wise and good men sought it, and Al wanted to be with them. One of them, the tireless Judge O'Neill, had given Al a tip years before in Criminal Court when Al had been particularly sickened by the plea-bargaining and the hardened recidivists' amusement with the system.

"Don't let this drive you crazy, Al," Judge O'Neill had said. "Don't make the mistake of looking for justice in these walls. Always remember that this is not a court of justice; this is merely a court of law."

And now on this Friday when the media were poised once more to try for information on the legs case, Alcibiades LoConti prepared to go to Long Island to pick his children up and perhaps to finally stop the one-sided war with Renee.

Back in the Four Six precinct, Rory O'Donnell told Pete DiCerrechia that he too was heading for the same destination on Long Island.

"I'm goin' to ask Renee to accompany me to a big shindig at the VFW for Saint Paddy's day," Rory had said.

"You should stay away from her, Rory," Pete said. "There are two kids involved, and maybe she and Al can get back together. I know from Vince that that's all she wants, and Al has started to come around."

"Oh, for Kerist sake, Pete, I'm just takin' her as a friend. I've been through a lot meself with Nam and my marriages. Renee is a friend and nothing more. You guys're all nuts. I never even tried to put a finger on her—me hand to God. I hope to hell Al goes back with her. But he's just a stupid and stubborn man and he never will."

When Rory left Pete picked up the phone. He made two calls: The first was to Vince LoConti and the second to Allie Boy Spano. He arranged to meet them and to drive to Long Island.

"Gotta try and prevent a disaster," Pete told Ruella Watkins as he ran down the stairs.

None of them would have guessed the outcome. Renee had refused Rory's invitation on the doorstep. She did not even invite him in. She knew that Al would arrive at any time, and she frankly was fed up with the company of the alcoholic Rory O'Donnell. As Rory walked back toward his car, Alcibiades LoConti drove up and stopped.

Rory stood in the driveway as Al got out of his car. Pete DiCerrechia parked his Chrysler New Yorker behind Al's car and got out with Vince and Allie Boy.

Rory took the initiative. "She won't have nothin' to do with the likes of me, Al," he said. "And I just want you to know she's just a good friend and it's been nothin' more. You're a goddamn fool if you believe otherwise."

No one spoke as Rory got into his car and drove off.

Renee, standing on the porch, said, "I think we could all use a cup of coffee."

Vince put his arm around his brother. "Let's go inside, Al. You've been outside too long. Make believe you're jumpin' from another airplane, take the plunge. What the hell you worryin' about, we all love ya."

And hours later, after hastily packing, three automobiles left the home of Renee LoConti's sister. Al drove one car with Renee beside him while their children slept in the backseat. Only they, the children, had neither fear nor reservation regarding this risky endeavor. Only they now felt secure, for their parents had been reconciled. Their countless prayers had finally been answered. God was truly looking down upon them, and once again the world was glorious.

IT WAS TEN IN the morning of the day after St. Patrick's Day and half the squad was drinking Alka Seltzer when Detective Pete DeCerrechia's telephone rang. The caller, a woman with a thick Irish brogue, stated that she had information concerning the missing female. The caller lived on Tenth Avenue in Manhattan under the Broadway El where Fordham Road in the Bronx became 207th Street in Manhattan. Even though the woman was so obviously Irish, Pete was not pleased to have Rory O'Donnell as his partner today. Rory, now forty-one, had come to America when he was seventeen and after twenty-four years he spoke as if he had never left County Cork. He had done too much "celebratin'," as he called it, and was in no condition to drive. As Pete drove over the Fordham Bridge into Manhattan, Rory begged him to stop next to Dr. McShanes' Saloon. "I need a wee prescription this morning, Petey," Rory had said.

DiCerrechia, following him into the bar, watched as Rory downed a shot of Bushmills with a beer chaser then pointed to the empty glasses and told the bartender to do it again.

The detectives then went across the street to the caller's apartment house and walked up to the third floor. The odors of boiling cabbage and frying rice and beans confirmed that the building was a mix of old Irish and young Hispanic. O'Donnell, desperate for another drink, had a rough time focusing on the name Keefe over the doorbell while Pete rang.

A lovely Irish woman whose beauty had not quite begun to fade ushered them into a railroad flat and through to the parlor. An old RCA floor-model TV stood in the corner against the far wall and a faded imitation Persian rug covered the floor. Pete liked its dark maroon colors and the intricate design. A coffee table with a vase of bright artificial flowers in its center stood in front of an old horsehair-stuffed coach. Clean white lace curtains hung from the window cornices setting off the darker, deeper hues of the furniture and rugs.

Some job keepin' them curtains so clean under the El, Pete thought.

The woman who identified herself as Margaret Keefe was a fifty-eight-year-old widow. A picture of herself with a large puffy-faced, mustachioed man stood on top of the TV set. The man wore the uniform of a lieutenant in the fire department. The woman, seeing Pete looking at the picture, said, "That's Michael, my husband, dead now for the last eighteen years."

Pete nodded, thinking to himself that every once in a while you ran into someone on the job whom you liked instantly. Margaret Keefe was one of those people. He was surprised to hear Rory speak out.

"It's a wonder a woman like yourself has not remarried," he said. Margaret blushed, her eyes shining as she heard the accent. She looked knowingly at Rory O'Donnell's bloodshot eyes and asked if he would have something to drink.

"Not when I'm on duty, ma'am."

"Come on now, my husband used to be on duty too."

"Well, maybe just a dram."

She went to a cabinet next to the television set and opened it to reveal a well-stocked liquor chest.

Funny . . . she doesn't look like a boozer, Pete thought.

She held up scotch and Irish whiskey and Rory asked for the Irish. She poured a double shot and placed it on the coffee table. Then she asked Pete if he would like a drink. After thanking her, Pete politely refused.

She walked into the kitchen, returning with a bottle of beer and a glass. She poured half the beer in the glass and set it in front of Rory.

"You're an angel of mercy, Mrs. Keefe," Rory said, sipping the whiskey and then the beer.

Pete began, "Could you tell us why you called, Mrs. Keefe?"

"Yes, well, down by 204th Street, just off Seaman Avenue, there was a woman I used to see in the market. She was from County Clare in Ireland and lived very near where I was born. We chatted from time to time in the Pathmark Supermarket around the corner, and I believe she lived in the house right off Seaman and 204th. If I'm right, it would be the house on the northwest corner of the street.

"Her name was Nora but I don't remember what her last name was. Married to a transit worker she was and I only saw him with her one time and he was very drunk. She complained to me all the times we met that her husband drank and drank. I was thinkin' only last week that I hadn't seen her for a long time when I read that article in the paper. I think that she had said somethin' about goin' back to Ireland to live with a sister and leavin' the drunk, but I don't know what she did. Anyway, I thought maybe that I'd be wastin' yer time but then I thought maybe if somethin' did really happen to her it would be me duty to call."

Pete thanked her and verified her phone number. She told them that she had a roast in the oven and invited them to stay, but they declined. On the way out she patted Rory affectionately on the back and Rory thanked her.

The detectives left the tenement and entered their car. It was only a few short blocks up 207th Street to Seaman Avenue, a dead-end road. Beyond was a park, which stretched down along the west side of Manhattan to the Hudson River. At 204th they stopped, and parked the car, and entered another apartment house. On the stoop outside they spotted a man in a winter coat drinking from a beer can wrapped in a brown paper bag. It was always legal to drink if you covered the can with a brown paper bag.

Pete flashed his tin. "Can you tell me where to find the super?"

"Sure. Go down the alley, there's a door into the basement. His apartment is down there but you better watch out for the dog."

When the detectives knocked on the super's door, a dog barked ferociously and a heavily muscled black man answered. His head was completely shaved and he wore muttonchop sideburns with a thick mustache. He looked menacingly at Pete, who extended his badge and ID card. The man held it and took a long look, then stared with contempt at the detectives.

"What do you want from me?"

"We are looking for a tenant, a woman who came from Ireland lived here with her husband, who works for the TA. Want to know if she still lives here."

"Can't help ya, man." He shrugged.

Rory stepped next to Pete, inches in front of the black man, and unhooked his suit jacket to show the gun in his waist holster. Rory looked into the man's eyes and belched loudly right into his face. The man, seeing the gun and the bloodshot eyes and smelling the liquor on Rory's breath, underwent an instant attitude adjustment.

"She didn't go to Ireland, man," he said.

"Do you know where she is?" Pete asked, his voice cold and flat. The man nodded,

"Well, where the fuck is she?" Pete asked.

"She lives down by Dyckman Street on Post Avenue, first house in; lives with another woman there whose husband works for the TA. The two husbands live here together, apartment four D. They like the sauce better'n the wives, you know."

Pete watched as Rory nodded in agreement.

"Are any of them home now?" DiCerrechia asked.

"I don't know, man, check it out if you want."

"Thanks," Rory said.

The detectives walked around to the elevator and rang the button. After entering, they pressed the button for the fourth floor. The elevator was as spotless as the basement and as clean as the hallway of the fourth floor. Pete thought to himself that the super, even though a militant, still did a damn good job.

The peephole of 4D opened after they rang the bell. The detectives held up their tins and ID cards, and the locks clicked and the door swung inward revealing a man dressed in a T-shirt and gray work pants. His face was beet red, his hair iron gray, and his nose erupted into an irregular glob from the ravages of alcohol. Pete noted with distaste the yellow stains from sweaty booze discoloring the gray undershirt.

The man smiled at the detectives, and Rory engaged him in conversation while DiCerrechia looked around the apartment. It was nicely furnished and surprisingly clean. The furniture appeared to have been recently dusted, and there were no signs of the disarray and slovenliness that one associated with heavy drinkers.

DiCerrechia walked down the hallway, past the man, and looked into the kitchen where another man was seated at the kitchen table. Steam rose from a hot mug of strong tea in front of him, and two open beer cans stood on the table.

This man seemed a few years older than the man talking to Rory—about fifty-five, Pete guessed. The man nodded to Pete, offering him a seat, and Pete shook his head no. Rory and the first man then joined them.

Rory reported the substance of their conversation. Their two wives lived on Post Road and regularly came over and cleaned and washed, but outside of an occasional cooked meal the men fended for themselves. The wives were reported to be in good health and the man had no idea what the police wanted.

Pete nodded to the two men and went to the door, and Rory muttered thanks. Pete DiCerrechia never said a word.

Forty-five minutes later Detective Pete DiCerrechia put away his notebook after leaving the apartment on Post Road. He had recorded a synopsis of the interviews with the wives of the transit workers, who had just confirmed their husbands' stories. DiCerrechia, now disgusted, would go to the Four Six precinct and prepare another DD5, the report of another day's work and another blind alley. Rory, sitting next to him, was in a far different mood. He was simply delighted. He had received offers from all three women today, and after due deliberation decided to accept Mrs. Keefe's. She had been able to do something for him that no woman had done in years. Rory smiled happily because the Widow Keefe had given him a woody, a diamond cutter, a real stiff hard-on.

After years of frustration caused by leads to blind alleys and paths to dead ends, the DA's job suddenly provided one of those fascinating, even freaky days on this Thursday, March 20, 1975. The first surprise came with news about Quiet Marvin, who had become the most important informer in the federal system. Not only had Marvin disclosed that Connie O'Toole was the Hat's rabbi and provided valuable insight into the assassination of Mickey Varino, the Admiral's son-in-law, but he had furnished an abundance of other bits and pieces that proved to be a true fountain of information. In fact, Marvin spouted so much that he became known as "Old Faithful."

But Marvin, despite his value to the criminal justice system, remained a source of ridicule to the DAs. They still spoke of Marvin's sale of drugs to a federal agent, which had been videotaped. After being arrested by the FBI, Marvin had predictably threatened them with lawsuits resulting in terrible consequences. They had answered by playing a videotape for him. After watching himself selling drugs on television and reading a copy of the laboratory analysis of the drugs he had sold, Marvin for only a split second became very, very quiet and then became a federal informant.

"He turned so quick—he almost spun," the FBI agent said.

Marvin had always been cocky, always calling the feds "guys with C averages," never impressed with their intelligence.

Today Farrell told Al the latest on Quiet Marvin. Two days before he had slipped his federal watchdogs and driven to Newark Airport. With a false passport and carry-on luggage filled with cash, he flew to Paraguay. Marvin knew that General Stroessner, the boss of Paraguay, was sensitive to the fact that there were many former fascists from Germany and Italy, including war criminals, enjoying life in his country. Desiring to improve his standing in the community of nations, Stroessner attempted to project a pro-Israeli image. To capitalize on this policy, Quiet Marvin disembarked at Asuncion Airport dressed as a rabbi and soon became a guest of the General.

Quiet Marvin was very pleased and only a little upset to find that the General required a pretty hefty downpayment for his hospitality.

Farrell and Al were laughing at the way Marvin had screwed the feds, but their laughter stopped when Pete DiCerrechia came in with the second fluky event of the day.

Pete was trailed by two detectives from the Four Three IU. There had been a shootout last night in a bar on Watson Avenue just off Bruckner Boulevard. The detectives had three white males in tow.

"Al, we escorted these three witnesses here so that they may be personally served by the DA with a grand jury subpoena."

"What case?" Al asked.

"Investigation into the shootout on Watson Avenue in the Tit for Tat Lounge." DiCerrechia said. "And the investigation into the death of one Jane Doe Female, DOA—the legs case."

Al wrote out three Grand Jury sobpoenas and asked the witnesses their names. Then he filled in the names and handed each of them a subpoena. "Please take these witnesses outside and then come back and fill me in," Al said quietly.

"Hey, man, I gotta go to work," one of the men said angrily. "These fuckin' cops been hasslin' me all day since last night. Who the fuck is gonna pay me if I lose my job."

Al looked at the copies of the subpoenas to get the man's name correct.

"Mr. Dinefresio," Al began, "I appreciate your predicament and in a few minutes I will be with you and I'll do everything I can to expedite the situation so that you will be minimally inconvenienced."

"Hey, fuck it, man, I didn't see nuthin' anyhow, I can't help ya."

"Please wait outside, Mr. Dinefresio."

"Look, Mr. DA, whatever the fuck your name is, I ain't got time to be fuckin' hassled so I'm leavin'. These fuckin' cops just about dragged me over here and I told them I didn't see nuthin' and I don't know shit, so you can put me in front of the Grand Jury or the fuckin' Grand Union and it ain't gonna change one fuckin' iota."

Al turned to his secretary. "Please prepare a material witness commitment for Mr. Dinefresio. Officer, please cuff Mr. Dinefresio if he refuses to accompany you to the anteroom."

As Dinefresio left, asking what a material witness commitment was, the detective told him he was going on a little vacation from his job and would soon be a guest of the People of the State of New York. The other detective sat down with Al and Pete.

DiCerrechia placed seven black-and-white mug shots and a colored passport-size photo on the desk in front of Al. All the faces were alike, all men in their early fifties, with gray hair and mustaches. The mug shots had numbers across the front. The color photo did not.

"The guy in the color photo shot up the bar on Watson Avenue last night. He's a Yugoslavian who's been here for about six years. There were two black guys in the bar who got into a pissin' contest with him. The black guys and the three kids outside are regulars in the bar. They all live in the neighborhood. Anyway, the black guys were breakin' the old guy's balls and the bartender started laughin' at some of their cracks, and so the Yugoslav takes off and comes back in fifteen minutes with a shotgun and fires five rounds of double-ought buck and blows a hand off one of the black guys and half the face off the other one. The bartender takes some pellets in the side, which went up into his chest wall, collapsing a lung. All three will probably live.

"So," Pete continued, "one of the witnesses outside—the quiet blond kid—follows the Yugoslav outside and gets a plate number. The car it turns out belongs to the brother-in-law of the perp, an Albanian.

"The brother-in-law gives us this color shot of the shooter and tells us his name is Josef Mroz, fifty-five years old and in the country for the last six years. I don't want to show the picture to the witnesses because I don't want the identification to be thrown out of court."

Al was pleased, for DiCerrechia was one of the very few detectives who realized that a case only began when an arrest was made and that the effectiveness of the prosecution depended on police conduct before the defendant got to court. Pete took the trouble to learn all the Supreme Court and Court of Appeals cases, keeping himself more current than most lawyers. He was only too well aware of the sanctions for suggestive identification procedures set forth in the Wade, Stovall, and Denno cases and their progeny. He knew that before the trial there would be a Wade hearing, which would explore the method in which the accused was identified and that the preferred method was a lineup.

Of course when the accused was at large, a photo array was permissible. To provide the hearing court with firsthand evidence of the photo array, the detectives would assemble a group of likely photos together with the photo of the accused and glue them into a brown file folder. The opened folder would be shown to the witness, who would be asked if he recognized anyone. The detectives would record the witness's response in his memo book and make up a DD5. The faces of course had to fairly resemble each other.

DiCerrechia knew he'd have a legal problem if his photo array consisted of black-and-white mug shots plus one color photo of the accused, so he asked Al to call the DA's technician. Within twenty minutes the technician had converted the color photo to black and white and covered all the B numbers of the mug shots. Then after inserting the photos into the folder, they showed them to the witnesses individually. Even Dinefresio picked out the Yugoslav.

Al led them to the Grand Jury and gave the case to Hornbein. After listening to the witnesses and DiCerrechia, the grand jury indicted Joseph Mroz for Attempted Murder. Assault First Degree, and Possession of a Weapon.

After Pete DiCerrechia had finished testifying, he began to discuss the legs case with Al.

"I was talking to the brother-in-law when I got the photo," DiCerrechia began, "and in the course of the conversation I find out that Mroz has a hair-trigger temper and is a horrendous drunk. When he's sober he is a good, stand-up, hard-working stiff, but when he's got his load on he's a fuckin' maniac. Anyway, the brother-in-law is married to Mroz's sister. I ask him if Mroz is married, and he tells me that he married an American woman when he came here from Yugoslavia and that the woman nagged the shit out of him especially when he drank. He thinks that the woman left him and I ask him when is the last time the woman was seen and it coincides with the time the golfers found the legs. He tells me that Mroz lives just south of the Yonkers line on Broadway and that he just took a plane to Yugoslavia this morning. He puts me onto Mroz's girlfriend, young Yugoslav kid in her twenties.

"So I dropped by the girl's apartment with two uniforms from the Five Oh in Riverdale and we bring her to the stationhouse. I tell her that we know all about her and Mroz and what happened to Mroz's wife and that she is involved. She's scared shitless and tells us right away that Mroz told her what he did to his wife . . . and when he did it . . . and she can prove that she didn't come to America until two months after—"

"After what?" Al asked.

"After Mroz killed his wife, put her in a bathtub filled with ice, and cut off her legs."

"She told you this?" Al asked, very excited.

"That's right, and then he dumped the legs at a golf course, and when the blood had drained from her torso he put her in a plastic bag and then into his freezer. He was a hunter and kept a wall freezer in his apartment. Years later he dumped her in the park."

"Didn't this worry the girl? I mean, she goes out with a guy about thirty years older who treats his wife like a slaughtered animal?" Al asked.

"No, funny enough, the girl was compassionate. She said that Josef cried and told her about this when he had something to drink and that he was afraid he would be punished in the afterlife. And the girl said that the wife nagged him constantly. The family bore this out, the wife was a real fuckin' nag. She apparently got off by nagging the living shit out of him."

"Well, she won't do that anymore," Al said.

"What do you think, Al?"

"Well, you have enough for an indictment, but I'd like to see you have him formally identified with the same folder. Since they knew each other it would technically not be required. See if the deceased had any family. I'd like to find some dental records to identify her."

"He knocked out all her teeth, Al. Remember, the corpse was toothless."

"I remember, but suppose there was a bridgework or false teeth made? We might have something."

"Okay, Al, I'll get on it, but if we get the indictment what do we do about Yugoslavia?"

"I'll take it up with the DA and O'Boyle. We'll probably have to request his extradition. In the meantime I'll set up the Grand Jury for tomorrow. Bring in the girl. The dental stuff I'd like for trial. I don't need it right now."

Al thought back to the scene when the corpse was discovered and almost laughed at himself for not eating leg of lamb since that day. He thought of Farrell's carrying on at the scene with the gorgeous blond ME, his former lover Dr. Linda Cristen.

As Al told the homicide coordinator to subpoena Cristen for the legs case for tomorrow, he wondered if anyone had told her that his wife and kids were back at home.

Dr. Linda Cristen arrived the next morning and testified before the Grand Jury. Al was not surprised that she seemed distant, and after she had testified and left the Grand Jury room Al followed her to call his next witness. She stopped and turned towards him.

"Good luck, Alcibiades LoConti. I really mean it," she said softly.

"Thanks, Doc," Al replied.

Dr. Linda Cristen took a seat in the anteroom. Al stepped inside the Grand Jury room and when the witness finished he came back outside and was shocked to see Dr. Linda Cristen kissing Jimmy Farrell. Farrell looked up and waved, then escorted the doctor from the anteroom.

Al went back into the grand jury with his last witness, Josef Mroz's girlfriend. After she testified to Mroz's confession, the Grand Jury voted an indictment. Al asked the foreman to accompany him to Part 12 where the indictment was handed up before the Justice Presiding and a bench warrant was issued for the arrest of Joseph Mroz.

To his surprise, Al was feeling no jealousy at all towards Jimmy Farrell.

I guess I'm lucky to be back with Renee, he thought.

AL WANTED TO SERVE the bench warrant on the Yugoslav Embassy and demand the extradition of Joseph Mroz. O'Boyle urged caution. "The United States government has to make the demand, the Bronx is not an independent nation with sovereign powers," he said.

The District Attorney, who was famous for never backing down and for loving to shoot from the hip, decided to follow Al's suggestion.

"Look, O'Boyle, why fuck around? . . . Get me the Yugoslav ambassador in Washington," he bellowed.

Minutes later the District Attorney was chatting with a member of the Ambassador's staff.

"This is Frank Caporosso, the District Attorney of Bronx County. One of your nationals named Josef Mroz has been shooting up my people. He is wanted on two indictments charging murder and attempted murder, and I want him back here for trial so I demand his extradition."

The Yugoslav official took the phone number and promised to call back the next day.

"Bring DiCerrechia back tomorrow," the DA ordered.

"You gonna at least check this out with the State Department?" O'Boyle asked.

"Nah, fuck 'em, this is my jurisdiction, I don't check with anyone."

The next day Al, O'Boyle, and a bemused DiCerrechia were summoned to the DA's office. The Yugoslav ambassador had just informed him that there was no extradition treaty between the United States and Yugoslavia. Therefore Mr. Mroz, who was a Yugoslavian citizen, would not be sent back to the United States.

"However, the Ambassador went on to say that if we sent over our investigator together with our evidence, then they would try him for us," the District Attorney related. "I decided to call their fuckin' bluff, so we'll send over DiCerrechia with the case file. They don't have the same rules of evidence that we do so a lot of the technical objections won't apply. Their prosecutor will try it for us. DiCerrechia, get your ass ready to leave for Dubrovnik."

"Hey, Mr. Caporosso, just a minute," DiCerrechia shouted in alarm. "That fuckin' place is behind the Iron Curtain."

"Come on, don't you have any balls, Pete? For Christ sake, don't worry. If anything happens to you we'll . . ." Caporosso sighed and paused while thinking, then suddenly his face lit up. ". . . We'll rename Lou Gehrig Square DiCerrechia Square, in your honor." He guffawed.

"I don't like it," DiCerrechia persisted.

"You want to go with him, Johnny?" the DA asked O'Boyle.

"Nah, I got too many things to look after."

"Okay then, Al, you go. Tell the bride you'll be home in four days."

The District Attorney had been right. In four days they returned from Yugoslavia, arriving on a Wednesday morning. The following Friday Al had felony duty. It had been a very long and busy night with four homicides, all Bronx divorces. Al had arrived at his home at 3 A.M. Saturday morning bone tired, after taking the last statement from the fourth Bronx divorcée. He quietly entered his kitchen and patted the German short-haired pointer who had trotted out to greet him. He opened the refrigerator and Sport sat smacking his lips. Al took out two pieces of ham, ate one, and threw the other to the dog. Sport caught it, wolfed it down, then nuzzled Al again. Al petted him and poured himself a cup of cold black coffee, drank it quickly, rinsed out the cup, and went into the living room. Just before he turned on the TV the beeper went off. After calling in, he dressed and left for the homicide scene on Davidson Avenue.

As Al was calling in, Rory O'Donnell, sitting in the Widow Keefe's living room, poured the second shot of Bushmill's over ice.

It was now 3:15 A.M. and Rory, radiant, slowly sipped the whiskey, reflecting on having just spent the most delightful evening in his life.

Miffed at his rejection by Renee LoConti, Rory had become despondent. He always struck out with women. For the last five years he hadn't even spoken to his third wife and had lost all contact with his fifteen-year-old son. Many was the night that Rory had put the barrel of his Smith & Wesson into his mouth and contemplated firing a final round.

Rory's sole recent sex experience had been two years ago and then only with a pinch-hit hooker from West Farms. He hadn't even tried with Al LoConti's wife, knowing that Al now hating him would never believe he was incapable of even getting up to bat.

But Rory's slump had ended last night when he hit a home run with the Widow Keefe. He had called her on his lunch break Friday and asked to take her to dinner, but she insisted on cooking for him.

Rory couldn't believe that he might be falling in love. The widow was very attractive and he, being a good detective, had done a check on her through the department of motor vehicles. She'd been born in 1917. That made her fifty-eight years old, some seventeen years his senior. He consoled himself that if things didn't work out he would still have provided a service.

Now some nine hours after he had arrived, Rory reflected on how clever he had been. He'd enjoyed the most delicious pot roast since his mother cooked for him and the accompanying Colcannan had transported him right back to Ireland. He could still taste the buttered greens and potato mixture with melted butter in the center, eating it together with the Widow Keefe in the manner taught in County Cork; taking the mixture with a fork from the outside and eating inwards. Then he had relished the carrots in cream, called *slieve na mban* in Gaelic, the mountain of the woman. Dessert had been Barmbrack or Irish fruit loaf. Rory had known that the term Barmbrack derived from the Gaelic words *aran breac*, or speckled bread. He had relished the meal and then lovingly sipped the Bushmill's-laced coffee.

After some desultory chatter he had persisted in helping the widow with the dishes then, after more drinks, had taken her to bed. The sex had been even better than the meal, and after much love playing and lovemaking they had fallen asleep. Rory had awoken some twenty minutes ago. The widow, naked next to him, was breathing softly, the beginning of a smile on her face. Rory gently left the bed and dressed. He was about to leave the house but thinking better of it poured another Bushmill's, opened a beer and sat in the living room, looking at the picture of the widow's husband while sipping the whiskey and the beer.

After the second Bushmill's he raised the can of beer in a salute at the picture. Fireman Keefe's eyes stared back from the frame. "Rest in peace, Keefe," Rory said. Then he belched with contentment. "Rest in peace," he repeated.

At the same time that Rory was looking at Keefe's picture, Al was driving right past the apartment house on his way to the homicide on Davidson Avenue.

He proceeded down University Avenue to Tremont then over to Davidson. He had never been on the street and never even heard its name despite having spent most of his thirty-one years in the county. Arriving, he was surprised to find the scene was in a private home.

A squad car was parked in front of the house, and Allie Boy Spano, in full uniform, was standing on the porch. Al parked and walked up to him. Allie Boy's partner, Richie Zemberelli, was out sick as a result of gardening in his father's backyard. Richie had stepped on the tines of a rake lying on the ground. His weight had rotated the tines, causing the hard wood handle to spring up and strike him in the face, knocking out two teeth.

Tonight Allie Boy was nervous because he had a new partner—Carleton, the former lover of the deceased Martha Valles. Al greeted his cousin warmly then walked past him into the vestibule. Three mailboxes were fastened to a wall above buttons that rang bells to two apartments on the ground floor and one upstairs.

The inner door opened and Al was greeted by Pete DiCerrechia and Ruella Watkins. He observed a blood-spattered wall to his left and a trail of blood leading through an open doorway to the corpse of a male sprawled on the floor. At the far end of the hallway another door led to the second apartment on the ground floor. The door to that apartment was closed. Detectives Munoz and Gutierrez were reading letters written in Spanish inside the apartment.

A bloodied bed stood next to a blood-splattered wall. Munoz and Gutierrez nodded to Al while continuing to read. Then Gutierrez put a letter down on the table and examined what appeared to be a diary. Al walked over and retrieved the letter.

The letter was written in Spanish in a small, meticulous hand. It had been written by the mother of the deceased. Al, finding his high-school Spanish inadequate, asked Munoz to translate. After a few minutes Munoz and Gutierrez reviewed the contents of the letters and the diary with Al. The writings established that the deceased was one Emmanuel Vildar, twenty-four years of age who had come to the mainland from Puerto Rico in January of this year 1975. He had been unable to adapt to the cold weather and had become very lonely missing his mother and his home. His mother, a widow, had written requesting him to return. DiCerrechia and Ruella listened to the translations of the deceased's private papers. There were no names mentioned, no leads to follow. A canvass by the detectives and uniformed officers had turned up zero.

The corpse was lying facedown, its head turned slightly to the right. Gutierrez knelt in front of the head, noting the multiple stab wounds mutilating the entire torso.

"Looks like our friend here has a little mascara on the eyes and a little powder on his face," Gutierrez said.

Al stepped gingerly around the pools of blood that had formed on the floor, careful of his new shoes and pressed suit. Kneeling next to Carl Gutierrez, he also detected the signs of female makeup.

DiCerrechia was kneeling at the other end staring at the partially exposed foot of the deceased, positioned so that the heel was facing the rear, thus shielding the toes from view. Pete took a pencil with a rubber eraser and, contrary to department regulations, moved the foot slightly. When he did he was able to see that the toenails were polished to a glossy red.

"Our boy probably took it up the ass," he said.

Munoz looked surprised but not Gutierrez. Ruella had already reached the same conclusion. "So we probably have a fag murder," she said.

"Yep. The guy's wallet is inside and it has money in it. He has a pay stub from a factory over on 140th Street and the amount in the wallet is only twenty short of the pay stub. The stub is dated yesterday. So he stopped somewhere to pick up someone, or he met someone, or he knew someone and whoever that was did him in," Gutierrez said.

"Jesus," Munoz shook his head. "What a slaughter."

"Yep, very vicious," Gutierrez agreed.

Ruella broke in. "The guy down the hall is a male black, sixty-seven years old. He owns the building and lives there with his wife. Upstairs is a young couple with a Hispanic last name. The owner tells me they left last night to visit relatives in Chicago, and he heard nothing and saw nothing. He doesn't even know when this kid got in. Oddly enough, we believe the old guy. I stayed in his apartment with the door shut and Petey went outside and slammed the doors. I heard nothing. The old man is also deaf as a coot, and the old lady was asleep. There was a bottle of Irish Rose wine next to her bed half empty so she was probably shit-faced when this happened."

"So we got bubkus," Munoz joined in.

"Well, I gotta wait for forensic and the ME now," Gutierrez said.

"Jeez, I thought they were here already since you guys were handling things in the apartment," Al said, annoyed.

"Those fucks in forensic couldn't find a spic in the barrio," Munoz said, smiling.

Al didn't laugh. "You guys don't have to explain to a jury why we manhandled a scene before it was dusted. I can't tell a jury that you guys think forensic is incompetent. Besides, you know it depends on who we get."

"Well, Al, we are waiting for almost three hours and they tell us that all forensic units are tied up in Manhattan. There had to be eight homicides there tonight," Gutierrez said.

I've had four in the Bronx tonight. All matrimonials," Al said.

"Matrimonials?" Munoz said, puzzled.

"Bronx divorces." Gutierrez explained.

"Oh." Munoz nodded, understanding.

Although it was now Saturday morning, March 29, the weather was cold and damp. Rain began spattering on the porch steps while the wind whipped down the street. The sight and smell of the corpse was making Al sick, and he was bone tired.

He walked out onto the porch and looked at the rain spattering on the asphalt of the deserted street. Allie Boy sat in the patrol car double-parked in front of the house and Carleton stood on the porch off to one side cupping a lit cigarette in his hand.

Al reached inside his jacket and withdrew a Parodi cigar, lit it, and blew the smoke out into the street while Carleton smiled at him.

"My grandfather smokes those things. I never get used to the smell."

Al nodded back. "I always liked the smell. They prevent cancer too."

"No shit," Carleton said. "Gee, I couldn't figure why anyone could smoke those things. No offense, Mr. DA, but I think the guy inside smells better."

"Yeah, well, I don't," Al said. "And I'll have you know that these things also put plenty of lead in your pencil."

"Really," Carleton said. "Well, maybe I should try them."

"Only try 'em if you have someone to write too." Al chuckled to himself. Then he turned to the street, noticing an olive-drab military sedan pulling up to the house directly opposite. Al looked down at his watch; it was 4:20 A.M.

The rain was pounding down as the door to the sedan opened and an army officer wearing captain's bars sprinted across the street, up the steps, and started to speak to Carleton.

"Mornin'. I'm Cap'n Moltry and I might need some help."

Carleton just continued to smoke, saying nothing.

Al walked over and introduced himself and they shook hands.

"I notified a woman across the street last week that her son was missing in action in Nam. Now I've got to tell her that they found him. The news is not good."

Al nodded. "Yeah, I know, Captain. I used to be a captain myself and I had this detail when I was in."

"Well, I'm lucky then, because you understand that I have to tell her now and I might need some assistance taking her to a hospital in case the news fucks her up."

"Well, I don't understand why you can't wait until the morning," Al said. "These police officers are assigned to guard this crime scene, they can't assist you."

"Look, I promised this woman I'd tell her as soon as I found out, and I'm going to keep that promise."

Carleton spoke for the first time. "This might be the last guy killed in Nam, huh, Cap'n?"

"Nah, he won't be the last. But he will be close to it. At least I hope so."

For the first time Al looked at the officer's uniform. He had the patch of the 101st Airborne and two rows of ribbons, which included the Vietnam service and campaign ribbons as well as a Bronze Star with a V for valor. Above the ribbons rested the silver musket on a blue shield surrounded by a silver wreath, the coveted combat infantryman badge. Topping all was the parachute insignia denoting the wearer as an Airborne soldier.

Then and there Al resolved to help the captain. He motioned for Allie Boy Spano to come over.

"What's up?" Allie Boy asked.

Allie Boy, who had spent beaucoup combat time in Nam, nodded at the captain.

"This officer here has to make a NOK job, a next-of-kin notification. Lady across the street lost a son. She'll probably be in bad shape after she gets the news. So the captain wants some police assistance to maybe rush her to the hospital if she needs it."

"Well, I can't leave here, you know, Al. I'll call it into the desk, but tonight we have that dipshit from Brooklyn, Boremisano. He won't dispatch another unit unless there is a job."

"Well, see what you can do, okay?" Al asked.

"Sure, Al." Allie Boy started for the steps.

"Say, Captain, does this lady happen to be a friend of the borough president?" Allie Boy asked.

The captain did not understand the question.

Al turned to the captain. "Tell him she is a relative of the borough president."

"She is related to him," the captain lied.

"Okay," Allie Boy said. "I just want to tell fuckhead Boremisano that we need another RMP to take the borough president's sister-in-law to the hospital because she is suffering from acute aging."

Allie Boy radioed in and two minutes later another RMP arrived with Fuckhead Boremisano himself in the passenger seat. The army officer joined the police sergeant in the rain, and together they went across the street into the apartment house. After five minutes they emerged with a woman in her early fifties. The woman's screams penetrated like darts into the marrow of Al Lo-Conti's bones. He puffed furiously on the Parodi until the cigar steamed from its wrapper while Allie Boy Spano rolled up the window to drown out the screams.

Carleton, horrified, pushed his back against the wall to the house as the four detectives inside ran out with revolvers drawn.

Al hurriedly explained what had happened. As Fuckhead Boremisano and the captain ushered the hysterical woman into the RMP, the forensic team and the ME arrived. The police car drove off, sirens blasting and lights rotating, followed by the army sedan.

No one laughed at the Brooklyn forensic team's jokes about being this far north. The night had been too long and gruesome.

Inside the house, the ME counted twenty-three stab wounds and said that they were inflicted by either an ice pick or a screwdriver.

When he flipped the body over on its back, a gush of blood spattered on Al LoConti's new suit and shoes.

Fifteen minutes later Al left the scene, returning to the Four Eight precinct with Munoz and Gutierrez. Inside the squad room the detectives helped him wipe the blood from his pants and shoes. While writing his reports for the tour, he drank a cup of black coffee, finally finishing at 6:30 A.M. He called the DA's night number to check if there were any other murders and was pleased to find out that he had covered them all.

He poured another cup of coffee and at 7 A.M. called the night number again. He left instructions to beep him en route to his home.

With two more hours remaining on his tour, he drove under the El at 10th Avenue in Manhattan. He passed the apartment of Margaret Keefe, who had awakened as she did each day to attend seven-thirty mass. Before leaving her apartment she had fondly placed a blanket over Rory O'Donnell, who was asleep on her couch.

WHEN AL, WOUND UP tighter than a coiled spring from the ordeals of the last twenty-four hours, opened the door to his apartment, he wondered if he could ever fall asleep. Renee greeted him from the kitchen and started cooking his breakfast.

Later that day they would formally remarry. Father Kiernan at Good Shepherd was to perform the ceremony, despite the divorce.

No one was to know and no one had been invited. Al would announce it as a *fait accompli,* wanting no fanfare, ceremony or gifts. Both were united in a desire to get on with their lives shunning the intervening wasteland of the divorce years.

Renee scrambled two eggs and threw some ham in the pan and served the combination to Al, sitting next to him while he ate. A quiet peace marked their relationship now and their discussions were considerate, tender, almost like the exchanges of teenagers in their first love. It was truly a remarkable situation.

At nine sharp Al signed off from felony duty, kissed Renee affectionately on the cheek, walked into the bedroom, took off his clothes, and flopped onto the bed, exhausted.

Yet sleep eluded him as he lay there thinking of his recent trip with Pete DiCerrechia to Yugoslavia.

At Dubrovnik, when the trial had been completed, they were treated by a colonel in the state police to the most interesting and delicious array of food they had ever seen.

The Colonel, very curious about America and the American justice system, asked one question after another which they promptly and clearly answered. The Colonel smiled at each of their responses. He compared the two systems of justice and concluded, as he always did, with a small speech extolling the superiority of the Yugoslav system. DiCerrechia had smiled back and replied that he was only a policeman, not a lawyer or a diplomat, and as a guest in the Colonel's country he could not disagree with an officer of such superior rank. The Colonel was quite pleased with this deference and raved on about the superiority of the Tito form of socialism. Al and Pete politely ignored him.

Finally the time arrived to leave for the airport. Pete, in the car's rear seat, asked if there was time to pass the American neighborhoods in Dubrovnik. The Colonel's brow furrowed. There were no concentrations of Americans anywhere in his country, he explained, and he was confused at Pete's comment. In his direct and forceful manner he asked why Pete had posed the question. Pete replied that he was just curious. Since there were many thousands of Yugoslavians in New York City, he anticipated that there might be a similar number of Americans in Yugoslavia. The sarcasm was lost on the Colonel.

Pete DiCerrechia and Alcibiades LoConti had left the country without incident. Except the colonel's boorish behavior, they had been treated as visiting royalty. Still, they were delighted to arrive at JFK with their reports on the trial completed. And now Al, soothed by his memories of those emotions and comforted by the presence of his wife and kids, finally unwound and fell asleep.

Less than a mile away, Rory O'Donnell woke up and looked through the apartment for the Widow Keefe but she was busy praying inside Good Shephard on Isham Street and Broadway. Rory, feeling a trifle hung over and still tired, stumbled into the kitchen in his stocking feet and opened the refrigerator. He withdrew a cold beer and poured it into a glass, downed the contents in two gulps, and then poured another. After throwing the empty can into the garbage pail under the sink, he took the beer glass and walked into the bedroom. He lay on the bed sipping the beer. Then he placed the glass on the night table next to him and fell asleep.

Margaret Keefe left Good Shephard after the mass, following her same daily routine. She walked from Isham to 207th Street, then went to the deli between Broadway and Seaman Avenue. This morning she purchased a blood pudding and a slab of Canadian bacon, some mushrooms, and a fresh tomato. Then she went to the bakery near the bus stop on Broadway to buy some fresh rolls and hot crumb buns. While strolling down 207th Street toward the El and mentally preparing a gourmet breakfast for Rory, she felt like a young colleen on this fine and lovely Saturday morning. Who would have thought that she, Margaret Keefe, fifty-eight years old, could ever enjoy such splendid intimacy with such a fine young man? She had thanked God for this blessing during the mass, feeling neither shame nor remorse and marveling with amazement at her own lack of guilt. She was feeling strong, good, and independent and looking forward to a fine breakfast and then who knew, perhaps even some more delight in the bed. Smiling to herself, she placed the key in the lock.

After taking off her coat and hanging it in the closet, she peeked into the bedroom to see that Rory was fast asleep. His mouth was hanging open and he was snoring. She saw the half-full glass of beer on the night table next to his holster with the gun. Then she closed the door and went back into the kitchen. She passed the picture of her husband whose eyes seemed to stare accusingly at her, then paused momentarily and placed the picture facedown.

In the kitchen she sliced the blood pudding and the Canadian bacon, and put them into a pan and began to fry them over a slow heat. She sliced mushrooms and fresh tomato then fried them together in another pan. After arranging rolls and buns in a breadbasket and placing butter in a dish, she set two places at the table and made tea and coffee. She held bottles of Irish Mist and Bushmills in reserve, should her guest desire his beverage laced.

She soft-boiled four eggs and let them sit in tepid water, surprised that the kitchen smells did not awake her guest. So while the coffee perked she started toward the bedroom to wake him up when the doorbell rang. She looked through the peephole and saw a UPS man dressed in the brown uniform, holding up a box and announcing UPS. She opened the door and he handed her the package, and she took it and placed it on a chair. He held out a clipboard and asked her to sign and she took the pen and started to write her name when suddenly the man kicked the door shut behind him and reached into his back pocket. He whipped out a lineoleum knife and started towards her, moaning and grinning insanely. Margaret Keefe froze in fear, feeling her bowels churn to water and her knees shuddering in long spasms. Managing to back up into the living room, she finally was able to scream and then as the man slashed her across the face and grabbed her hair, she screamed again and again in pure terror.

Rory O'Donnell, thinking he was dreaming, bolted upright at the second scream and hearing another shriek that penetrated to the marrow of his bones drew his revolver from the holster on the night table. He opened the bedroom door and gazed in shock.

A young blond man, vaguely familiar, wearing a UPS uniform, was holding Margaret's hair with one hand. His other hand held a lineoleum knife, and Rory watched him slash at her neck. Her head ducked and Rory saw the knife slice across her forehead. A crimson line of blood appeared and began to pour down her face.

Margaret sagged as her legs collapsed. The man snatched her head upright by a handful of hair. With his right hand he drew his arm across his body with the knife parallel to Margaret's exposed throat and Rory O'Donnell started to act. The man's back was to him when some sixth sense triggered DePew's psyche and he pivoted so that Margaret became a shield between Rory and himself. Rory couldn't help staring at Margaret's face, her eyes bulging in terror and the blood streaming down.

Rory grasped DePew's wrist, which held the knife, and fired a shot at DePew's head. DePew ducked to the left, the bullet only grazing his cheek and yanked his right arm violently in an effort to cut Margaret's throat. Rory pulled the wrist back, he was losing his grip to the much younger and stronger Ronald DePew. DePew, who was not hung over, again raised Margaret as a shield between himself and the man with the gun and Rory put the gun against DePew's temple and fired, but DePew moved and received only a grazing scalp wound. He slipped and as he did his right hand was freed from Rory's grasp. The tension release caught him momentarily off balance. Rory also lost his footing and swayed then fell. Margaret fell. DePew lunged at the fallen Margaret screaming insanely, as he had been taught in army bayonet drill. With a final burst of adrenaline Rory jumped at DePew placing the barrel of the revolver in DePew's screaming mouth and fired his remaining three shots in rapid succession.

DePew, dying, plunged the blade into Rory. As Rory collapsed he knew that he had seen this killer in person before.

The following Monday when Al arrived at work he was shocked to see that all offices in the Homicide Bureau were manned by detectives assigned to the media task force. A press conference was scheduled for ten-thirty that morning and would include New York City's five DAs and police brass from all over the metropolitan area.

Similar press conferences were being held throughout the United States and Canada, and law enforcement officials were eager to announce the end of the reign of terror caused by Ronald DePew.

Detectives assigned to the media task force were receiving calls from across the country inquiring if the homicide coordinator, Timmy Flanagan, had established any other links, and media persons from out of state were calling to ask if various names appeared on his list. Al walked over to his desk and saw that it had two extra phones on it. In his seat sat one of the Hat's bag man detectives. Al jerked his thumb indicating the detective should get up. The detective, in his early forties, about ten years Al's senior, and weighing about fifty pounds less than the stocky DA, replied in a snotty snappy voice. "Inspector McDaniel told me to man these phones and that's exactly what I'm goin' to do."

"Get the fuck out of my seat," Al said.

The detective ignored him. Al walked over and picked up the chair with the detective still seated and pivoted it, dumping the detective on the floor. Then he sat down behind his desk. The Hat, who had been walking around with his Cheshire cat grin, came over and ordered the detective away, screaming and humiliating him.

The phone rang and Al picked it up. "*Cleveland Daily Star.* Is there a Phillips from Cleveland on Flanagan's list?" Al walked over to the list and came back. "No, we don't have any Phillips," he said, annoyed.

Another call came in. "*Austin Daily Ranger* here. Do y'all have a Rogers from Austin, Texas?" Al again checked the list and came back with a negative response. The calls kept on coming and each time Al checked the list. By the time Hanratty and Jimmy Farrell joined him, he was getting really aggravated.

"What a fuckin' zoo," Farrell said as O'Boyle sat down too. Flanagan had cleared over a hundred homicides and assaults so far. Hanratty and Hornbein felt that DePew could realistically be linked to no more than sixty-eight. Al was getting disgusted with the circus.

He lit an anisette-flavored Denobili and soon the police personnel began giving him dirty looks. Farrell and Hanratty, noticing the cops' displeasure with the cigar fumes, borrowed DeNobilis from Al and lit up as well. O'Boyle and Hornbein soon followed. By the time the cameras got set for the press conference, the five assembled DAs were choking and windows were ordered open. As the cameras started to roll, one of the phones on Al's desk started to ring.

"*Harrisburg Harbinger* here, do you guys have a Sexauer?"

"What do you want to know for?" Al said, annoyed.

"We are reporting to the public on the linking of Ronald DePew to crimes in our city, and we would like to know if you have a Sexauer up there."

"Well, I've been getting calls all morning and I am getting a little pissed off," Al said.

"I'd like to have your name if it's not too much trouble," the reporter asked.

"Chief Cornelius O'Toole," Al responded. The mere mentioning of the rank softened the reporter's tone.

"Well, Chief, could you tell me if you have a Sexauer up there?" the reporter repeated.

"A Sex hour . . . are you shittin' me?" Al said. "We don't even get a fuckin' coffee break."

Al hung up, laughing to himself, and walked out of his office to see the Hat standing smiling in front of the cameras.

Two days later at the same time that Rory O'Donnell and Margaret Keefe were discharged from Jewish Memorial Hospital at 190th Street and Broadway, Al, Pete DiCerrechia, and Johnny O'Boyle were present in the office of the DA while Al reported the events of the Yugoslav expedition.

"First we were met at Dubrovnik by their state police. They treated us like kings. We were put up in a beautiful hotel and given great food. The next day we were taken to the trial. There were three judges and no jury, and they listened to everything Pete had to say. At the end they asked me if I had any scientific evidence linking the defendant to the crimes. The defendant took the stand and said that he didn't go into bars because he was a Moslem and didn't drink alcohol. They wouldn't let me cross examine him.

"Their prosecutor asked him a few questions, which went to the reasons why he came back to Yugoslavia. He said he just wanted to visit his sons. So they acquitted him. They were very cordial, telling us that they placed great stock in scientific evidence and they believed that this Moslem would not be drinking in any bar and there must have been a case of mistaken identity.

"They asked me if I had anything else and I said no. So they spent five hours showing us the country and then we came home. It is a real beautiful place and the people are very friendly to Americans.

"The only other thing of significance is that their DA and defense lawyer asked me a lot of questions about double jeopardy. Then they let it slip that they were in contact with Rhinequist—you know, the guy that handles most of the Bronx gambling cases—and they also talked to Frankie Hammon, the lawyer. Well, Rhinequist referred them to Hammon and Hammon told them that the guy could never be tried in America after they acquitted him. So maybe he'll be confident enough to come back. We're waiting with something he hasn't been tried on—a real nice murder indictment."

Two weeks later and some six hours after he had arrived back in the United States, Josef Mroz was spotted by a friend of his late wife, who promptly called the police. An hour after the call Josef Mroz was in the Four Six precinct with Detective DiCerrechia and Alcibiades LoConti.

Mroz recognized them both as having attended his recent acquittal in Yugoslavia and he was genuinely surprised that he had been arrested for the murder of his wife but refused to answer any questions. He was arrogant in his certitude that he could never again be tried for any old crimes in America.

"My lawyer in Yugoslavia is a professor of law and he studied here in America also. He says that I can't be tried here and to make sure he called Mr. Hammon, who also say I can't be tried here. So why don't you let me go and stop thinking I am a stupid or a foolish man?"

"Let me ask you one thing, Josef," Al said.

"Sure, go ahead, ask what you want," Mroz replied.

"Did you speak with Frankie Hammon?"

"Yes, I did."

"And what did Frankie Hammon say to you?"

"He said that he agreed with my lawyer and that . . . let's see . . . and that it was his very, very best guess that I could not be tried here."

"His very, very best guess?" Alcibiades LoConti asked.

"Yes, his very best guess," Josef Mroz answered.
"When you see Frankie Hammon, I want you to tell him something for me, okay?" Al asked.
"Sure, I called him before and he is coming here now. What do you want me to tell him?"
"Tell him that Al LoConti says . . . guess again."

Two weeks later after Josef Mroz pled guilty to Man One in exchange for an eight-and-a-third- to twenty-five-year sentence, Al spoke to Fast Frankie Hammon.
"How could you tell this guy he could never be tried here again?" Al asked.
"Hey, Al," Frankie said, "what do you think I'm fuckin' stupid? I never give an opinion that could result in me losing business."

The Hat was particularly miffed at DiCerrechia for his Yugoslavian excursion, done without the Hat's knowledge or permission. And this was not the first time Pete had defied the Hat's authority. Moreover, his rabbi, Connie O'Toole, had told the Hat to try to discredit a select few cops and ADAs, including Pete and Al LoConti. So the Hat planned on taking care of DiCerrechia. And he thought to himself while he was at it he would take care of that fuck Solwin and his pal Detective Wotter. The Hat conferred with one of his detective bag man and soon a plan was hatched. Ira Schmorkler, a plainclothes officer from the commissioner's confidential investigating squad, was enlisted. The confidential squad consisted of the finest and most intelligent men in the department. The monthly take of the eight members of this squad would be enough to build a nuclear aircraft carrier.

Ira's forté was dressing as a rabbi and visiting various markets in the city. He particularly liked to visit the Hunt's Point Market where he would pose as one of the rabbis inspecting the kosher meat plants. From time to time he would approach bookmakers taking action from the thousands of truck drivers and market employees. Ira would sometimes place bets with the bookmakers, who were very pleased to take action from a rabbi. They were so pleased that they even made jokes about it. They were not so pleased when Ira's backup squad put handcuffs on them.

Ira was one smart son of a bitch who loved being a cop. He familiarized himself with the kosher food industry and the requirements of the dietary laws of his own religion. Within a short period of time Ira discovered that there were a plethora of violations of the kosher dietary laws with a good deal of meat marketed as kosher actually being trafe, pork and lamb products routinely passed off as pure kosher.

In his spare time Ira developed the evidence and then presented it to the Consumer Affairs and Department of Health bureaus of the city government. He also informed the Bronx DA and various influential Jewish leaders, thus assuring himself of being a lifelong member of the Commissioner's confidential investigating squad.

Ira conferred with the Hat, who arranged for Dicerrechia, Solwin, and Wotter to be assigned to the same tour in the Four Six. The Hat made sure that the three were sent on a follow-up investigation. En route they were met by a rabbi who reported that he had been mugged by three teenagers. They treated the rabbi with the utmost deference as they took his report. The following week, unknown to Ira, who had posed as the rabbi, a former narcotics-dealing cop from Brooklyn who had become an informer delivered three boxes of steaks and three boxes of prime veal cutlets to DiCerrechia, Solwin, and Wotter. "The rabbi sent these over," he said, but when the three detectives refused he left the boxes on the desktop and ran downstairs yelling that they should not insult a rabbi. When their tour of duty was up the three detectives brought the boxes down to their cars. There they were met by IAD officers and taken down to headquarters for questioning.

Although only minor charges were brought against them there was justification for the Hat to flop them back to the bag and return them to uniform patrol; the ultimate disgrace for a detective.

DiCerrechia went to see Al LoConti and O'Boyle. The DAs wrote letters to the commissioner on behalf of the three detectives. Al went so far as to implicate the Hat.

This was unacceptable to Connie O'Toole, and soon health department inspectors began to make daily visits to Al's uncle's restaurant, giving him many violations and reporting them to the daily papers. Business began to fall off. Each and every violation was a phony, and on Al's advice his uncle hired a former FBI agent who was now a private eye. The former agent was present surreptitiously when the health department inspector arrived and was able to tape-record evidence to prove the conspiracy against Al's uncle. But they still couldn't implicate the Hat. Ultimately all of the violations against Al's uncle were thrown out of court, and the Manhattan DA began an investigation into the Department of Health. The total cost to Al's uncle, including attorney's fees, was $15,000.

Alcibiades LoConti spoke to Johnny O'Boyle, and the joint federal-state investigation into the Hat and the Admiral went into high gear.

Six months later, despite their greatest efforts, they still could not make a case against the Hat. So Al, O'Boyle, and the feds decided to make the Hat a federal witness.

They had followed him for six months, videotaping him at all of his many known stops. Since no one would testify against the Hat and no undercover could get next to him, Al decided that maybe the Federal Grand Jury might be interested to find out why the Hat made all these stops. If the Hat refused to tell them, he would be held for contempt and imprisoned. If he lied he would be indicted for perjury. So on the advice of Frankie Hammon, the day after he received a federal grand jury subpoena the Hat put in his retirement papers. They would be effective in thirty days. Within that time forty senior members of the department, including Connie O'Toole, also put in their papers.

The Hat was really surprised when Fast Frankie Hammon and a team of lawyers arrived at his office and told him not to worry because all his legal expenses had been paid. Frankie Hammon did two things. First he had the Hat visit a cardiologist, and second, he obtained an adjournment of the Hat's grand jury appearance. Within that time the Hat's retirement became effective as did the retirements of all the other brass who had applied. With pensions now assured, the legal consequences could be faced.

The Hat had finally been trapped. He was scheduled to appear before a federal Grand Jury on Monday, November 3, 1975. On

Friday night, October 31—Halloween—the Hat was haunted by the apparitions of children dressed as hobgoblins and monsters. His fear was making him shake, and he became even more sick and afraid when he recalled the admonitions of Frankie Hammon. The lawyer had explained the Federal Grand Jury system. The Hat was shocked to find out that unlike the State system, you did not get automatic immunity. If you were guilty and you were subpoenaed before the State Grand Jury you should be happy, Frankie had explained, because you thumb your nose and tell the grand jury that you did it and nothing could ever happen to you. You had full transactional immunity. So Frankie had said if you commit murder and you get subpoenaed before a state grand jury, you should tell them the whole truth, tell them you did it and why you did it and how you did it. And after you finished telling them, you walked out a free man. If you are called before a federal grand jury, however, you first have to invoke your fifth amendment privilege against self-incrimination. Then, if you insisted, you would be given use immunity. This meant that the feds could compel the testimony and that they could not use your own words against you nor leads developed from your own words, but if they got independent evidence then you could be prosecuted. And, Frankie had gone on, sometimes the investigators, like some police, would lie about where they got the leads. The Hat then shit his pants.

Mrs. Hat, alarmed at her husband's excessive drinking since the subpoena had been served, began to nag him incessantly. He had taken to leaving shot glasses and cans of beer behind the curtains throughout his house. In this way he could have a drink no matter where his wife happened to be. On Sunday morning Mrs. Hat began to nag the Hat to go to mass at St. Benedict's to pray for a miracle the next day. Not wanting to have anything interfering with his drinking, the Hat refused.

The wife nagged and nagged, and finally got a concession from her husband. He agreed to shave and shower and after he finished, he went down to the corner to buy the Sunday papers. His wife had been right, he was feeling a little better. After stopping at his car parked in his driveway, he took a hidden pint bottle from the glove compartment and had a long pull. He put the whiskey back inside and went into his house. His wife was in the bathroom getting ready for mass. She had left a cup of coffee for him on the table and while he was drinking the hot coffee his stomach started to rumble.

When his wife started nagging him to go to mass with her he left the kitchen and went into the bedroom, laid down, and lit a cigarette. His wife, still in the bathroom, fully dressed and running very late, opened a new can of hairspray. Hurriedly she rammed down hard on the aerosol nozzle but the excessive pressure jammed the valve wide open. The spray would not stop, and in a fury she flung the can into the toilet bowl where it expended its entire contents. While it was discharging all its spray into the water Mrs. Hat put a touch of rouge on her cheeks and adjusted her makeup. When the can had emptied she picked it out of the toilet bowl and dropped it into the garbage pail. She left the house telling the Hat she would pray for him.

When the door slammed shut the Hat looked out the window to make sure his wife had gone. Then he opened his closet and took out a bottle, and refilled the empty shot glasses all around the house. After a long pull at the bottle he went back to the kitchen to finish his coffee as a chaser. He lit a super-king-size cigarette and started to read the funnies. His stomach began to rumble again and he was feeling a little better. He went to the bathroom, elated that now he was alone, free to drink, and at peace.

He sat on the bowl maneuvering his buttocks until he was comfortable. Smoking and reading the funnies, he squeezed and voided his bowels. After a while, feeling much better, he even began to chuckle. A cartoon struck him and he howled in glee, opening his legs and ditching the cigarette between them into the toilet bowl. The cigarette hit off the porcelain interior and the sparks sprayed onto the volatile, combustible contents of the emptied aerosol can. Ignition was instantly followed by lift-off.

As he was being launched like a rocket, the Hat heard an enormous explosion. The deafening roar was accompanied by an excruciating burning of his roasting ass. The force was horrendous, cracking the toilet bowl and propelling the Hat ten feet straight up. Had the Hat's nose not smashed into the ceiling, he might have made it all the way to the church where his wife was praying for the miracle that had just occurred.

Mrs. Hat arrived back from mass to see fire engines and police in front of her house. The Hat had been removed to Jacobi Hospital suffering a concussion, a broken nose, and second-degree burns on his ass and balls. The burns would eventually heal, but the hair on his privates would never grow back. The Hat would later claim amnesia, and Frankie Hammon would provide the necessary medical backup. As a result of his takeoff the Hat would never have to appear before the Federal Grand Jury.

Timmy Flanagan had cleared the chart. Virtually every outstanding case that could be remotely connected to DePew had been marked off. O'Boyle's team of Al, Hanratty, and Hornbein had drawn up a list of homicides which they felt had not been cleared. The DA wrote to the Police Commissioner and the Mayor. The mayor replied that he would stand by the decision of the Commissioner. The Commissioner replied that it was in his department's purview to decide when a case was cleared and that the DA should not interfere with the internal mechanisms of the department. The DA answered by getting a court order requiring the Mayor and the Commissioner to show cause why an order should not be entered enjoining the commissioner and his department from marking these cases closed. Unfortunately on the return date of the order to show cause, the presiding judge was none other than the Mayor's brother-in-law whose only qualification for a position on the bench was that he had managed to seduce and marry the mayor's very ugly sister. The judge, of course, promptly denied the relief. The DA appealed, and a divided appellate division compromised by permitting the police department to mark cases closed but with asterisks indicating that the DA did not regard the cases as solved. The state's highest court in Albany refused the DA's request for a further appeal. So O'Boyle and Al read the decision and looked from O'Boyle's window onto Yankee stadium some two long blocks away.

"Now you know how Roger Maris felt, Al," O'Boyle said.

"Roger Maris?" Al replied.

"Yeah. They gave him an asterisk when he hit sixty-one and broke the Babe's record."

"Yeah," Al replied, "I see what you mean."

Only Carleton's case was now unsolved. Al was still not sure whether the man was guilty or innocent. It remained a cloud on Carleton too. He had passed the sergeant's exam but the brass refused to appoint him. Al knew that Carleton was an excellent police officer with an enviable record, but he still didn't know if Carleton's efforts were the result of trying to make amends for the murder or if he was truly a victim, just like the poor hairdresser whose life was blown from her body. The department had attributed the death of Martha Valles to Ronald DePew. Alcibiades LoConti felt certain that without any detectives trying to find him, the identity of her killer would never be known.

AL LOCONTI, JUST PAST his fortieth birthday on this twenty-second day of November, 1983, drove down the Bronx River Parkway from his home in the city of White Plains, where he now practiced law, Renee sat beside him. Today was Johnny O'Boyle's investiture as a judge of the criminal court. On a merit basis it was long overdue and a miracle, since O'Boyle was not active in any political party.

Circumstances had compelled the mayor to include competence as a factor to be considered before appointing one to the bench. A series of newspaper articles by Jimmy Phelan the journalist had driven the citizens to outrage.

The journalist had written of Judge Gruck, who found everyone not guilty on Friday afternoons. Soon the DA ceased putting cases before Judge Gruck on Friday afternoons and Judge Gruck could then adjourn to the Shady Rest Gold Course in Pelham Manor each Friday, which was exactly what Judge Gruck desired.

And Jimmy Phelan also wrote of Judge Fleck, who had been transferred to the civil Parts of the court. This judge had one stack of motions where he ruled for the plaintiff and another stack where he ruled for the defendant. The journalist was investigating the reasons why Judge Fleck had no backlog of pending motions, while all of his other colleagues had. In fact, it took between six and eight weeks to get a decision from the other judges whereas with Fleck it took just three days. In an interview with Phelan, Fleck had proudly announced his system. It was simplicity itself. On Monday, Wednesday, and Fridays all the plaintiffs won. On Tuesday and Thursdays all the defendants won.

"But, Judge," Phelan had said, aghast. "You rule for plaintiffs on three days and the defendants on two days . . . how do you justify that?"

"Shit," his honor had replied. "I alternate, three days for plaintiffs one week, three days for defendants the next week. This way I know I am being absolutely fair."

Although this revelation did not help the mayor's reelection chances, the next story almost buried him.

One of the judges assigned to Part 3, the youth Part of the criminal court, had taken to paroling youths charged with serious felonies. He would have these youths accompany him to his home for counseling. It turned out that the judge, who was a bachelor and lived alone, had done far more to the youths than administer advice.

Although the specter of nonjudicial behavior was apparent, no independent crime could be established, because the youths wisely refused to implicate the judge who had dismissed the charges against them.

When word came down for the judge to cease and desist, he had refused.

The judge's refusal sparked calls for his impeachment. Soon a court of inquiry commenced proceedings to remove him from the bench. Two weeks after that O'Boyle was notified he would be invested on November 22.

And so Al, accompanied by Renee this Tuesday afternoon, traveled to the Bronx County courthouse for the investiture of his friend and former boss, Johnny O'Boyle. On the Grand Concourse he observed the decay of the fine apartment houses that had lined this once-majestic boulevard. The streets were strewn with broken glass and beer and soda bottles. Graffiti marred each wall. Al parked at a meter opposite the courthouse on 161st Street with his car facing Yankee Stadium. As he put the coin in the meter, he observed a graffiti-encrusted train heading north on the Jerome Avenue line.

"Look at that," Al said in disgust. "Just look at that."

Renee grabbed his arm as they walked across the wide street and up the courthouse steps.

Minutes later the couple stood in the courtroom on the seventh floor and watched Al's friend being sworn in. O'Boyle made a brief acceptance speech, which was followed by a long-winded speech by the leading member of the party in the Bronx who went on *ad nauseum* about how politics played no part in the judicial selection process.

Al leaned over and whispered to his wife, "We'd better get out of here."

"Why?" she asked.

"Because I don't want to get hit when lightning strikes this lying fuck."

At the conclusion of the speech, Al and his wife walked up and congratulated the O'Boyles. They didn't stay for the reception. He would see the couple at the private party he was hosting for them at the Last Supper that weekend. The guest list included Detective First Grade Elrod Harrison and his wife, Lieutenant Ruella Watkins Harrison, the Executive Assistant to the Deputy Chief Inspector for Plans and Operations. Elrod and Ruella were enjoying life and living in Scarsdale, minutes from Al and Renee's home. Also expected to attend was Lieutenant Pete DiCerrechia, deputy commander of the Five Three investigation unit; Detective First Grade William Wotter of the CitiWide Homicide Task Force. Detective First Grade Rory O'Donnell and his wife, the former Margaret Keefe, were on vacation in Ireland and could not attend. Hanratty and Farrell, both attorneys in private practice, were expected to attend. Hardass Hornbein, famous for indicting his mother-in-law and now the head of the Rackets Bureau, would be a little late due to an ongoing investigation into the Building Department.

Finally Lieutenant Allie Boy Spano of the Four Four would be coming with his former partner, retired police officer Richie Zemberelli, now employed as a United States marshal.

"Please address me as Marshal Zemberelli," he said to anyone who spoke to him.

The LoContis left the courthouse and Al drove north on the Grand Concourse.

"Do you know," Al said, "this Concourse was a magnificent boulevard, built at the turn of the century? Later they planted trees along it that carried metal name plates of guys from the Bronx killed in the First World War. Imagine how different people were in those days."

"Where are the name plates now?" Renee asked.

"They built the IND subway under the Concourse and removed the trees to Pelham Bay Park. I don't know what happened to the name plates."

They drove north, made a left just before Fordham Road, and made another left onto University Avenue passing St. Nicholas of Tolentine Church. Renee, who knew this was not the way back home, asked, "Where are we going?"

"Just a little out of the way, kid, just a little bit today."

Renee looked at him and although she really wanted to go home she didn't argue. Al pointed to an apartment house.

"That is where we found the old lady who had lost three sons in two wars. She was one of DePew's victims."

A short while later Al pulled up in front of the former uptown campus of NYU, parked his car, and walked up the stairs from the street to the grounds where he had earned his undergraduate degree. It was now Bronx Community College. A tradition of over a hundred years had ended when NYU abandoned this tranquil, lovely campus. Al stood and looked out at Ohio Field, which stood between him and the former student center. It was dark now.

Ohio Field was where Al had been marching twenty years ago this very day. Marching at shortly after one-thirty in the afternoon, in command of one of the two full companies of cadets that made up the ROTC battalion, marching as Cadet Captain LoConti, the third ranking cadet on campus.

And then the sudden command from the battalion commander to halt and fall in. Then standing at parade rest in front of the regular army colonel assigned to the battalion, who informed them that President Kennedy had been shot, and then the dismissal.

Al recalled walking to the student center and seeing students gathering near radios. Upstairs in the lounge a TV played as Al and many cadets walked among their fellow students. Students were crowding around in shock, which was followed by grief and hysteria, when the news spread that the President had died. Al had left the student center, walked to his old Chevy parked near the river, and driven home. He would never forget that day.

Twenty years later Al now turned and walked back off the campus with Renee next to him.

They walked down the steps onto University Avenue and got into the Oldsmobile and Al swung a U-turn heading north. He turned right at Fordham Road. At a red light next to a burned-out building Renee followed his glance. "They used to call it the borough of universities," he said. "Imagine that, the borough of universities."

Renee grasped his hand and gave it a tug. The light changed and they drove on. Once driving north on the Bronx River Parkway, Al's thoughts turned to a conversation he'd had with O'Boyle just last week.

Al had asked if there were any changes in the status of the murder of hairdresser Martha Valles where the cop Carleton had been implicated, and O'Boyle, who had forgotten the case, had checked and replied that the status remained unchanged.

May 1988

THE LARGE RECREATIONAL VEHICLE rode up the Deegan Expressway returning from a weekend of shark killing off Montauk Point.

Nineteen-year-old Ray LoConti was still driving and his father, Alcibiades LoConti, was sitting next to him. Behind them Lieutenant Allie Boy Spano, Vince LoConti, Willie Wotter, and Pete DiCerrechia were standing drinking beer.

They had started this May weekend in 1988 speaking of their adventures in Bronx County many years ago. At first Ray had been more fascinated with the stories than he had been with the search for sharks, but the schools of makos and hammerheads had changed all that. Now, though, Ray wanted to hear the conclusions.

"So you never found out who killed the hairdresser?" Ray said.

"It's unsolved," Allie Boy said.

"What happened to Judge Flay?" Ray asked.

His father, chuckling, said, "There is a God. Flay was lucky enough to guess the right number of seats in Yankee Stadium but he was unlucky that my good friend, Pete DiCerrechia here, picked up the conversation on a bug."

The others also chuckled as they passed Yankee Stadium. The square imposing monolith of the Bronx County Courthouse stood granite still overlooking the stadium and the Deegan Expressway.

"That's the courthouse where your father worked for many years." Al pointed to his son. The boy looked.

"See on the top floor there is a library. From the library you can look down into Yankee Stadium. Well, if you wanted to get a judgeship, you had to guess the number of seats in the stadium. You were really bidding dollars from the political boss to get the job. So if you guessed there were thirty thousand seats and someone else in contention guessed forty thousand, then he got the job for forty grand, which he paid to the bosses."

Al went on. "Samuel Flay went up to the library and met the boss. He guessed there were fifty thousand seats in Yankee stadium. And he got the nomination. But Judge O'Boyle had the library bugged. And O'Boyle had a turned Bronx politico as an informant. So Flay was indicted, tried, convicted, and sent to prison."

"Who turned O'Boyle onto the judge?" Ray asked.

Al turned his head quickly. The kid was real sharp, and Al was proud of this son, this son he had lost and then reclaimed.

"No one will ever know," Al LoConti said.

EPILOGUE

ON A RAINY SATURDAY morning in May 1990, Al, Renee, their children left the funeral parlor in South Brooklyn where Al's great-uncle was lying in state. The man had lived until ninety-two and had always treated Al with a little special affection.

Al undid his tie as they drove through the Brooklyn streets to the Prospect Expressway and then on 278 to the Brooklyn Bridge.

"That old man was here from 1904 when he was seven years old. He was a laborer all his life except when he went back to Italy in 1914 to fight for his homeland. The priests from Italy told all the young men to go home to fight for Italia. He was seventeen and lucky to have survived. You see, in 1917 he was at the battle of Caporetto, which today is Kobarid in Yugoslavia. At that time it was part of Italy. The Germans and the Austrians made a breakthrough and the Italian armies collapsed, retreating far into Italy. The French and British troops saved the Italians from utter defeat. The Italians lost over 300,000 men, killed, wounded, and missing. Thank God the old man wasn't one of them."

"You really loved him, Dad didn't you?" his daughter asked.

"He was the kindest man I knew."

"He taught you about the garden and the wine, Dad?" she asked again.

"Yep, he taught me. He made the best wine and gave me two gallons every Easter. When he stopped driving his car about ten years ago, he would send his son up. I used to go and see him a few times a year to say hello. Today I'm sorry I didn't go more often."

After getting off the Brooklyn Bridge they drove up the FDR Drive and over the Willis Avenue Bridge into the Bronx. Then Al drove up the Bruckner Expressway.

"How did you ever live here, Dad?" Ray asked.

"It was a great place to live, Ray, a great place."

"Jeez, look at all the burned-out buildings."

"Yeah, Ray, but if you look you will see that some are being refurbished and others have been restored."

The young man looked and nodded.

"It's coming back, Ray, the Bronx is coming back. Just look at the single-family homes on Charlotte Street and Boston Road. It's unbelievable. Ten years ago it looked like Hiroshima after the bomb, and now you have cut green lawns. People are nicer and times are getting better."

Al went off the Bruckner Expressway to the service road and picked up the Bronx River Parkway north. They exited at Burke Avenue and Al stopped and went into an Italian bakery, where bread was baked in a coal-fired oven. Al came out with a bag of hot bread and passed it to his son.

Ray broke off a piece of the crusty hot bread, sighed as he ate it, and passed the bag to his sister. Al smiled as he drove home. He didn't notice the police car with Lieutenant Allie Boy Spano and Patrolman Roy Carleton pass him. It was 12:30 P.M.

Carleton told Lieutenant Spano that he thought he saw former DA LoConti pass them, but Allie Boy told him he was mistaken, LoConti had moved to White Plains and did not come from this neighborhood. Allie Boy also told Carleton that he had used Al's legal services and found that he was a truly excellent lawyer. Carleton knew that LoConti was Allie Boy's first cousin.

"In fact, in seventy-six when he left the DA's office I got him his first estate case," Allie Boy went on. "I knew a widow from Morris Park, grew up with her. She'd been married to a bartender in the Old Bailey, right near the courthouse, you know. Guy's name was Paddy Fay. Lot of rumors about the guy. Anyway, one day he goes up to the El on 161st and Jerome next to Yankee Stadium, stands on the railing, and steps off into the air flapping his arms. He couldn't fly so he came down into the roadway and got run over by two trucks. The autopsy showed a ton of LSD in his blood. They figure someone laced Paddy's drink while he was working. Anyway, Al did a good job for the widow."

As Carleton retold the story of how LoConti had prevented him from being railroaded, Allie Boy got a sudden pain in his stomach and side. He groaned.

"What's the matter, Loo?" Carleton asked, alarmed.

"Nothin', nothin', it's my wife, she put fuckin' Tabasco in my meatballs. It tasted so good last night but I'm in fuckin' purgatory now, fuckin' purgatory." Allie Boy opened a Thermos and took a long pull. He wiped his mouth. The cocktail of Maalox and Mylanta in ginger ale soothed his stomach. Carleton looked out the corner of his eyes at the lieutenant. He'd been Allie Boy's driver for many years now. Allie Boy was the patrol supervisor for this area of the Bronx and, unlike other supervisors, he was always on the streets. The other units knew when Allie Boy was working, and they made many arrests. Allie Boy had a flaming temper, and Carleton's job was to tame him down. Allie Boy was a cop's cop, now on the Captain's list and the toughest customer in Bronx county.

As they went north under the El, Allie Boy saw an old derelict Chevy make a sharp turn. The car had not signaled and had narrowly missed a woman walking in the rain with a baby carriage.

"Get that fuck," Allie Boy told Carleton.

Carleton turned on the light and the siren and pursued. The Chevy did not stop when the RMP was behind it, so Carleton pulled alongside. Allie Boy, calling that they were in pursuit, transmitted the license plate of the car.

As he motioned for the car to pull over, he noticed two males inside.

The LoContis arrived home just as the rain stopped. Al walked out to the garden in his backyard while his two dogs played in the wet grass beside him. He looked at the fenced area where his plants were and went back inside. His wife and daughter went inside. His son stayed outside and played with the dogs and Al picked up the day's newspaper. Inside on page four he read an article that shocked him. The story concerned Guido Insalata, the Admiral. Thursday last, the Admiral was acquitted for the fourth time on federal racketeering charges. It was he, Al LoConti, who had obtained the first indictments against the Admiral years before.

Despite massive efforts, the feds just couldn't get him. Yesterday the Admiral had driven with his wife to New Jersey to celebrate his most recent acquittal. Now at long last, he had been assured by his attorneys, the feds would leave him alone. The Admiral was to inspect two recently acquired racehorses. On the Jersey turnpike a tractor trailer jackknifed, rolling over the Admiral's Mercedes convertible. The Admiral was crushed to death; his wife lingered for four hours before joining him.

Allie Boy Spano had the driver spreadeagled over the hood of the car and Carleton did the same with the passenger. Then Allie Boy trained his gun on both, while Carleton searched the vehicle. Two other RMPs pulled up and the officers jumped out and assisted.

Allie Boy Spano always told his men that the fourth amendment was bullshit. "Search the fucks if you have any doubt. Fuck the Supreme Court. Fuck the judges. They want to throw it out, let them. But you protect your ass. Search for the drugs. Search for the weapons. Let your wives have husbands, your kids fathers, not memories." This was the gospel according to Spano, and today he practiced what he preached. But the search was totally negative. Allie Boy wanted to get something more on this guy than reckless driving.

Finally he told the driver to produce his license and registration. The car had not been reported stolen and the registration was current. Allie Boy examined the license, which was issued to Hamshooz Rajehvi.

"Hey, Hamshooz," Allie Boy said. "What kind of fuckin' name is Hamshooz? What are you, a fuckin' Swami?"

"What?" the driver asked.

"A fuckin' Swami, Hamshooz, you know, a fuckin' Indian or Pakistani, you one of those?"

The officers were cringing.

"No, I am not," the driver said insolently. "I am neither Indian nor Pakistani."

"Well, Hamshooz, that accent of yours ain't from the Bronx, so where you from?"

"Are you arresting me, Officer?" the man said.

"Bet your fuckin' ass, Swami, you just missed that woman and baby there. Did you see them, you fuckin' Swami, or are you too used to drivin' a magic carpet?"

Some cops began to snicker and the passenger started to sweat.

"Where you from, Hamshooz?"

"I am Iranian."

Allie Boy's eyes brightened. Ever since the hostage crisis in 1979 he had wanted to arrest an Iranian. Now his prayers were answered. There is a God, he thought.

"Well, well, boys," Allie Boy said. "A fuckin' Iranian. One of the Ayatollah's little followers. One of the guys that made this country eat shit. It's a fuckin' pleasure to lock you up, Hamshooz. Too bad it's only for a misdemeanor."

One of the officers, formerly of the tactical patrol force, had looked at the license. The TPF was famous for locking up gypsy cab drivers.

"Hey, Lieutenant," the TPF officer said, "this license is a phony, it's a forgery."

Allie Boy was beaming now. He looked at the license and the officer pointed out the telltale signs of a forgery. Unknown to Hamshooz, a forged license in the Bronx was routinely disposed of by a plea to a traffic infraction.

"Well, Hamshooz, now you are going to do about four years. Those guys in Attica are goin' to love havin' a little Ayatollah on their hands."

"I am not a supporter of Khomeini nor was I a supporter of the Shah."

"Yeah, yeah, just like we found no Nazis in Germany and when I was in Nam and we kicked ass, we couldn't find a communist. Every fuckin' gook believed in free enterprise. Nothin' changes. Cuff him, Carleton."

Hamshooz was cuffed and placed in the back of Spano's RMP.

An officer from another RMP got in beside him.

"Sir," Hamshooz entreated.

"What?" Allie Boy growled.

"Sir, if you let me go I will tell you who murdered the hairdresser on Sedgwick Avenue in 1973."

"What?" Allie Boy said, flabbergasted.

"There was a woman who was a hairdresser and she was shot in 1973 in her apartment on Sedgwick Avenue. I know who her murderer is."

"Yeah, well, who the fuck is it?"

"It is the man who is with me, my brother-in-law."

"Take them in," Allie Boy said.

At the Four Seven precinct the man confessed. His name was William Portman, and he was an American with a long history of mental health problems. He had been visiting a friend in Martha's apartment house and had gone up to the roof for some air. While there he had smoked a joint and looked down. He saw Martha come home in her white uniform and noticing her beautiful figure, he resolved to have some of her that night. So he had snapped off some clotheslines from the roof and tied them together, then hung from the roof by the line and opened the only window that was unlocked. Martha had been in the shower, and he had searched the apartment. He had a .38 with him, which was still in his apartment in Yonkers. He had shot her and then sodomized her and left the same way he came in, out the window and up the rope to the roof.

Then he had taken the clothesline, rolled it up, and walked downstairs, discarding it in a garbage pail.

Allie Boy Spano, who had summoned a DA and a stenographer, treated Portman with kid gloves. He was solicitous to the point of sycophancy. Portman loved the attention. Allie Boy's instincts paid off, because before the DA had finished, Portman confessed to killing eight other women in the five boroughs of the City of New York. A check of the details showed that only the killer would have the knowledge Portman possessed.

Just before 5 P.M. that day as he was getting ready to leave the bench, Judge O'Boyle was informed by the bridgeman that one more arraignment had just come in. Soon a breathless Allie Boy accompanied by a beaming Carleton strode into the court from the pens with Portman. The DA recited the facts. The Legal Aid attorney requested reasonable bail. O'Boyle asked his old friend Allie Boy a few questions and realized that this was Al LoConti's old case. He looked at Portman. Unbelievable, he thought. After all this time to be caught because of a traffic infraction, unbelievable. O'Boyle remanded Portman for a 730 exam to see if he was mentally fit to proceed to trial. Court was adjourned. In the robing room, O'Boyle picked up the phone and dialed Al's home number.

In White Plains Al was in his garden. Renee heard the phone ring and answered it. She yelled to Al that O'Boyle had some news as Al picked some basil and walked to the house motioning for his son to follow. The herbs would go great with the tomatoes, he thought.